Enid Blyton

MORE ADVENTURES OF THE
FAMOUS FIVE

TREASURE PRESS

First published in this format in 1986
under the title *Enid Blyton's Fun with the Famous Five*
This edition published in 1988 by
Treasure Press
Michelin House
81 Fulham Road
London SW3 6RB

Reprinted 1989, 1991

by arrangement with Hodder and Stoughton Children's Books

ISBN 1 85051 329 5

Printed in Czechoslovakia

52176/5

Enid Blyton's

FIVE GO OFF IN A CARAVAN

ILLUSTRATED BY JOLYNE KNOX

CONTENTS

1
The beginning of the holidays

'I do love the beginning of the summer hols,' said Julian. 'They always seem to stretch out ahead for ages and ages.'

'They go so nice and slowly at first,' said Anne, his little sister. 'Then they start to gallop.'

The others laughed. They knew exactly what Anne meant. 'Woof,' said a deep voice, as if someone else thoroughly agreed too.

'Timmy thinks you're right, Anne,' said George, and patted the big dog lying panting beside them. Dick patted him, too, and Timmy licked them both.

The four children were lying in a sunny garden in the first week of the holidays. Usually they went to their cousin Georgina's home for holidays, at Kirrin – but this time, for a change, they were all at the home of Julian, Dick and Anne.

Julian was the oldest, a tall, sturdy boy with a strong

and pleasant face. Dick and Georgina came next. Georgina looked more like a curly-headed boy than a girl, and she insisted on being called George. Even the teachers at school called her George. Anne was the youngest, though, much to her delight, she was really growing taller now.

'Daddy said this morning that if we didn't want to stay here all the hols we could choose what we wanted to do,' said Anne. 'I vote for staying here.'

'We could go off somewhere just for two weeks, perhaps,' said Dick. 'For a change.'

'Shall we go to Kirrin, and stay with George's mother and father for a bit?' said Julian, thinking that perhaps George would like this.

'No,' said George at once. 'I went home at half-term, and Mother said Father was just beginning one of his experiments in something or other – and you know what *that* means. If we go there we'd have to walk about on tiptoe, and talk in whispers, and keep out of his way the whole time.'

'That's the worst of having a scientist for a father,' said Dick, lying down on his back and shutting his eyes. 'Well, your mother couldn't cope with us and with your father, too, in the middle of one of his experiments at the same time. Sparks would fly.'

'I like Uncle Quentin, but I'm afraid of him when he's in one of his tempers,' said Anne. 'He shouts so.'

'It's decided that we won't go to Kirrin, then,' said Julian, yawning. 'Not these hols, anyhow. You can always go and see Mother for a week or so, George, when you want to. What shall we do, then? Stay here all the time?'

They were now all lying down on their backs in the sun, their eyes shut. What a hot afternoon! Timmy sat up by George, his pink tongue hanging out, panting loudly.

'Don't, Timmy,' said Anne. 'You sound as if you have been running for miles, and you make me feel hotter than ever.'

8

Timmy put a friendly paw on Anne's middle and she squealed. 'Oh, Timmy – your paw's heavy. Take it off.'

'You know, I think if we were allowed to go off by ourselves somewhere, it would be rather fun,' said George, biting a blade of grass and squinting up into the deep blue sky. 'The biggest fun we've ever had was when we were alone on Kirrin Island, for instance. Couldn't we go off somewhere all by ourselves?'

'But where?' said Dick. 'And how? I mean we aren't old enough to take a car – though I bet I could drive one. It wouldn't be much fun going on bicycles, because Anne can't ride as fast as we can.'

'And somebody always get a puncture,' said Julian.

'It would be jolly good fun to go off on horses,' said George. 'Only we haven't got even one.'

'Yes, we have – there's old Dobby down in the field,' said Dick. 'He is ours. He used to draw the pony-cart, but we don't use it any more now he's turned out to grass.'

'Well, one horse wouldn't take four of us, silly,' said George. 'Dobby's no good.'

There was a silence, and everyone thought lazily about holidays. Timmy snapped at a fly, and his teeth came together with a loud click.

'Wish I could catch flies like that,' said Dick, flapping away a blue-bottle. 'Come and catch this one, Timmy, old thing.'

'What about a walking tour?' said Julian after a pause. There was a chorus of groans.

'What! In this weather! You're mad!'

'We shouldn't be allowed to.'

'All right, all right,' said Julian. 'Think of a better idea, then.'

'I'd like to go somewhere where we could bathe,' said Anne. 'In a lake, for instance, if we can't go to the sea.'

'Sounds nice,' said Dick. 'My goodness, I'm sleepy.

Let's hurry up and settle this matter, or I shall be snoring hard.'

But it wasn't easy to settle. Nobody wanted to go off to an hotel, or to rooms. Grown-ups would want to go with them and look after them. And nobody wanted to go walking or cycling in the hot August weather.

'Looks as if we'll have to stay at home all the hols, then,' said Julian. 'Well – I'm going to have a snooze.'

In two minutes they were all asleep on the grass except Timmy. If his family fell asleep like this, Timmy considered himself on guard. The big dog gave his mistress George a soft lick and sat up firmly beside her, his ears cocked, and his eyes bright. He panted hard, but nobody heard him. They were all snoozing deliciously in the sun, getting browner and browner.

The garden sloped up a hillside. From where he sat Timmy could see quite a long way, both up and down the road that ran by the house. It was a wide road, but not a very busy one, for it was a country district.

Timmy heard a dog barking in the distance, and his ears twitched in that direction. He heard people walking down the road and his ears twitched again. He missed nothing, not even the robin that flew down to get a caterpillar on a bush not far off. He growled softly in his throat at the robin – just to tell it that he was on guard, so beware.

Then something came down the wide road, something that made Timmy shake with excitement, and sniff at the strange smells that came floating up to the garden. A big procession came winding up the road, with a rumble and clatter of wheels – a slow procession, headed by a very strange thing.

Timmy had no idea what it was that headed the procession. Actually it was a big elephant, and Timmy smelt its smell, strange and strong, and didn't like it. He smelt the scent of the monkeys in their travelling cage, too,

10

and he heard the barking of the performing dogs in their van.

He answered them defiantly. 'WOOF, WOOF, WOOF.'

The loud barking awoke all four children at once. 'Shut up, Timmy,' said George crossly. 'What a row to make when we're all having a nap.'

'WOOF,' said Timmy obstinately, and pawed at his mistress to make her sit up and take notice. George sat up. She saw the procession at once and gave a yell.

'Hey, you others. There's a circus procession going by. 'Look.'

They all sat up, wide awake now. They stared down at the caravans going slowly along, and listened to an animal howling, and the dogs barking.

'Look at that elephant, pulling the caravan along,' said Anne. 'He must be jolly strong.'

'Let's go down to the gate of the drive and watch,' said Dick. So they all got up and ran down the garden, then round the house and into the drive that led to the road. The procession was just passing the gates.

It was a gay sight. The caravans were painted in brilliant colours, and looked spick and span from the

11

outside. Little flowery curtains hung at the windows. At the front of each caravan sat the man or woman who owned it, driving the horse that pulled it. Only the front caravan was pulled by an elephant.

'Golly – doesn't it look exciting?' said George. 'I wish I belonged to a circus that went wandering all over the place all the year. That's just the sort of life I'd like.'

'Fat lot of good you'd be in the circus,' said Dick rudely. 'You can't even turn a cart-wheel.'

'What's a cart-wheel?' said Anne.

'What that boy's doing over there,' said Dick. 'Look.'

He pointed to a boy who was turning cart-wheels very quickly, going over and over on his hands and feet, turning himself like a wheel. It looked so easy, but it wasn't, as Dick very well knew.

'Oh, is he turning a cart-wheel?' said Anne admiringly. 'I wish I could do that.'

The boy came up to them and grinned. He had two terrier dogs with him. Timmy growled and George put her hand on his collar.

'Don't come too near,' she called. 'Timmy isn't quite sure about you.'

'We won't hurt him!' said the boy, and grinned again. He had an ugly, freckled face, with a shock of untidy hair. 'I won't let my dogs eat your Timmy.'

'As if they could!' began George scornfully, and then laughed. The terriers kept close to the boy's heels. He clicked and both dogs rose at once on their hind legs and walked sedately behind him with funny little steps.

'Oh – are they performing dogs?' said Anne. 'Are they yours?'

'These two are,' said the boy. 'This is Barker and this is Growler. I've had them from pups – clever as paint they are!'

'Woof,' said Timmy, apparently disgusted at seeing

12

dogs walk in such a peculiar way. It had never occurred to him that a dog could get up on his hind legs.

'Where are you giving your next show?' asked George eagerly. 'We'd like to see it.'

'We're off for a rest,' said the boy. 'Up in the hills, where there's a blue lake at the bottom. We're allowed to camp there with our animals – it's wild and lonely and we don't disturb nobody. We just camp there with our caravans.'

'It sounds fine,' said Dick. 'Which is your caravan?'

'This one, just coming,' said the boy, and he pointed to a brightly painted van, whose sides were blue and yellow, and whose wheels were red. 'I live in it with my Uncle Dan. He's the chief clown of the circus. There he is, sitting on the front, driving the horse.'

The children stared at the chief clown, and thought that they had never seen anyone less like a clown. He was dressed in dirty grey flannel trousers and a dirty red shirt open at an equally dirty neck.

He didn't look as if he could make a single joke, or do anything in the least funny. In fact, he looked really bad-tempered, the children thought, and he scowled so fiercely as he chewed on an old pipe that Anne felt quite scared. He didn't look at the children at all, but called in a sharp voice to the boy:

'Nobby! You come on along of us. Get in the caravan and make me a cup of tea.'

The boy Nobby winked at the children and ran to the caravan. It was plain that Uncle Dan kept him in order all right! He poked his head out of the little window in the side of the caravan nearest to the children.

'Sorry I can't ask you to tea too!' he called. 'And the dog. Barker and Growler wouldn't half like to know him!'

The caravan passed on, taking the scowling clown with it, and the grinning Nobby. The children watched the others going by, too; it was quite a big circus. There was a cage of monkeys, a chimpanzee sitting in a corner of a dark cage, asleep, a string of beautiful horses, sleek and shining, a great wagon carrying benches and forms and tents, caravans for the circus folk to live in, and a host of interesting people to see, sitting on the steps of their vans or walking together outside to stretch their legs.

At last the procession was gone and the children went slowly back to their sunny corner in the garden. They sat down – and then George announced something that made them sit up straight.

'*I* know what we'll do these hols! We'll hire a caravan and go off in it by ourselves. Do let's! Oh, do let's!'

2

George's great idea

The others stared at George's excited face. She had gone quite red. Dick thumped on the ground.

'A jolly good idea! Why didn't we think of it before?'

'Oh, *yes*! A caravan to ourselves! It sounds too good to be true!' said Anne, and her eyes shone.

'Well, I must say it would be something we've never done before,' said Julian, wondering if it was really possible. 'I say – wouldn't it be gorgeous if we could go off into the hills – where that lake is that the boy spoke about? We could bathe there – and we could perhaps get to know the circus folk. I've always wanted to know about circuses.'

'Oh, *Julian*! That's a better idea still!' said George, rubbing her hands together in delight. 'I liked that boy Nobby, didn't you!'

'Yes,' said everyone.

'But I didn't like his uncle,' said Dick. 'He looked a nasty bit of work. I bet he makes Nobby toe the mark and do what he's told.'

'Julian, do you think we'd be allowed to go caravanning

by ourselves?' asked Anne earnestly. 'It does seem to me to be the most marvellous idea we've ever had.'

'Well – we can ask and see,' said Julian. 'I'm old enough to look after you all.'

'Pooh!' said George. 'I don't want any looking after, thank you. And anyway, if we want looking after, Timmy-can do that. I bet the grown-ups will be glad to be rid of us for a week or two. They always think the summer hols are too long.'

'We'll take Dobby with us to pull the caravan!' said Anne suddenly, looking down at the field where Dobby stood, patiently flicking away the flies with his long tail. 'Dobby would love that! I always think he must be lonely, living in that field all by himself, just being borrowed by people occasionally.'

'Of course – Dobby could come,' said Dick. 'That would be fine. Where could we get the caravan from? Are they easy to hire?'

'Don't know,' said Julian. 'I knew a chap at school – you remember him, Dick, that big fellow called Perry – he used to go caravanning every hols with his people. They used to hire caravans, I know. I might find out from him where he got them from.'

'Daddy will know,' said Anne. 'Or Mummy. Grown-ups always know things like that. I'd like a nice large caravan – red and blue – with a little chimney, and windows each side, and a door at the back, and steps to go up into the caravan, and . . .'

The others interrupted with their own ideas, and soon they were all talking excitedly about it – so loudly that they didn't see someone walking up and standing near by, laughing at the excitement.

'Woof,' said Timmy politely. He was the only one who had ears and eyes for anything else at the moment. The children looked up.

'Oh, hallo, Mother!' said Julian. 'You've just come at

the right moment. We want to tell you about an idea we've got.'

His mother sat down, smiling. 'You seem very excited about something,' she said. 'What is it?'

'Well, it's like this, Mummy,' said Anne, before anyone else could get a word in, 'we've made up our minds that we'd like to go off in a caravan for a holiday by ourselves! Oh, Mummy – it would be such fun!'

'By yourselves?' said her mother doubtfully. 'Well, I don't know about that.'

'Julian can look after us,' said Anne.

'So can Timmy,' put in George at once, and Timmy thumped the ground with his tail. Of course he could look after them! Hadn't he done it for years, and shared all their adventures? Thump, thump, thump!

'I'll have to talk it over with Daddy,' said Mother. 'Now don't look so disappointed – I can't decide a thing like this all by myself in a hurry. But it may fit in quite well because I know Daddy has to go up north for a little while, and he would like me to go with him. So he might think a little caravanning quite a good idea. I'll talk to him tonight.'

'We could have Dobby to pull the caravan, Mummy,' said Anne, her eyes bright. 'Couldn't we? He'd love to come. He has such a dull life now.'

'We'll see, we'll see,' said her mother, getting up. 'Now you'd better all come in and wash. It's nearly tea-time. Your hair is terrible, Anne. What *have* you been doing?'

Everyone rushed indoors to wash, feeling distinctly cheerful. Mother hadn't said NO. She had even thought it might fit in quite well. Golly, to go off in a caravan all alone – doing their own cooking and washing – having Dobby for company, and Timmy as well, of course. How simply gorgeous.

The children's father did not come home until late that evening, which was a nuisance, for nobody felt that they could wait for very long to know whether they might or might not go. Everyone but Julian was in bed when he came home, and even when he, too, came to bed he had nothing to report.

He stuck his head into the girls' bedroom. 'Daddy's tired and he's having a late supper, and Mother won't bother him till he's feeling better. So we shan't know till morning, worse luck!'

The girls groaned. How could they possibly go to sleep with thoughts of caravans floating deliciously in their heads – not knowing whether or not they would be allowed to go!

'Blow!' said George. 'I shan't go to sleep for ages. Get off my feet, Timmy. Honestly, it's too hot to have you anywhere near me this weather.'

In the morning good news awaited the four children. They sat down at the breakfast-table, all very punctual for once, and Julian looked expectantly at his mother. She smiled at him and nodded.

'Yes, we've talked it over,' she said. 'And Daddy says he doesn't see why you shouldn't have a caravan holiday. He thinks it would be good for you to go off and rough it a bit. But you will have to have two caravans, not one. We couldn't have all four of you, and Timmy too, living in one caravan.'

'Oh – but Dobby couldn't pull *two* caravans, Mummy,' said Anne.

'We can borrow another horse,' said Julian. 'Can't we, Mother? Thanks awfully, Daddy, for saying we can go. It's jolly sporting of you.'

'Absolutely super,' said Dick.

'Wizard!' said George, her fingers scratching Timmy's head excitedly. 'When can we go? Tomorrow?'

'Of course not!' said Julian. 'We've got to get the caravans – and borrow a horse – and pack – and all sorts of things.'

'You can go next week, when I take your mother up north with me,' said his father. 'That will suit us very well. We can give Cook a holiday, too, then. You will have to send us a card every single day to tell us how you are and where you are.'

'It does sound thrilling,' said Anne. 'I really don't feel as if I can eat any breakfast, Mummy.'

'Well, if that's the effect the idea of caravanning has on you, I don't think you'd better go,' said her mother. Anne hastily began to eat her shredded wheat, and her appetite soon came back. It was too good to be true – to have *two* caravans – and *two* horses – and sleep in bunks perhaps –

and cook meals outside in the open air – and . . .

'You will be in complete charge, you understand, Julian,' said the boy's father. 'You are old enough now to be really responsible. The others must realise that you are in charge and they must do as you say.'

'Yes, sir,' said Julian, feeling proud. 'I'll see to things all right.'

'And Timmy will be in charge, too,' said George. 'He's just as responsible as Julian.'

'Woof,' said Timmy, hearing his name, and thumping the floor with his tail.

'You're a darling, Timmy,' said Anne. 'I'll always do what *you* say, as well as what Julian says!'

'Idiot!' said Dick. He patted Timmy's head. 'I bet we wouldn't be allowed to go without you, Timothy. You are a jolly good guard for anyone.'

'You certainly wouldn't be allowed to go without Timmy,' said his mother. 'We know you'll be safe with him.'

It was all most exciting. The children went off to talk things over by themselves when breakfast was finished.

'I vote we go caravanning up into the hills that boy spoke of, where the lake lies at the bottom – and camp there,' said Julian. 'We'd have company then – jolly exciting company, too. We wouldn't live *too* near the circus camp – they might not like strangers butting in – but we'll live near enough to see the elephant going for his daily walk, and the dogs being exercised . . .'

'And we'll make friends with Nobby, won't we?' said Anne eagerly. 'I liked him. We won't go near his uncle, though. I think it's queer that such a bad-tempered looking man should be the chief clown in a circus.'

'I wonder when and where Mother will get the caravans!' said Julian. 'Gosh, won't it be fun when we see them for the first time!'

20

'Let's go and tell Dobby!' said Anne. 'He is sure to be excited, too!'

'Baby! He won't understand a word you tell him!' said George. But off she went with Anne just the same, and soon Dobby was hearing all about the wonderful holiday plan. Hrrrrumph! So long as it included him, too, he was happy!

3

The caravans arrive

At last the great day came when the two caravans were due to arrive. The children stood at the end of the drive for hours, watching for them.

Mother had managed to borrow them from an old friend of hers. The children had promised faithfully to look after them well, and not to damage anything. Now they stood at the end of the drive, watching eagerly for the caravans to arrive.

'They are being drawn by cars today,' said Julian. 'But they are fitted up to be horse-drawn, too. I wonder what they are like – and what colour they are?'

'Will they be like gypsy caravans, on high wheels, do you think?' asked Anne. Julian shook his head.

'No, they're modern, Mother says. Streamlined and all that. Not too big either, because a horse can't draw too heavy a van.'

'They're coming, they're coming! I can see them!' suddenly yelled George, making them all jump. 'Look, isn't that them, far down the road?'

22

They all looked hard into the distance. No one had such good eyes as George, and all they could see was a blotch, a moving speck far away on the road. But George's eyes saw two caravans, one behind the other.

'George is right,' said Julian, straining his eyes. 'It's our caravans. They're each drawn by a small car.'

'One's red and the other's green,' said Anne. 'Bags I the red one. Oh, hurry up, caravans!'

At last they were near enough to see properly. The children ran to meet them. They certainly were very nice ones, quite modern and 'streamlined', as Julian had said, well built and comfortable.

'They almost reach the ground!' said Anne. 'And look at the wheels, set so neatly into the side of the vans. I do like the red one, bags I the red one.'

Each van had a little chimney, long, narrow windows down the two sides, and tiny ones in front by the driver's seat. There was a broad door at the back and two steps down. Pretty curtains fluttered at the open windows.

'Red curtains for the green caravan, and green ones for the red caravan!' said Anne. 'Oh, I want to go inside!'

But she couldn't because the doors were locked. So she had to be content to run with the others up the drive after the two caravans, shouting loudly:

'Mummy! They're here, the caravans are here.'

Her mother came running down the steps to see. Soon the doors were unlocked and the children went inside the caravans. Delighted shouts came from both vans.

'Bunks along one side – is that where we sleep? How gorgeous!'

'Look at this little sink – we can really wash up. And golly, water comes out of these taps!'

'There's a proper stove to cook on – but I vote we cook out of doors on a camp fire. I say, look at the bright frying-pans – and all the cups and saucers hanging up!'

'It's like a proper little house inside. Doesn't it seem

nice and *big*? Mother, isn't it beautifully planned? Don't you wish you were coming with us?'

'Hey, you girls! Do you see where the water comes from? Out of that tank on the roof. It must collect rainwater. And look at this gadget for heating water. Isn't it all super?'

The children spent hours examining their caravans and finding out all the secrets. They certainly were very well fitted, spotlessly clean, and very roomy. George felt as if she couldn't wait to start out. She really must get Dobby and set out at once!

'No, you must wait, silly,' said Julian. 'You know we've to get the other horse. He's not coming till tomorrow.'

The other horse was a sturdy little black fellow called Trotter. He belonged to the milkman, who often lent him out. He was a sensible little horse, and the children knew him very well and liked him. They all learnt riding at school, and knew how to groom and look after a horse, so there would be no difficulty over their managing Dobby and Trotter.

Mother was thrilled over the caravans, too, and looked very longingly at them. 'If I wasn't going with Daddy I should be most tempted to come with you,' she said. 'Don't look so startled, Anne dear – I'm not really coming!'

'We're jolly lucky to get such decent caravans,' said Julian. 'We'd better pack our things today, hadn't we, Mother – and start off tomorrow, now we've got the caravans.'

'You won't need to pack,' said his mother. 'All you have to do is to pop your things straight into the cupboards and drawers – you will only want clothes and books and a few games to play in case it's rainy.'

'We don't need any clothes except our night things, do we?' said George, who would have lived in a jersey and jeans all day and every day if she had been allowed to.

'You must take plenty of jerseys, another pair of jeans each, in case you get wet, your rain-coats, bathing-things, towels, a change of shoes, night things, and some cool shirts or blouses,' said Mother. Everyone groaned.

'What a frightful lot of things!' said Dick. 'There'll never be room for all those.'

'Oh yes there will,' said Mother. 'You will be sorry if you take too few clothes, get soaked through, have nothing to change into, and catch fearful colds that will stop you from enjoying a lovely holiday like this.'

'Come on, let's get the things,' said Dick. 'Once Mother starts off about catching cold there's no knowing what else she'll make us take – is there, Mother?'

'You're a cheeky boy,' said his mother, smiling. 'Yes, go and collect your things. I'll help you to put them into the cupboards and drawers. Isn't it marvellous how everything folds so neatly into the walls of the caravans – there seems to be room for everything, and you don't notice the cupboards.'

'I shall keep everything very clean,' said Anne. 'You know how I like *playing* at keeping house, don't you, Mother – well, it will be real this time. I shall have two caravans to keep clean, all by myself.'

'All by yourself!' said her mother. 'Well, surely the boys will help you – and certainly George must.'

'Pooh, the boys!' said Anne. 'They won't know how to wash and dry a cup properly – and George never bothers about things like that. If I don't make the bunks and wash the crockery, they would never be made or washed, I know that!'

'Well, it's a good thing that one of you is sensible!' said her mother. 'You'll find that everyone will share in the work, Anne. Now off you go and get your things. Bring all the rain-coats, to start with.'

It was fun taking things down to the caravans and packing them all in. There were shelves for a few books and games, so Julian brought down snap cards, ludo, lexicon, happy families and dominoes, as well as four or five books for each of them. He also brought down some maps of the district, because he meant to plan out where they were to go, and the best roads to follow.

Daddy had given him a useful little book in which were the names of farms that would give permission to caravanners to camp in fields for the night. 'You must always choose a field where there is a stream, if possible,' said his father, 'because Dobby and Trotter will want water.'

'Remember to boil every drop of water you drink,' said the children's mother. 'That's very important. Get as much milk from the farms as they will let you have. And remember that there is plenty of ginger-beer in the locker under the second caravan.'

'It's all so thrilling,' said Anne, peering down to look at the locker into which Julian had put the bottles of ginger-beer. 'I can't believe we're really going tomorrow.'

But it was true. Dobby and Trotter were to be taken to the caravans the next day and harnessed. How exciting for them, too, Anne thought.

Timmy couldn't quite understand all the excitement, but he shared in it, of course, and kept his tail on the wag all day long. He examined the caravans thoroughly from end to end, found a rug he liked the smell of, and lay down on it. 'This is *my* corner,' he seemed to say. 'If you go off in these peculiar houses on wheels, this is my own little corner.'

'We'll have the red caravan, George,' said Anne. 'The boys can have the green one. They don't care what colour they have – but I love red. I say, won't it be sport to sleep in those bunks? They look jolly comfortable.'

At last tomorrow came – and the milkman brought the sturdy little black horse, Trotter, up the drive. Julian fetched Dobby from the field. The horses nuzzled one another and Dobby and 'Hrrrumph' in a very civil horsy voice.

'They're going to like each other,' said Anne. 'Look at them nuzzling. Trotter, you're going to draw *my* caravan.'

The two horses stood patiently while they were harnessed. Dobby jerked his head once or twice as if he was impatient to be off and stamped a little.

'Oh, Dobby, I feel like that, too!' said Anne. 'Don't you, Dick, don't you, Julian?'

'I do rather,' said Dick with a grin. 'Get up there, Dobby – that's right. Who's going to drive, Julian – take it in turns, shall we?'

'I'm going to drive *our* caravan,' said George. 'Anne

27

wouldn't be any good at it, though I'll let her have a turn at it sometimes. Driving is a man's job.'

'Well, you're only a girl!' said Anne indignantly. 'You're not a man, nor even a boy!'

George put on one of her scowls. She always wanted to be a boy, and even thought of herself as one. She didn't like to be reminded that she was only a girl. But not even George could scowl for long that exciting morning! She soon began to caper round and about again, laughing and calling out with the others:

'We're ready! Surely we're ready!'

'Yes. Do let's go! JULIAN! He's gone indoors, the idiot, just when we want to start.'

'He's gone to get the cakes that Cook has baked this morning for us. We've heaps of food in the larder. I feel hungry already.'

'Here's Julian. Do come on, Julian. We'll drive off without you. Good-bye, Mother! We'll send you a card every single day, we faithfully promise.'

Julian got up on the front of the green caravan. He clicked to Dobby. 'Get on, Dobby! We're off! Good-bye, Mother!'

Dick sat beside him, grinning with pure happiness. The caravans moved off down the drive. George pulled at Trotter's reins and the little horse followed the caravan in front. Anne, sitting beside George, waved wildly.

'Good-bye, Mother! We're off at last on another adventure. Hurrah! Three cheers! Hurrah!'

28

4

Away they go!

The caravans went slowly down the wide road. Julian was so happy that he sang at the top of his voice, and the others joined in the choruses. Timmy barked excitedly. He was sitting on one side of George and as Anne was on the other George was decidedly squashed. But little things like that did not bother her at all.

Dobby plodded on slowly, enjoying the sunshine and the little breeze that raised the hairs on his mane. Trotter followed at a short distance. He was very much interested in Timmy, and always turned his head when the dog barked or got down for a run. It was fun to have two horses and a dog to travel with.

It had been decided that they should make their way towards the hills where they hoped to find the circus. Julian had traced the place in his map. He was sure it must be right because of the lake that lay in the valley at the foot of the hills.

'See?' he said to the others, pointing. 'There it is – Lake Merran. I bet we'll find the circus camp somewhere near it. It would be a very good place for all their animals – no one to interfere with the camp, plenty of water for both animals and men, and probably good farms to supply them with food.'

'We'll have to find a good farm ourselves tonight,' said Dick. 'And ask permission to camp. Lucky we've got that little book telling us where to go and ask.'

Anne thought with delight of the coming evening, when they would stop and camp, cook a meal, drowse over a camp fire, and go to sleep in the little bunks. She didn't know which was nicer – ambling along down country lanes with the caravans – or preparing to settle in for the night. She was sure it was going to be the nicest holiday they had ever had.

'Don't you think so?' she asked George as they sat together on the driving-seat, with Timmy, for once, trotting beside the caravan, and leaving them a little more room than usual. 'You know, most of our hols have been packed with adventures – awfully exciting, I know – but I'd like an *ordinary* holiday now, wouldn't you – not *too* exciting.'

'Oh, I like adventures,' said George, shaking the reins and making Trotter do a little trot. 'I wouldn't a bit mind having another one. But we shan't this time, Anne. No such luck!'

They stopped for a meal at half-past twelve, all of them feeling very hungry. Dobby and Trotter moved towards a ditch in which long, juicy grass grew, and munched away happily.

The children lay on a sunny bank and ate and drank. Anne looked at George. 'You've got more freckles these hols, George, than you ever had in your life before.'

'That doesn't worry *me*!' said George, who never cared in the least how she looked, and was even angry with her hair for being too curly, and making her look too much like a girl. 'Pass the sandwiches, Anne – the tomato ones –

golly, if we always feel as hungry as this we'll have to buy eggs and bacon and butter and milk at every farm we pass!'

They set off again. Dick took his turn at driving Dobby, and Julian walked to stretch his legs. George still wanted to drive, but Anne felt too sleepy to sit beside her with safety.

'If I shut my eyes and sleep I shall fall off the seat,' she said. 'I'd better go into the caravan and sleep there.'

So in she went, all by herself. It was cool and dim inside the caravan, for the curtains had been pulled across the window to keep the inside cool. Anne climbed on to one of the bunks and lay down. She shut her eyes. The caravan rumbled slowly on, and the little girl fell asleep.

Julian peeped in at her and grinned. Timmy came and looked, too, but Julian wouldn't let him go in and wake Anne by licking her.

'You come and walk with me, Tim,' he said. 'You're getting fat. Exercise will do you good.'

'He's *not* getting fat!' called George, indignantly. 'He's a very nice shape. Don't you listen to him, Timmy.'

'Woof,' said Timmy, and trotted along at Julian's heels.

The two caravans covered quite a good distance that day, even though they went slowly. Julian did not miss the way once. He was very good indeed at map-reading. Anne was disappointed that they could not see the hills they were making for, at the end of the day.

'Goodness, they're miles and miles away!' said Julian. 'We shan't arrive for at least four or five days, silly! Now, look out for a farm, kids. There should be one near here, where we can ask permission to camp for the night.'

'There's one, surely,' said George, after a few minutes. She pointed to where a red-roofed building with moss-covered barns, stood glowing in the evening sun. Hens clucked about it, and a dog or two watched them from a gateway.

31

'Yes, that's the one,' said Julian, examining his map. 'Longman's Farm. There should be a stream near it. There it is, look – in that field. Now, if we could get permission to camp just here, it would be lovely.'

Julian went to the farm to see the farmer, and Anne went with him to ask for eggs. The farmer was not there, but the farmer's wife, who liked the look of the tall well-spoken Julian very much, gave them permission at once to spend the night in the field by the stream.

'I know you won't leave a lot of litter, or go chasing the

farm animals,' she said. 'Or l[...]
ill-bred campers do. An[...]
some new-laid eggs? [...]
and you can pick the [...]
with your supper!'

There was bacon in th[...]
Anne said she would fry that [...]
She was very proud of being a[...]
taken a few lessons from Cook in [...]
very anxious to show the others w[...]

Julian said it was too hot to cook [...]
built her a fine fire in the field. Dick se[...]
and they wandered off to the stream, [...]
knee-high in the cool water, enjoying it i[...]
ter muzzled against Dobby, and then tried [...]
to Timmy, too, when the big dog came to [...]
him.

'Doesn't the bacon smell lovely?' called [...]
George, who was busy getting plates and mugs ou[...]
red caravan. 'Let's have ginger-beer to drink, George[...]
jolly thirsty. Watch me crack these eggs on the edge of [...]
cup, everybody, so that I can get out the yolk and whi[...]
and fry them.'

Crack! The egg broke against the edge of the cup – but
its contents unfortunately fell outside the cup instead of
inside. Anne went red when everyone roared with laughter.

Timmy came and licked up the mess. He was very
useful for that sort of thing. 'You'd make a good dust-bin,
Timmy,' said Anne. 'Here's a bit of bacon-rind, too.
Catch!'

Anne fried the bacon and eggs really well. The others
were most admiring, even George, and they all cleared
their plates well, wiping the last bit of fat off with bread, so
that they would be easy to wash.

'Do you think Timmy would like me to fry him a few

cuits, instead of having them cold?' said Anne,
ly. 'Fried things are so nice. I'm sure Timmy
like fried biscuits better than ordinary ones.'
ell, he wouldn't,' said George. 'They would just
e him sick.'
How do you know?' said Anne. 'You can't possibly
.'
I always know what Timmy would really like and
what he wouldn't,' said George. 'And he wouldn't like
his biscuits fried. Pass the plums, Dick. They look
super.'

They lingered over the little camp-fire for a long
time, and then Julian said it was time for bed. Nobody
minded, because they all wanted to try sleeping on the
comfortable-looking bunks.

'Shall I wash at the stream or in the little sink where I
washed the plates?' said Anne. 'I don't know which would
be nicer.'

'There's more water to spare in the stream,' said Julian.
'Hurry up, won't you, because I want to lock your caravan
door so that you'll be safe.'

'Lock our door!' said George, indignantly. 'You jolly
well won't! Nobody's going to lock *me* in! I might think I'd
like to take a walk in the moonlight or something.'

'Yes, but a tramp or somebody might . . .' began Julian. George interrupted him scornfully.

'What about Timmy? You know jolly well he'd never let
anyone come *near* our caravans, let alone into them! I
won't be locked in, Julian. I couldn't bear it. Timmy's
better than any locked door.'

'Well, I suppose he is,' said Julian. 'All right, don't look
so furious, George. Walk half the night in moonlight if you
want to – though there won't be any moon tonight, I'm
sure. Golly, I'm sleepy!'

They climbed into the two caravans, after washing in
the stream. They all undressed, and got into the inviting

34

bunks. There was a sheet, one blanket and a rug – but all the children threw off both blanket and rug and kept only a sheet over them that hot night.

At first Anne tried sleeping in the lower bunk, beneath George – but Timmy would keep on trying to clamber up to get to George. He wanted to lie on her feet as usual. Anne got cross.

'George! You'd better change places with me. Timmy keeps jumping on me and walking all over me trying to get up to your bunk. I'll never get to sleep.'

So George changed places, and after that Timmy made no more noise, but lay contentedly at the end of George's bunk on the rolled-up blanket, while Anne lay in the bunk above, trying not to go to sleep because it was such a lovely feeling to be inside a caravan that stood by a stream in a field.

Owls hooted to one another, and Timmy growled softly. The voice of the stream, contented and babbling, could be quite clearly heard now that everything was so quiet. Anne felt her eyes closing. Oh dear – she would simply *have* to go to sleep.

But something suddenly awoke her with a jump, and Timmy barked so loudly that both Anne and George almost fell out of their bunks in fright. Something bumped violently against the caravan, and shook it from end to end! Was somebody trying to get in?

Timmy leapt to the floor and ran to the door, which George had left open a little because of the heat. Then the voices of Dick and Julian were heard.

'What's up? Are you girls all right? We're coming!' And over the wet grass raced the two boys in their dressing-gowns. Julian ran straight into something hard and warm and solid. He yelled.

Dick switched on his torch and began to laugh help-lessly. 'You ran straight into Dobby. Look at him staring at you! He must have lumbered all round our caravans making the bumps we heard. It's all right, girls. It's only Dobby.'

So back they all went again to sleep, and this time they slept till the morning, not even stirring when Trotter, too, came to nuzzle round the caravan and snort softly in the night.

5

The way to Merran Lake

The next three or four days were absolutely perfect, the children thought. Blue skies, blazing sun, wayside streams to paddle or bathe in, and two houses on wheels that went rumbling for miles down roads and lanes quite new to them – what could be lovelier for four children all on their own?

Timmy seemed to enjoy everything thoroughly, too, and had made firm friends with Trotter, the little black horse. Trotter was always looking for Timmy to run beside him, and he whinnied to Timmy whenever he wanted him. The two horses were friends, too, and when they were set free at night they made for the stream together, and stood in the water side by side, nuzzling one another happily.

'I like this holiday better than any we've ever had,' said Anne, busily cooking something in a pan. 'It's exciting without being adventurous. And although Julian thinks he's in charge of us, *I* am really! You'd never get your

bunks made, or your meals cooked, or the caravans kept
clean if it wasn't for me!'

'Don't boast!' said George, feeling rather guilty because
she let Anne do so much.

'I'm not boasting!' said Anne, indignantly. 'I'm just

telling the truth. Why, you've never even made your own bunk once, George. Not that I mind doing it. I love having two houses on wheels to look after.'

'You're a very good little housekeeper,' said Julian. 'We couldn't possibly do without you!'

Anne blushed with pride. She took the pan off the camp-fire and put the contents on to four plates. 'Come along!' she called, in a voice just like her mother's. 'Have your meal while it's hot.'

'I'd rather have mine when it's cold thank you,' said George. 'It doesn't seem to have got a bit cooler, even though it's evening-time.'

They had been on the road four days now, and Anne had given up looking for the hills where they hoped to find the circus folk camping. In fact she secretly hoped they wouldn't find them, because she was so much enjoying the daily wanderings over the lovely countryside.

Timmy came to lick the plates. The children always let him do that now because it made them so much easier to wash. Anne and George took the things down to a little brown brook to rinse, and Julian took out his map.

He and Dick pored over it. 'We're just about here,' said Julian, pointing. 'And if so, it looks as if tomorrow we ought to come to those hills above the lake. Then we should see the circus.'

'Good!' said Dick. 'I hope Nobby will be there. He would love to show us round, I'm sure. He would show us a good place to camp, too, perhaps.'

'Oh, we can find that ourselves,' said Julian, who now rather prided himself on picking excellent camping-sites. 'Anyway, I don't want to be *too* near the circus. It might be a bit smelly. I'd rather be up in the hills some way above it. We'll get a place with a lovely view.'

'Right,' said Dick, and Julian folded up the map. The two girls came back with the clean crockery, and Anne put it neatly back on the shelves in the red caravan. Trotter came to look for Timmy, who was lying panting under George's caravan.

Timmy wouldn't budge, so Trotter tried to get under the caravan too. But he couldn't possibly, of course, for he was much too big. So he lay down on the shady side, as near to Timmy as he could get.

'Trotter's really a comic horse,' said Dick. 'He'd be quite good in a circus, I should think! Did you see him chasing Timmy yesterday – just as if they were playing "He"?'

The word 'circus' reminded them of Nobby and his circus, and they began to talk eagerly of all the animals there.

'I liked the look of the elephant,' said George. 'I wonder what his name is. And wouldn't I like to hold a monkey!'

'I bet that chimpanzee's clever,' said Dick. 'I wonder what Timmy will think of him. I hope he'll get on all right with all the animals, especially the other dogs.'

'I hope we don't see much of Nobby's uncle,' said Anne. 'He looked as if he'd like to box anybody's ears if they so much as answered him back.'

'Well, he won't box *mine*,' said Julian. 'We'll keep out of his way. He doesn't look a very pleasant chap, I must say. Perhaps he won't be there.'

'Timmy, come out from under the caravan!' called George. 'It's quite cool and shady where we are. Come on!'

He came, panting. Trotter immediately got up and came with him. The little horse lay down beside Timmy and nuzzled him. Timmy gave his nose a lick and then turned away, looking bored.

'Isn't Trotter funny?' said Anne. 'Timmy, what *will* you think of all the circus animals, I wonder! I do hope we see the circus tomorrow. Shall we get as far as the hills, Julian? Though really I shan't mind a bit if we don't; it's so nice being on our own like this.'

40

They all looked out for the hills the next day as the caravans rumbled slowly down the lanes, pulled by Trotter and Dobby. And, in the afternoon, they saw them, blue in the distance.

'There they are!' said Julian. 'Those must be the Merran Hills – and Merran Lake must lie at the foot. I say, I hope the two horses are strong enough to pull the caravans a good way up. There should be an absolutely marvellous view over the lake if we get up high enough.'

The hills came nearer and nearer. They were high ones, and looked lovely in the evening light. Julian looked at his watch.

'We shan't have time to climb them and find a camping site there tonight, I'm afraid,' he said. 'We'd better camp a little way on this evening, and then make our way up into the hills tomorrow morning.'

'All right,' said Dick. 'Anything you say, Captain! There should be a farm about two miles on, according to the book. We'll camp there.'

They came to the farm, which was set by a wide stream that ran swiftly along. Julian went as usual to ask permission to camp, and Dick went with him, leaving the two girls to prepare a meal.

Julian easily got permission, and the farmer's daughter, a plump jolly girl, sold the boys eggs, bacon, milk, and butter, besides a little crock of yellow cream. She also offered them raspberries from the garden if they liked to pick them and have them with the cream.

'Oh, I say, thanks awfully,' said Julian. 'Could you tell me if there's a circus camping in those hills? Somewhere by the lake.'

'Yes, it went by about a week ago,' said the girl. 'It goes camping there every year, for a rest. I always watch the caravans go by – quite a treat in a quiet place like this! One year they had lions, and at nights I could hear them roaring away. That fair frizzled my spine!'

The boys said good-bye and went off, chuckling to think of the farm-girl's spine being 'fair frizzled' by the roars of the distant lions.

'Well, it looks as if we'll pass the circus camp tomorrow all right,' said Julian. 'I shall enjoy camping up in the hills, won't you, Dick? It will be cooler up there, I expect – usually there's a breeze on the hills.'

'I hope we shan't get our spines fair frizzled by the noise of the circus animals at night,' grinned Dick. 'I feel fair frizzled up by the sun today, I must say!'

The next morning the caravans set off again on what the children hoped would be the last lap of their journey. They would find a lovely camping-place and stay there till they had to go home.

Julian had remembered to send a post-card each day to his parents, telling them where he was, and that everything was fine. He had found out from the farm-girl the right address for that district, and he planned to arrange with the nearest post office to take in any letters for them that came. They had not been able to receive any post, of course, when they were wandering about in their caravans.

Dobby and Trotter walked sedately down the narrow country lane that led towards the hills. Suddenly George caught sight of something flashing blue between the trees.

'Look! There's the lake! Merran Lake!' she shouted. 'Make Dobby go more quickly, Ju. I'm longing to come out into the open and see the lake.'

Soon the lane ended in a broad cart-track that led over a heathery common. The common sloped right down to the edge of an enormous blue lake that lay glittering in the August sunshine.

'I say! Isn't it magnificent?' said Dick, stopping Dobby with a pull. 'Come on, let's get down and go to the edge, Julian. Come on, girls!'

'It's lovely!' said Anne, jumping down from the driving-seat of the red caravan. 'Oh, do let's bathe straight away!'

'Yes, let's,' said Julian, and they all dived into their caravans, stripped off jeans and blouses and pulled on bathing-things. Then, without even a towel to dry themselves on, they tore down to the lake-side, eager to plunge into its blue coolness.

It was very warm at the edge of the water, but further in, where it was deep, the lake was deliciously cold. All the children could swim strongly, and they splashed and yelled in delight. The bottom of the lake was sandy, so the water was as clear as crystal.

When they were tired they all came out and lay on the warm sandy bank of the lake. They dried at once in the sun. Then as soon as they felt too hot in they went again, squealing with joy at the cold water.

'What gorgeous fun to come down here every day and bathe!' said Dick. 'Get away, Timmy, when I'm swimming on my back. Timmy's enjoying the bathe as much as we are, George.'

'Yes, and old Trotter wants to come in, too,' shouted Julian. 'Look at him – he's brought the red caravan right down to the edge of the lake. He'll be in the water with it if we don't stop him!'

They decided to have a picnic by the lake, and to set the horses free to have a bathe if they wanted one. But all they wanted was to drink and to stand knee-high in the water, swishing their tails to keep away the flies that worried them all day long.

'Where's the circus camp?' said George suddenly as they sat munching ham and tomato sandwiches. 'I can't see it.'

The children looked all round the edge of the lake, which stretched as far as they could see. At last George's sharp eyes saw a small spire of smoke rising in the air about a mile or so round the lake.

'The camp must be in that hollow at the foot of the hills over there,' she said. 'I expect the road leads round to it. We'll go that way, shall we, and then go up into the hills behind?'

'Yes,' agreed Julian. 'We shall have plenty of time to have a word with Nobby, and to find a good camping-place before night comes – and to find a farm, too, that will let us have food. Won't Nobby be surprised to see us?'

They cleared up, put the horses into their harness again and set off for the circus camp. Now for a bit of excitement!

6

The circus camp and Nobby

It did not take the caravans very long to come in sight of the circus camp. As George had said, it was in a comfortable hollow, set at the foot of the hills – a quiet spot, well away from any dwelling-places, where the circus animals could enjoy a certain amount of freedom and be exercised in peace.

The caravans were set round in a wide circle. Tents had been put up here and there. The big elephant was tied by a thick rope to a stout tree. Dogs ran about everywhere, and a string of shining horses was being paraded round a large field nearby.

'There they all are!' said Anne, excitedly, standing up on a the driving-seat to see better. 'Golly, the chimpanzee is loose, isn't he? No, he isn't – someone has got him on a rope. Is it Nobby with him?'

'Yes, it is. I say, fancy walking about with a live chimp like that!' said Julian.

The children looked at everything with the greatest interest as their caravans came nearer to the circus camp. Few people seemed to be about that hot afternoon. Nobby was there with the chimpanzee, and one or two women were stirring pots over small fires – but that seemed to be all.

The circus dogs set up a great barking as the red and green caravans drew nearer. One or two men came out of the tents and looked up the track that led to the camp. They pointed to the children's caravans and seemed astonished.

Nobby, with the chimpanzee held firmly by the paw,

came out of the camp in curiosity to meet the strange caravans. Julian hailed him.

'Hi, Nobby! You didn't think you'd see *us* here, did you?'

Nobby was amazed to hear his name called. At first he did not remember the children at all. Then he gave a yell.

'Jumping Jiminy, it's you kids I saw away back on the road! What are *you* doing here?'

Timmy growled ominously and George called to Nobby. 'He's never seen a chimpanzee before. Do you think they'll be friends?'

'Don't know,' said Nobby doubtfully. 'Old Pongo likes the circus dogs all right. Anyway, don't you let your dog fly at Pongo, or he'll be eaten alive! A chimp is very strong, you know.'

'Could I make friends with Pongo, do you think?' asked George. 'If he would shake hands with me, or something, Timmy would know I was friends with him and he'd be all right. Would Pongo make friends with me?'

' 'Course he will!' said Nobby. 'He's the sweetest-tempered chimp alive – ain't you, Pongo? Now, shake hands with the lady.'

Anne didn't feel at all inclined to go near the chimpanzee, but George was quite fearless. She walked up to the big animal and held out her hand. The chimpanzee took it at once, raised it to his mouth and pretended to nibble it, making friendly noises all the time.

George laughed. 'He's nice, isn't he?' she said. 'Timmy, this is Pongo, a friend. Nice Pongo, good Pongo!'

She patted Pongo on the shoulder to show Timmy that she liked the chimpanzee, and Pongo at once patted her on the shoulder, too, grinning amiably. He then patted her on the head and pulled one of her curls.

Timmy wagged his tail a little. He looked very doubtful indeed. What was this strange creature that his mistress appeared to like so much. He took a step towards Pongo.

47

'Come on, Timmy, say how do you do to Pongo,' said George. 'Like this.' And she shook hands with the chimpanzee again. This time he wouldn't let her hand go, but went on shaking it up and down as if he was pumping water with a pump-handle.

'He won't let go,' said George.

'Don't be naughty, Pongo,' said Nobby in a stern voice. Pongo at once dropped George's hand and covered his face with a hairy paw as if he was ashamed. But the children saw that he was peeping through his fingers with wicked eyes that twinkled with fun.

'He's a real monkey!' said George, laughing.

'You're wrong – he's an ape!' said Nobby. 'Ah, here comes Timmy to make friends. Jumping Jiminy, they're shaking paws!'

So they were. Timmy, having once made up his mind that Pongo was to be a friend, remembered his manners and held out his right paw as he had been taught. Pongo seized it and shook it vigorously. Then he walked round to the back of Timmy and shook hands with his tail. Timmy didn't know what to make of it all.

The children yelled with laughter, and Timmy sat down firmly on his tail. Then he stood up again, his tail wagging, for Barker and Growler had come rushing up. Timmy remembered them, and they remembered him.

'Well, *they're* making friends all right,' said Nobby, pleased. 'Now they'll introduce Timmy to all the other dogs, and there'll be no trouble. Hey, look out for Pongo, there!'

The chimpanzee had stolen round to the back of Julian and was slipping his hand into the boy's pocket. Nobby went to him and slapped the chimpanzee's paw hard.

'Naughty! Bad boy! Pickpocket!'

The children laughed again when the chimpanzee covered his face with his paws, pretending to be ashamed.

'You'll have to watch out when Pongo's about,' said

Nobby. 'He loves to take things out of people's pockets. I say – do tell me – are those your caravans? Aren't they posh?'

'They've been lent to us,' said Dick. 'As a matter of fact, it was seeing your circus go by, with all its gay caravans, that made us think of borrowing caravans, too, and coming away for a holiday.'

'And as you'd told us where you were going we thought we'd follow you and find you out, and get you to show us round the camp,' said Julian. 'Hope you don't mind.'

'I'm proud,' said Nobby, going a bright red. ' 'Tisn't often folks want to make friends with a circus fellow like me – not gentlefolk like you, I mean. I'll be proud to show you round – and you can make friends with every blessed monkey, dog and horse on the place!'

'Oh, thanks!' said all four at once.

'Jolly decent of you,' said Dick. 'Gosh, look at that chimp – he's trying to shake hands with Timmy's tail again. I bet he's funny in the circus ring, isn't he, Nobby?'

'He's a scream,' said Nobby. 'Brings the house down. You should see him act with my Uncle Dan. He's the chief clown, you know. Pongo is just as big a clown as my uncle is – it's a fair scream to see them act the fool together.'

'I wish we *could* see them,' said Anne. 'Acting in the ring, I mean. Will your uncle mind you showing us all the animals and everything?'

'Why should he?' said Nobby. 'Shan't ask him! But you'll mind and act polite to him, won't you? He's worse than a tiger when he's in a temper. They call him Tiger Dan because of his rages.'

Anne didn't like the sound of that at all – Tiger Dan! It sounded very fierce and savage.

'I hope he isn't about anywhere now,' she said nervously, looking round.

'No. He's gone off somewhere,' said Nobby. 'He's a

49

lonesome sort of chap – got no friends much in the circus, except Lou, the acrobat. That's Lou over there.'

Lou was a long-limbed, loose-jointed fellow with an ugly face, and a crop of black shining hair that curled tightly. He sat on the steps of a caravan, smoking a pipe and reading a paper. The children thought that he and Tiger Dan would make a good pair – bad-tempered, scowling and unfriendly. They all made up their minds that they would have as little as possible to do with Lou the acrobat and Tiger Dan the clown.

'Is he a very good acrobat?' said Anne in a low voice, though Lou was much too far away to hear her.

'Fine. First class,' said Nobby with admiration in his voice. 'He can climb anything anywhere – he could go up that tree there like a monkey – and I've seen him climb a drainpipe straight up the side of a tall building just like a cat. He's a marvel. You should see him on the tight-rope, too. He can dance on it!'

The children gazed at Lou with awe. He felt their glances, looked up and scowled. 'Well,' thought Julian, 'he may be the finest acrobat that ever lived – but he's a jolly nasty-looking fellow. There's not much to choose between him and Tiger Dan!'

Lou got up, uncurling his long body like a cat. He moved easily and softly. He loped to Nobby, still with the ugly scowl on his face.

'Who are these kids?' he said. 'What are they doing messing about here?'

'We're not messing about,' said Julian politely. 'We came to seee Nobby. We've seen him before.'

Lou looked at Julian as if he was something that smelt nasty. 'Them your caravans?' he asked jerking his head towards them.

'Yes,' said Julian.

'Posh, aren't you?' said Lou sneeringly.

'Not particularly,' said Julian, still polite.

50

'Any grown-ups with you?' asked Lou.

'No. I'm in charge,' said Julian, 'and we've got a dog that flies at people he doesn't like.'

Timmy clearly didn't like Lou. He stood near him, growling in his throat. Lou kicked out at him.

George caught hold of Timmy's collar just in time. 'Down Tim, down!' she cried. Then she turned on Lou, her eyes blazing.

'Don't you dare kick my dog!' she shouted. 'He'll have you down on the ground if you do. You keep out of his way, or he'll go for you now.'

Lou spat on the ground in contempt and turned to go. 'You clear out,' he said. 'We don't want no kids messing about here. And I ain't afraid of no dog. I got ways of dealing with bad dogs.'

'What do you mean by that?' yelled George, still in a furious temper. But Lou did not bother to reply. He went up the steps of his caravan and slammed the door shut. Timmy barked angrily and tugged at his collar, which George was still holding firmly.

'Now you've torn it!' said Nobby dismally. 'If Lou catches you about anywhere he'll hoof you out. And you be careful of that dog of yours, or he'll disappear.'

George was angry and alarmed. 'Disappear! What do you mean? If you think Timmy would let anyone steal him, you're wrong.'

'All right, all right. I'm only telling you. Don't fly at me like that!' said Nobby. 'Jumping Jiminy, look at that chimp. He's gone inside one of your caravans!'

The sudden storm was forgotten as everyone rushed to the green caravan. Pongo was inside, helping himself liberally from a tin of sweets. As soon as he saw the children he groaned and covered his face with his paws – but he sucked hard at the sweets all the time.

'Pongo! Bad boy! Come here!' scolded Nobby. 'Shall I whip you?'

'Oh, no, don't,' begged Anne. 'He's a scamp, but I do like him. We've plenty of sweets to spare. You have some, too, Nobby.'

'Well, thank you,' said Nobby, and helped himself. He grinned round at everyone. 'Nice to have friends like you,' he said. 'Ain't it, Pongo?'

7

A tea-party – and a visit in the night

Nobody particularly wanted to see round the camp just then, as Lou had been so unpleasant. So instead they showed the admiring Nobby over the two caravans. He had never seen such beauties.

'Jumping Jiminy, they're like palaces!' he said. 'Do you mean to say them taps turn on and water comes out? Can I turn on a tap? I've never turned a tap in my life!'

He turned the taps on and off a dozen times, exclaiming in wonder to see the water come gushing out. He thumped the bunks to see how soft they were. He admired the gay soft rugs and the shining crockery. He was, in fact, a very nice guest to have, and the children like him more and more. They liked Barker and Growler, too, who were both well-behaved, obedient, merry dogs.

Pongo, of course, wanted to turn the taps on and off, too, and he threw all the coverings off the two bunks to see what was underneath. He also took the kettle off the stove

3

put the spout to his thick lips and drank all the water out of it very noisily indeed.

'You're forgetting your manners, Pongo!' said Nobby in horror, and snatched the kettle away from him. Anne squealed with laughter. She loved the chimpanzee, and he seemed to have taken a great fancy to Anne, too. He followed her about and stroked her hair and made funny affectionate noises.

'Would you like to stay and have tea here with us?' asked Julian, looking at his watch. 'It's about time.'

'Coo – I don't have tea as a rule,' said Nobby. 'Yes, I'd like to. Sure you don't mind me staying, though? I ain't got your manners, I know, and I'm a bit dirty, and not your sort at all. But you're real kind.'

'We'd love to have you stay,' said Anne in delight. 'I'll cut some bread and butter and make some sandwiches. Do you like potted meat sandwiches, Nobby?'

'Don't I just!' said Nobby. 'And Pongo does, too. Don't you let him get near them or he'll finish up the lot.'

It was a pleasant and amusing little tea-party. They all sat out on the heather, on the shady side of the caravan. Barker and Growler sat with Timmy. Pongo sat beside Anne, taking bits of sandwich from her most politely. Nobby enjoyed his tea immensely, eating more sandwiches than anyone and talking all the time with his mouth full.

He made the four children yell with laughter. He imitated his Uncle Dan doing some of his clown tricks. He turned cart-wheels all round the caravan while he was waiting for Anne to cut more sandwiches. He stood solemnly on his head and ate a sandwich like that, much to Timmy's amazement. Timmy walked round and round him, and sniffed at his face as if to say: 'Strange! No legs! Something's gone wrong.'

At last nobody could eat any more. Nobby stood up to go, suddenly wondering if he had stayed too long.

54

'I was enjoying myself so much I forgot the time,' he said awkwardly. 'Bet I've stayed too long and you've been too polite to tell me to get out. Coo, that wasn't half a good tea! Thanks, Miss, awfully, for all them delicious sandwiches. 'Fraid my manners aren't like yours, kids, but thanks for a very good time.'

'You've got very good manners indeed,' said Anne, warmly. 'You've been a splendid guest. Come again, won't you?'

'Well, thanks, I will,' said Nobby, forgetting his sudden awkwardness, and beaming round. 'Where's Pongo? Look at that chimp! He's got one of your hankies, and he's blowing his nose!'

Anne squealed in delight. 'He can keep it!' she said. 'It's only an old one.'

'Will you be here camping for long?' asked Nobby.

'Well, not just exactly *here*,' said Julian. 'We thought of going up higher into the hills. It will be cooler there. But we might camp here just for tonight. We meant to go up higher this evening, but we might as well stay here and go tomorrow morning now. Perhaps we could see round the camp tomorrow morning.'

'Not if Lou's there you can't,' said Nobby. 'Once he's told people to clear out he means it. But it will be all right if he's not. I'll come and tell you.'

'All right,' said Julian. 'I'm not afraid of Lou – but we don't want to get *you* into any trouble, Nobby. If Lou's there tomorrow morning, we'll go on up into the hills, and you can always signal to us if he's out of the camp, and we can come down any time. And mind you come up and see us when you want to.'

'And bring Pongo,' said Anne.

'You bet!' said Nobby. 'Well – so long!'

He went off with Barker and Growler at his heels and with Pongo held firmly by the paw. Pongo didn't want to go at all. He kept pulling back like a naughty child.

'I do like Nobby and Pongo,' said Anne. 'I wonder what Mummy would say if she knew we'd made friends with a chimpanzee. She'd have a fit.'

Julian suddenly looked rather doubtful. He was wondering if he had done right to follow the circus and let Anne and the others make friends with such queer folk and even queerer animals. But Nobby was so nice. He was sure his mother would like Nobby. And they could easily keep away from Tiger Dan and Lou the acrobat.

'Have we got enough to eat for supper tonight and breakfast tomorrow?' he asked Anne. 'Because there doesn't seem to be a farm near enough to go to just here. But Nobby says there's one up on the hill up there – the circus folk get their supplies from it, too – what they don't get from the nearest town. Apparently somebody goes in each day to shop.'

'I'll just see what we've got in the larder, Julian,' said Anne, getting up. She knew perfectly well what there was in the larder – but it made her feel grown-up and important to go and look. It was nice to feel like that when she so often felt small and young, and the others were big and knew so much.

She called back to them: 'I've got eggs and tomatoes and potted meat, and plenty of bread, and a cake we bought today, and a pound of butter.'

'That's all right then,' said Julian. 'We won't bother about going to the farm tonight.'

When darkness fell that night, there were clouds across the sky for the first time. Not a star showed and there was no moon. It was pitch-black, and Julian, looking out of the window of his caravan, before clambering into his bunk, could not even see a shimmer of water from the lake.

He got into his bunk and pulled the covers up. In the other caravan George and Anne were asleep. Timmy was, as usual, on George's feet. She had pushed him off them once or twice, but now that she was asleep he was undisturbed, and lay heavily across her ankles, his head on his paws.

Suddenly his ears cocked up. He raised his head cautiously. Then he growled softly in his throat. He had heard something. He sat there stiffly, listening. He could hear footsteps from two different directions. Then he heard voices – cautious voices, low and muffled.

Timmy growled again, more loudly. George awoke and reached for his collar. 'What's the matter?' she whispered. Timmy listened and so did she. They both heard the voices.

George slipped quietly out of the bunk and went to the half-open door of the caravan. She could not see anything outside at all because it was so dark. 'Don't make a noise, Tim,' she whispered.

Timmy understood. He did not growl again, but George could feel the hairs rising all along the back of his neck.

The voices seemed to come from not very far away. Two men must be talking together, George thought. Then she heard a match struck, and in its light she saw two men lighting their cigarettes from the same match. She recognised them at once – they were Nobby's Uncle Dan and Lou the acrobat.

What were they doing there? Had they got a meeting-place there – or had they come to steal something from the caravans? George wished she could tell Julian and Dick – but she did not like to go out of her caravan in case the men heard her.

At first she could not hear anything the men said. They were discussing something very earnestly. Then one raised his voice.

'Okay, then – that's settled,' Then came the sound of footsteps again, this time towards George's caravan. The men walked straight into the side of it, exclaimed in

surprise and pain, and began to feel about to find out what they had walked into.

'It's those posh caravans!' George heard Lou exclaim. 'Still here! I told those kids to clear out!'

'What kids?' asked Tiger Dan, in surprise. Evidently he had come back in the dark and did not know they had arrived.

'Some kids Nobby knows,' said Lou in an angry voice. He rapped loudly on the walls of the caravan, and Anne woke up with a jump. George, just inside the caravan with Timmy, jumped in fright, too. Timmy barked in rage.

Julian and Dick woke up. Julian flashed on his torch and went to his door. The light picked out the two men standing by George's caravan.

'What are you doing here at this time of night?' said Julian. 'Making a row like that! Clear off!'

This was quite the wrong thing to have said to Dan and Lou, both bad-tempered men who felt that the whole of the camping-ground around belonged to them and the circus.

'Who do you think you're talking to?' shouted Dan angrily. 'You're the ones to clear off! Do you hear?'

'Didn't I tell you to clear out this afternoon?' yelled Lou, losing his temper, too. 'You do as you're told, you young rogue, or I'll set the dogs on you and have you chased for miles.'

Anne began to cry. George trembled with rage. Timmy growled. Julian spoke calmly but determinedly.

'We're going in the morning, as we meant. But if you're suggesting we should go now, you can think again. This is as much our camping-ground as yours. Now get off, and don't come disturbing us again.'

'I'll give you a leathering, you young cockerel!' cried Lou, and began to unfasten the leather belt from round his waist.

George let go her hold of Timmy's collar. 'Go for

them, Timmy,' she said. 'But don't bite. Just worry them!'

Timmy sprang down to the ground with a joyful bark. He flung himself at the two men. He knew what George wanted him to do, and although he longed to snap at the two rogues with his sharp teeth, he didn't. He pretended to, though, and growled so fiercely that they were scared out of their wits.

Lou hit out at Timmy, threatening to kill him. But Timmy cared for no threats of that kind. He got hold of Lou's right trouser-leg, pulled, and ripped it open from knee to ankle.

'Come on – the dog's mad!' cried Dan. 'He'll have us by the throat if we don't go. Call him off, you kids. We're going. But mind you clear out in the morning, or we'll see you do! We'll pay you out one day.'

Seeing that the men really meant to go, George whistled to Timmy. 'Come here, Tim. Stand on guard till they're really gone. Fly at them if they come back.'

But the men soon disappeared – and nothing would have made either of them come back and face Timmy again that night!

8

Up in the hills

The four children were upset and puzzled by the behaviour of the two men. George told how Timmy had wakened her by growling and how she had heard the men talking together in low voices.

'I don't really think they had come to steal anything,' she said. 'I think they were just meeting near here for a secret talk. They didn't know the caravans were here and walked straight into ours.'

'They're bad-tempered brutes,' said Julian. 'And I don't care what you say, George, I'm going to lock your caravan door tonight. I know you've got Timmy – but I'm not running any risk of these men coming back, Timmy or no Timmy.'

Anne was so scared that George consented to let Julian lock the red caravan door. Timmy was locked in with them. The boys went back to their own caravan, and Julian locked his door, too, from the inside. He wanted to be on the safe side.

'I'll be glad to get away from here up into the hills,' he

said. 'I shan't feel safe as long as we are quite so near the camp. We'll be all right up in the hills.'

'We'll go first thing after breakfast,' said Dick, settling down to his bunk again. 'Gosh, it's a good thing the girls had Timmy tonight. Those fellows looked as if they meant to go for you properly, Ju.'

'Yes. I shouldn't have had much chance against the two of them either,' said Julian. 'They are both hefty, strong fellows.'

The next morning all the four awoke early. Nobody felt inclined to lie and snooze – all of them were anxious to get off before Lou and Dan appeared again.

'You get the breakfast, Anne and George, and Dick and I will catch the horses and put them in the caravan shafts,' said Julian. 'Then we shall be ready to go off immediately after breakfast.'

They had breakfast and cleared up. They got up on to the driving-seats and were just about to drive away when Lou and Dan came down the track towards them.

'Oh, you're going, are you?' said Dan, with an ugly grin on his face. 'That's right. Nice to see kids so obedient. Where you going?'

'Up into the hills,' said Julian. 'Not that it's anything to do with you where we go.'

'Why don't you go round the foot of the hills, instead of over the top?' said Lou. 'Silly way to go – up there, with the caravans dragging them horses back all the way.'

Julian was just about to say that he didn't intend to go right up to the top of the hills and over to the other side, when he stopped himself. No – just as well not to let these fellows know that he meant to camp up there, or they might come and worry them all again.

He clicked to Dobby. 'We're going the way we want to go,' he said to Lou in a curt voice. 'And that's up the hill. Get out of the way, please.'

As Dobby was walking straight at them, the men had to

jump to one side. They scowled at the four children. Then they all heard the sound of running footsteps and along came Nobby, with Barker and Growler at his heels as usual.

'Hey, what you going so early for?' he yelled. 'Let me come part of the way with you.'

'No, you don't,' said his uncle, and gave the surprised boy an unexpected cuff. 'I've told these kids to clear out, and they're going. I won't have no meddling strangers round this camp. And don't you kid yourself they want to make friends with you, see! You go and get out those dogs and exercise them, or I'll give you another box on the ears that'll make you see all the stars in the sky.'

Nobby stared at him, angry and afraid. He knew his uncle too well to defy him. He turned on his heel sullenly and went off back to the camp. The caravans overtook him on the way. Julian called to him in a low voice:

'Cheer up, Nobby. We'll be waiting for you up in the hills – don't tell Lou and your uncle about it. Let them think we've gone right away. Bring Pongo up sometime!'

Nobby grinned. 'Right you are!' he said. 'I can bring the dogs up to exercise them, too – but not today. I dursent today. And as soon as them two are safely out for the day I'll bring you down to the camp and show you round, see? That all right?'

'Fine,' said Julian, and drove on. Neither Lou nor Dan had heard a word, or even guessed that this conversation was going on, for Nobby had been careful to walk on all the time and not even turn his face towards the children.

The road wound upwards into the hills. At first it was not very steep, but wound to and fro across the side of the hill. Half-way up the caravans crossed a stone bridge under which a very swift stream flowed.

'That stream's in a hurry!' said George, watching it bubble and gurgle downwards. 'Look – is that where it starts from – just there in the hillside?'

63

She pointed some way up the hill, and it seemed as if the stream really did suddenly start just where she pointed.

'But it can't suddenly start here – not such a big fast stream as this!' said Julian, stopping Dobby on the other side of the bridge. 'Let's go and see, I'm thirsty, and if there's a spring there, it will be very cold and clear – lovely to drink from. Come on, we'll go and see.'

But there was no spring. The stream did not 'begin' just there, but flowed out of a hole in the hillside, as big and as fast as it was just under the stone bridge. The children bent down and peered into the water-filled hole.

'It comes out from inside the hill,' said Anne, surprised. 'Fancy it running around in the hill itself. It must be glad to find a way out!'

They didn't like to drink it as it was not the clear, fresh spring they had hoped to find. But, wandering a little farther on, they came to a real spring that gushed out from beneath a stone, cold and crystal clear. They drank from this and voted that it was the nicest drink they had ever had in their lives. Dick followed the spring-water downwards and saw that it joined the little rushing stream.

'I suppose it flows into the lake,' he said. 'Come on. Let's get on and find a farm, Julian. I'm sure I heard the crowing of a cock just then, so one can't be far away.'

They went round a bend of the hill and saw the farm, a rambling collection of old buildings sprawling down the hillside. Hens ran about, clucking. Sheep grazed above the farm, and cows chewed the cud in fields nearby. A man was working not far off, and Julian hailed him. 'Good morning! Are you the farmer?'

'No. Farmer's over yonder,' said the man, pointing to a barn near the farm house. 'Be careful of the dogs.'

The two caravans went on towards the farm. The farmer heard them coming and came out with his dogs. When he saw that there were only children driving the two caravans he looked surprised.

64

Julian had a polite, well-

all the grown-ups liked

the man, with most

willing to sup—

wanted, and th

any time. His wi—

they asked her to,

'Perhaps I could

Julian. 'I'd like to pay

'That's right, son,' sa—

way as you go along, and

You go and see my old wo—

she'll make you right welcom—

camp?'

'I'd like to camp somewhere w—

lake,' said Julian. 'We can't see it fro—

bit farther on we'll get just the view I w—

'Yes, you go on about half a mile,' said

track goes that far – and when you come to

birch trees you'll see a sheltered hollow, se—

hillside, with a wonderful fine view over the lak—

pull your caravans in there, son, and you'll be

from the winds.'

'Thanks awfully,' said all the children together, t—

ing what a nice man this old farmer was. How differ—

from Lou and Dan, with their threats and rages!

'We'll go and see your wife first, sir,' said Julian. 'Then

we'll go on and pull into the hollow you suggest. We'll be

seeing you again some time, I expect.'

They went to see the farmer's wife, a fat, round-cheeked

old woman, whose little curranty eyes twinkled with good

humour. She made them very welcome, gave them hot

buns from the oven and told them to help themselves to

the little purple plums on the tree outside the old farm

house.

Julian arranged to pay on the spot for anything they

ch day. The prices the farmer's wife asked
ry low indeed, but she would not hear of taking
money for her goods.
e a pleasure to see your bonny faces at my door!'
. 'That'll be part of my payment, see? I can tell
well-brought-up children by your nice manners
ays. You'll not be doing any damage or foolishness
e farm, *I* know.'
he children came away laden with all kinds of food,
n eggs and ham to scones and ginger cakes. She pushed
bottle of raspberry syrup into Anne's hand when the
ttle girl said good-bye. But when Julian turned back to
pay her for it she was quite annoyed.

'If I want to make a present to somebody I'll do it!' she
said. 'Go on with you . . . paying for this and paying for
that. I'll have a little something extra for you each time,
and don't you dare to ask to pay for it, or I'll be after you
with my rolling pin!'

'Isn't she awfully nice?' said Anne as they made their
way back to the caravans. 'Even Timmy offered to shake
hands with her without you telling him to, George – and
he hardly ever does that to anyone, does he?'

They packed the things away into the larder, got up into
the driving-seats, clicked to Dobby and Trotter and set off
up the track again.

Just over half a mile away was a clump of birch trees.
'We'll find that sheltered hollow near them,' said Julian.

'Yes, look – there it is – set back into the hill, a really
cosy place! Just right for camping in – and oh, what a
magnificent view!'

It certainly was. They could see right down the steep
hillside to the lake. It lay spread out, flat and smooth, like
an enchanted mirror. From where they were they could
now see right to the opposite banks of the lake – and it was
indeed a big stretch of water.

'Isn't it blue?' said Anne, staring. 'Bluer even than the

sky. Oh, won't it be lovely to see this marvellous view every single day we're here?'

Julian backed the caravans into the hollow. Heather grew there, like a springy purple carpet. Harebells, pale as an evening sky, grew in clumps in crevices of the hill behind. It was a lovely spot for camping in.

George's sharp ears caught the sound of water and she went to look for it. She called back to the others. 'What do you think? There's another spring here, coming out of the hill. Drinking and washing water laid on! Aren't we lucky?'

'We certainly are,' said Julian. 'It's a lovely place – and nobody will disturb us here!'

But he spoke too soon!

9

An unpleasant meeting

It really was fun settling into that cosy hollow. The two
caravans were backed in side by side. The horses were
taken out and led to a big field where the farmer's horses
were kept when they had done their day's work. Trotter
and Dobby seemed very pleased with the green, sloping
field. It had a spring of its own that ran into a stone trough
and out of it, keeping it always filled with fresh cold water.
Both horses went to take a long drink.

'Well, that settles the two horses all right,' said Julian.
'We'll tell the farmer he can borrow them if he wants
to – he'll be harvesting soon and may like to have Dobby
and Trotter for a few days. They will enjoy hobnobbing
with other horses again.'

At the front of the hollow was a rocky ledge, hung with
heathery tufts. 'This is the front seat for Lake View!' said
Anne. 'Oh, it's warm from the sun! How lovely!'

'I vote we have all our meals on this ledge,' said George,
sitting down too. 'It's comfortable and roomy – and flat
enough to take our cups and plates without spilling

anything – and honestly the view from here is too gorgeous for words. Can anyone see anything of the circus from up here?'

'There's a spire or two of smoke over yonder,' said Dick, pointing. 'I should think that's where the camp is. And look – there's a boat pushing out on the lake – doesn't it look tiny?'

. 'Perhaps Nobby is in it,' said Anne. 'Haven't we brought any field-glasses, Julian? I thought we had.'

'Yes – we have,' said Julian, remembering. 'I'll get them.' He went to the green caravan, rummaged about in the drawers, and came out with his field-glasses swinging on the end of their straps.

'Here we are!' he said, and set them to his eyes. 'Yes – I can see the boat clearly now – and it *is* Nobby in it – but who's with him? Golly, it's Pongo!'

Everyone had to look through the glasses to see Nobby and Pongo in the boat. 'You know, we could always get Nobby to signal to us somehow from his boat when he wanted to tell us that Lou and his uncle were away,' said Dick. 'Then we should know it was safe, and we could pop down to the camp and see round it.'

'Yes. Good idea,' said George. 'Give me the glasses, Dick. Timmy wants to have a turn at seeing, too.'

'He can't see through glasses like these, idiot,' said Dick, handing them to George. But Timmy most solemnly glued his eyes to the glasses, and appeared to be looking through them very earnestly indeed.

'Woof,' he remarked, when he took his eyes away at last.

'He says he's seen Nobby and Pongo, too,' said George, and the others laughed. Anne half-believed that he had. Timmy was such an extraordinary dog, she thought, as she patted his smooth head.

It was a terribly hot day. Too hot to do anything – even to walk down to the lake and bathe! The children were glad they were up in the hills, for at least there was a little breeze that fanned them now and again. They did not expect to see Nobby again that day, but they hoped he would come up the next day. If not they would go down and bathe in the lake and hope to see him somewhere about there.

Soon the rocky ledge got too hot to sit on. The children retreated to the clump of birch trees, which at least cast some shade. They took books with them, and Timmy came along, too, panting as if he had run for miles. He kept going off to the little spring to drink. Anne filled a big bowl with the cold water, and stood it in a breezy place near by, with a cup to dip into it. They were thirsty all day long, and it was pleasant to dip a cup into the bowl of spring-water and drink.

The lake was unbelievably blue that day, and lay as still as a mirror. Nobby's boat was no longer in the water. He and Pongo had gone. There was not a single movement to be seen down by the lake.

'Shall we go down to the lake this evening, when it's cooler, and bathe there?' said Julian, at tea-time. 'We haven't had much exercise today, and it would do us good to walk down and have a swim. We won't take Timmy in case we happen to come across Lou or Dan. He'd certainly fly at them today. We can always keep an eye open for those two and avoid them ourselves – but Timmy would go for them as soon as he spotted them. We might be in the water and unable to stop him.'

'Anyway, he'll guard the caravans for us,' said Anne. 'Well, I'll just take these cups and plates and rinse them in the stream. Nobody wants any more to eat, do they?'

'Too hot,' said Dick, rolling over on to his back. 'I wish we were by the lake at this moment – I'd go straight into the water now!'

At half-past six it was cooler, and the four children set off down the hill. Timmy was angry and hurt at being left behind.

'You're to be on guard, Timmy,' said George firmly. 'See? Don't let anyone come near our caravans. On guard, Timmy!'

'Woof,' said Timmy dismally, and put his tail down. On guard! Didn't George know that the caravans wouldn't walk off by themselves, and that he wanted a good splash in the lake?

Still, he stayed behind, standing on the rocky ledge to see the last of the children, his ears cocked to hear their voices and his tail still down in disgust. Then he went and lay down beneath George's caravan, and waited patiently for his friends to return.

The children went down the hill with their bathing-things, taking short cuts, and leaping like goats over the steep bits. It had seemed quite a long way up when they had gone so slowly in the caravans with Dobby and Trotter – but it wasn't nearly so far when they could go on their own legs, and take rabbit-paths and short cuts whenever they liked.

There was one steep bit that forced them back on to the track. They went along it where the track turned a sharp corner round a cliff-like bend – and to their surprise and dismay they walked almost straight into Lou and Tiger Dan!

'Take no notice,' said Julian, in a low voice. 'Keep together and walk straight on. Pretend that Timmy is somewhere just behind us.'

'Tim, Tim!' called George, at once.

Lou and Dan seemed just as surprised to see the children, as they had been to see the two men. They stopped and looked hard at them, but Julian hurried the others on.

'Hey, wait a minute!' called Dan. 'I thought you had gone off – over the hill-top!'

'Sorry we can't stop!' called back Julian. 'We're in rather a hurry!'

71

Lou looked round for Timmy. He wasn't going to lose his temper and start shouting in case that mad dog came at him again. He spoke to the children loudly, forcing himself to appear good-tempered.

'Where are your caravans? Are you camping up here anywhere?'

But the children still walked on, and the men had to go after them to make them hear.

'Hey! What's the matter? We shan't hurt you! We only want to know if you're camping here. It's better down below, you know.'

'Keep on walking,' muttered Julian. 'Don't tell them anything. Why do they tell us it's better to camp down below when they were so anxious for us to clear out yesterday? They're mad!'

'Timmy, Timmy!' called George, again, hoping that the men would stop following them if they heard her calling for her dog.

It did stop them. They gave up going after the children, and didn't shout any more. They turned angrily and went on up the track.

'Well, we've thrown them off all right,' said Dick, with relief. 'Don't look so scared, Anne. I wonder what they want up in the hills. They don't look the sort that would go walking for pleasure.'

'Dick – we're not going to have another adventure, are we?' said Anne suddenly, looking very woebegone. 'I don't want one. I just want a nice ordinary, peaceful holiday.'

' 'Course we're not going to have an adventure!' said Dick, scornfully. 'Just because we meet two bad-tempered fellows from a circus camp you think we're in for an adventure, Anne! Well, *I* jolly well wish we were! Every hols we've been together so far we've had adventures – and you must admit that you love talking about them and remembering them.'

72

'Yes, I do. But I don't like it much when I'm in the *middle* of one,' said Anne. 'I don't think I'm a very adventurous person, really.'

'No, you're not,' said Julian, pulling Anne over a very steep bit. 'But you're a very nice little person, Anne, so don't worry about it. And, anyway, you wouldn't like to be left out of any of our adventures, would you?'

'Oh *no*,' said Anne. 'I couldn't bear it. Oh, look – we're at the bottom of the hill – and there's the lake, looking icy-cold!'

It wasn't long before they were all in the water – and suddenly there was Nobby too, waving and yelling. 'I'm coming in! Lou and my uncle have gone off somewhere. Hurray!'

Barker and Growler were with Nobby, but not Pongo the chimpanzee. Nobby was soon in the water, swimming like a dog, and splashing George as soon as he got up to her.

'We met Lou and your uncle as we came down,' called George. 'Shut up, Nobby, and let me talk to you. I said, we met Lou and your uncle just now – going up into the hills.'

'Up into the hills?' said Nobby, astonished. 'Whatever for? They don't go and fetch things from the farm. The women do that, early each morning.'

'Well, we met those two,' said Dick swimming up. 'They seemed jolly surprised to see us. I hope they aren't going to bother us any more.'

'I've had a bad day,' said Nobby, and he showed black bruises on his arms. 'My uncle hit me like anything for making friends with you. He says I'm not to go talking to strangers no more.'

'Why ever not?' said Dick. 'What a surly, selfish fellow he is! Well, you don't seem to be taking much notice of him now!'

' 'Course not!' said Nobby. 'He's safe up in the hills, isn't he? I'll have to be careful he doesn't see me with you, that's all. Nobody else at the camp will split on me – they all hate Lou and Tiger Dan.'

'We saw you out in your boat with Pongo,' said Julian, swimming up to join in the conversation. 'We thought that if ever you wanted to signal to us you could easily do it by going out in your boat, and waving a handkerchief or something. We've got field-glasses, and we can easily see you. We could come along down if you signalled. We'd know it would be safe.'

'Right,' said Nobby. 'Come on, let's have a race. Bet you I'm on the shore first!'

He wasn't, of course, because he didn't swim properly. Even Anne could race him. Soon they were all drying themselves vigorously.

'Golly, I'm hungry!' said Julian. 'Come on up the hill with us, Nobby, and share our supper!'

10

A curious change of mind

Nobby felt very much tempted to go and have a meal up in the hills with the children. But he was afraid of meeting Lou and his uncle coming back from their walk.

'We can easily look out for them and warn you if we see or hear them,' said Dick, 'and you can flop under a bush and hide till they go past. You may be sure we'll be on the look-out for them ourselves, because *we* don't want to meet them either!'

'Well, I'll come,' said Nobby. 'I'll take Barker and Growler too. They'll like to see Timmy.'

So all five of them, with the two dogs, set off up the hill. They climbed up short cuts at first, but they were soon panting, and decided to take the track, which, although longer, was easier to follow.

They all kept a sharp look-out for the two men, but they could see no sign of them. 'We shall be at our caravans soon,' said Julian. Then he heard Timmy barking in the distance. 'Hallo! What's old Tim barking for? I wonder if those fellows have been up to our caravans?'

'Good thing we left Timmy on guard if so,' said Dick. 'We might have missed something if not.'

Then he went red, remembering that it was Nobby's uncle he had been talking of. Nobby might feel upset and offended to hear someone speaking as if he thought Tiger Dan would commit a little robbery.

But Nobby wasn't at all offended. 'Don't you worry about what you say of my uncle,' he said, cheerfully. 'He's a bad lot. I know that. Anyway, he's not really my uncle, you know. When my father and mother died, they left a little money for me – and it turned out that they had asked Tiger Dan to look after me. So he took the money, called himself my uncle, and I've had to be with him ever since.'

'Was he in the same circus, then?' asked Julian.

'Oh yes. He and my father were both clowns,' said Nobby. 'Always have been clowns, in my family. But wait till I'm old enough, and I'll do a bunk – clear off and join another circus, where they'll let me look after the horses. I'm mad on horses. But the fellow at our circus won't often let me go near them. Jealous because I can handle them, I suppose!'

The children gazed at Nobby in wonder. He seemed an extraordinary boy to them – one who walked about with a tame chimpanzee, exercised hordes of performing dogs, lived with the chief clown in the circus, could turn the most marvellous cart-wheels, and whose only ambition was to work with horses! What a boy! Dick half-envied him.

'Haven't you ever been to school?' he asked Nobby.

The boy shook his head. 'Never! I can't write. And I can only read a bit. Most circus folk are like that, so nobody minds. Jumping Jiminy, I bet *you're* all clever, though! I bet even little Anne can read a book!'

'I've been able to read for *years*,' said Anne. 'And I'm up to fractions now in numbers.'

'Coo! What fractions?' said Nobby, impressed.

76

'Well – quarters and halves and seven-eighths, and things like that,' said Anne. 'But I'd rather be able to turn a cart-wheel like you can, Nobby, than know how to do fractions.'

'Whatever *is* Timmy barking for?' said George as they came near the clump of birch trees. Then she stopped suddenly, for she had seen two figures lying down in the grass below the trees. Lou – and Tiger Dan!

It was too late for Nobby to hide. The men saw him at once. They got up and waited for the children to come near. George felt thankful that Timmy was within whistling distance. He would come at the first call or whistle, she knew.

Julian looked at the men. To his surprise they appeared to be quite amiable. A faint scowl came over Tiger Dan's face when he caught sight of Nobby, but it passed at once.

'Good evening,' said Julian curtly, and would have passed on without another word, but Lou stepped up to him.

'We see you're camping up by here,' said Lou, and smiled showing yellow teeth. 'Ain't you going over the hill?'

'I don't need to discuss my affairs with either you or your friend,' said Julian, sounding extremely grown-up. 'You told us to clear out from down below, and we have. What we do now is nothing to do with you.'

'Ho yes, it is,' said Tiger Dan, sounding as if he was being polite with great difficulty. 'We come up here tonight to plan a place for some of our animals, see? And we don't want you to be in no danger.'

'We shan't be,' said Julian, scornfully. 'And there is plenty of room on these hills for you and your animals and for us, too. You won't scare us off, so don't think it. We shall stay here as long as we want to – and if we want help there's the farmer and his men quite near by – to say nothing of our dog.'

'Did you leave that there dog on guard?' asked Lou, as he heard Timmy barking again. 'He ought to be destroyed, that dog of yours. He's dangerous.'

'He's only dangerous to rogues and scamps,' said George, joining in at once. 'You keep away from our caravans when Timmy's on guard. He'll maul you if you go near.'

Lou began to lose his temper. 'Well, are you going or ain't you?' he said. 'We've told you we want this here bit of the hill. You can come down and camp by the lake again if you want to.'

78

'Yes – you come,' said Tiger Dan to the children's growing astonishment. 'You come, see? You can bathe in the lake every day, then – and Nobby here can show you round the camp, and you can make friends with all the animals, see?'

Now it was Nobby's turn to look amazed.

'Jumping Jiminy! Didn't you beat me black and blue for making friends with these kids?' he demanded. 'What's the game, now? You've never had animals up in the hills before. You've . . .'

'Shut up,' said Tiger Dan in such a fierce voice that all the children were shocked. Lou nudged Dan, and he made an effort to appear pleasant again.

'We didn't want Nobby to make friends with posh folk like you,' he began again. 'But it seems as if you want to pal up with him – so it's okay with us. You come on down and camp by the lake, and Nobby'll show you everything in the circus. Can't say fairer than that.'

'You've got other reasons for making all these suggestions,' said Julian, scornfully. 'I'm sorry – but our plans are made, and I am not going to discuss them with you.'

'Come on,' said Dick. 'Let's go and find Timmy. He's barking his head off because he can hear us, and it won't be long before he comes flying along here. Then we shall find it difficult to keep him off these two fellows.'

The four children began to move off. Nobby looked doubtfully at his uncle. He didn't know whether to go with them or not. Lou nudged Dan again.

'You go, too, if you want to,' said Tiger Dan, trying to grin amiably at the surprised Nobby. 'Keep your fine friends, see! Much good may they do you!' The grin vanished into a scowl, and Nobby skipped smartly out of reach of his uncle's hand. He was puzzled and wondered what was behind his uncle's change of mind.

He tore after the children. Timmy came to meet them, barking his head off, waving his plumy tail wildly in joy.

79

'Good dog, good dog!' said George, patting him. 'You keep on guard beautifully. You know I would have whistled for you if I'd wanted you, didn't you, Timmy? Good dog!'

'I'll get you some supper,' said Anne to everyone. 'We're all famishing. We can talk while we eat. George, come and help. Julian, can you get some ginger-beer? And, Dick, do fill up the water-bowl for me.'

The boys winked at one another. They always thought that Anne was very funny when she took command like this, and gave her orders. But everyone went obediently to work.

Nobby went to help Anne. Together they boiled ten eggs hard in the little saucepan. Then Anne made tomato sandwiches with potted meat and got out the cake the farmer's wife had given them. She remembered the raspberry syrup, too – how lovely!

Soon they were all sitting on the rocky ledge, which was still warm, watching the sun go down into the lake. It was a most beautiful evening, with the lake as blue as a cornflower and the sky flecked with rosy clouds. They held their hard-boiled eggs in one hand and a piece of bread and butter in the other, munching happily. There was a dish of salt for everyone to dip their eggs into.

'I don't know why, but the meals we have on picnics always taste so much nicer than the ones we have indoors,' said George. 'For instance, even if we had hard-boiled eggs and bread and butter indoors, they wouldn't taste as nice as these.'

'Can everyone eat two eggs?' asked Anne. 'I did two each. And there's plenty of cake – and more sandwiches and some plums we picked this morning.'

'Best meal I've ever had in my life,' said Nobby, and picked up his second egg. 'Best company I've ever been in, too!'

'Thank you,' said Anne, and everyone looked pleased.

Nobby might not have their good manners, but he always seemed to say just the right thing.

'It's a good thing your uncle didn't make you go back with him and Lou,' said Dick. 'Funny business – changing his mind like that!'

They began to talk about it. Julian was very puzzled indeed, and had even begun to wonder if he hadn't better find another camping site and go over the hill.

The others raised their voices scornfully.

'JULIAN! We're not cowards. We'll jolly well stay here!'

'What, leave now – why should we? We're in nobody's way, whatever those men say!'

'*I'm* not moving *my* caravan, whatever *anyone* says!' That was George, of course.

'No, don't you go,' said Nobby. 'Don't you take no notice of Lou and my uncle. They can't do nothing to you at all. They're just trying to make trouble for you. You stay and let me show you over the camp, see?'

'It isn't that I *want* to give in to those fellows' ideas,' said Julian. 'It's just that – well, I'm in charge of us all – and I *don't* like the look of Lou and Tiger Dan – and, well . . .'

'Oh, have another egg and forget about it,' said Dick. 'We're going to stay here in this hollow, however much Dan and Lou want us out of it. And, what's more, I'd like to find out why they're so keen to push us off. It seems jolly queer to me.'

The sun went down in a blaze of orange and red, and the lake shimmered with its fiery reflection. Nobby got up regretfully, and Barker and Growler, who had been hobnobbing with Timmy, got up, too.

'I'll have to go,' said Nobby. 'Still got some jobs to do down there. What about you coming down tomorrow to see the animals? You'll like Old Lady, the elephant. She's a pet. And Pongo will be pleased to see you again.'

'Your uncle may have changed his mind again by tomorrow, and not want us near the camp,' said Dick.

'Well – I'll signal to you,' said Nobby. 'I'll go out in the boat, see? And wave a hanky. Then you'll know it's all right. Well – so long! I'll be seeing you.'

11

Fun at the circus camp

Next morning, while Anne cleared up the breakfast things with George, and Dick went off to the farm to buy whatever the farmer's wife had ready for him, Julian took the field-glasses and sat on the ledge to watch for Nobby to go out on the lake in his boat.

Dick sauntered along, whistling. The farmer's wife was delighted to see him, and showed him two big baskets full of delicious food.

'Slices of ham I've cured myself,' she said, lifting up the white cloth that covered one of the baskets. 'And a pot of brawn I've made. Keep it in a cool place. And some fresh lettuces and radishes I pulled myself this morning early. And some more tomatoes.'

'How gorgeous!' said Dick, eyeing the food in delight. 'Just the kind of things we love! Thanks awfully, Mrs Mackie. What's in the other basket?'

'Eggs, butter, milk, and a tin of shortbread I've baked,' said Mrs Mackie. 'You should do all right till tomorrow, the four of you! And in that paper there is a bone for the dog.'

'How much do I owe you?' asked Dick. He paid his bill and took up the baskets. Mrs Mackie slipped a bag into his pocket.

'Just a few home-made sweets,' she said. That was her little present. Dick grinned at her.

'Well, I won't offer to pay you for them because I'm afraid of that rolling-pin of yours,' he said. 'But thank you very, very much.'

He went off delighted. He thought of Anne's pleasure when she came to unpack the baskets. How she would love to put the things in the little larder – and pop the butter in a dish set in a bowl of cold water – and set the eggs in the little rack!

When he got back Julian called to him: 'Nobby's out in his boat. Come and look. He's waving something that can't possibly be a hanky. It must be the sheet off his bed!'

'Nobby doesn't sleep in sheets,' said Anne. 'He didn't know what they were when he saw them in our bunks. Perhaps it's a table-cloth.'

'Anyway, it's something big, to tell us that it's absolutely all right to come down to the camp,' said Julian. 'Are we ready?'

'Not quite,' said Anne, unpacking the baskets Dick had brought. 'I must put away these things – and do you want to take a picnic lunch with you? Because if so I must prepare it. Oh – look at all these gorgeous things!'

They all came back to look. 'Mrs Mackie is a darling,' said Anne. 'Honestly, these things are super – look at this gorgeous ham. It smells heavenly.'

'Here's her little present – home-made sweets,' said Dick, remembering them and taking them out of his pocket. 'Have one!'

Anne had everything ready in half an hour. They had decided to take a picnic lunch with them for themselves and for Nobby as well. They took their bathing-things and towels, too.

84

'Are we going to take Timmy or not?' said George. 'I want to. But as these two men seem rather interested in our caravans, perhaps we had better leave him on guard again. We don't want to come back and find the caravans damaged or half the things stolen.'

'I should think not!' said Dick. 'They're not our things, nor our caravans. They belong to somebody else and we've got to take extra good care of them. I think we ought to leave Timmy on guard, don't you, Ju?'

'Yes, I do,' said Julian at once. 'These caravans are too valuable to leave at the mercy of any passing tramp – though I suppose we could lock them up. Anyway – we'll leave Timmy on guard today – poor old Timmy, it's a shame, isn't it?'

Timmy didn't answer. He looked gloomy and miserable. What! They were all going off without him again? He knew what 'on guard' meant – he was to stay here with these houses on wheels till the children chose to come back. He badly wanted to see Pongo again. He stood with his ears and tail drooping, the picture of misery.

But there was no help for it. The children felt that they couldn't leave the caravans unguarded while they were still so uncertain about Lou and Tiger Dan. So they all patted poor Timmy and fondled him, and then said good-bye. He sat down on the rocky ledge with his back to them and wouldn't even watch them go.

'He's sulking,' said George. 'Poor Timothy!'

It didn't take them very long to get down to the camp, and they found Nobby, Pongo, Barker and Growler waiting for them. Nobby was grinning from ear to ear.

'You saw my signal all right?' he said. 'Uncle hasn't changed his mind – in fact, he seems quite to have taken to you, and says I'm to show you all round and let you see anything you want to. That was his shirt I waved. I thought if I waved something enormous you'd know things were absolutely safe.'

'Where shall we put the bathing-things and the picnic baskets while we see round the camp?' asked Anne. 'Somewhere cool, if possible.'

'Put them in my caravan,' said Nobby, and led them to a caravan painted blue and yellow, with red wheels. The children remembered having seen it when the procession passed by their house a week or two before.

They peeped inside. It wasn't nearly so nice as theirs. It was much smaller, for one thing, and very untidy. It looked dirty, too, and had a nasty smell. Anne didn't like it very much.

'Not so good as yours!' said Nobby. 'I wish I had a caravan like yours. I'd feel like a prince. Now what do you want to see first? The elephant? Come on, then.'

They went to the tree to which Old Lady the elephant was tied. She curled her trunk round Nobby and looked at the children out of small, intelligent eyes.

'Well, Old Lady!' said Nobby. 'Want a bathe?'

The elephant trumpeted and made the children jump. 'I'll take you later on,' promised Nobby. 'Now then – hup, hup, hup!'

At these words the elephant curled her trunk tightly round Nobby's waist and lifting him bodily into the air, placed him gently on her big head!

Anne gasped.

'Oh! Did he hurt you, Nobby?'

' 'Course not!' said Nobby. 'Old Lady wouldn't hurt anyone, would you, big one?'

A small man came up. He had bright eyes that shone as if they had been polished, and a very wide grin. 'Good morning,' he said. 'How do you like my Old Lady? Like to see her play cricket?'

'Oh, *yes*!' said everyone, and the small man produced a cricket bat and held it out to Old Lady. She took it in her trunk and waved it about. Nobby slipped deftly off her head to the ground.

'I'll play with her, Larry,' he said, and took the ball
from the small man. He threw it to Old Lady and she hit it
smartly with the bat. It sailed over their heads!

Julian fetched the ball. He threw it at the elephant, and
again the great creature hit the ball with a bang. Soon all
the children were playing with Old Lady and enjoying the
game very much.

Some small camp children came up to watch. But they
were as scared as rabbits as soon as Julian or George spoke
to them and scuttled off to their caravans at once. They
were dirty and ragged, but most of them had beautiful
eyes and thick curly hair, though it wanted brushing and
washing.

Nobby went to fetch Pongo, who was dancing to and fro
in his cage, making anguished sounds, thinking he was

forgotten. He was simply delighted to see the children again, and put his arm right round Anne at once. Then he pulled George's hair and hid his face behind his paws, peeping out mischievously.

'He's a caution, aren't you, Pongo?' said Nobby. 'Now you keep with me, Pongo, or I'll put you back into your cage, see?'

They went to see the dogs and let them all out. They were mostly terrier dogs, or mongrels, smart, well-kept little things who jumped up eagerly at Nobby, and made a great fuss of him. It was clear that they loved him and trusted him.

'Like to see them play football?' asked Nobby. 'Here, Barker – fetch the ball. Go on, quick!'

Barker darted off to Nobby's caravan. The door was shut, but the clever little dog stood on his hind legs and jerked the handle with his nose. The door opened and in went Barker. He came out dribbling a football with his nose. Down the steps it went and into the camp field. All the dogs leapt on it with howls of delight.

'Yap-yap-yap! Yap-yap!' They dribbled that football to and fro, while Nobby stood with his legs open to make a goal for them.

It was Barker's job and Growler's to score the goals, and the task of the other dogs to stop them. So it was a most amusing game to watch. Once, when Barker scored a goal by hurling himself on the ball and sending it rolling fast between Nobby's arched legs, Pongo leapt into the fray, picked up the ball and ran off with it.

'Foul, foul!' yelled Nobby and all the dogs rushed after the mischievous chimpanzee. He leapt on to the top of a caravan and began to bounce the ball there, grinning down at the furious dogs.

'Oh, this is such fun!' said Anne, wiping the tears of laughter from her eyes. 'Oh, dear! I've got such a pain in my side from laughing.'

Nobby had to climb up to the roof of the caravan to get the ball. Pongo jumped down the other side, but left the ball balanced neatly on the chimney. He was really a most mischievous chimpanzee.

Then they went to see the beautiful horses. All of them had shining satiny coats. They were being trotted round a big field by a slim, tall young fellow called Rossy, and they obeyed his slightest word.

'Can I ride Black Queen, Rossy?' asked Nobby eagerly. 'Do let me!'

'Okay,' said Rossy, his black hair shining like the horses' coats. Then Nobby amazed the watching children, for he leapt on to a great black horse, stood up on her back and trotted all round the field like that!

'He'll fall!' cried Anne. But he didn't, of course. Then he suddenly swung himself down on to his hands and rode Black Queen standing upside down.

'Good, good!' cried Rossy. 'You are good with horses, young one! Now ride Fury!'

Fury was a small, fiery-looking little horse, whose gleaming eyes showed a temper. Nobby ran to her and leapt on her bare-backed. She rose up, snorting and tried to throw him off. But he wouldn't be thrown off. No matter what she did, Nobby clung on like a limpet to a rock.

At last Fury tired of it, and began to canter round the field. Then she galloped – and suddenly she stopped absolutely dead, meaning to fling Nobby over her head!

But the boy was waiting for that trick and threw himself backwards at once. 'Good, good!' cried Rossy. 'She will soon eat out of your hand, Nobby! Good boy.'

'Nobby, Nobby, you're terribly clever!' yelled Anne. 'Oh, I wish I could do the things you do! I wish I could.'

Nobby slid off Fury's back, looking pleased. It was nice to show off a little to his 'posh' friends. Then he looked round and about. 'I say – where's that chimp? Up to some mischief, I'll be bound! Let's go and find him.'

12

A lovely day – with a horrid end

They soon saw Pongo. He was coming round one of the caravans, looking exceedingly pleased with himself. He went to Anne and held out his paw to her, making little affectionate noises.

Anne took what he held. She looked at it. 'It's a hard-boiled egg! Oh, Nobby, he's been at the picnic baskets!'

So he had! Two of the eggs were gone, and some of the tomatoes! Nobby smacked the chimpanzee and took him back to his cage. He was very sad and made a noise as if he was crying, hiding his face in his paws. Anne was upset.

'Is he really crying? Oh, do forgive him, Nobby. He didn't mean to be naughty.'

'He's not crying. He's only pretending,' said Nobby. 'And he *did* mean to be naughty. I know him!'

The morning soon went in visiting the circus animals. It

90

was dinner-time before they had had time to see the monkeys. 'We'll see them afterwards,' said Nobby. 'Let's have a meal now. Come on. We'll go and have it by the lake.'

The children hadn't seen Lou or Tiger Dan at all, much to their joy. 'Where are they?' asked Julian. 'Gone out for the day?'

'Yes, thank goodness,' said Nobby. 'Gone out on one of their mysterious jaunts. You know, when we're on the road, going from place to place, my uncle sometimes disappears at night. I wake up – and he's not there.'

'Where does he go?' asked George.

'I wouldn't dare to ask,' said Nobby. 'Anyway, he and Lou are out of the way today. I don't expect they'll be back till night.'

They had their meal by the lake. It glittered at their feet, calm and blue, and looked very inviting.

'What about a swim?' asked Dick when they had eaten as much as they could. Julian looked at his watch.

'Can't swim directly after a good meal,' he said. 'You know that, Dick. We'll have to wait a bit.'

'Right,' said Dick, and lay down. 'I'll have a snooze – or shall we go and see the monkeys?'

They all had a short nap and then got up to go and see the monkeys. When they got back to the camp they found it alive with people, all excited and yelling.

'What's up?' said Nobby. 'Jumping Jiminy, the monkeys are all loose!'

So they were. Wherever they looked the children saw a small brown monkey, chattering to itself, on the roof of a caravan or tent!

A brown-faced woman with sharp eyes came up to Nobby. She caught him by the shoulder and shook him. 'See what that chimp of yours has done!' she said. 'You put him in his cage and couldn't have locked it properly. He got out and let all the monkeys loose. Drat that chimp – I'll take a broomstick to him if ever I catch him!'

'Where's Lucilla then?' asked Nobby, dragging himself away from the cross woman. 'Can't she get them in?'

'Lucilla's gone to the town,' scolded the woman. 'And fine and pleased she'll be to hear this when she comes back!'

'Aw, let the monkeys be!' said Nobby. 'They won't come to any harm. They'll wait for Lucilla all right!'

'Who's Lucilla?' asked Anne, thinking that life in a circus camp was very exciting.

'She owns the monkeys,' said Nobby. 'Hi, look – there's Lucilla coming back! Now we'll be all right!'

A little wizened old woman was hurrying towards the camp. She really looked rather like a monkey herself, Anne thought. Her eyes were bright and sharp, and her tiny hands clutched a red shawl round her. They looked like brown paws.

'Your monkeys are out!' yelled the camp children. 'LUCILLA! Your monkeys are out.'

Lucilla heard and, raising her voice, she scolded everyone in sight fully and shrilly. Then she stood still and held out her arms. She spoke some soft words in a language the children didn't know – magic words, Anne said afterwards.

One by one the wandering monkeys came scampering over to her, flinging themselves down from the caravan roofs, making little chattering sounds of love and welcome. They leapt on to Lucilla's shoulders and into her arms, cuddling against her like tiny brown children. Not one monkey was left out – all went to Lucilla as if drawn by some enchantment.

She walked slowly towards their cage, murmuring her soft words as she went. Everyone watched in silence.

'She's a queer one,' said the brown-faced woman to Nobby. 'She don't love nobody but her monkeys – and there's nobody loves her but them. You mind out she doesn't go for that chimp of yours, letting out her precious monkeys!'

'I'll take him and Old Lady down to bathe,' said Nobby, hastily. 'By the time we're back, Lucilla will have forgotten.'

They fetched Old Lady and discovered where naughty Pongo was hiding under a caravan. As quickly as possible they went back to the lake, Old Lady stepping out well, looking forward to her bathe.

'I suppose things like that are always happening in a circus camp,' said Anne. 'It's not a bit like real life.'

'Isn't it?' said Nobby, surprised. 'It's real life all right to *me!*'

It was cool in the lake and they all enjoyed themselves very much, swimming and splashing. Pongo wouldn't go in very far, but splashed everyone who came within reach, laughing and cackling loudly. He gave Old Lady a shock by leaping up on to her back, and pulling one of her big ears.

She dipped her trunk into the lake, sucked up a lot of water, turned her trunk over her back, and squirted the water all over the startled chimpanzee! The children yelled with laughter, and roared again to see Pongo falling in fright off Old Lady's back. Splash! He went right in and got himself wet from head to foot – a thing he hated doing.

'Serves you right, you scamp!' shouted Nobby. 'Hey, Old Lady, stop it! Don't squirt at me!'

The elephant, pleased with her little joke, didn't want to stop it. So the children had to keep well away from her, for her aim was very good.

'I've never had such a lovely time in my life!' said Anne, as she dried herself. 'I shall dream all night of monkeys and elephants, horses, dogs and chimpanzees!'

Nobby turned about twenty cart-wheels by the edge of the lake from sheer good spirits – and Pongo at once did the same. He was even better at it than Nobby. Anne tried and fell down flop immediately.

They went back to the camp. 'Sorry I can't offer you any tea,' said Nobby, 'but we never seem to have tea, you know – we circus folk, I mean. Anyway, I'm not hungry after that enormous lunch. Are you?'

Nobody was. They shared out Mrs Mackie's home-made toffees, and gave one to Pongo. It stuck his teeth together, and he looked so comically alarmed when he found that he couldn't open his mouth that the children roared at him.

He sat down, swayed from side to side, and began to groan dismally. But the toffee soon melted away, and he found that he could open his mouth after all. He sucked the rest of the sweet noisily, but wouldn't have another.

They wandered round the camp, looking at the different caravans. Nobody took much notice of them now. They were just Nobby's 'posh' friends – that was all. Some of the smaller children peeped out and stuck out their little red tongues – but at Nobby's roar they vanished.

'Got no manners at all!' said Nobby. 'But they're all right really.'

They came to where big wagons stood, stored with all kinds of circus things. 'We don't bother to unpack these when we're resting in camp like this,' said Nobby. 'Don't need them here. One of my jobs is to help to unpack this stuff when we're camping to give a show. Have to get out all them benches and set them up in the big top – that's the circus tent, you know. We're pretty busy then, I can tell you!'

'What's in *this* cart?' asked Anne, coming to a small wagon with a tightly-fitting hood of tarpaulin.

'Don't know,' said Nobby. 'That cart belongs to my uncle. He won't never let me unpack it. I don't know what

94

he keeps there. I've wondered if it was things belonging to my Dad and Mum. I told you they were dead. Anyway, I thought I'd peep and see one day; but Uncle Dan caught me and half-killed me!'

'But if they belonged to your parents, they ought to be yours!' said George.

'Funny thing is, sometimes that cart's crammed full,' said Nobby. 'And sometimes it isn't. Maybe Lou puts some of his things there too.'

'Well, nobody could get anything else in there at the moment!' said Julian. 'It's full to bursting!'

They lost interest in the little wagon and wandered round to see the 'props' as Nobby called them. Anne pictured these as clothes-props, but they turned out to be gilt chairs and tables, the shining poles used for the tight-rope, gaily-painted stools for the performing dogs to sit on, and circus 'props' of that kind.

'*Prop*erties, Anne,' said Julian. 'Circus *prop*erties. Props for short. Look here, isn't it about time we went back? My watch has stopped. Whatever time is it?'

'Golly, it's quite late!' said Dick, looking at his watch. 'Seven o'clock. No wonder I feel jolly hungry. Time we went back. Coming with us, Nobby? You can have supper up there if you like. I bet you could find your way back in the dark.'

'I'll take Pongo with me, and Barker and Growler,' said Nobby, delighted at the invitation. 'If *I* lose the way back, *they* won't!'

So they all set off up the hill, tired with their long and exciting day. Anne began to plan what she would give the little company for supper. Ham, certainly – and tomatoes – and some of that raspberry syrup diluted with icy-cold spring-water.

They all heard Timmy barking excitedly as soon as they came near the caravans. He barked without ceasing, loudly and determinedly.

'He sounds cross,' said Dick. 'Poor old Tim! He must think we've quite deserted him.'

They came to the caravans and Timmy flung himself on George as if he hadn't seen her for a year. He pawed her and licked her, then pawed her again.

Barker and Growler were pleased to see him too, and as for Pongo, he was delighted. He shook hands with Timmy's tail several times, and was disappointed that Timmy took no notice of him.

'Hallo! What's Barker gnawing at?' suddenly said Dick. 'Raw meat! How did it come here? Do you suppose the farmer has been by and given Timmy some? Well, why didn't he eat it, then?'

They all looked at Barker, who was gnawing some meat on the ground. Growler ran to it too. But Timmy would

96

not go near it. Nor would Pongo. Timmy put his tail down and Pongo hid his furry face behind his paws.

'Funny,' said the children, puzzled at the queer behaviour of the two animals. Then suddenly they understood – for poor Barker suddenly gave a terrible whine, shivered from head to foot, and rolled over on his side.

'Jiminy – it's poisoned!' yelled Nobby, and kicked Growler away from the meat. He picked Barker up, and to the children's utter dismay they saw that Nobby was crying.

'He's done for,' said the boy, in a choking voice. 'Poor old Barker.'

Carrying Barker in his arms, with Growler and Pongo behind him, poor Nobby stumbled down the hill. No one liked to follow him. Poisoned meat! What a terrible thing.

13

Julian thinks of a plan

George was trembling. Her legs felt as if they wouldn't hold her up, and she sank down on the ledge. She put her arms round Timmy.

'Oh, Timmy! That meat was meant for you! Oh, thank goodness, thank goodness you were clever enough not to touch it! Timmy, you might have been poisoned!'

Timmy licked his mistress soberly. The others stood round, staring, not knowing what to think. Poor Barker! Would he die? Suppose it had been old Timmy? They had left him all alone, and he might have eaten the meat and died.

'I'll never, never leave you up here alone again!' said George.

'Who threw him the poisoned meat, do you think?' said Anne, in a small voice.

'Who do you suppose?' said George, in a hard, scornful voice. 'Lou and Tiger Dan!'

'They want to get us away from here, that's plain,' said Dick. 'But again – why?'

'What can there be about this place that makes the men want to get rid of us all?' wondered Julian. 'They're real rogues. Poor Nobby. He must have an awful life with them. And now they've gone and poisoned his dog.'

Nobody felt like eating very much that evening. Anne got out the bread and the butter and a pot of jam. George wouldn't eat anything. What a horrid end to a lovely day!

They all went to bed early, and nobody objected when Julian said he was going to lock both the caravans. 'Not that I think either Lou or Dan will be up here tonight,' he said. 'But you never know!'

Whether they came or not the children didn't know, for although Timmy began to bark loudly in the middle of the night, and scraped frantically at the shut door of George's caravan, there was nothing to be seen or heard when Julian opened his door and flashed on his torch.

Timmy didn't bark any more. He lay quite quietly sleeping with one ear cocked. Julian lay in bed and thought hard. Probably Lou and Dan had come creeping up in the dark, hoping that Timmy had taken the meat and been poisoned. But when they heard him bark, they knew he was all right, and they must have gone away again. What plan would they make next?

'There's something behind all this,' Julian thought, again and again. 'But what can it be? Why do they want us out of this particular spot?'

He couldn't imagine. He fell asleep at last with a vague plan in his mind. He would tell it to the others tomorrow. Perhaps if he could make Lou and Dan think they had all gone off for the day – with Timmy – but really, he, Julian, would be left behind, in hiding – maybe he could find out something, if Lou and Dan came along . . .

Julian fell asleep in the middle of thinking out his plan. Like the others, he dreamt of elephants squirting him with water, of Pongo chasing the monkeys, of the dogs playing football with excited yaps – and then into the dream came lumps of poisoned meat! Horrid.

Anne woke with a jump, having dreamt that someone had put poison into the hard-boiled eggs they were going to eat. She lay trembling in her bunk, and called to George in a small voice.

'George! I've been having an awful dream!'

George woke up, and Timmy stirred and stretched himself. George switched on her torch.

'I've been having beastly dreams, too,' she said. 'I dreamt that those men were after Timmy. I'll leave my torch on for a bit and we'll talk. I expect that with all the excitement we've had today, and the horrid end to it this evening, we're just in the mood for horrid dreams! Still – they are only dreams.'

'Woof,' said Timmy, and scratched himself.

'Don't,' said George. 'You shake the whole caravan when you do that, Timmy. Stop it.'

Timmy stopped. He sighed and lay down heavily. He put his head on his paws and looked sleepily at George, as if to say, 'put that torch out. I want to go to sleep.'

The next morning was not so warm, and the sky was cloudy. Nobody felt very cheerful, because they kept thinking of Nobby and poor Barker. They ate their breakfast almost in silence, and then Anne and George began to stack the plates, ready to take them to the spring to rinse.

'*I'll* go to the farm this morning,' said Julian. 'You sit on the ledge and take the field-glasses, Dick. We'll see if Nobby goes out in his boat and waves. I've an idea that he won't want us down in the camp this morning. If he suspects his Uncle Dan and Lou of putting down the meat that poisoned Barker, he'll probably have had a frightful row with them.'

He went off to the farm with two empty baskets. Mrs Mackie was ready for him, and he bought a further supply of delicious-looking food. Her present this time was a round ginger cake, warm from the oven!

'Do the circus folk come up here often to buy food?' asked Julian, as he paid Mrs Mackie.

'They come sometimes,' said Mrs Mackie. 'I don't mind the women or the children – dirty though they are, and not above taking one of my chickens now and again – but it's the men I can't abide. There were two here last year, messing about in the hills, that my husband had to send off quick.'

Julian pricked up his ears. 'Two men? What were they like?'

'Ugly fellows,' said Mrs Mackie. 'And one had the yellowest teeth I ever saw. Bad-tempered chaps, both of them. They came up here at night, and we were afraid our chickens would go. They swore they weren't after our chickens – but what else would they be up here at night for?'

'I can't imagine,' said Julian. He was sure that the two men Mrs Mackie spoke of were Lou and Tiger Dan. Why did they wander about in the hills at night?

He went off with the food. When he got near the camping-place, Dick called to him excitedly.

'Hey, Julian! Come and look through the glasses. Nobby's out in his boat with Pongo, and I simply can't make out what it is they're both waving.'

Julian took the glasses and looked through them. Far down the hill, on the surface of the lake, floated Nobby's little boat. In it was Nobby, and with him was Pongo. Both of them were waving something bright red.

'Can't see what they're waving – but that doesn't matter,' said Julian. 'The thing is – what they're waving is red, not white. Red for danger. He's warning us.'

'Golly – I didn't think of that. What an idiot I am! said Dick. 'Yes – red for danger. What's up, I wonder?'

'Well, it's clear we'd better not go down to the camp

today,' said Julian. 'And it's also clear that whatever danger there is, is pretty bad – because both he *and* Pongo are waving red cloths – doubly dangerous!'

'Julian, you're jolly sharp,' said George, who was listening. 'You're the only one of us who tumbled to all that. Double-danger. What can it be?'

'Perhaps it means danger down at the camp, and danger here too,' said Julian, thoughtfully. 'I hope poor old Nobby is all right. Tiger Dan is so jolly beastly to him. I bet he's had a beating or two since last night.'

'It's a shame!' said Dick.

'Don't tell Anne we think there is double-danger about,' said Julian, seeing Anne coming back from the spring. 'She'll be scared. She was hoping we wouldn't have an adventure these hols – and now we seem to be plunged into the middle of one. Golly I really think we ought to leave these hills and go on somewhere else.'

But he only said this half-heartedly, because he was burning to solve the curious mystery behind Lou's behaviour and Dan's. The others pounced on him at once.

'We can't leave! Don't be a coward, Ju!'

'I *won't* leave. Nor will Timmy.'

'Shut up,' said Julian. 'Here comes Anne.'

They said no more. Julian watched Nobby for a little while longer. Then the boy and the chimpanzee drew in to the shore and disappeared.

When they were all sitting together on the ledge, Julian proposed the plan he had been thinking out the night before.

'I'd like to find out what there is about this place that attracts Lou and Dan,' he said. 'There is *something* not far from here that makes the men want to get rid of us. Now suppose we four and Timmy go off down the hill and pass the camp, and yell out to Nobby that we're *all – all* of us – going to the town for the day – and you three do go, but I slip back up the hill – maybe Lou and Dan will come up here, and if I'm hiding I shall see what they're up to!'

'You mean, we'll all four pretend to go to town – but really only three of us go, and you get back and hide,' said Dick. 'I see. It's a good idea.'

'And you'll hide somewhere and watch for the men to come,' said George. 'Well, for goodness sake don't let them see you, Julian. You won't have Timmy, you know! Those men could make mincemeat of you if they wanted to.'

'Oh, they'd want to all right. I know that,' said Julian grimly. 'But you can be sure I'll be jolly well hidden.'

'I don't see why we can't have a good look round and see if we can't find the cave or whatever it is the men want to come to,' said Dick. 'If they can find it, we can, too!'

'We don't know that it *is* a cave,' said Julian. 'We haven't any idea at all what attracts the men up here. Mrs Mackie said they were up here last year, too, and the farmer had to drive them away. They thought the men were after the chickens – but I don't think so. There's *some*thing in these hills that makes the men want to get us away.'

'Let's have a good look round,' said George, feeling suddenly thrilled. 'I've gone all adventurous again!'

'Oh dear!' said Anne. But she couldn't help feeling rather thrilled, too. They all got up and Timmy followed, wagging his tail. He was pleased that his friends hadn't gone off and left him on guard by himself that morning.

'We'll all go different ways,' said Julian. 'Up, down and sideways. I'll go up.'

They separated and went off, George and Timmy together, of course. They hunted in the hillside for possible caves, or even for some kind of hiding-place. Timmy put his head down every rabbit-hole and felt very busy indeed.

After about half an hour the others heard Julian yelling.

103

They ran back to the caravans, sure that he had found something exciting.

But he hadn't. He had simply got tired of hunting and decided to give it up. He shook his head when they rushed up to him, shouting to know what he had found.

'Nothing,' he said. 'I'm fed up with looking. There's not a cave anywhere here. I'm sure of that! Anyone else found anything?'

'Not a thing,' said everyone in disappointment. 'What shall we do now?'

'Put our plan into action,' said Julian, promptly. 'Let the men themselves show us what they're after. Off we go down the hills, and we'll yell out to Nobby that we're off for the day – and we'll hope that Lou and Tiger Dan will hear us!'

14

A very good hiding-place

They went down the hill with Timmy. Julian gave Dick some instructions. 'Have a meal in the town,' he said. 'Keep away for the day, so as to give the men a chance to come up the hill. Go to the post office and see if there are any letters for us – and buy some tins of fruit. They'll make a nice change.'

'Right, Captain!' said Dick. 'And just you be careful, old boy. These men will stick at nothing – bad-tempered brutes they are.'

'Look after the girls,' said Julian. 'Don't let George do anything mad!'

Dick grinned. 'Who can stop George doing what she wants to? Not me!'

They were now at the bottom of the hills. The circus camp lay nearby. The children could hear the barking of the dogs and the shrill trumpeting of Old Lady.

They looked about for Nobby. He was nowhere to be seen. Blow! It wouldn't be any good setting off to the town and laying such a good plan if they couldn't tell Nobby they were going!

Nobody dared to go into the camp. Julian thought of the two red cloths that Nobby and Pongo had waved. Double-danger! It would be wise not to go into the camp that morning. He stood still, undecided what to do.

Then he opened his mouth and yelled:

'Nobby! NOBBY!'

No answer and no Nobby. The elephant man heard him shouting and came up. 'Do you want Nobby? I'll fetch him.'

'Thanks,' said Julian.

The little man went off, whistling. Soon Nobby appeared from behind a caravan, looking rather scared. He didn't come near Julian, but stood a good way away, looking pale and troubled.

'Nobby! We're going into the town for the day,' yelled Julian at the top of his voice. 'We're . . .'

Tiger Dan suddenly appeared behind Nobby and grabbed his arm fiercely. Nobby put up a hand to protect his face, as if he expected a blow. Julian yelled again:

'We're going into the town, Nobby! We shan't be back till evening. Can you hear me? WE'RE GOING TO THE TOWN!'

The whole camp must have heard Julian. But he was quite determined that, whoever else didn't hear, Tiger Dan certainly should.

Nobby tried to shake off his uncle's hand, and opened his mouth to yell back something. But Dan roughly put his hand across Nobby's mouth and hauled him away, shaking him as a dog shakes a rat.

'HOW'S BARKER?' yelled Julian. But Nobby had disappeared, dragged into his uncle's caravan by Dan. The little elephant man heard, however.

'Barker's bad,' he said. 'Not dead yet. But nearly. Never saw a dog so sick in my life. Nobby's fair upset!'

The children walked off with Timmy. George had had to hold his collar all the time, for once he saw Dan he

106

growled without stopping, and tried to get away from George.

'Thank goodness Barker isn't dead,' said Anne. 'I do hope he'll get better.'

'Not much chance,' said Julian. 'That meat must have been chock-full of poison. Poor old Nobby. How awful to be under the thumb of a fellow like Tiger Dan.'

'I just simply can't *imagine* him as a clown – Tiger Dan, I mean,' said Anne. 'Clowns are always so merry and gay and jolly.'

'Well, that's just acting,' said Dick. 'A clown needn't be the same out of the ring as he has to be when he's in it. If you look at photographs of clowns when they're just being ordinary men, they've got quite sad faces.'

'Well, Tiger Dan hasn't got a sad face. He's got a nasty, ugly, savage, cruel, fierce one,' said Anne, looking quite fierce herself.

That made the others laugh. Dick turned round to see if anyone was watching them walking towards the bus-stop, where the buses turned to go to the town.

'Lou the acrobat is watching us,' he said. 'Good! Can he see the bus-stop from where he is, Ju?'

Julian turned round. 'Yes, he can. He'll watch to see us all get into the bus – so I'd better climb in, too, and I'll get out at the first stop, double back, and get into the hills by some path he won't be able to see.'

'Right,' said Dick, enjoying the thought of playing a trick on Lou. 'Come on. There's the bus. We'll have to run for it.'

They all got into the bus. Lou was still watching, a small figure very far away. Dick felt inclined to wave cheekily to him, but didn't.

The bus set off. They took three tickets for the town and one for the nearest stop. Timmy had a ticket, too, which he wore proudly in his collar. He loved going in a bus.

Julian got out at the first stop. 'Well, see you this

evening!' he said. 'Send Timmy on ahead to the caravans when you come back – just in case the men are anywhere about. I may not be able to warn you.'

'Right,' said Dick. 'Good-bye – and good luck!'

Julian waved and set off back down the road he had come. He saw a little lane leading off up into the hills and decided to take it. It led him not very far from Mrs Mackie's farm, so he soon knew where he was. He went back to the caravans, and quickly made himself some sandwiches and cut some cake to take to his hiding-place. He might have a long wait!

'Now – where shall I hide?' thought the boy. 'I want somewhere that will give me a view of the track so that I can see when the men come up it. And yet it must be somewhere that gives me a good view of their doings, too. What would be the best place?'

A tree? No, there wasn't one that was near enough or thick enough. Behind a bush? No, the men might easily come round it and see him. What about the middle of a thick gorse bush? That might be a good idea.

But Julian gave that up very quickly, for he found the bush far too prickly to force his way into the middle. He scratched his arms and legs terribly.

'Blow!' he said. 'I really must make up my mind, or the men may be here before I'm in hiding!'

And then he suddenly had a real brainwave, and he crowed in delight. Of course! The very place!

'I'll climb up on to the roof of one of the caravans!' thought Julian. 'Nobody will see me there – and certainly nobody would guess I was there! That really is a fine idea. I shall have a fine view of the track and a first-rate view of the men and where they go!'

It wasn't very easy to climb up on to the high roof. He had to get a rope, loop it at the end, and try to lasso the chimney in order to climb up.

He managed to lasso the chimney, and the rope hung

down over the side of the caravan, ready for him to swarm up. He threw his packet of food up on to the roof and then climbed up himself. He pulled up the rope and coiled it beside him.

Then he lay down flat. He was certain that nobody could see him from below. Of course, if the men went higher up the hill and looked down on the caravans, he could easily be spotted – but he would have to chance that.

He lay there quite still, watching the lake, and keeping eyes and ears open for anyone coming up the hillside. He was glad that it was not a very hot sunny day, or he would have been cooked up on the roof. He wished he had thought of filling a bottle with water in case he was thirsty.

He saw spires of smoke rising from where the circus camp lay, far below. He saw a couple of boats on the lake, a good way round the water – people fishing, he supposed. He watched a couple of rabbits come out and play on the hillside just below.

The sun came out from behind the clouds for about ten minutes and Julian began to feel uncomfortably hot. Then it went in again and he felt better.

He suddenly heard somebody whistling and stiffened himself in expectation – but it was only someone belonging to the farm, going down the hill some distance away. The whistle had carried clearly in the still air.

Then he got bored. The rabbits went in, and not even a butterfly sailed by. He could see no birds except a yellowhammer that sat on the topmost spray of a bush and sang: 'Little-bit-of-bread-and-no-cheese', over and over again in a most maddening manner.

Then it gave a cry of alarm and flew off. It had heard something that frightened it.

Julian heard something, too, and glued his eyes to the track that led up the hill. His heart began to beat. He could see two men. Were they Lou and Dan?

He did not dare to raise his head to see them when they came nearer in case they spotted him. But he knew their voices when they came near enough!

Yes – it was Lou and Tiger Dan all right. There was no mistaking those two harsh, coarse voices. The men came right into the hollow, and Julian heard them talking.

'Yes, there's nobody here. Those kids have really gone off for the day at least – and taken that wretched dog with them!'

'I saw them get on the bus, dog and all, I told you,' growled Lou. 'There'll be nobody here for the day. We can get what we want to.'

110

'Let's go and get it, then,' said Dan.

Julian waited to see where they would go to. But they didn't go out of the hollow. They stayed there, apparently beside the caravans. Julian did not dare to look over the edge of the roof to see what they were up to. He was glad he had fastened all the windows and locked the doors.

Then there began some curious scuffling sounds, and the men panted. The caravan on which Julian was lying began to shake a little.

'What *are* they doing?' thought Julian in bewilderment. In intense curiosity he slid quietly to the edge of the caravan roof and cautiously peeped over, though he had firmly made up his mind not to do this on any account.

He looked down on the ground. There was nobody there at all. Perhaps the men were the other side. He slid carefully across and peeped over the opposite side of the caravan, which was still shaking a little, as if the men were bumping against it.

There was nobody the other side either! How very extraordinary! 'Golly! They must be underneath the caravan!' thought Julian, going back to the middle of the roof. 'Underneath! What in the wide world for?'

It was quite impossible to see underneath the caravan from where he was, so he had to lie quietly and wonder about the men's doings. They grunted and groaned, and seemed to be scraping and scrabbling about, but nothing happened. Then Julian heard them scrambling out from underneath, angry and disappointed.

'Give us a cigarette,' said Lou in a disagreeable voice. 'I'm fed up with this. Have to shift this van. Those tiresome brats! What did they want to choose this spot for?'

Julian heard a match struck and smelt cigarette smoke. Then he got a shock. The caravan he was on began to move! Heavens! Were the men going to push it over the ledge and send it rolling down the hillside?

111

15

Several things happen

Julian was suddenly very scared. He wondered if he had better slide off the roof and run. He wouldn't have much chance if the caravan went hurtling down the hill! But he didn't move. He clung to the chimney with both hands, whilst the men shoved hard against the caravan.

It ran a few feet to the rocky ledge, and then stopped. Julian felt his forehead getting very damp, and he saw that his hands were trembling. He felt ashamed of being so scared, but he couldn't help it.

'Hey! Don't send it down the hill!' said Lou in alarm, and Julian's heart felt lighter. So they didn't mean to destroy the caravan in that way! They had just moved it to get at something underneath. But what could it be? Julian racked his brains to try and think what the floor of the hollow had been like when Dobby and Trotter pulled their caravans into it. As far as he could remember it was just an ordinary heathery hollow.

The men were now scrabbling away again by the back steps of the caravan. Julian was absolutely eaten up with curiosity, but he did not dare even to move. He could find out the secret when the men had gone. Meantime he really must be patient or he would spoil everything.

There was some muttered talking, but Julian couldn't catch a word. Then, quite suddenly, there was complete and utter silence. Not a word. Not a bump against the caravan. Not a pant or even a grunt. Nothing at all.

Julian lay still. Maybe the men were still there. He wasn't going to give himself away. He lay for quite a long time, waiting and wondering. But he heard nothing.

Then he saw a robin fly to a nearby bramble spray. It flicked its wings and looked about for crumbs. It was a robin that came around when the children were having a meal – but it was not as tame as most robins, and would not fly down until the children had left the hollow.

Then a rabbit popped out of a hole on the hillside and capered about, running suddenly up to the hollow.

'Well,' thought Julian, 'it's plain the men aren't here now, or the birds and animals wouldn't be about like this. There's another rabbit. Those men have gone somewhere – though goodness knows where. I can peep over now and have a look, quite safely, I should think.'

He slid himself round and peered over the roof at the back end of the caravan. He looked down at the ground. There was absolutely nothing to be seen to tell him what the men had been doing, or where they had gone! The heather grew luxuriantly there as it did everywhere else. There was nothing so show what the men had been making such a disturbance about.

'This is really very queer,' thought Julian, beginning to wonder if he had been dreaming. 'The men are certainly gone – vanished into thin air, apparently! Dare I get down and explore a bit? No, I daren't. The men may appear at any moment, and it's quite on the cards they'll lose their temper if they find me here, and chuck both me and the caravans down the hill! It's pretty steep just here, too.'

He lay there, thinking. He suddenly felt very hungry and thirsty. Thank goodness he had been sensible enough to take food up to the roof! He could at least have a meal while he was waiting for the men to come back – if they ever did!

He began to eat his sandwiches. They tasted very good indeed. He finished them all and began on the cake. That was good, too. He had brought a few plums up as well, and was very glad of them because he was thirsty. He flicked the plum stones from the roof before he thought what he was doing.

'Dash! Why did I do that? If the men notice them they may remember they weren't there before. Still, they've most of them gone into the heather!'

The sun came out a little and Julian felt hot. He wished the men would come again and go down the hill. He was tired of lying flat on the hard roof. Also he was terribly sleepy. He yawned silently and shut his eyes.

How long he slept he had no idea – but he was suddenly awakened by feeling the caravan being moved again! He clutched the chimney in alarm, listening to the low voices of the two men.

They were pulling the caravan back into place again. Soon it was in the same position as before. Then Julian heard a match struck and smelt smoke again.

The men went and sat on the rocky ledge and took out food they had brought. Julian did not dare to peep at them, though he felt sure they had their backs to him. The men ate, and talked in low voices, and then, to Julian's dismay, they lay down and went to sleep! He knew that they were asleep because he could hear them snoring.

'Am I going to stay on this awful roof all day long?' he thought. 'I'm getting so cramped, lying flat like this. I want to sit up!'

'R-r-r-r-r-r!' snored Lou and Dan. Julian felt that surely it would be all right to sit up now that the men were obviously asleep. So he sat up cautiously, stretching himself with pleasure.

He looked down on the two men, who were lying on their backs with their mouths open. Beside them were two neat sacks, strong and thick. Julian wondered what was inside them. They certainly had not had them when they came up the track.

The boy gazed down the hillside, frowning, trying to probe the mystery of where the men had been, and what they were doing up here – and suddenly he jumped violently. He stared as if he could not believe his eyes.

A squat and ugly face was peering out from a bramble bush there. There was almost no nose, and an enormous mouth. Who could it be? Was it someone spying on Lou and Dan? But what a face! It didn't seem human.

A hand came up to rub the face – and Julian saw that it was hairy. With a start he knew who the face belonged to – Pongo the chimpanzee! No wonder he had thought it such an ugly, inhuman face. It was all right on a chimp, of course – quite a nice face – but not on a man.

Pongo stared at Julian solemnly, and Julian stared back, his mind in a whirl. What was Pongo doing there? Was Nobby with him? If so, Nobby was in danger, for at any moment the men might wake up. He couldn't think what to do. If he called out to warn Nobby, he would wake the men.

Pongo was pleased to see Julian, and did not seem to think the roof of a caravan a curious place to be in at all. After all, *he* often went up on the roofs of caravans. He nodded and blinked at the boy, and then scratched his head for a long time.

Then beside him appeared Nobby's face – a tear-stained face, bruised and swollen. He suddenly saw Julian looking over the roof of the caravan, and his mouth fell open in surprise. He seemed about to call out, and Julian shook his head frantically to stop him, pointing downwards to try and warn Nobby that somebody was there.

But Nobby didn't understand. He grinned and, to Julian's horror, began to climb up the hillside to the rocky ledge! The men were sleeping there, and Julian saw with dismay that Nobby would probably heave himself up right on top of them.

'Look out!' he said, in a low, urgent voice. 'Look out, you fathead!'

But it was too late. Nobby heaved himself up on to the ledge, and, to his utmost horror, found himself sprawling on top of Tiger Dan! He gave a yell and tried to slide away – but Dan, rousing suddenly, shot out a hand and gripped him.

Lou woke up, too. The men glared at poor Nobby, and the boy began to tremble, and to beg for mercy.

'I didn't know you were here, I swear it! Let me go, let me go! I only came up to look for my knife that I lost yesterday!'

Dan shook him savagely. 'How long have you been here? You been spying?'

'No, no! I've only just come! I've been at the camp all morning – you ask Larry and Rossy. I been helping them!'

'You been spying on us, that's what you've been doing!' said Lou, in a cold, hard voice that filled the listening Julian with dread. 'You've had plenty of beatings this week, but seemingly they ain't enough. Well, up here, there's nobody to hear your yells, see? So we'll show you what a real beating is! And if you can walk down to the camp after it, I'll be surprised.'

Nobby was terrified. He begged for mercy, he promised to do anything the men asked him, and tried to jerk his poor swollen face away from Dan's hard hands.

Julian couldn't bear it. He didn't want to give away the

116

fact that it was he who had been spying, nor did he want to fight the men at all, for he was pretty certain he would get the worst of it. But nobody could lie in silence, watching two men treat a young boy in such a way. He made up his mind to leap off the roof right on to the men, and to rescue poor Nobby if he could.

Nobby gave a anguished yell as Lou gave him a flick with his leather belt – but before Julian could jump down to help him, somebody else bounded up! Somebody who bared his teeth and made ugly animal noises of rage, somebody whose arms were far stronger than either Lou's or Dan's – somebody who loved poor Nobby, and wasn't going to let him be beaten any more!

It was Pongo. The chimpanzee had been watching the scene with his sharp little eyes. He had still hidden himself in the bush, for he was afraid of Lou and Dan – but now, hearing Nobby's cries, he leapt out of the brambles and flung himself on the astonished men.

He bit Lou's arm hard. Then he bit Dan's leg. The men yelled loudly, much more loudly than poor Nobby had. Lou lashed out with his leather belt, and it caught Pongo on the shoulder. The chimpanzee made a shrill chattering noise, and leapt on Lou with his arms open, clasping the man to him, trying to bite his throat.

Tiger Dan rushed down the hill at top speed, terrified of the angry chimpanzee. Lou yelled to Nobby.

'Call him off! He'll kill me!'

'Pongo!' shouted Nobby. 'Stop it! Pongo! Come here.'

Pongo gave Nobby a look of the greatest surprise. 'What!' he seemed to say, 'you won't let me punish this bad man who beat you? Well, well – whatever you say must be right!'

And the chimpanzee, giving Lou one last vicious nip, let the man go. Lou followed Dan down the hill at top speed, and Julian heard him crashing through the bushes as if a hundred chimpanzees were after him.

Nobby sat down, trembling. Pongo, not quite sure if his beloved friend was angry with him or not, crept up to him putting a paw on the boy's knee. Nobby put his arm round the anxious animal, and Pongo chattered with joy.

Julian slid down from the roof of the caravan and went to Nobby. He, too, sat down beside him. He put his arm round the trembling boy and gave him a hug.

'I was just coming to give you a hand, when Pongo shot up the hill,' he said.

'Were you really?' said Nobby, his face lighting up. 'You're a real friend, you are. Good as Pongo, here.'

And Julian felt quite proud to be ranked in bravery with the chimpanzee!

16

A surprising discovery

'Listen – somebody's coming!' said Nobby, and Pongo gave an ugly growl. The sound of voices could be heard coming up the hill. Then a dog barked.

'It's all right. It's Timmy – and the others,' said Julian, unspeakably glad to welcome them back. He stood up and yelled.

'All right! Come along!'

George, Timmy, Dick and Anne came running up the track. 'Hallo!' shouted Dick. 'We thought it would be safe, because we saw Lou and Dan in the distance, running along at the bottom of the.hill. I say – there's Pongo!'

Pongo shook hands with Dick, and then went to the back of Timmy, to shake hands with his tail. But Timmy was ready for him, and backing round, he held out his paw to Pongo instead. It was very funny to see the two animals solemnly shaking hands with one another.

'Hallo, Nobby!' said Dick. 'Goodness – what have you been doing to yourself? You look as if you've been in the wars.'

'Well, I have, rather,' said Nobby, with a feeble grin. He was very much shaken, and did not get up. Pongo ran to Anne and tried to put his arms round her.

'Oh, Pongo – you squeeze too hard,' said Anne. 'Julian, did anything happen? Did the men come? Have you any news?'

'Plenty,' said Julian. 'But what I want first is a jolly good drink. I've had none all day. Ginger-beer, I think.'

'We're all thirsty. I'll get five bottles – no, six, because I expect Pongo would like some.'

Pongo loved ginger-beer. He sat down with the children on the rocky ledge, and took his glass from Anne just like a child. Timmy was a little jealous, but as he didn't like ginger-beer he couldn't make a fuss.

Julian began to tell the others about his day, and how he had hidden on the caravan roof. He described how the men had come – and had gone under the caravan – and then moved it. They all listened with wide eyes. What a story!

Then Nobby told his part. 'I butted in and almost gave the game away,' he said, when Julian had got as far as the men falling asleep and snoring. 'But, you see, I had to come and warn you. Lou and Dan swear they'll poison Timmy somehow, even if they have to dope him, put him into a sack and take him down to the camp to do it. Or they might knock him on the head.'

'Let them try!' said George, in her fiercest voice, and put her arm round Timmy. Pongo at once put his arm round Timmy too.

'And they said they'd damage your caravans too – maybe put a fire underneath and burn them up,' went on Nobby.

The four children stared at him in horror. 'But they wouldn't do a thing like that, surely?' said Julian, at last. 'They'd get into trouble with the police if they did.'

120

'Well, I'm just telling you what they said,' Nobby went on. 'You don't know Lou and Tiger Dan like I do. They'll stick at nothing to get their way – or to get anybody *out* of their way. They tried to poison Timmy, didn't they? And poor old Barker got it instead.'

'Is – is Barker – all right?' asked Anne.

'No,' said Nobby. 'He's dying, I think. I've given him to Lucilla to dose. She's a marvel with sick animals. I've put Growler with the other dogs. He's safe with them.'

He stared round at the other children, his mouth trembling, sniffing as if he had a bad cold.

'I dursent go back,' he said, in a low voice, 'I dursent. They'll half-kill me.'

'You're not going back, so that's settled,' said Julian, in a brisk voice. 'You're staying here with us. We shall love to have you. It was jolly decent of you to come up and warn us – and bad luck to have got caught like that. You're our friend now – and we'll stick together.'

Nobby couldn't say a word, but his face shone. He rubbed a dirty hand across his eyes, then grinned his old grin. He nodded his head, not trusting himself to speak, and the children all thought how nice he was. Poor old Nobby.

They finished their ginger-beer and then Julian got up. 'And now,' he said, 'we will do a little exploring and find out where those men went, shall we?'

'Oh yes!' cried George, who had sat still quite long enough. 'We *must* find out! Do we have to get under the caravan, Julian?'

' 'Fraid so,' said Julian. 'You sit there quietly, Nobby, and keep guard in case Lou or Dan come back.'

He didn't think for a moment that they would, but he could see that Nobby needed to sit quietly for a while. Nobby, however, had different ideas. He was going to share this adventure!

'Timmy's guard enough, and so is Pongo,' he said.

121

'They'll hear anyone coming half a mile away. I'm in on this!'

And he was. He went scrabbling underneath the low-swung base of the caravan with the others, eager to find out anything he could.

But it was impossible to explore down in the heather, with the caravan base just over their heads. They had no room at all. Like Dan and Lou they soon felt that they would have to move the van.

It took all five of them, with Pongo giving a shove, too, to move the caravan a few feet away. Then down they dropped to the thick carpet of heather again.

The tufts came up easily by the roots, because the men had already pulled them up once that day and then replanted them. The children dragged up a patch of heather about five feet square, and then gave an exclamation.

'Look! Boards under the heather!'

'Laid neatly across and across. What for?'

'Pull them up!'

The boys pulled up the planks one by one and piled them on one side. Then they saw that the boards had closed up the entrance of a deep hole. 'I'll get my torch,' said Julian. He fetched it and flashed it on.

The light showed them a dark hole, going down into the hillside, with footholds sticking out of one side. They all sat and gazed down in excitement.

'To think we went and put our caravan *exactly* over the entrance of the men's hiding-place!' said Dick. 'No wonder they were wild! No wonder they changed their minds and told us we could go down to the lake and camp there instead of here!'

'Gosh!' said Julian, staring into the hole. 'So that's where the men went! Where does it lead to? They were down there a mighty long time. They were clever enough to replace the planks and drag some of the heather over

122

them, too, to hide them when they went down.'

Pongo suddenly took it into his head to go down the hole. Down he went, feeling for the footholds with his hairy feet, grinning up at the others. He disappeared at the bottom. Julian's torch could not pick him out at all.

'Hey, Pongo! Don't lose yourself down there!' called Nobby, anxiously. But Pongo had gone.

'Blow him!' said Nobby. 'He'll never find his way back, if he goes wandering about underground. I'll have to go after him. Can I have your torch, Julian?'

'I'll come too,' said Julian. 'George, get me your torch as well, will you?'

'It's broken,' said George. 'I dropped it last night. And nobody else has got one.'

'What an awful nuisance!' said Julian. 'I want us to go and explore down there – but we can't with only one torch. Well, I'll just go down with Nobby and get Pongo – have a quick look round and come back. I may see something worth seeing!'

Nobby went down first, and Julian followed, the others all kneeling round the hole, watching them enviously. They disappeared.

'Pongo!' yelled Nobby. 'Pongo! Come here, you idiot!'

Pongo had not gone very far. He didn't like the dark down there very much, and he came to Nobby as soon as he saw the light of the torch. The boys found themselves in a narrow passage at the bottom of the hole, which widened as they went further into the hill.

'Must be caves somewhere,' said Julian, flashing his torch round. 'We know that a lot of springs run out of this hill. I daresay that through the centuries the water has eaten away the softer stuff and made caves and tunnels everywhere in the hill. And somewhere in a cave Lou and Dan store away things they don't want anyone to know about. Stolen goods, probably.'

The passage ended in a small cave that seemed to have no other opening out of it at all. There was nothing in it. Julian flashed his torch up and down the walls.

He saw footholds up one part, and traced them to a hole in the roof, which must have been made, years before, by running water. 'That's the way we go!' he said. 'Come on.'

'Wait!' said Nobby. 'Isn't your torch getting rather faint?'

'Goodness – yes!' said Julian in alarm, and shook his torch violently to make the lighter brighter. But the battery had almost worn out, and no better light came. Instead the light grew even fainter, until it was just a pin-prick in the torch.

'Come on – we'd better get back at once,' said Julian, feeling a bit scared. 'I don't want to wander about here in the pitch dark. Not my idea of fun at all.'

Nobby took firm hold of Pongo's hairy paw and equally firm hold of Julian's jersey. He didn't mean to lose either of them! The light in the torch went out completely. Now they must find their way back in black darkness.

Julian felt round for the beginning of the passage that led back to the hole. He found it and made his way up it, feeling the sides with his hands. It wasn't a pleasant experience at all, and Julian was thankful that he and Nobby had only gone a little way into the hill. It would have been like a nightmare if they had gone well in, and then found themselves unable to see the way back.

They saw a faint light shining further on and guessed it was the daylight shining down the entrance-hole. They stumbled thankfully towards it. They looked up and saw the anxious faces of the other three peering down at them, unable to see them.

'We're back!' called Julian, beginning to climb up. 'My torch went out, and we daren't go very far. We've got Pongo, though.'

The others helped to pull them out at the top of the hole. Julian told them about the hole in the roof of the little cave.

'That's were the men went,' he said. 'And tomorrow, when we've all bought torches, and matches and candles, that's where we're going, too! We'll go down to the town and buy what we want, and come back and do a Really Good Exploration!'

'We're going to have an adventure after all,' said Anne, in rather a small voice.

' 'Fraid so,' said Julian. 'But you can stay at the farm with Mrs Mackie for the day, Anne dear. Don't you come with us.'

'If you're going on an adventure, I'm coming, too,' said Anne. 'So there! I wouldn't *dream* of not coming.'

'All right,' said Julian. 'We'll all go together. Golly, things are getting exciting!'

17

Another visit from Lou and Dan

Nobody disturbed the children that night, and Timmy did not bark once. Nobby slept on a pile of rugs in the boys' caravan, and Pongo cuddled up to him. The chimpanzee seemed delighted at staying with the caravanners. Timmy was rather jealous that another animal should be with them, and wouldn't take any notice of Pongo at all.

The next morning, after breakfast, the children discussed who was to go down to the town. 'Not Nobby and Pongo, because they wouldn't be allowed in the bus together,' said Julian. 'They had better stay behind.'

'Not by ourselves?' said Nobby, looking alarmed. 'Suppose Lou and Uncle Dan come up? Even if I've got Pongo I'd be scared.'

'Well, I'll stay here, too,' said Dick. 'We don't all need to go to buy torches. Don't forget to post that letter to Daddy and Mother, Julian.'

They had written a long letter to their parents, telling them of the exciting happenings. Julian put it into his pocket. 'I'll post it all right,' he said. 'Well, I suppose we might as well go now. Come on, girls. Keep a look-out, Dick, in case those rogues come back.'

George, Timmy, Anne and Julian went down the hill together, Timmy running on in front, his tail wagging nineteen to the dozen. Pongo climbed up to the roof of the red caravan to watch them go. Nobby and Dick sat down in the warm sun on the ledge, their heads resting on springy clumps of heather.

'It's nice up here,' said Nobby. 'Much nicer than down below. I wonder what everyone is thinking about Pongo and me. I bet Mr Gorgio, the head of the circus, is wild that the chimpanzee's gone. I bet he'll send up to fetch us.'

Nobby was right. Two people were sent up to get him – Lou and Tiger Dan. They came creeping up through the bracken and heather, keeping a sharp eye for Timmy or Pongo.

Pongo sensed them long before they could be seen and warned Nobby. Nobby went very pale. He was terrified of the two scoundrels.

'Get into one of the caravans,' said Dick in a low voice. 'Go on. I'll deal with those fellows – if it *is* them. Pongo will help me if necessary.'

Nobby scuttled into the green caravan and shut the door. Dick sat where he was. Pongo squatted on the roof of the caravan, watching.

Lou and Dan suddenly appeared. They saw Dick, but did not see Pongo. They looked all round for the others.

'What do you want?' said Dick.

'Nobby and Pongo,' said Lou with a scowl. 'Where are they?'

'They're going to stay on with us,' said Dick.

'Oh, no, they're not!' said Tiger Dan. 'Nobby's in my charge, see? I'm his uncle.'

'Funny sort of uncle,' remarked Dick. 'How's that dog you poisoned, by the way?'

Tiger Dan went purple in the face. He looked as if he would willingly have thrown Dick down the hill.

'You be careful what you say to me!' he said, beginning to shout.

Nobby, hidden in the caravan, trembled when he heard his uncle's angry yell. Pongo kept quite still, his face set and ugly.

'Well, you may as well say good-bye and go,' said Dick in a calm voice to Dan. 'I've told you that Nobby and Pongo are staying with us for the present.'

'Where *is* Nobby?' demanded Tiger Dan, looking as if he would burst with rage at any moment. 'Wait till I get my hands on him. Wait . . .'

He began to walk towards the caravans – but Pongo was not having any of that! He leapt straight off the roof on to the horrified man, and flung him to the ground. He made such a terrible snarling noise that Dan was terrified.

'Call him off!' he yelled. 'Lou, come and help.'

'Pongo won't obey *me*,' said Dick still sitting down looking quite undisturbed. 'You'd better go before he bites big pieces out of you.'

Dan staggered to the rock ledge, looking as if he would box Dick's ears. But the boy did not move, and somehow Dan did not dare to touch him. Pongo let him go and stood glowering at him, his great hairy arms hanging down his sides, ready to fly at either of the men if they came near.

Tiger Dan picked up a stone – and as quick as lightning Pongo flung himself on him again and sent the man rolling down the hill. Lou fled in terror. Dan got up and fled, too, yelling furiously as he went. Pongo chased them in delight. He, too, picked up stones and flung them with a very accurate aim, so that Dick kept hearing yells of pain.

Pongo came back, looking extremely pleased with himself. He went to the green caravan, as Dick shouted to Nobby.

'All right, Nobby. They've gone. Pongo and I won the battle!'

Nobby came out. Pongo put his arm round him at once and chattered nonsense in his ear. Nobby looked rather ashamed of himself.

'Bit of a coward, aren't I?' he said. 'Leaving you out here all alone.'

'I enjoyed it,' said Dick truthfully. 'And I'm sure Pongo did!'

'You don't know what dangerous fellows Lou and Dan are,' said Nobby, looking down the hillside to make sure the men were really gone. 'I tell you they'd stick at nothing. They'd burn your caravans, hurl them down the hill, poison your dog, and do what harm they could to you, too. You don't know them like I do!'

'Well, as a matter of fact, we've had some pretty exciting adventures with men just as tough as Dan and Lou,' said Dick. 'We always seem to be falling into the middle of some adventure or other. Now, last hols we went to a place called Smuggler's Top – and, my word, the adventures we had there! You wouldn't believe them!'

'You tell me and Pongo,' said Nobby, sitting down beside Dick. 'We've plenty of time before the others come back.'

So Dick began to tell the tale of all the other thrilling adventures that the five of them had had, and the time flew. Both boys were surprised when they heard Timmy barking down the track, and knew that the others were back.

George came tearing up with Timmy at her heels. 'Are you all right? Did anything happen while we were away? Do you know, we saw Lou and Tiger Dan getting on the bus when we got off it! They were carrying bags as if they meant to go away and stay somewhere.'

130

Nobby brightened up at once. 'Did you really? Good! They came up here, you know, and Pongo chased them down the hill. They must have gone back to the camp, collected their bags, and gone to catch the bus. Hurrah!'

'We've gone fine torches,' said Julian, and showed Dick his. 'Powerful ones. Here's one for you, Dick – and one for you, Nobby.'

'Oooh – thanks,' said Nobby. Then he went red. 'I haven't got enough money to pay you for such a grand torch,' he said awkwardly.

'It's a present for you,' said Anne at once, 'a present for a friend of ours, Nobby!'

'Coo! Thanks awfully,' said Nobby, looking quite over-come. 'I've never had a present before. You're decent kids, you are.'

Pongo held out his hand to Anne and made a chattering noise as if to say: 'What about one for me, too?'

'Oh – we didn't bring one for Pongo!' said Anne. 'Why ever didn't we?'

'Good thing you didn't,' said Nobby. 'He would have put it on and off all day long and wasted the battery in no time!'

'I'll give him my old torch,' said George. 'It's broken, but he won't mind that!'

Pongo was delighted with it. He kept pressing down the knob that should make the light flash – and when there was no light he looked all about on the ground as if the light must have dropped out! The children roared at him. He liked them to laugh at him. He did a little dance all round them to show how pleased he was.

'Look here – wouldn't it be a jolly good time to explore underground now that we know Lou and Dan are safely out of the way?' asked Julian suddenly. 'If they've got bags with them, surely that means they're going to spend the night somewhere and won't be back till tomorrow at least. We'd be quite safe to go down and explore.'

'Yes, we would,' said George eagerly. 'I'm longing to get down there and Make Discoveries!'

'Well, let's have something to eat first,' said Dick. 'It's long past our dinner-time. It must be about half-past one. Yes, it is!'

'George and I will get you a meal,' said Anne. 'We called at the farm on our way up and got a lovely lot of food. Come on, George.'

George got up unwillingly. Timmy followed her, sniffing expectantly. Soon the two girls were busy getting a fine meal ready, and they all sat on the rocky ledge to eat it.

'Mrs Mackie gave us this enormous bar of chocolate for a present today,' said Anne, showing a great slab to Dick and Nobby. 'Isn't it lovely? No, Pongo, it's not for you. Eat your sandwiches properly, and don't grab.'

'I vote we take some food down into the hill with us,' said Julian. 'We may be quite a long time down there, and we shan't want to come back at tea-time.'

'Oooh – a picnic inside the hill!' said Anne. 'That would be thrilling. I'll soon pack up some food in the kit-bag. I won't bother to make sandwiches. We'll take a new loaf, butter, ham and a cake, and cut what we want. What about something to drink?'

'Oh, we can last out till we get back,' said Julian. 'Just take something to eat to keep us going till we have finished exploring.'

George and Nobby cleared up and rinsed the plates. Anne wrapped up some food in greased paper, and packed it carefully into the kitbag for Julian to carry. She popped the big bar of chocolate into the bag, too. It would be nice to eat at odd moments.

At last they were all ready. Timmy wagged his tail. He knew they were going somewhere.

The five of them pushed the caravan back a few feet to expose the hole. They had all tugged the van back into the

132

place the night before, in case Lou and Dan came to go down the hole again. No one could get down it if the caravan was over it.

The boards had been laid roughly across the hole and the boys took them off, tossing them to one side. As soon as Pongo saw the hole he drew back, frightened.

'He's remembered the darkness down there,' said George. 'He doesn't like it. Come on, Pongo. You'll be all right. We've all got torches!'

But nothing would persuade Pongo to go down the hole again. He cried like a baby when Nobby tried to make him.

'It's no good,' said Julian. 'You'll have to stop up here with him.'

'What – and miss all the excitement!' cried Nobby indignantly. 'I jolly well won't. We can tie old Pongo up to a wheel of the van so that he won't wander off. Lou and Dan are away somewhere, and no one else is likely to tackle a big chimp like Pongo. We'll tie him up.'

So Pongo was tied firmly to one of the caravan wheels. 'You stay there like a good chimp till we come back,' said Nobby, putting a pail of water beside him in case he should want a drink. 'We'll be back soon!'

Pongo was sad to see them go – but nothing would have made him go down that hole again! So he sat watching the children disappear one by one. Timmy jumped down, too, and then they were all gone. Gone on another adventure. What would happen now?

18

Inside the hill

The children had all put on extra jerseys, by Julian's orders, for he knew it would be cold inside the dark hill. Nobby had been lent an old one of Dick's. They were glad of them as soon as they were walking down the dark passage that led to the first cave, for the air was very chilly.

They came to the small cave and Julian flashed his torch to show them where the footholds went up the wall to a hole in the roof.

'It's exciting,' said George, thrilled. 'I like this sort of thing. Where does that hole in the roof lead to, I wonder? I'll go first, Ju.'

'No, you won't,' said Julian firmly. 'I go first. You don't know what might be at the top!'

Up he went, his torch held in his mouth, for he needed both hands to climb. The footholds were strong nails driven into the rock of the cave-wall, and were fairly easy to climb.

He got to the hole in the roof and popped his head through. He gave a cry of astonishment.

'I say! There's a most ENORMOUS cavern here – bigger than six dance-halls – and the walls are all glittering with something – phosphorescence, I should think.'

He scrambled out of the hole and stood on the floor of the immense cave. Its walls twinkled in their queer light, and Julian shut off his torch. There was almost enough phosphorescent light in the cavern to see by!

One by one the others came up and stared in wonder. 'It's like Aladdin's cave!' said Anne. 'Isn't that a queer light shining from the walls – and from the roof, too, Julian?'

Dick and George had rather a difficulty in getting Timmy up to the cavern, but they managed it at last. Timmy put his tail down at once when he saw the curious light gleaming everywhere. But it went up again when George patted him.

'What an enormous place!' said Dick. 'Do you suppose this is where the men hide their stuff, whatever it is?'

Julian flashed his torch on again and swung it round and about, picking out the dark, rocky corners. 'Can't see anything hidden,' he said. 'But we'd better explore the cave properly before we go on.'

So the five children explored every nook and cranny of the gleaming cave, but could find nothing at all. Julian gave a sudden exclamation and picked something up from the floor.

'A cigarette end!' he said. 'That shows that Lou and Dan have been here. Come on let's see if there's a way out of this great cave.'

Right at the far end, half-way up the gleaming wall was a large hole, rather like a tunnel. Julian climbed up to it and called to the others. 'This is the way they went. There's a dead match just at the entrance to the tunnel or whatever this is.'

It was a curious tunnel, no higher than their shoulders in some places, and it wound about as it went further into

the hill. Julian thought that at one time water must have
run through it. But it was quite dry now. The floor of the
tunnel was worn very smooth, as if a stream had hollowed
it out through many, many years.

'I hope the stream won't take it into its head to begin
running suddenly again!' said George. 'We should get
jolly wet!'

The tunnel went on for some way, and Anne was
beginning to feel it must go on for ever. Then the wall at
one side widened out and made a big rocky shelf. Julian,
who was first, flashed his torch into the hollow.

'I say!' he shouted. 'Here's where those fellows keep
their stores! There's a whole pile of things here!'

136

The others crowded up as closely as they could, each of them flashing their torch brightly. On the wide, rocky shelf lay boxes and packages, sacks and cases. The children stared at them. 'What's in them?' said Nobby, full of intense curiosity. 'Let's see!'

He put down his torch and undid a sack. He slid in his hand – and brought it out holding a piece of shining gold plate!

'Coo!' said Nobby. 'So that's what the police were after last year when they came and searched the camp! And it was hidden safely here. Coo, look at all these things. Jumping Jiminy, they must have robbed the Queen herself!'

The sack was full of exquisite pieces of gold plate – cups, dishes, small trays. The children set them all out on the ledge. How they gleamed in the light of their torches!

'They're thieves in a very big way,' said Julian. 'No doubt about that. Let's look in this box.'

The box was not locked, and the lid opened easily. Inside was a piece of china, a vase so fragile that it looked as if it might break at a breath!

'Well, I don't know anything about china,' said Julian, 'but I suppose this is a very precious piece, worth thousands of pounds. A collector of china would probably give a very large sum for it. What rogues Lou and Dan are!'

'Look here!' suddenly said George, and she pulled leather boxes out of a bag. 'Jewellery!'

She opened the boxes. The children exclaimed in awe. Diamonds flashed brilliantly, rubies glowed, emeralds shone green. Necklaces, bracelets, rings, brooches – the beautiful things gleamed in the light of the five torches.

There was a tiara in one box that seemed to be made only of big diamonds. Anne picked it out of its box gently. Then she put it on her hair.

'I'm a princess! It's my crown!' she said.

'You look lovely,' said Nobby admiringly. 'You look as grand as Delphine the Bareback Rider when she goes into the ring on her horse, with jewels shining all over her!'

Anne put on necklaces and bracelets and sat there on the ledge like a little princess, shining brightly in the magnificent jewels. Then she took them off and put them carefully back into their satin-lined boxes.

'Well – what a haul those two rogues have made!' said Julian, pulling out some gleaming silver plate from another package. 'They must be very fine burglars!'

'*I* know how they work,' said Dick. 'Lou's a wonderful acrobat, isn't he? I bet he does all the climbing about up walls and over roofs and into windows – and Tiger Dan stands below and catches everything he throws down.'

'You're about right,' said Nobby, handling a beautiful silver cup. 'Lou could climb anywhere – up ivy, up pipes – even up the bare wall of a house, I shouldn't wonder! And jump! He can jump like a cat. He and Tiger Dan have been in this business for a long time, I expect. That's where Uncle Dan went at night, of course, when we were on tour, and I woke up and found him gone out of the caravan!'

'And I expect he stores the stolen goods in that wagon of his you showed us,' said Julian, remembering. 'You told us how angry he was with you once when you went and rummaged about in it. He probably stored it there, and then he and Lou came up here each year and hid the stuff underground – waiting till the police had given up the search for the stolen things – and then they come and get it and sell it somewhere safe.'

'A jolly clever plan,' said Dick. 'What a fine chance they've got – wandering about from place to place like that hearing of famous jewels or plate – slipping out at night – and Lou climbing up to bedrooms like a cat. I wonder how they found this place – it's a most wonderful hidey-hole!'

'Yes. Nobody would ever dream of it!' said George.

'And then we go and put our caravan bang on the top of the entrance – just when they want to put something in and take something out!' said Julian. 'I *must* have annoyed them.'

'What are we going to do about it?' said Dick.

'Tell the police, of course,' said Julian, promptly. 'What

do you suppose? My word, I'd like to see the face of the policeman who first sees this little haul.'

They put everything back carefully. Julian shone his torch up the tunnel. 'Shall we explore a bit further, or not?' he said. 'It still goes on. Look!'

'Better get back,' said Nobby. 'Now we've found this we'd better do something about it.'

'Oh, let's just see where the tunnel goes to,' said George. 'It won't take a minute!'

'All right,' said Julian, who wanted to go up the tunnel as much as she did. He led the way, his torch shining brightly.

The tunnel came out into another cave, not nearly as big as the one they had left behind. At one end something gleamed like silver, and seemed to move. There was a curious sound there, too.

'What is it?' said Anne, alarmed. They stood and listened.

'Water!' said Julian, suddenly. 'Of course! Can't you hear it flowing along? It's an underground stream, flowing through the hill to find an opening where it can rush out.'

'Like that stream we saw before we came to our caravan camping-place,' said George. 'It rushed out of the hill. Do you remember? This may be the very one!'

'I expect it is!' said Dick. They went over to it and watched it. It rushed along in its own hollowed out channel, close to the side of the cave-wall.

'Maybe at one time it ran across this cave and down the tunnel we came up by,' said Julian. 'Yes, look – there's a big kind of groove in the floor of the cave here – the stream must have run there once. Then for some reason it went a different way.'

'Let's get back,' said Nobby. 'I want to know if Pongo's all right. I don't somehow feel very comfortable about him. And I'm jolly cold, too. Let's go back to the sunshine and have something to eat. I don't want a picnic down here, after all.'

'All right,' said Julian, and they made their way back through the tunnel. They passed the rock shelf on which lay the treasure, and came at last to the enormous gleaming cavern. They went across it to the hole that led down into the small cave. Down they went, Julian and George trying to manage Timmy between them. But it was very awkward, for he was a big dog.

Then along the passage to the entrance-hole. They all felt quite pleased at the idea of going up into the sunshine again.

'Can't see any daylight shining down the hole,' said Julian puzzled. 'It would be near here.'

He came up against a blank wall, and was surprised. Where was the hole? Had they missed their way? Then he flashed his torch above him and saw the hole there – but there was no daylight shining in!

'I say!' said Julian, in horror. 'I say! What do you think's happened?'

'What?' asked everyone, in panic.

'The hole is closed!' said Julian. 'We can't get out!' Somebody's been along and put those planks across – and I bet they've put the caravan over them, too. We can't get out!'

Everyone stared up at the closed entrance in dismay. They were prisoners.

'Whatever are we to do?' said George. 'Julian – what *are* we going to do?'

19

Prisoners underground

Julian didn't answer. He was angry with himself for not thinking that this might happen! Although Lou and Dan had been seen getting on the bus with bags, they might easily not have been spending the night away – the bags might contain things they wanted to sell – stolen goods of some kind.

'They came back quickly – and came up the hill, I suppose, to have another try at getting Nobby and Pongo back,' said Julian, out loud. 'What an idiot I am to leave things to chance like that. Well – I'll have a try at shifting these planks. I should be able to, with luck.'

He did his best, and did shift them to a certain extent – but, as he feared, the caravan had been run back over the hole, and even if he managed to shift some of the planks it was impossible to make a way out.

'Perhaps Pongo can help,' he said suddenly. He shouted loudly: 'Pongo! Pongo! Come and help!'

Everyone stood still, hoping that they would hear Pongo chattering somewhere near, or scraping at the planks above. But there was no sign or sound of Pongo.

Everyone called, but it was no use. Pongo didn't come. What had happened to him? Poor Nobby felt very worried.

'I wish I knew what has happened,' he kept saying. 'I feel as if something horrid has happened to poor old Pongo. Where can he be?'

Pongo was not very far away. He was lying on his side, his head bleeding. He was quite unconscious, and could not hear the frantic calls of the children at all. Poor Pongo!

What Julian had feared had actually happened. Lou and Dan had come back up the hill, bringing money with them to tempt Nobby and Pongo back. When they had got near to the hollow, they had stood still and called loudly.

'Nobby! Nobby! We've come to make friends, not to hurt you! We've got money for you. Be a sensible boy and come back to the camp. Mr Gorgio is asking for you.'

When there had been no reply at all, the men had gone nearer. Then thcy had seen Pongo and had stopped. The chimpanzee could not get at them because he was tied up. He sat there snarling.

'Where have those kids gone?' asked Lou. Then he saw that the caravan had been moved back a little, and he at once guessed.

'They've found the way underground! The interfering little brutes! See, they've moved one of the caravans off the hole. What do we do *now*!'

'This first,' said Tiger Dan, in a brutal voice, and he picked up an enormous stone. He threw it with all his force at poor Pongo, who tried to leap out of the way. But the rope prevented him, and the stone hit him full on the head.

He gave a loud scream and fell down at once, lying quite still.

'You've gone and killed him,' said Lou.

143

'So much the better!' said Tiger Dan. 'Now let's go and see if the entrance-hole is open. Those kids want their necks wringing!'

They went to the hollow and saw at once that the hole had been discovered, opened, and that the children must have gone down it.

'They're down there now,' said Tiger Dan, almost choking with rage. 'Shall we go down and deal with them – and get our stuff and clear off? We meant to clear off tomorrow, anyway. We might as well get the stuff out now.'

'What – in the daylight – with any of the farm men about to see us!' said Lou with a sneer. 'Clever, aren't you?'

'Well, have you got a better idea?' asked Tiger Dan.

'Why not follow our plan?' said Lou. 'Go down when it's dark and collect the stuff. We can bring our wagon up as we planned to do tonight. We don't need to bother about forcing the children to go now – they're underground – and we can make them prisoners till we're ready to clear off!'

'I see,' said Dan, and he grinned suddenly, showing his ugly teeth. 'Yes – we'll close up the hole and run the caravan back over it – and come up tonight in the dark with the wagon – go down – collect everything – and shut up the hole again with the children in it. We'll send a card to Gorgio when we're safe and tell him to go up and set the kids free.'

'Why bother to do that?' said Lou, in a cruel voice. 'Let 'em starve underground, the interfering little beasts. Serve 'em right.'

'Can't do that,' said Dan. 'Have the police after us worse than ever. We'll have to chuck some food down the hole, to keep them going till they're set free. No good starving them, Lou. There'd be an awful outcry if we do anything like that.'

144

The two men carefully put back the boards over the top of the hole and replaced the heather tufts. Then they ran the caravan back over the place. They looked at Pongo. The chimpanzee was still lying on his side, and the men could see what a nasty wound he had on his head.

'He ain't dead,' said Lou, and gave him a kick. 'He'll come round all right. Better leave him here. He might come to himself if we carried him back to camp, and fight us. He can't do us any harm tonight, tied up like that.'

They went away down the track. Not ten minutes afterwards the children came to the hole and found it blocked up! If only they hadn't stopped to explore that tunnel a bit further, they would have been able to get out and set Timmy on the two men.

But it was too late now. The hole was well and truly closed. No one could get out. No one could find poor Pongo and bathe his head. They were real prisoners.

They didn't like it at all. Anne began to cry, though she tried not to let the others see her. Nobby saw that she was upset, and put his arm round her.

'Don't cry, little Anne,' he said. 'We'll be all right.'

'It's no good staying here,' said Julian, at last. 'We might as well go somewhere more comfortable, and sit down and talk and eat. I'm hungry.'

They all went back down the passage, up through the hole in the roof, and into the enormous cavern. They found a sandy corner and sat down. Julian handed Anne the kitbag and she undid it to get the food inside.

'Better only have one torch going,' said Julian. 'We don't know how long we'll be here. We don't want to be left in the dark!'

Everybody immediately switched off their torches. The idea of being lost in the dark inside the hill wasn't at all nice! Anne handed out slices of bread and butter, and the children put thin slices of Mrs Mackie's delicious ham on them.

They felt distinctly better when they had all eaten a good meal. 'That was jolly good,' said Dick. 'No, we won't eat that chocolate, Anne. We may want it later on. Golly, I'm thirsty!'

'So am I,' said Nobby. 'My tongue's hanging out like old Timmy's. Let's go and get a drink.'

'Well, there was a stream in that other cave beyond the tunnel, wasn't there?' said Nobby. 'We can drink from that. It'll be all right.'

'Well, I hope it will,' said Julian. 'We were told not to drink water that wasn't boiled while we were caravanning – but we didn't know this sort of thing was going to happen! We'll go through the tunnel and get some water to drink from the stream.'

They made their way through the long, winding tunnel, and passed the shelf of stolen goods. Then on they went and came out into the cave through which the stream rushed so quickly. They dipped in their hands and drank thirstily. The water tasted lovely – so clear and cold.

Timmy drank too. He was puzzled at this adventure, but so long as he was with George he was happy. If his mistress suddenly took it into her head to live underground like a worm, that was all right – so long as Timmy was with her!

'I wonder if this stream *does* go to that hole in the hillside, and pours out there,' said Julian, suddenly. 'If it does, and we could follow it, we might be able to squeeze out.'

'We'd get terribly wet,' said George, 'but that wouldn't matter. Let's see if we can follow the water.'

They went to where the stream disappeared into a tunnel rather like the dry one they had come along. Julian shone his torch into it.

'We could wade along, I think,' he said. 'It is very fast but not very deep. I know – I'll go along it myself and see where it goes, and come back and tell you.'

146

'No,' said George, at once. 'If you go, we all go. You might get separated from us. That would be awful.'

'All right,' said Julian. 'I thought there was no sense in us all getting wet, that's all. Come on, we'll try now.'

One by one they waded into the stream. The current tugged at their legs, for the water ran very fast. But it was only just above the knees there. They waded along by the light of their torches, wondering where the tunnel would lead to.

Timmy half-waded, half-swam. He didn't like this water-business very much. It seemed silly to him. He pushed ahead of Julian and then a little further down, jumped up to a ledge that ran beside the water.

'Good idea, Tim,' said Julian, and he got up on to it too. He had to crouch down rather as he walked because his head touched the roof of the tunnel if he didn't – but at least his legs were out of the icy-cold water! All the others did the same, and as long as the ledge ran along beside the stream they all walked along it.

But at times it disappeared and then they had to wade in the water again, which now suddenly got deeper. 'Gracious! It's almost to my waist,' said Anne. 'I hope it doesn't get any deeper. I'm holding my clothes up as high as I can, but they'll get soaked soon.'

Fortunately the water got no deeper, but it seemed to go faster. 'We're going down hill a bit,' said Julian at last. 'Perhaps we are getting near to where it pours out of the hill.'

They were! Some distance ahead of him Julian suddenly saw a dim light, and wondered whatever it could be. He soon knew! It was daylight creeping in through the water that poured out of the hole in the hillside – poured out in a torrent into the sunshine.

'We're almost there!' cried Julian. 'Come on.'

With light hearts the children waded along in the water. Now they would soon be out in the warm sunshine. They would find Pongo, and race down the hill in the warmth, catch the first bus, and go to the police station.

But nothing like that happened at all. To their enormous disappointment the water got far too deep to wade through, and Nobby stopped in fright. 'I dursent go no further,' he said. 'I'm almost off my feet now with the water rushing by.'

'I am, too,' said Anne, frightened.

'Perhaps I can swim out,' said Julian, and he struck out. But he gave it up in dismay, for the torrent of water was too much for him, and he was afraid of being hurled against the rocky sides and having his head cracked.

'It's no good,' he said, gloomily. 'No good at all. All that wading for nothing. It's far too dangerous to go any further – and yet daylight is only a few yards ahead. It's too sickening for words.'

'We must go back,' said George. 'I'm afraid Timmy will be drowned if we don't. Oh, dear – we must go all that way back!'

20
More excitement

It was a very sad and disappointed little company that made their way back to the cave. Along the tunnel they went, painfully and slowly, for it was not so easy against the current. Julian shivered; he was wet through with trying to swim.

At last they were back in the cave through which the stream flowed so swiftly. 'Let's run round and round it to get warm,' said Julian. 'I'm frozen. Dick, let me have one of your dry jerseys. I must take off these wet ones.'

The children ran round and round the cave, pretending to race one another, trying to get warm. They did get warm in the end, and sank down in a heap on some soft sand in a corner, panting. They sat there for a little while to get their breath.

Then they heard something. Timmy heard it first and growled. 'Jumping Jiminy, what's up with Timmy?' said Nobby, in fright. He was the most easily scared of the children, probably because of the frights he had had the last few days.

They all listened, George with her hand on Timmy's collar. He growled again, softly. The noise they all heard was a loud panting coming from the stream over at the other side of the cave!

'Someone is wading up the stream,' whispered Dick, in astonishment. 'Did they get in at the place where we couldn't get out? They must have!'

'But who is it?' asked Julian. 'Can't be Lou or Dan. They wouldn't come that way when they could come the right way. Sh! Whoever it is, is arriving in the cave. I'll shut off my torch.'

Darkness fell in the cave as the light from Julian's torch was clicked off. They all sat and listened, and poor Nobby shook and shivered. Timmy didn't growl any more, which was surprising. In fact, he even wagged his tail!

There was a sneeze from the other end of the cave – and then soft footsteps padded towards them. Anne felt as if she must scream. WHO was it?

Julian switched on his torch suddenly, and its light fell on a squat, hairy figure, halting in the bright glare. It was Pongo!

'It's *Pongo!*' everyone yelled, and leapt up at once. Timmy ran over to the surprised chimpanzee and sniffed round him in delight. Pongo put his arms round Nobby and Anne.

'Pongo! You've escaped! You must have bitten through your rope!' said Julian. 'How clever you are to find your way through the hole where the stream pours out. How did you know you would find us here! Clever Pongo.'

Then he saw the big wound on poor Pongo's head. 'Oh look!' said Julian. 'He's been hurt! I expect those brutes threw a stone at him. Poor old Pongo.'

'Let's bathe his head,' said Anne. 'I'll use my hanky.'

But Pongo wouldn't let anyone touch his wound, not even Nobby. He didn't snap or snarl at them, but simply held their hands away from him, and refused to leave go. So nobody could bathe his head or bind it up.

'Never mind,' said Nobby at last, 'animals' wounds often heal up very quickly without any attention at all. He won't let us touch it, that's certain. I expect Lou and Dan hit him with a stone, and knocked him unconscious when they came. They then shut up the hole and made us prisoners. Beasts!'

'I say,' suddenly said Dick. 'I say! I've got an idea. I don't know if it will work – but it really *is* an idea.'

'What?' asked everyone, thrilled.

'Well – what about tying a letter round Pongo's neck and sending him out of the hole again, to take the letter to the camp?' said Dick. 'He won't go to Lou or Dan because he's scared of them – but he'd go to any of the others all right, wouldn't he? Larry would be the best one. He seems to be a good fellow.'

'Would Pongo understand enough to do all that though?' asked Julian, doubtfully.

'We could try him,' said Nobby. 'I do send him here and there sometimes, just for fun – to take the elephant's bat to Larry, for instance – or to put my coat away in my caravan.'

'Well, we could certainly try,' said Dick. 'I've got a notebook and a pencil. I'll write a note and wrap it up in another sheet, pin it together and tie it round Pongo's neck with a bit of string.'

So he wrote a note. It said:

'To whoever gets this note – please come up the hill to the hollow where there are two caravans. Under the red one is the entrance to an underground passage. We are prisoners inside the hill. Please rescue us soon.

Julian, Dick, George, Anne and Nobby.'

He read it out to the others. Then he tied the note round

Pongo's neck. Pongo was surprised, but fortunately did not try to pull if off.

'Now, you give him his orders,' said Dick to Nobby. So Nobby spoke slowly and importantly to the listening chimpanzee.

'Where's Larry? Go to Larry, Pongo. Fetch Larry. Go. GO!'

Pongo blinked at him and made a funny little noise as if he was saying: 'Please, Nobby, I don't want to go.'

Nobby repeated everything again. 'Understand Pongo? I think you do. GO, then, GO. GO!'

And Pongo turned and went! He disappeared into the stream, splashing along by himself. The children watched him as far as they could by the light of their torches.

'He really is clever,' said Anne. 'He didn't want to go a bit, did he? Oh, I do hope he finds Larry, and that Larry sees the note and reads it and sends someone to rescue us.'

'I hope the note doesn't get all soaked and pulpy in the water,' said Julian, rather gloomily. 'Gosh, I wish I wasn't so cold. Let's run round a bit again, then have a piece of chocolate.'

They ran about and played 'he' for a time till they all felt warm again. Then they decided to sit down and have some chocolate, and play some sort of guessing game to while away the time. Timmy sat close to Julian, and the boy was very glad.

'He's like a big hot-water bottle,' he said. 'Sit closer, Tim. That's right. You'll soon warm me up!'

It was dull after a time, sitting in the light of one torch, for they dared not use them all. Already it seemed as if Julian's torch was getting a little dim. They played all the games they could think of and then yawned.

'What's the time? I suppose it must be getting dark outside now. I feel quite sleepy.'

'It's nine o'clock almost,' said Julian. 'I hope Pongo has

got down to the camp all right and found someone. We could expect help quite soon, if so.'

'Well, then, we'd better get along to the passage that leads to the hole,' said Dick, getting up. 'It's quite likely that if Larry or anyone else comes they'll not see the foot-holds leading up the wall out of that first little cave. They might not know where we were!'

This seemed very likely. They all made their way down the tunnel that led past the hidden store of valuables, and came out into the enormous cave. There was a nice sandy corner just by the hole that led down into the first small cave, and the children decided to sit there, rather than in the passage or in the first rocky and uncomfortable little cave. They cuddled up together for warmth, and felt hungry.

Anne and Nobby dozed off to sleep. George almost fell asleep, too. But the boys and Timmy kept awake, and talked in low voices. At least, Timmy didn't talk, but wagged his tail whenever either Dick or Julian said anything. That was his way of joining in their conversation.

After what seemed a long while Timmy growled, and the two boys sat up straight. Whatever it was that Timmy's sharp ears had heard, they had heard nothing at all. And they continued to hear nothing. But Timmy went on growling.

Julian shook the others awake. 'I believe help has come,' he said. 'But we'd better not go and see in case it's Dan and Lou come back. So wake up and look lively!'

They were all wide awake at once. Was it Larry come in answer to their note – or was it those horrid men, Tiger Dan and Lou the acrobat?

They soon knew! A head suddenly poked out of the hole nearby, and a torch shone on them. Timmy growled ferociously and struggled to fly at the head, but George held on firmly to his collar, thinking it might be Larry.

But it wasn't! It was Lou the acrobat, as the children

154

knew only too well when they heard his voice. Julian shone his torch on to him.

'I hope you've enjoyed your little selves,' came Lou's harsh voice. 'And you keep that dog under control, boy, or I'll shoot him. See? I'm not standing no nonsense from that dog this time. Have a look at this here gun!'

To George's horror she saw that Lou was pointing a gun at poor Timmy. She gave a scream and flung herself in front of him. 'Don't you dare to shoot my dog! I'll – I'll – I'll . . .'

She couldn't think of anything bad enough to do to the man who could shoot Timmy, and she stopped, choked by tears of rage and fear. Timmy, not knowing what the gun was, couldn't for the life of him understand why George wouldn't let him get at his enemy – such a nice position, too, with his head poking through a hole like that. Timmy felt he could deal with that head very quickly.

'Now, you kids, get up and go into that tunnel,' said Lou. 'Go on – go right ahead of me, and don't dare to stop. We've got work to do here tonight, and we're not going to have any more interference from kids like you. See?'

The children saw quite well. They began to walk towards the entrance of the tunnel. One by one they climbed into it. George first with Timmy. She dared not let his collar go for an instant. A few paces behind them came Lou with his revolver, and Dan with a couple of big sacks.

The children were made to walk right past the shelf on which were the hidden goods.

Then Lou sat down in the tunnel, his torch switched on fully so that he could pick out each child. He still pointed his revolver at Timmy.

'Now we'll get on,' he said to Tiger Dan. 'You know what to do. Get on with it.'

Tiger Dan began to stuff the things into one of the big sacks he had brought. He staggered off with it. He came back in about ten minutes and filled the other sack. It was plain that the men meant to take everything away this time.

'Thought you'd made a very fine discovery, didn't you?' said Lou, mockingly, to the children. 'Ho, yes – very smart you were! See what happens to little smarties like you – you're prisoners – and here you'll stay for two or three days!'

'What do you mean?' said Julian, in alarm. 'Surely you wouldn't leave us here to starve?'

'Not to starve. We're too fond of you,' grinned Lou. 'We'll chuck you down some food into the tunnel. And in two or three days maybe someone will come and rescue you.'

Julian wished desperately that Pongo would bring help before Lou and Dan finished their business in the tunnel and went, leaving them prisoners. He watched Tiger Dan, working quickly, packing everything, carrying it off, coming back again, and packing feverishly once more. Lou sat still with his torch and revolver, enjoying the scared faces of the girls and Nobby. Julian and Dick put on a brave show which they were far from feeling.

Tiger Dan staggered away with another sackful. But he hadn't been gone for more than half a minute before a wail echoed through the tunnel.

'Lou! Help! Help! Something's attacking me! HELP.'

Lou rose up and went swiftly down the tunnel. 'It's Pongo, I bet it's old Pongo,' said Julian thrilled.

21
Dick has a great idea!

'Listen,' said Dick in an urgent voice. 'It may be Pongo by himself – he may not have gone back to the camp at all – he may have wandered about and at last gone down the entrance-hole by the caravans, and come up behind Tiger Dan. If so he won't have much chance because Lou's got a gun and will shoot him. And we shan't be rescued. So I'm going to slip down the tunnel while there's a chance and hide in a big cave.'

'What good will that do?' said Julian.

'Well, idiot, I may be able to slip down into the passage that leads to the entrance hole and hop out without the others seeing me,' said Dick, getting up. 'Then I can fetch help, see? You'd better all clear off somewhere and hide – find a good place, Julian, in case the men come after you when they find one of us is gone. Go on.'

Without another word the boy began to walk down the tunnel, past the rocky shelf on which now very few goods were left, and then came to the enormous cave.

Here there was a great noise going on, for Pongo

157

appeared to have got hold of both men at once! Their torches were out, and Lou did not dare to shoot for fear of hurting Dan. Dick could see very little of this; he could only hear snarlings and shouting. He took a wide course round the heaving heap on the floor and made his way as quickly as he could in the dark to where he thought the hole was that led down into the first passage. He had to go carefully for fear of falling down it. He found it at last and let himself down into the cave below, and then, thinking it safe to switch on his torch in the passage, he flashed it in front of him to show him the way.

It wasn't long before he was out of the hole and was speeding round the caravans. Then he stopped. A thought struck him. He could fetch help all right – but the men would be gone by then! They had laid their plans for a getaway with all the goods; there was no doubt about that.

Suppose he put the boards over the hole, ramming them in with all his strength, and then rolled some heavy stones on top? He couldn't move the caravan over the boards, for it was far too heavy for a boy to push. But heavy stones would probably do the trick. The men would imagine that it was the caravan overhead again!

In great excitement Dick put back the boards, lugging them into place, panting and puffing. Then he flashed his torch round for stones. There were several small rocks nearby. He could not lift them, but he managed to roll them to the boards. Plonk! They went on to them one by one. Now nobody could move the boards at all.

'I know I've shut the others in with the men,' thought Dick. 'But I hope Julian will find a very safe hiding-place just for a time. Gosh, I'm hot! Now, down the hill I go – and I hope I don't lose my way in the darkness!'

Down below, the two men had at last freed themselves from the angry chimpanzee. They were badly bitten and mauled, but Pongo was not as strong and savage as usual because of his bad head-wound. The men were able to

158

drive him off at last, and he went limping in the direction of the tunnel, sniffing out the children.

He would certainly have been shot if Lou could have found his revolver quickly enough. But he could not find it in the dark. He felt about for his torch, and found that although it was damaged, he could still put on the light by knocking it once or twice on the ground. He shone it on to Dan.

'We ought to have looked out for that ape when we saw he was gone,' growled Dan. 'He had bitten his rope through. We might have known he was somewhere about. He nearly did for me, leaping on me like that out of the darkness. It was lucky he flung himself on to my sack and not me.'

'Let's get the last of the things and clear out,' said Lou, who was badly shaken up. 'There's only one more load. We'll get back to the tunnel, scare the life out of those kids once more, shoot Pongo if we can, and then clear out. We'll chuck a few tins of food down the hole and then close it up.'

'I'm not going to risk meeting that chimp again,' said Dan. 'We'll leave the rest of the things. Come on. Let's go.'

Lou was not particularly anxious to see Pongo again either. Keeping his torch carefully switched on and his revolver ready, he followed Dan to the hole that led down to the first cave. Down they went, and then along the passage, eager to get out into the night and go with their wagon down the track.

They got a terrible shock when they found that the hole was closed. Lou shone his torch upwards, and gazed in amazement at the underside of the boards. Someone had put them back into place again. *They* were prisoners now!

Tiger Dan went mad. One of his furious rages overtook him, and he hammered against those boards like a madman. But the heavy stones held them down, and the raging man dropped down beside Lou.

'Can't budge the boards! Someone must have put the caravan overhead again. We're prisoners!'

'But who's made us prisoners? Who's put back those boards?' shouted Lou, almost beside himself with fury. 'Could those kids have slipped by us when we were having that fight with the chimp?'

'We'll go and see if the kids are still there,' said Tiger Dan, grimly. 'We'll find out. We'll make them very, very sorry for themselves. Come on.'

The two men went back again to the tunnel. The children were not there. Julian had taken Dick's advice and had gone off to try and find a good hiding-place. He had suddenly thought that perhaps Dick might get the idea of shutting up the entrance-hole – in which case the two men would certainly be furious!

So up the tunnel the children went, and into the cave with the stream. It seemed impossible to find any hiding-place there at all.

'I don't see where we can hide,' said Julian, feeling rather desperate. 'It's no good wading down that stream again – we shall only get wet and cold – and we have no escape from there at all if the men should come after us!'

'I can hear something,' said George, suddenly. 'Put your light out, Julian – quick!'

The torch was snapped off, and the children waited in the darkness. Timmy didn't growl. Instead George felt that he was wagging his tail.

'It's someone friendly,' she whispered. 'Over there. Perhaps it's Pongo. Put the torch on again.'

The light flashed out, and picked out the chimpanzee, who was coming towards them across the cave. Nobby gave a cry of joy.

'Here's old Pongo again!' he said. 'Pongo, did you go to the camp? Did you bring help?'

'No – he hasn't been down to the camp,' said Julian, his eyes catching sight of the note still tied round the chim-

160

panzee's neck. 'There's our letter still on him. Blow!'

'He's clever – but not clever enough to understand a difficult errand like that,' said George.

'Oh, Pongo – and we were depending on you! Never mind – perhaps Dick will escape and bring help. Julian, where *shall* we hide?'

'*Up* the stream?' suddenly said Anne. 'We've tried going *down* it. But we haven't tried going up it. Do you think it would be any good?'

'We could see,' said Julian, doubtfully. He didn't like this business of wading through water that might suddenly get deep. 'I'll shine my torch up the stream and see what it looks like.'

He went to the stream and shone his light up the tunnel from which it came. 'It seems as if we might walk along the ledge beside it,' he said. 'But we'd have to bend almost double – and the water runs so fast just here we must be careful not to slip and fall in.'

'I'll go first,' said Nobby. 'You go last, Julian. The girls can go in the middle with Pongo and Timmy.'

He stepped on to the narrow ledge inside the rocky tunnel, just above the rushing water. Then came Pongo. Then Anne, then George and Timmy – and last of all Julian.

But just as Julian was disappearing, the two men came into the cave, and by chance Lou's torch shone right on to the vanishing Julian. He gave a yell.

'There's one of them – look, over there! Come on!'

The men ran to where the stream came out of the tunnel, and Lou shone his torch up it. He saw the line of children, with Julian last of all. He grabbed hold of the boy and pulled him back.

Anne yelled when she saw Julian being pulled back. Nobby had a dreadful shock. Timmy growled ferociously, and Pongo made a most peculiar noise.

'Now look here,' came Lou's voice, 'I've got a gun, and

161

I'm going to shoot that dog and that chimp if they so much as put their noses out of here. So hang on to them if you want to save their lives!'

He passed Julian to Tiger Dan, who gripped the boy firmly by the collar. Lou shone his torch up the tunnel again to count the children. 'Ho, there's Nobby,' he said. 'You come on out here, Nobby.'

'If I do, the chimp will come out too,' said Nobby. 'You know that. And he may get *you* before you get him!'

Lou thought about that. He was afraid of the big chimpanzee. 'You stay up there with him, then,' he said. 'And the girl can stay with you, holding the dog. But the other boy can come out here.'

He thought that George was a boy. George didn't mind. She liked people to think she was a boy. She answered at once.

'I can't come. If I do the dog will follow me, and I'm not going to have him shot.'

'You come on out,' said Lou, threateningly. 'I'm going to show you two boys what happens to kids who keep spying and interfering. Nobby knows what happens, don't you, Nobby? He's had his lesson. And you two boys are going to have yours, too.'

Dan called to him. 'There ought to be another girl there, Lou. I thought Nobby said there were two boys and two girls. Where's the other girl?'

'Gone further up the tunnel, I suppose,' said Lou, trying to see. 'Now, you boy – come on out!'

Anne began to cry. 'Don't go, George; don't go. They'll hurt you. Tell them you're a . . .'

'Shut up,' said George, fiercely. She added, in a whisper: 'If I say I'm a girl they'll know Dick is missing, and will be all the angrier. Hang on to Timmy.'

Anne clutched Timmy's collar in her trembling hand. George began to walk back to the cave. But Julian was not going to let George be hurt. She might like to think of

162

herself as a boy, but he wasn't going to let her be treated like one. He began to struggle.

Lou caught hold of George as she came out of the tunnel – and at the same moment Julian managed to kick high in the air, and knocked Lou's torch right out of his hand. It flew up into the roof of the cave and fell somewhere with a crash. It went out. Now the cave was in darkness.

'Get back into the tunnel, George, with Anne,' yelled Julian. 'Timmy, Timmy, come on! Pongo, come here!'

'I don't want Timmy to be shot!' cried out George, in terror, as the dog shot past her into the cave.

Even as she spoke a shot rang out. It was Lou, shooting blindly at where he thought Timmy was. George screamed.

'Oh, Timmy, Timmy! You're not hurt, are you?'

22
The end of the adventure

No, Timmy wasn't hurt. The bullet zipped past his head and struck the wall of the cave. Timmy went for Lou's legs. Down went the man with a crash and a yell, and the revolver flew out of his hand. Julian heard it slithering across the floor of the cave, and he was very thankful.

'Put on your torch, George, quickly!' he yelled. 'We must see what we're doing. Goodness, here's Pongo now!'

Tiger Dan gave a yell of fright when the torch flashed on and he saw the chimpanzee making straight for him. He dealt the ape a smashing blow on the face that knocked him down, and then turned to run. Lou was trying to keep Timmy off his throat, kicking frantically at the excited dog.

Dan ran to the tunnel – and then stopped in astonishment. Four burly policemen were pushing their way out of the tunnel, led by Dick! One of them carried a revolver in his hand. Dan put his hands up at once.

'Timmy! Come off!' commanded George, seeing that there was now no need for the dog's delighted help.

164

Timmy gave her a reproachful glance that said: 'Mistress! I'm really enjoying myself! Let me eat him all up!'

Then the dog caught sight of the four policemen and yelped furiously. More enemies! He would eat the lot.

'What's all this going on?' said the first man, who was an Inspector. 'Get up, you on the floor. Go on, get up!'

Lou got up with great difficulty. Timmy had nipped him in various places. His hair was over his eyes, his clothes were torn. He stared at the policemen, his mouth open in the utmost surprise. How had they come here? Then he saw Dick.

'So one of you kids slipped out – and shut the boards on us!' he said, savagely. 'I might have guessed. You . . .'

'Hold your tongue, Lewis Allburg,' rapped out the Inspector. 'You can talk when we tell you. You'll have quite a lot of talking to do, to explain some of the things we've heard about you.'

'Dick! How did you get here so soon?' cried Julian, going over to his brother. 'I didn't expect you for hours! Surely you didn't go all the way to the town and back?'

'No. I shot off to the farm, woke up the Mackies, used their telephone and got the police up here double-quick in their car,' said Dick, grinning. 'Everyone all right? Where's Anne? And Nobby?'

'There they are – just coming out of the tunnel, up-stream,' said Julian, and swung his torch round. Dick saw Anne's white, scared face, and went over to her.

'It's all right,' he said. 'The adventure is over, Anne! You can smile again!'

Anne gave a watery sort of smile. Pongo took her hand and made little affectionate noises, and that made her smile a little more. George called Timmy to her, afraid that he might take a last nip at Lou.

Lou swung round and stared at her. Then he looked at Dick and Julian. Then at Anne.

'So there *was* only one girl!' he said. 'What did you want to tell me there were two boys and two girls for?' he said to Nobby.

'Because there were,' answered Nobby. He pointed to George. 'She's a girl, though she looks like a boy. And she's as good as a boy any day.'

George felt proud. She stared defiantly at Lou. He was now in the grip of a stout policeman, and Tiger Dan was being hustled off by two more.

'I think we'll leave this rather gloomy place,' said the Inspector, putting away the notebook he had been hastily scribbling in. 'Quick march!'

Julian led the way down the tunnel. He pointed out the shelf where the men had stored their things, and the Inspector collected the few things that were still left. Then on they went, Tiger Dan muttering and growling to himself.

'Will they go to prison?' whispered Anne to Dick.

'You bet,' said Dick. 'That's where they ought to have gone long ago. Their burglaries have been worrying the police for four years!'

Out of the tunnel and into the cave with gleaming walls. Then down the hole and into the small cave and along the narrow passage to the entrance-hole. Stars glittered over the black hole, and the children were very thankful to see them. They were tired of being underground!

Lou and Dan did not have a very comfortable journey along the tunnels and passages, for their guards had a very firm hold of them indeed. Once out in the open they were handcuffed and put into the large police car that stood a little way down the track.

'What are you children going to do?' asked the big Inspector, who was now at the wheel of the car. 'Hadn't you better come down into the town with us after this disturbing adventure?'

'Oh, no thanks,' said Julian politely. 'We're quite used

to adventures. We've had plenty, you know. We shall be all right here with Timmy and Pongo.'

'Well, I can't say I'd like a chimpanzee for company myself,' said the Inspector. 'We'll be up here in the morning, looking round and asking a few questions, which I'm sure you'll be pleased to answer. And many thanks for your help in capturing two dangerous thieves!'

'What about the wagon of goods?' asked Dick. 'Are you going to leave it up here? It's got lots of valuables in it.'

'Oh, one of the men is driving down,' said the Inspector, nodding towards a policeman, who stood near by. 'He'll follow us. He can drive a horse all right. Well, look after yourselves. See you tomorrow!'

The car started up suddenly. The Inspector put her into gear, took off the brake and the car slid quietly down the hill, following the winding track. The policeman with the wagon followed slowly, clicking to the horse, which didn't seem at all surprised to have a new driver.

'Well, that's that!' said Julian thankfully. 'I must say we were well out of that. Gosh, Dick. I was glad to see you back with those bobbies so quickly. That was a brain wave of yours to telephone from the farm.'

Dick suddenly yawned. 'It must be frightfully late!' he said. 'Long past the middle of the night. But I'm so fearfully hungry that I simply must have something to eat before I fall into my bunk!'

'Got anything, Anne?' asked Julian.

Anne brightened up at once. 'I'll see,' she said. 'I can find something, I'm sure!'

And she did, of course. She opened two tins of sardines and made sandwiches, and she opened two tins of peaches, so they had a very nice meal in the middle of the night! They ate it sitting on the floor of George's caravan. Pongo had as good a meal as anyone, and Timmy crunched at one of his bones.

It didn't take them long to go to sleep that night. In fact they were all so sleepy when they had finished their meal that nobody undressed! They clambered into the bunks just as they were and fell asleep at once. Nobby curled up with Pongo, and Timmy, as usual, was on George's feet. Peace reigned in the caravans – and tonight no one came to disturb them!

All the children slept very late the next morning. They were awakened by a loud knocking on Julian's caravan. He woke up with a jump and yelled out:

'Yes! Who is it?'

'It's us,' said a familiar voice, and the door opened. Farmer Mackie and his wife peeped in, looking rather anxious.

'We wondered what had happened,' said the farmer. 'You rushed out of the farmhouse when you had used the 'phone last night and didn't come back.'

'I ought to have slipped back and told you,' said Dick, sitting up with his hair over his eyes. He pushed it back. 'But I forgot. The police went down into the hills with us and got the two men. They're well-known burglars. The police got all the goods, too. It was a very thrilling night. Thanks most awfully for letting me use the 'phone.'

'You're very welcome,' said Mrs Mackie. 'And look – I've brought you some food.'

She had two baskets stacked with good things. Dick felt wide awake and very hungry when he saw them. 'Oh, thanks,' he said gratefully. 'You *are* a good sort!'

Nobby and Pongo suddenly uncurled themselves from their pile of rugs, and Mrs Mackie gave a squeal.

'Land-snakes, what's that? A monkey?'

'No, an ape, Mam,' said Nobby politely. 'He won't hurt you. Hi, take your hand out of that basket!'

Pongo, who had been hoping to find a little titbit unnoticed, covered his face with his hairy paw and looked through his fingers at Mrs Mackie.

'Look at that now – he's like a naughty child!' said Mrs Mackie. 'Isn't he, Ted?'

'He is that,' said the farmer. 'Queer sort of bedfellow, I must say!'

'Well, I must be getting along,' said Mrs Mackie, nodding and smiling at George and Anne, who had now come out of their caravan with Timmy to see who the visitors were. 'You come along to the farm if you want anything. We'll be right pleased to see you.'

'Aren't they nice?' said Anne as the two farm-folk went down the cart-track. 'And oh, my goodness – what a breakfast we're going to have! Cold bacon – tomatoes – fresh radishes – curly lettuces – and who wants new honey?'

'Marvellous!' said Julian. 'Come on – let us have it now, before we clean up.'

But Anne made them wash and tidy themselves first! 'You'll enjoy it much more if you're clean,' she said. 'We all look as black as sweeps! I'll give you five minutes – then you can come to a perfectly wonderful breakfast!'

'All right, Ma!' grinned Nobby, and he went off with the others to wash at the spring. Then back they all went to the sunny ledge to feast on the good things kind Mrs Mackie had provided.

23

Good-bye, Nobby – good-bye, caravanners!

Before they had finished their breakfast the Inspector came roaring up the track in his powerful police car. There was one sharp-eyed policeman with him to take down notes.

'Hallo, hallo!' said the Inspector, eyeing the good things set out on the ledge. 'You seem to do yourselves well, I must say!'

'Have some new bread and honey?' said Anne in her best manner. 'Do! There's plenty!'

'Thanks,' said the Inspector, and sat down with the children. The other policeman wandered round the caravans, examining everything. The Inspector munched away at honey and bread, and the children talked to him, telling him all about their extraordinary adventure.

170

'It must have been a most unpleasant shock for those two fellows when they found that your caravan was immediately over the entrance to the place where they hid their stolen goods,' said the Inspector. 'Most unpleasant.'

'How you examined the goods?' asked Dick eagerly. 'Are they very valuable?'

'Priceless,' answered the Inspector, taking another bit of bread and dabbing it thickly with honey. 'Quite priceless. Those rogues apparently stole goods they knew to be of great value, hid them here for a year or two till the hue and cry had died down, then got them out and quietly disposed of them to friends in Holland and Belgium.'

'Tiger Dan used to act in circuses in Holland,' said Nobby. 'He often told me about them. He had friends all over Europe – people in the circus line, you know.'

'Yes. It was easy for him to dispose of his goods abroad,' said the Inspector. 'He planned to go across to Holland today, you know – got everything ready with Lou – or, to give him the right name, Lewis Allburg – and was going to sell most of those things. You just saved them in time!'

'What a bit of luck!' said George. 'They almost got away with it. If Dick hadn't managed to slip out when Pongo was attacking them, we'd still have been prisoners down in the hill, and Lou and Dan would have been half-way to Holland!'

'Smart bit of work you children did,' said the Inspector approvingly, and looked longingly at the honey-pot. 'That's fine honey, I must buy some from Mrs Mackie.'

'Have some more,' said Anne, remembering her manners. 'Do. We've got another loaf.'

'Well, I will,' said the Inspector, and took another slice of bread, spreading it with the yellow honey. It looked as if there wouldn't even be enough left for Pongo to lick out! Anne thought it was nice to see a grown-up enjoying bread and honey as much as children did.

'You know, that fellow Lou did some very remarkable

171

burglaries,' said the Inspector. 'Once he got across from the third floor of one house to the third floor of another *across the street* – and nobody knows how!'

'That would be easy for Lou,' said Nobby, suddenly losing his fear of the big Inspector. 'He'd just throw a wire rope across, lasso something with the end of it, top of a gutter-pipe, perhaps, draw tight, and walk across! He's wonderful on the tight-rope. There ain't nothing he can't do on the tight-rope.'

'Yes – that's probably what he did,' said the Inspector. 'Never thought of that! No, thanks, I really won't have any more honey. That chimpanzee will eat me if I don't leave some for him to lick out!'

Pongo took away the jar, sat himself down behind one of the caravans, and put a large pink tongue into the remains of the honey. When Timmy came running up to see what he had got, Pongo held the jar high above his head and chattered at him.

'Yarra-yarra-yarra-yarra!' he said. Timmy looked rather surprised and went back to George. She was listening with great interest to what the Inspector had to tell them about the underground caves.

'They're very old,' he said. 'The entrance to them used to be some way down the hill, but there was a landslide and it was blocked up. Nobody bothered to unblock it because the caves were not particularly interesting.'

'Oh, but they *are*,' said Anne, 'especially the one with the gleaming walls.'

'Well, I imagine that quite by accident one day Dan and Lou found another way in,' said the Inspector. 'The way you know – a hole going down into the hill. They must have thought what a fine hiding-place it would make for any stolen goods – perfectly safe, perfectly dry, and quite near the camping-place here each year. What could be better?'

'And I suppose they would have gone on burgling for

172

years and hiding the stuff if we hadn't just happened to put our caravan over the very spot!' said Julian. 'What a bit of bad luck for them!'

'And what a bit of good luck for us!' said the Inspector. 'We did suspect those two, you know, and once or twice we raided the circus to try and find the goods – but they must always have got warning of our coming and got them away in time – up here!'

'Have you been down to the camp, mister?' asked Nobby suddenly.

The Inspector nodded. 'Oh, yes. We've been down already this morning – seen everyone and questioned them. We created quite a stir!'

Nobby looked gloomy.

'What's the matter, Nobby?' said Anne.

'I shan't half cop it when I get back to the camp,' said Nobby. 'They'll say it's all my fault the coppers going there. We don't like the bobbies round the camp. I shall get into a whole lot of trouble when I go back. I don't want to go back.'

Nobody said anything. They all wondered what would happen to poor Nobby now his Uncle Dan was in prison.

Then Anne asked him: 'Who will you live with now in the camp, Nobby?'

'Oh, somebody will take me in and work me hard,' said Nobby. 'I wouldn't mind if I could be with the horses – but Rossy won't let me. I know that. If I could be with horses I'd be happy. I love them and they understand me all right.'

'How old are you, Nobby?' asked the Inspector, joining in the talk. 'Oughtn't you to be going to school?'

'Never been in my life, mister,' said Nobby. 'I'm just over fourteen, so I reckon I never will go now!'

He grinned. He didn't look fourteen. He seemed more like twelve by his size. Then he looked solemn again.

'Reckon I won't go down to the camp today,' he said.

'I'll be proper set on by them all – about you going there and snooping round like. And Mr Gorgio, he won't like losing his best clown and best acrobat!'

'You can stay with us as long as you like,' said Julian. 'We'll be here a bit longer, anyway.'

But he was wrong. Just after the Inspector had left, taking his policeman with him, Mrs Mackie came hurrying up to them with a little orange envelope in her hand.

'The telegraph boy's just been up,' she said. 'He was looking for you. He left this telegram for you. I hope it's not bad news.'

Julian tore the envelope open and read the telegram out loud.

'AMAZED TO GET YOUR LETTER ABOUT THE EXTRAORDINARY HAPPENINGS YOU DESCRIBE. THEY SOUND DANGEROUS. COME HOME AT ONCE.   DADDY.'

'Oh dear,' said Anne. 'Now we shall have to leave. What a pity!'

'I'd better go down to the town and telephone Daddy and tell him we're all right,' said Julian.

'You can 'phone from my house,' said Mrs Mackie, so Julian thought he would. They talked as they went along and suddenly a bright idea struck Julian.

'I say – I suppose Farmer Mackie doesn't want anyone to help him with his horses, does he?' he asked. 'He wouldn't want a boy who really loves and understands them and would work hard and well?'

'Well, now, I dare say he would,' said Mrs Mackie. 'He's a bit short-handed now. He was saying the other day he could do with a good lad, just leaving school.'

'Oh, do you think he'd try our friend Nobby from the circus camp?' said Julian. 'He's mad on horses. He can do anything with them. And he's been used to working very hard I'm sure he'd do well.'

174

Before Julian had left the farmhouse after telephoning to his amazed parents, he had had a long talk with Farmer Mackie – and now he was running back with the good news to the caravans.

'Nobby!' he shouted as he got near. 'Nobby! How would you like to go and work for Farmer Mackie and help with the horses? He says you can start tomorrow if you like – and live at the farm!'

'Jumping Jiminy!' said Nobby, looking startled and disbelieving. 'At the farm? Work with the horses? Coo – I wouldn't half like that. But Farmer Mackie wouldn't have the likes of me.'

'He will. He says he'll try you,' said Julian. 'We've got to start back home tomorrow, and you can be with us till then. You don't need to go back to the camp at all.'

'Well – but what about Growler?' said Nobby. 'I'd have to have him with me. He's my dog. I expect poor old Barker's dead. Would the farmer mind me having a dog?'

'I shouldn't think so,' said Julian. 'Well, you'll have to go down to the camp, I suppose, to collect your few things – and to get Growler. Better go now, Nobby, and then you'll have the rest of the day with us.'

Nobby went off, his face shining with delight. 'Well, I never!' he kept saying to himself. 'Well, I never did! Dan and Lou gone, so they'll never hurt me again – and me not going to live in the camp any more – and going to have charge of them fine farm horses. Well, I never!'

The children had said good-bye to Pongo because he had to go back with Nobby to the camp. He belonged to Mr Gorgio, and Nobby could not possibly keep him. Anyway, it was certain that even if he could have kept him, Mrs Mackie wouldn't have let him live at the farm.

Pongo shook hands gravely with each one of them, even with Timmy. He seemed to know it was good-bye. The children were really sorry to see the comical chimpanzee go. He had shared in their adventure with them and seemed much more like a human being than an animal.

When he had gone down the hill a little way he ran back to Anne. He put his arms round her and gave her a gentle squeeze, as if to say: 'You're all nice, the lot of you, but little Anne's the nicest!'

'Oh, Pongo, you're really a dear!' said Anne, and gave him a tomato. He ran off with it, leaping high for joy.

The children cleared up everything, put the breakfast things away, and cleaned the caravans, ready for starting off the next day. At dinner-time they looked out for Nobby. Surely he should be back soon?

They heard him whistling as he came up the track. He carried a bundle on his back. Round his feet ran two dogs. Two!

'Why – one of them is Barker!' shouted George in delight. 'He must have got better! How simply marvellous!'

Nobby came up, grinning. They all crowded round him, asking about Barker.

'Yes, it's fine, isn't it?' said Nobby, putting down his bundle of belongings. 'Lucilla dosed him all right. He almost died – then he started to wriggle a bit, she said, and the next she knew he was as lively as could be – bit weak on his legs at first – but he's fine this morning.'

Certainly there didn't seem anything wrong with Barker. He and Growler sniffed round Timmy, their tails wagging fast. Timmy stood towering above them, but his tail wagged, too, so Barker and Growler knew he was friendly.

'I was lucky,' said Nobby. 'I only spoke to Lucilla and Larry. Mr Gorgio has gone off to answer some questions at the police station, and so have some of the others. So I just told Larry to tell Mr Gorgio I was leaving, and I got my things and hopped it.'

'Well, now we can really enjoy our last day,' said Julian. 'Everybody's happy!'

176

And they did enjoy that last day. They went down to the lake and bathed. They had a fine farmhouse tea at Mrs Mackie's, by special invitation. They had a picnic supper on the rocky ledge, with the three dogs rolling over and over in play. Nobby felt sad to think he would so soon say good-bye to his 'posh' friends – but he couldn't help feeling proud and pleased to have a fine job of his own on the farm – with the horses he loved so much.

Nobby, Barker, Growler, Farmer Mackie and his wife

all stood on the cart-track to wave good-bye to the two caravans the next morning.

'Good-bye!' yelled Nobby. 'Good luck! See you again some time!'

'Good-bye!' shouted the others. 'Give our love to Pongo when you see him.'

'Woof! woof!' barked Timmy, but only Barker and Growler knew what *that* meant. It meant, 'Shake paws with Pongo for me!'

Good-bye, five caravanners . . . till your next exciting adventure!

Enid Blyton's

FIVE ON
KIRRIN
ISLAND
AGAIN

ILLUSTRATED BY JOLYNE KNOX

CONTENTS

CONTENTS

1
A letter for George

Anne was trying to do some of her prep in a corner of the common-room when her cousin George came bursting in.

George was not a boy; she was a girl called Georgina, but because she had always wanted to be a boy she insisted on being called George. So George she was. She wore her curly hair cut short, and her bright blue eyes gleamed angrily now as she came towards Anne.

'Anne! I've just had a letter from home – and what do you think? Father wants to go and live on my island to do some special work – and he wants to build a sort of tower or something in the castle yard!'

The other girls looked up in amusement, and Anne held out her hand for the letter that George was waving at her. Everyone knew about the little island off Kirrin Bay that belonged to George. Kirrin Island was a tiny place with an old ruined castle in the middle of it: the home of rabbits and gulls and jackdaws.

It had underground dungeons in which George and her cousins had had one or two amazing adventures. It had once belonged to George's mother, and she had given it to George – and George was very fierce where her precious Kirrin Island was concerned! It was *hers*. Nobody else must live there, or even land there without her permission.

And now, dear me, here was her father proposing to go to her island, and even build some sort of workshop there! George was red with exasperation.

'It's just like grown-ups; they go and give you things and then act as though the things were theirs all the time. I don't *want* Father living on my island, and building nasty messy sheds and things there.'

'Oh George – you know your father is a very famous scientist, who needs to work in peace,' said Anne, taking the letter. 'Surely you can lend him your island for a bit?'

'There are plenty of other places where he can work in peace,' said George. 'Oh dear – I was so hoping we could go and stay there in the Easter hols – take our boat there, and food and everything, just like we've done before. Now we shan't be able to if Father really does go there.'

Anne read the letter. It was from George's mother.

'My darling George,

'I think I must tell you at once that your father proposes to live on Kirrin Island for some little time in order to finish some very important experiments he is making. He will have to have some kind of building erected there – a sort of tower, I believe. Apparently he needs a place where he can have absolute peace and isolation, and also, for some reason, where there is water all around him. The fact of being surrounded by water is necessary to his experiment.

'Now, dear, don't be upset about this. I know that you consider Kirrin Island is your very own, but you must allow your family to share it, especially when it is for something as important as your father's scientific work. Father thinks you will be very pleased indeed to lend him Kirrin Island, but I know your funny feelings about it, so I thought I had better write and tell you, before you arrive home and see him installed there, complete with his tower.'

184

The letter then went on about other things, but Anne did not bother to read these. She looked at George.

'Oh, George! I don't see why you mind your father borrowing Kirrin Island for a bit! I wouldn't mind *my* father borrowing an island from me – if I was lucky enough to have one!'

'*Your* father would talk to you about it first, and ask your permission, and see if you minded,' said George, sulkily. 'My father never does anything like that. He just does exactly as he likes without asking anybody anything. I really do think he might have written to me himself. He just puts my back up.'

'You've got a back that is very easily put up, George,' said Anne, laughing. 'Don't scowl at me like that. *I'm* not borrowing your island without your gracious permission.'

But George wouldn't smile back. She took her letter and read it again gloomily. 'To think that all my lovely holiday plans are spoilt!' she said. 'You know how super Kirrin Island is at Easter time – all primroses and gorse and baby rabbits. And you and Julian and Dick were coming to stay, and we haven't stayed together since last summer when we went caravanning.'

'I know. It *is* hard luck!' said Anne. 'It would have been wizard to go and stay on the island these hols. But perhaps your father wouldn't mind if we did? We needn't disturb him.'

'As if living on Kirrin Island with Father there would be the same as living there all by ourselves,' said George, scornfully. 'You know it would be horrid.'

Well yes – Anne didn't think on the whole that Kirrin Island would be much fun with Uncle Quentin there. George's father was such a hot-tempered, impatient man, and when he was in the middle of one of his experiments he was quite unbearable. The least noise upset him.

'Oh dear – how he will yell at the jackdaws to keep quiet, and shout at the noisy gulls!' said Anne, beginning to giggle. 'He won't find Kirrin quite so peaceful as he imagines!'

George gave a watery sort of smile. She folded up the letter and turned away. 'Well, I think it's just the limit,' she said. 'I wouldn't have felt so bad if only Father had asked my permission.'

'He'd never do that!' said Anne. 'It just wouldn't occur to him. Now George, don't spend the rest of the day brooding over your wrongs, for goodness' sake. Go down to the kennels and fetch Timmy. He'll soon cheer you up.'

Timothy was George's dog, whom she loved with all her heart. He was a big black and white mongrel dog, with a ridiculously long tail, and a wide mouth that really seemed to smile. All the four cousins loved him. He was so friendly and loving, so lively and amusing, and he had shared so very many adventures with them all. The five of them had had many happy times together.

George went to get Timmy. Her school allowed the children to keep their own pets. If it hadn't allowed this, it is quite certain that George would not have gone to boarding-school! She could not bear to be parted from Timmy for even a day.

Timmy began to bark excitedly as soon as she came near. George lost her sulky look and smiled. Dear Timmy, dear trustable Timmy – he was better than any person! He was always on her side, always her friend whatever she did, and to Timmy there was no one in the world so wonderful as George.

They were soon going through the fields together, and George talked to Timmy as she always did. She told him about her father borrowing Kirrin Island. Timmy agreed with every word she said. He listened as if he understood everything, and not even when a rabbit shot across his path did he leave his mistress's side. Timmy always knew when George was upset.

He gave her hand a few little licks every now and again.

186

By the time that George was back at school again she felt much better. She took Timmy into school with her smuggling him in at a side door. Dogs were not allowed in the school building, but George, like her father, often did exactly as she liked.

She hurried Timmy up to her dormitory. He scuttled under her bed quickly and lay down. His tail thumped the floor gently. He knew what this meant. George wanted the comfort of his nearness that night! He would be able to jump on her bed, when lights were out, and snuggle into the crook of her knees. His brown eyes gleamed with delight.

'Now, lie quiet,' said George, and went out of the room to join the other girls. She found Anne, who was busy writing a letter to her brothers, Julian and Dick, at their boarding-school.

'I've told them about Kirrin Island, and your father wanting to borrow it,' she said. 'Would you like to come and stay with *us*, George, these hols, instead of us coming to Kirrin? Then you won't feel cross all the time because your father is on your island.'

'No thanks,' said George, at once. 'I'm going home. I want to keep an eye on Father! I don't want him blowing up Kirrin Island with one of his experiments. You know he's messing about with explosives now, don't you?'

'Ooooh – atom bombs, or things like that?' said Anne.

'I don't know,' said George. 'Anyway, quite apart from keeping an eye on Father and my island, we ought to go and stay at Kirrin to keep Mother company. She'll be all alone if Father's on the island. I suppose he'll take food and everything there.'

'Well, there's one thing, we shan't have to creep about on tiptoe and whisper, if your father isn't at Kirrin Cottage!' said Anne. 'We can be as noisy as we like. Do cheer up, George!'

But it took George quite a long time to get over the fit of gloom caused by her mother's letter. Even having Timmy on her bed each night, till he was discovered by an angry teacher, did not quite make up for her disappointment.

The term ran swiftly on to its end. April came in, with sunshine and showers. Holidays came nearer and nearer! Anne thought joyfully of Kirrin, with its lovely sandy beach, its blue sea, its fishing-boats and its lovely cliffside walks.

Julian and Dick thought longingly of them too. This term both they and the girls broke up on the same day.

They could meet in London and travel down to Kirrin together. Hurrah!

The day came at last. Trunks were piled in the hall. Cars arrived to fetch some of the children who lived fairly near. The school coaches drew up to take the others down to the station. There was a terrific noise of yelling and shouting everywhere. The teachers could not make themselves heard in the din.

'Anyone would think that every single child had gone completely mad,' said one of them to another. 'Oh, thank goodness, they're getting into the coaches. George! *Must* you rush along the corridor at sixty miles an hour, with Timmy barking his head off all the time!'

'Yes, I must, I must!' cried George. 'Anne, where are you? Do come and get into the coach. I've got Timmy. He knows it's holidays now. Come on, Tim!'

Down to the station went the singing crowd of children. They piled into the train. 'Bags I this seat! Who's taken my bag? Get out, Hetty, you know you can't bring your dog in here with mine. They fight like anything. Hurrah, the guard's blowing his whistle! We're off!'

The engine pulled slowly out of the station, its long train of carriages behind it, filled to bursting with girls off for their holidays. Through the quiet countryside it went, through small towns and villages, and at last ran through the smoky outskirts of London.

'The boys' train is due in two minutes before ours,' said Anne, leaning out of the window, as the train drew slowly into the London station. 'If it was punctual, they might be on our platform to meet us. Oh look, George, look – there they are!'

George hung out of the window too. 'Hi, Julian!' she yelled. 'Here we are! Hi, Dick, Julian!'

2

Back at Kirrin Cottage

Julian, Dick, Anne, George and Timmy went straight-away to have buns and ginger-beer at the station tearoom. It was good to be all together again. Timmy went nearly mad with joy at seeing the two boys. He kept trying to get on to their knees.

'Look here, Timmy, old thing, I love you very much and I'm jolly glad to see you,' said Dick, 'but that's twice you've upset my ginger-beer all over me. Has he behaved himself this term, George?'

'Fairly well,' said George, considering. 'Hasn't he, Anne? I mean – he only got the joint out of the larder once – and he didn't do so *much* harm to that cushion he chewed – and if people *will* leave their goloshes all over the place nobody can blame Timmy for having a good old game with them.'

'And that was the end of the goloshes, I suppose,' said Julian, with a grin. 'On the whole, Timmy, you have a rather poor report. I'm afraid our Uncle Quentin will not award you the usual twenty-five pence we get for good reports.'

At the mention of her father, George scowled. 'I see George has not lost her pretty scowl,' said Dick, in a teasing voice. 'Dear old George! We shouldn't know her unless she put on that fearsome scowl half a dozen times a day!'

'Oh, she's better than she was,' said Anne hurrying to George's defence at once. George was not so touchy as she had once been, when she was being teased. All the same, Anne knew that there might be sparks flying over her father taking Kirrin Island these holidays, and she didn't want George to fly into a temper too soon!

Julian looked at his cousin. 'I say, old thing, you're not going to take this business of Kirrin Island too much to heart, are you?' he said. 'You've just got to realise that your father's a remarkably clever man, one of the finest scientists we've got – and *I* think that those kind of fellows ought to be allowed as much freedom as they like, for their work. I mean – if Uncle Quentin wants to work on Kirrin Island for some peculiar reason of his own, then you ought to be pleased to say "Go ahead, Father!" '

George looked a little mutinous after this rather long speech; but she thought a great deal of Julian, and usually went by what he said. He was older than any of them, a tall, good-looking boy, with determined eyes and a strong chin. George scratched Timmy's head, and spoke in a low voice.

'All right. I won't go up in smoke about it, Julian. But I'm frightfully disappointed. I'd planned to go to Kirrin Island ourselves these hols.'

'Well, we're all disappointed,' said Julian. 'Buck up with your bun, old thing. We've got to get across London and catch the train for Kirrin. We shall miss it if we don't look out.'

Soon they were in the train for Kirrin. Julian was very

good at getting porters and taxis. Anne gazed admiringly at her big brother as he found them all corner-seats in a carriage. Julian did know how to tackle things!

'Do you think I've grown, Julian?' she asked him. 'I did hope I'd be as tall as George by the end of this term, but she grew too!'

'Well, I should think you might be a quarter of an inch taller than last term,' said Julian. 'You can't catch us up, Anne – you'll always be the smallest! But I like you small.'

'Look at Timmy, putting his head out of the window as usual!' said Dick. 'Timmy you'll get a grit in your eye. Then George will go quite mad with grief and think you're going blind!'

'Woof,' said Timmy, and wagged his tail. That was the nice part about Timmy. He always knew when he was being spoken to, even if his name was not mentioned, and he answered at once.

Aunt Fanny was at the station to meet them in the pony-trap. The children flung themselves on her, for they were very fond of her. She was kind and gentle, and did her best to keep her clever, impatient husband from finding too much fault with the children.

'How's Uncle Quentin?' asked Julian, politely, when they were setting off in the trap.

'He's very well,' said his aunt. 'And terribly excited. Really, I've never known him to be so thrilled as he has been lately. His work has been coming along very success-fully.'

'I suppose you don't know what his latest experiment is?' said Dick.

'Oh no. He never tells me a word,' said Aunt Fanny. 'He never tells anyone anything while he is at work, except his colleagues, of course. But I do know it's very im-portant – and I know, of course, that the last part of the experiment has to be made in a place where there

192

is deep water all round. Don't ask me why! I don't know.'

'Look! There's Kirrin Island!' said Anne, suddenly. They had rounded a corner, and had come in sight of the bay. Guarding the entrance to it was the curious little island topped by the old ruined castle. The sun shone down on the blue sea, and the island looked most enchanting.

George looked earnestly at it. She was looking for the building, whatever it was, that her father said he needed for his work. Everyone looked at the island, seeking the same thing.

They saw it easily enough! Rising from the centre of the castle, probably from the castle yard, was a tall thin tower, rather like a lighthouse. At the top was a glass-enclosed room, which glittered in the sun.

'Oh Mother! I don't like it! It spoils Kirrin Island,' said George, in dismay.

'Darling, it can come down when your father has finished his work,' said her mother. 'It's a very flimsy, temporary thing. It can easily be pulled down. Father promised me he would scrap it as soon as his work was done. He says you can go across and see it, if you like. It's really rather interesting.'

'Ooooh – I'd *love* to go and see it,' said Anne, at once. 'It looks so queer. Is Uncle Quentin all alone on Kirrin Island, Aunt Fanny?'

'Yes, I don't like him to be alone,' said her aunt. 'For one thing I am sure he doesn't get his meals properly, and for another, I'm always afraid some harm might come to him when he's experimenting – and if he's alone, how would I know if anything happened to him?'

'Well, Aunt Fanny, you could always arrange for him to signal to you each morning and night, couldn't you?' said Julian, sensibly. 'He could use that tower easily. He could flash a signal to you in the morning, using a mirror, you know – heliographing that he was all right – and at night he could signal with a lamp. Easy!'

'Yes. I did suggest that sort of thing,' said his aunt. 'I said I'd go over with you all tomorrow, to see him and perhaps, Julian dear, you could arrange something of the sort with your uncle? He seems to listen to you now.'

'Gracious! Do you mean to say Father wants us to invade his secret lair, and actually to see his strange tower?' asked George, surprised. 'Well – I don't think I want to go. After all, it's *my* island – and it's horrid to see someone else taking possession of it.'

'Oh, George, don't begin all that again,' said Anne, with a sigh. 'You and your island! Can't you even *lend* it to your own father! Aunt Fanny, you should have seen George when your letter came. She looked so fierce that I was quite scared!'

Everyone laughed except George and Aunt Fanny. She looked distressed. George was always so difficult! She found fault with her father, and got up against him time after time – but dear me, how very, very like him she was, with her scowls, her sudden temper, and her fierceness! If only George was as sweet-tempered and as easy-going as these three cousins of hers!

George looked at her mother's troubled face, and felt ashamed of herself. She put her hand on her knee. 'It's all right Mother! I won't make a fuss. I'll try and keep my feelings to myself, really I will. I know Father's work is important. I'll go with you to the island tomorrow.'

Julian gave George a gentle clap on the back. 'Good old George! She's actually learned, not only to give in, but to give in gracefully! George, you're more like a boy than ever when you act like that.'

George glowed. She liked Julian to say she was like a boy. She didn't want to be petty and catty and bear malice as so many girls did. But Anne looked a little indignant.

'It isn't *only* boys that can learn to give in decently, and things like that,' she said. 'Heaps of girls do. Well, I jolly well hope I do myself!'

'My goodness, here's another fire-brand!' said Aunt Fanny, smiling. 'Stop arguing now, all of you – here's Kirrin Cottage. Doesn't it look sweet with all the primroses in the garden, and the wallflowers coming out, and the daffodils peeping everywhere?'

It certainly did. The four children and Timmy tore in at the front gate, delighted to be back. They clattered into the house, and, to their great delight, found Joanna, the old cook there. She had come back to help for the holidays. She beamed at the children, and fondled Timmy when he leapt round her barking.

'Well, there now! Haven't you all grown again? How big you are, Master Julian – taller than I am, I declare. And little Miss Anne, why, she's getting quite big.'

That pleased Anne, of course. Julian went back to the front door to help his aunt with the small bags in the trap.

The trunks were coming later. Julian and Dick took everything upstairs.

Anne joined them, eager to see her old bedroom again. Oh, how good it was to be in Kirrin Cottage once more! She looked out of the windows. One looked on to the moor at the back. The other looked sideways on to the sea. Lovely! Lovely! She began to sing a little song as she undid her bag.

'You know,' she said to Dick, when he brought George's bag in, 'you know, Dick, I'm really quite pleased that Uncle Quentin has gone to Kirrin Island, even if it means we won't be able to go there much! I feel much freer in the house when he's away. He's a very clever man and he can be awfully nice – but I always feel a bit afraid of him.'

Dick laughed. 'I'm not afraid of him – but he's a bit of a wet blanket in a house, I must say, when we're here for the holidays. Funny to think of him on Kirrin Island all alone.'

A voice came up the stairs. 'Come down to tea, children, because there are hot scones for you, just out of the oven.'

'Coming, Aunt Fanny!' called Dick. 'Hurry, Anne. I'm awfully hungry. Julian, did you hear Aunt Fanny calling?'

George came up the stairs to fetch Anne. She was pleased to be home, and as for Timmy, he was engaged in going round every single corner of the house, sniffing vigorously.

'He always does that!' said George. 'As if he thought that there *might* be a chair or a table that didn't smell quite the same as it always did. Come on, Tim. Teatime! Mother, as Father isn't here, can Timmy sit beside me on the floor? He's awfully well-behaved now.'

'Very well,' said her mother, and tea began. What a tea! It looked as if it was a spread for a party of twenty. Good old Joanna! She must have baked all day. Well, there wouldn't be much left when the Five had finished!

196

3
Off to Kirrin Island

Next day was fine and warm. 'We can go across to the island this morning,' said Aunt Fanny. 'We'll take our own food, because I'm sure Uncle Quentin will have forgotten we're coming.'

'Has he a boat there?' asked George. 'Mother – he hasn't taken *my* boat, has he?'

'No, dear,' said her mother. 'He's got another boat. I was afraid he would never be able to get it in and out of all those dangerous rocks round the island, but he got one of the fishermen to take him, and had his own boat towed behind, with all its stuff in.'

'Who built the tower?' asked Julian.

'Oh, he made out the plans himself and some men were sent down from the Ministry of Research to put the tower up for him,' said Aunt Fanny. 'It was all rather hush-hush really. The people here were most curious about it, but they don't know any more than I do! No local man helped in the building, but one or two fishermen were hired to take the material to the island, and to land the men and so on.'

'It's all very mysterious,' said Julian. 'Uncle Quentin leads rather an exciting life, really, doesn't he? I wouldn't mind being a scientist myself. I want to be something really worthwhile when I grown up – I'm not just going into somebody's office. I'm going to be on my own.'

'I think I shall be a doctor,' said Dick.

'I'm off to get my boat,' said George, rather bored with this talk. She knew what *she* was going to do when she was grown-up – live on Kirrin Island with Timmy!

Aunt Fanny had got ready plenty of food to take across to the island. She was quite looking forward to the trip. She had not seen her husband for some days, and was anxious to know that he was all right.

They all went down to the beach, Julian carrying the bag of food. George was already there with her boat. James, a fisher-boy friend of George's, was there too, ready to push the boat out for them.

He grinned at the children. He knew them all well. In the old days he had looked after Timmy for George when her father had said the dog must be given away. George had never forgotten James's kindness to Timmy, and always went to see him every holidays.

'Going off to the island?' said James. 'That's a queer thing in the middle of it, isn't it? Kind of lighthouse, it looks. Take my hand, Miss, and let me help you in.'

Anne took his hand and jumped into the boat. George was already there with Timmy. Soon they were all in. Julian and George took the oars. James gave them a shove and off they went on the calm, clear water. Anne could see every stone on the bottom!

Julian and George rowed strongly. They sent the boat along swiftly. George began to sing a rowing song and they all took it up. It was lovely to be on the sea in a boat again. Oh holidays, go slowly, don't rush away too fast!

'George,' said her mother nervously, as they came near to Kirrin Island, 'you *will* be careful of these awful rocks, won't you? The water's so clear today that I can see them all – and some of them are only just below the water.'

'Oh Mother! You know I've rowed hundreds of times to Kirrin Island!' laughed George. 'I simply *couldn't* go on a rock! I know them all, really I do. I could almost row blindfold to the island now.'

There was only one place to land on the island in safety. This was a little cove, a natural little harbour running up to a stretch of sand. It was sheltered by high rocks all round. George and Julian worked their way to the east side of the island, rounded a low wall of very sharp rocks, and there lay the cove, a smooth inlet of water running into the shore!

Anne had been looking at the island as the others rowed. There was the old ruined Kirrin Castle in the centre, just the same as ever. Its tumbledown towers were full of jackdaws as usual. Its old walls were gripped by ivy.

'It's a lovely place!' said Anne, with a sigh. Then she gazed at the curious tower that now rose from the centre of the castle yard. It was not built of brick but some smooth, shiny material, that was fitted together in sections. Evidently the tower had been made in that way so that it might be brought to the island easily, and set up there quickly.

'Isn't it queer?' said Dick. 'Look at that little glass room at the top – like a look-out room! I wonder what it's for?'

'Can anyone climb up inside the tower?' asked Dick, turning to Aunt Fanny.

'Oh yes. There is a narrow spiral staircase inside,' said his aunt. 'That's about all there is inside the tower itself. It's the little room at the top that is important. It has got some extraordinary wiring there, essential to your uncle's experiments. I don't think he *does* anything with the tower – it just has to be there, doing something on its own, which has a certain effect on the experiments he is making.'

Anne couldn't follow this. It sounded too complicated. 'I should like to go up the tower,' she said.

'Well, perhaps your uncle will let you,' said her aunt.

'If he's in a good temper,' said George.

'Now George – you're not to say things like that,' said her mother.

The boat ran into the little harbour, and grounded softly. There was another boat there already – Uncle Quentin's.

George leapt out with Julian and they pulled it up a little further, so that the others could get out without wetting their feet. Out they all got, and Timmy ran up the beach in delight.

'Now, Timmy!' said George, warningly, and Timmy turned a despairing eye on his mistress. Surely she wasn't going to stop him looking to see if there were any rabbits? Only just *looking*! What harm was there in that?

Ah – there was a rabbit! And another and another! They sat all about, looking at the little company coming up from the shore. They flicked their ears and twitched their noses, keeping quite still.

'Oh, they're as tame as ever!' said Anne in delight. 'Aunty Fanny, aren't they lovely? Do look at the baby one over there. He's washing his face!'

They stopped to look at the rabbits. They really were astonishingly tame. But then very few people came to Kirrin Island, and the rabbits multiplied in peace, running about where they liked, quite unafraid.

'Oh, that one is . . .' began Dick, but then the picture was spoilt. Timmy, quite unable to do nothing but look, had suddenly lost his self-control and was bounding on the surprised rabbits. In a trice nothing could be seen but white bobtails flashing up and down as rabbit after rabbit rushed to its burrow.

'*Timmy!*' called George, crossly, and poor Timmy put his tail down, looking round at George miserably. 'What!' he seemed to say. 'Not even a scamper after the rabbits? What a hard-hearted mistress!'

'Where's Uncle Quentin?' asked Anne, as they walked to the great broken archway that was the entrance to the old castle. Behind it were the stone steps that led towards the centre. They were broken and irregular now. Aunt Fanny went across them carefully, afraid of stumbling, but the children, who were wearing rubber shoes, ran over them quickly.

They passed through an old ruined doorway into what looked like a great yard. Once there had been a stone-paved floor, but now most of it was covered by sand, and by close-growing weeds or grass.

The castle had had two towers. One was almost a complete ruin. The other was in better shape. Jackdaws circled round it, and flew above the children's heads, crying 'chack, chack, chack'.

'I suppose your father lives in the little old room with the two slit-like windows,' said Dick to George. 'That's the only place in the castle that would give him any shelter. Everywhere else is in ruins except that one room. Do you remember we once spent a night there?'

'Yes,' said George. 'It was fun. I suppose that's where Father lives. There's nowhere else – unless he's down in the dungeons!'

'Oh, no one would live in the dungeons surely, unless they simply *had* to!' said Julian. 'They're so dark and cold. Where *is* your father, George? I can't see him anywhere.'

'Mother, where would Father be?' asked George. 'Where's his workshop – in that old room there?' She pointed to the dark, stone-walled, stone-roofed room, which was really all that was left of the part in which people had long ago lived. It jutted out from what had once been the wall of the castle.

'Well, really, I don't exactly know,' said her mother. 'I suppose he works over there. He's always met me down at the cove, and we've just sat on the sand and had a picnic and talked. He didn't seem to want me to poke round much.'

'Let's call him,' said Dick. So they shouted loudly.

'Uncle QUEN-tin! Uncle QUEN-tin! Where are you?'

The jackdaws flew up in fright, and a few gulls, who had been sitting on part of the ruined wall, joined in the noise, crying 'ee-oo, ee-oo, ee-oo' over and over again. Every rabbit disappeared in a trice.

No Uncle Quentin appeared. They shouted again. 'UNCLE QUENTIN! WHERE ARE YOU?'

'What a noise!' said Aunt Fanny, covering her ears. 'I should think that Joanna must have heard that at home. Oh dear – where is your uncle? This is most annoying of him. I *told* him I'd bring you across today.'

'Oh well – he must be somewhere about,' said Julian, cheerfully. 'If Mahomet won't come to the mountain, then the mountain must go to Mahomet. I expect he's deep in some book or other. We'll hunt for him.'

202

'We'll look in that little dark room,' said Anne. So they all went through the stone doorway, and found themselves in a little dark room, lit only by two slits of windows. At one end was a space, or recess, where a fireplace had once been, going back into the thick stone wall.

'He's not here,' said Julian in surprise. 'And what's more – there's nothing here at all! No food, no clothes, no books, no stores of any sort. This is not his workroom, nor even his store!'

'Then he must be down in the dungeons,' said Dick. 'Perhaps it's necessary to his work to be underground – and with water all round! Let's go and find the entrance. We know where it is – not far from the old well in the middle of the yard.'

'Yes. He must be down in the dungeons. Mustn't he, Aunt Fanny?' said Anne. 'Are you coming down?'

'Oh no,' said her aunt. 'I can't bear those dungeons. I'll sit out here in the sun, in this sheltered corner, and unpack the sandwiches. It's almost lunch-time.'

'Oh good,' said everyone. They went towards the dungeon entrance. They expected to see the big flat stone that covered the entrance, standing upright, so that they might go down the steps underground.

But the stone was lying flat. Julian was just about to pull on the iron ring to lift it up when he noticed something peculiar.

'Look,' he said. 'There are weeds growing round the edges of the stone. Nobody has lifted it for a long time. Uncle Quentin isn't down in the dungeons!'

'Then where *is* he?' said Dick. 'Wherever *can* he be?'

4

Where is Uncle Quentin?

The four of them, with Timmy nosing round their legs, stood staring down at the big stone that hid the entrance to the dungeons. Julian was perfectly right. The stone could not have been lifted for months, because weeds had grown closely round the edges, sending their small roots into every crack.

'No one is down there,' said Julian. 'We need not even bother to pull up the stone and go down to see. If it had been lifted lately, those weeds would have been torn up as it was raised.'

'And anyway, we know that no one can get *out* of the dungeon once the entrance stone is closing it,' said Dick. 'It's too heavy. Uncle Quentin wouldn't be silly enough to shut himself in! He'd leave it open.'

'Of course he would,' said Anne. 'Well – he's not there, then. He must be somewhere else.'

'But *where*?' said George. 'This is only a small island, and we know every corner of it. Oh – would he be in that cave we hid in once? The only cave on the island.'

204

'Oh yes – he might be,' said Julian. 'But I doubt it. I can't see Uncle Quentin dropping down through the hole in the cave's roof – and that's the only way of getting into it unless you're going to clamber and slide about the rocks on the shore for ages. I can't see him doing that, either.'

They made their way beyond the castle to the other side of the island. Here there was a cave they had once lived in. It could be entered with difficulty on the seaward side, as Julian had said, by clambering over slippery rocks, or it could be entered by dropping down a rope through a hole in the roof to the floor some way below.

They found the hole, half hidden in old heather. Julian felt about. The rope was still there. 'I'll slide down and have a look,' he said.

He went down the rope. It was knotted at intervals so that his feet found holding-places and he did not slide down too quickly and scorch his hands.

He was soon in the cave. A dim light came in from the seaward side. Julian took a quick look round. There was absolutely nothing there at all, except for an old box that they must have left behind when they were last here themselves.

He climbed up the rope again, his head appearing suddenly out of the hole. Dick gave him a hand.

'Well?' he said. 'Any sign of Uncle Quentin?'

'No,' said Julian. 'He's not there, and hasn't been there either, I should think. It's a mystery! Where is he, and if he's really doing important work where is all his stuff? I mean, we know that plenty of stuff was brought here because Aunt Fanny told us so.'

'Do you think he's in the tower?' said Anne, suddenly. 'He might be in that glass room at the top.'

'Well, he'd see us at once, if he were!' said Julian, scornfully. '*And* hear our yells too! Still, we might as well have a look.'

So back to the castle they went and walked to the queer

tower. Their aunt saw them and called to them. 'Your lunch is ready. Come and have it. Your uncle will turn up, I expect.'

'But Aunt Fanny where is he?' said Anne, with a puzzled face. 'We've looked simply *every*where!'

Her aunt did not know the island as well as the children did. She imagined that there were plenty of places to shelter in, or to work in. 'Never mind,' she said, looking quite undisturbed. 'He'll turn up later. You come along and have your meal.'

'We think we'll go up the tower,' said Julian. 'Just in case he's up there working.'

The four children and Timmy went to where the tower rose up from the castle yard. They ran their hands over the smooth, shining sections, which were fitted together in curving rows. 'What's this stuff it's built of?' said Dick.

'Some kind of new plastic material, I should think,' said Julian. 'Very light and strong, and easily put together.'

'I should be afraid it would blow down in a gale,' said George.

'Yes, so should I,' said Dick. 'Look – here is the door.'

The door was small, and rounded at the top. A key was in the keyhole. Julian turned it and unlocked the door. It opened outwards not inwards. Julian put his head inside and looked round.

There was not much room in the tower. A spiral staircase, made of the same shiny stuff as the tower itself, wound up and up and up. There was a space at one side of it, into which projected curious hook-like objects made of what looked like steel. Wire ran from one to the other.

'Better not touch them,' said Julian, looking curiously at them. 'Goodness, this is like a tower out of a fairy-tale. Come on – I'm going up the stairs to the top.'

He began to climb the steep, spiral stairway. It made him quite giddy to go up and round, up and round so many, many times.

206

The others followed him. Tiny, slit-like windows, set sideways not downwards, were let into the side of the tower here and there, and gave a little light to the stairway. Julian looked through one, and had a wonderful view of the sea and the mainland.

He went on up to the top. When he got there he found himself in a small round room, whose sides were of thick, gleaming glass. Wires ran right into the glass itself, and then pierced through it, the free ends waving and glittering in the strong wind that blew round the tower.

There was nothing in the little room at all! Certainly Uncle Quentin was not there. It was clearly only a tower meant to take the wires up on the hook-like things, and to run them through the strange, thick glass at the top, and set them free in the air. What for? Were they catching some kind of wireless waves? Was it to do with Radar? Julian wondered, frowning, what was the meaning of the tower and the thin, shining wires?

The others crowded into the little room. Timmy came too, having managed the spiral stairs with difficulty.

'Gracious! What a queer place!' said George. 'My goodness, what a view we've got from here. We can see miles and miles out to sea – and on this other side we can see miles and miles across the bay, over the mainland to the hills beyond.'

'Yes. It's lovely,' said Anne. 'But – *where* is Uncle Quentin? We still haven't found him. I suppose he *is* on the island.'

'Well, his boat was pulled up in the cove,' said George. 'We saw it.'

'Then he must be here somewhere,' said Dick. 'But he's not in the castle, he's not in the dungeons, he's not in the cave and he's not up here. It's a first-class mystery.'

'The Missing Uncle. Where is he?' said Julian. 'Look there's poor Aunt Fanny still down there, waiting with the lunch. We'd better go down. She's signalling to us.'

'I should like to,' said Anne. 'It's an awful squash in this tiny glass room. I say – did you feel the tower sway then, when that gust of wind shook it? I'm going down quickly, before the whole thing blows over!'

She began to go down the spiral stairs, holding on to a little hand-rail that ran down beside them. The stairs were so steep that she was afraid of falling. She nearly *did* fall when Timmy pushed his way past her, and disappeared below at a remarkably fast pace.

Soon they were all down at the bottom. Julian locked the door again. 'Not much good locking a door if you leave the key in,' he said. 'Still – I'd better.'

They walked over to Aunt Fanny. 'Well, I thought you were never coming!' she said. 'Did you see anything interesting up there?'

'Only a lovely view,' said Anne. 'Simply magnificent. But we didn't find Uncle Quentin. It's very mysterious, Aunt Fanny – we really have looked everywhere on the island – but he's just not here.'

'And yet his boat is in the cove,' said Dick. 'So he can't have gone.'

'Yes, it does sound queer,' said Aunt Fanny, handing round the sandwiches. 'But you don't know your uncle as well as I do. He always turns up all right. He's forgotten I was bringing you, or he would be here. As it is, we may not see him, if he's quite forgotten about your coming. If he remembers, he'll suddenly turn up.'

'But where from?' asked Dick, munching a potted meat sandwich. 'He's done a jolly good disappearing trick, Aunt Fanny.'

'Well, you'll see where he comes from, I've no doubt, when he arrives,' said Aunt Fanny. 'Another Sand-wich George? No, *not* you, Timmy. You've had three already. Oh george, do keep Timmy's head out of that plate.'

'He's hungry too, Mother,' said George.

'Well, I've brought dog-biscuits for him,' said her mother.

'Oh, Mother! As if Timmy would eat *dog* biscuits when he can have sandwiches,' said George. 'He only eats dog biscuits when there's absolutely nothing else and he's so ravenous he can't help eating them.'

They sat in the warm April sunshine, eating hungrily. There was orangeade to drink, cool and delicious. Timmy wandered over to a rock pool he knew, where rain-water collected, and he could be heard lapping there.

'Hasn't he got a good memory?' said George proudly. 'It's ages since he was here – and yet he remembered that pool at once, when he felt thirsty.'

'It's funny Timmy hasn't found Uncle Quentin, isn't it?' said Dick, suddenly. 'I mean – when we were hunting for him, and got "Warm" you'd think Timmy would bark or scrape about or something. But he didn't.

'I think it's jolly funny that Father can't be found anywhere,' said George. 'I do really. I can't think how you can take it so calmly, Mother.'

'Well, dear, as I said before, I know your father better than you do,' said her mother. 'He'll turn up in his own good time. Why, I remember once when he was doing some sort of work in the stalactite caves at Cheddar, he disappeared in them for over a week – but he wandered out all right when he had finished his experiments.'

'It's very queer,' began Anne, and then stopped suddenly. A curious noise came to their ears – a rumbling grumbling, angry noise, like a giant hidden dog, growling in fury. Then there was a hissing noise from the tower, and all the wires that waved at the top were suddenly lit up as if by lightning.

'There now – I knew your father was somewhere about,' said George's mother. 'I heard that noise when I was here before – but I couldn't make out where it came from.'

209

'Where *did* it come from?' said Dick. 'It sounded almost as if it was underneath us, but it couldn't have been. Gracious, this is most mysterious.'

No more noises came. They each helped themselves to buns with jam in the middle. And then Anne gave a squeal that made them all jump violently.

'Look! *There's* Uncle Quentin! Standing over there, near the tower. He's watching the jackdaws! Wherever *did* he come from?'

5

A mystery

Everyone stared at Uncle Quentin. There he was, intently watching the jackdaws, his hands in his pockets. He hadn't seen the children or his wife.

Timmy leapt to his feet, and gambolled over to George's father. He barked loudly. Uncle Quentin jumped and turned round. He saw Timmy – and then he saw all the others, staring at him in real astonishment.

Uncle Quentin did not look particularly pleased to see anyone. He walked slowly over to them, a slight frown on his face. 'This *is* a surprise,' he said. 'I had no idea you were all coming today.'

'Oh *Quentin!*' said his wife, reproachfully. 'I wrote it down for you in your diary. You know I did.'

'Did you! Well, I haven't looked at my diary since, so it's no wonder I forgot,' said Uncle Quentin, a little peevishly. He kissed his wife, George and Anne, and shook hands with the boys.

'Uncle Quentin – where did you come from?' asked Dick, who was eaten up with curiosity. 'We've looked for you for ages.'

'Oh, I was in my workroom,' said Uncle Quentin, vaguely.

'Well, but where's that?' demanded Dick. 'Honestly, Uncle, we can't imagine where you hide yourself. We even went up the tower to see if you were in that funny glass room at the top.'

'*What!*' exploded his uncle, in a sudden surprising fury. 'You dared to go up there? You might have been in great danger. I've just finished an experiment, and all those wires in there were connected with it.'

'Yes, we saw them acting a bit queerly,' said Julian.

'You've no business to come over here, and interfere with my work,' said his uncle, still looking furious. 'How did you get into that tower? I locked it.'

'Yes, it was locked all right,' said Julian. 'But you left the key in, you see, Uncle – so I thought it wouldn't matter if . . .'

'Oh, that's where the key is, is it?' said his uncle. 'I thought I'd lost it. Well, don't you ever go into that tower again. I tell you, it's dangerous.'

'Uncle Quentin, you haven't told us yet where your workroom is,' said Dick, who was quite determined to know. 'We can't imagine where you suddenly came from.'

'I told them you would turn up, Quentin,' said his wife. 'You look a bit thin, dear. Have you been having regular meals. You know, I left you plenty of good soup to heat up.'

'Did you?' said her husband. 'Well, I don't know if I've had it or not. I don't worry about meals when I'm working. I'll have some of those sandwiches now, though, if nobody else wants them.'

He began to devour the sandwiches, one after another, as if he was ravenous. Aunt Fanny watched him in distress.

'Oh Quentin – you're starving. I shall come over here and stay and look after you!'

212

Her husband looked alarmed. 'Oh no! Nobody is to come here. I can't have my work interfered with. I'm working on an extremely important discovery.'

'Is it a discovery that nobody else knows about?' asked Anne, her eyes wide with admiration. How clever Uncle Quentin was!

'Well – I'm not sure about that,' said Uncle Quentin, taking two sandwiches at once. 'That's partly why I came over here – besides the fact that I wanted water round me and above me. I have a feeling that somebody knows a bit more than I want them to know. But there's one thing – they can't come here unless they're shown the way through all those rocks that lie round the island. Only a few of the fishermen know that, and they've been given orders not to bring anyone here at all. I think you're the only other person that knows the way, George.'

'Uncle Quentin – please do tell us where your work-room is,' begged Dick, feeling that he could not wait a single moment more to solve the mystery.

'Don't keep bothering your uncle,' said his aunt, annoyingly. 'Let him eat his lunch. He can't have had anything for ages!'

'Yes, but Aunt Fanny, I . . .' began Dick and was interrupted by his uncle.

'You obey your aunt, young man. I don't want to be pestered by any of you. What does it matter where I work?'

'Oh, it doesn't really matter a bit, sir,' said Dick, hurriedly. 'It's only that I'm awfully curious to know. You see, we looked for you simply everywhere.'

'Well, you're not quite so clever as you thought you were then,' said Uncle Quentin, and reached for a jammy bun. 'George, take this dog of yours away from me. He keeps breathing down my neck, hoping I shall give him a tit-bit. I don't approve of tit-bits at meal-times.'

George pulled Timmy away. Her mother watched her father gobbling up the rest of the food. Most of the sandwiches she had saved for tea-time had gone already. Poor Quentin! How very hungry he must be.

'Quentin, you don't think there's any danger for you here, do you?' she said. 'I mean – you don't think anyone would try to come spying on you, as they did once before?'

214

'No. How could they?' said her husband. 'No plane can land on this island. No boat can get through the rocks unless the way through is known, and the sea's too rough round the rocks for any swimmer.'

'Julian, see if you can make him promise to signal to me night and morning,' said Aunt Fanny, turning to her nephew. 'I feel worried about him somehow.'

Julian tackled his uncle manfully. 'Uncle, it wouldn't be too much of a bother to you to signal to Aunt Fanny twice a day, would it?'

'If you don't, Quentin, I shall come over every single day to see you,' said his wife.

'And we might come too,' said Anne mischievously. Her uncle looked most dismayed at the idea.

'Well, I could signal in the morning and in the evening when I go up to the top of the tower,' he said, 'I have to go up once every twelve hours to re-adjust the wires. I'll signal then. Half past ten in the morning and half past ten at night.'

'How will you signal?' asked Julian. 'Will you flash with a mirror in the morning?'

'Yes – that would be quite a good idea,' said his uncle. 'I could do that easily. And I'll use a lantern at night. I'll shine it out six times at half past ten. Then perhaps you'll all know I'm all right and will leave me alone! But don't look for the signal tonight. I'll start tomorrow morning.'

'Oh Quentin dear, you do sound cross,' said his wife. 'I don't like you being all alone here, that's all. You look thin and tired. I'm sure you're not . . .'

Uncle Quentin put on a scowl exactly like George sometimes put on. He looked at his wrist-watch. 'Well I must go,' he said. 'Time to get to work again. I'll see you to your boat.'

'We're going to stay to tea here, Father,' said George.

'No, I'd rather you didn't,' said her father, getting up. 'Come on – I'll take you to your boat.'

215

'But Father – I haven't been on my island for ages!' said George, indignantly. 'I want to stay here a bit longer. I don't see why I shouldn't.'

'Well, I've had enough interruption to my work,' said her father. 'I want to get on.'

'We shan't disturb you, Uncle Quentin,' said Dick, who was still terribly curious to know where his uncle had his workroom. Why wouldn't he tell them! Was he just being annoying? Or didn't he want them to know?

Uncle Quentin led them all firmly towards the little cove. It was plain that he meant them to go and to go quickly.

'When shall we come over and see you again, Quentin?' asked his wife.

'Not till I say so,' said her husband. 'It won't take me long now to finish what I'm on. My word, that dog's got a rabbit at last!'

'Oh *Timmy*!' yelled George in distress. Timmy dropped the rabbit he had actually managed to grab. It scampered away unhurt. Timmy came to his mistress looking very sheepish.

'You're a very bad dog. Just because I took my eye off you for half a second! No, it's no good licking my hand like that. I'm cross.'

They all came to the boat. 'I'll push her off,' said Julian. 'Get in, all of you. Well, good-bye, Uncle Quentin. I hope your work goes well.'

Everyone got into the boat. Timmy tried to put his head on George's knee, but she pushed it away.

'Oh, be kind to him and forgive him,' begged Anne. 'He looks as if he's going to cry.'

'Are you ready?' cried Julian. 'Got the oars, George? Dick, take the other pair.'

He shoved the boat off and leapt in himself. He cupped his hands round his mouth. 'Don't forget to signal, sir! We'll be watching out morning and evening!'

216

'And if you forget, I shall come over the very next day!' called his wife.

The boat slid away down the little inlet of water, and Uncle Quentin was lost to sight. Then round the low wall of rocks went the boat, and was soon on the open sea.

'Ju, watch and see if you can make out where Uncle Quentin is, when we're round these rocks,' said Dick. 'See what direction he goes in.'

Julian tried to see his uncle, but the rocks just there hid the cove from sight, and there was no sign of him at all.

'*Why* didn't he want us to stay? Because he didn't want us to know his hiding-place!' said Dick. 'And *why* doesn't he want us to know? Because it's somewhere *we* don't know, either!'

'But I thought we knew every single corner of my island,' said George. 'I think it's mean of Father not to tell me, if it's somewhere I don't know. I can't think *where* it can be!'

Timmy put his head on her knee again. George was so absorbed in trying to think where her father's hiding place could be that she absent-mindedly stroked Timmy's head. He was almost beside himself with delight. He licked her fingers lovingly.

'Oh Timmy – I didn't mean to pet you for ages,' said George. 'Stop licking my hands. You make them feel wet and horrid. Dick, it's very mysterious, isn't it – where *can* Father be hiding?'

'I can't imagine,' said Dick. He looked back at the island. A cloud of jackdaws rose up into the air calling loudly, 'Chack, chack, chack!'

The boy watched them. What had disturbed them? Was it Uncle Quentin? Perhaps his hiding-place was somewhere about that old tower then, the one the jackdaws nested in? On the other hand, the jackdaws often rose into the air together for no reason at all.

'Those jackdaws are making a bit of fuss,' he said.

'Perhaps Uncle's hiding-place is not far from where they roost together, by that tower.'

'Can't be,' said Julian. 'We went all round there today.'

'Well, it's a mystery,' said George, gloomily, 'and I think it's horrible having a mystery about my very own island – and to be forbidden to go to it, and solve it. It's really *too* bad!'

6

Up on the cliff

The next day was rainy. The four children put on their
macintoshes and sou'-westers and went out for a walk
with Timmy. They never minded the weather. In fact
Julian said that he really *liked* the feel of the wind and rain
buffeting against his face.

'We forgot that Uncle Quentin couldn't flash to us if the
weather wasn't sunny!' said Dick. 'Do you suppose he'll
find some way to signal instead?'

'No,' said George. 'He just won't bother. He thinks
we're awful fussers anyway, I'm sure. We'll have to watch
at half past ten tonight to see if he signals.'

'I say! Shall I be able to stay up till then?' said Anne
pleased.

'I shouldn't think so,' said Dick. 'I expect Julian and I
will stay up – but you kids will have to buzz off to bed!'

George gave him a punch. 'Don't call us *"kids"*! I'm
almost as tall as you are now.'

'It's not much use waiting about till half past ten now to
see if Uncle signals to us in any way, is it?' said Anne. 'Let's

go up on the cliff – it'll be lovely and blowy. Timmy will like that. I love to see him racing along in the wind, with his ears blown back straight!'

'Woof,' said Timmy.

'He says he likes to see you with yours blown back too,' said Julian, gravely. Anne gave a squeal of laughter.

'You really are an idiot, Ju! Come on – let's take the cliff-path!'

They went up the cliff. At the top it was very windy indeed. Anne's sou'-wester was blown to the back of her head. The rain stung their cheeks and made them gasp.

'I should think we must be about the only people out this morning!' gasped George.

'Well, you're wrong,' said Julian. 'There are two people coming towards us!'

So there was. They were a man and a boy, both well wrapped up in macintoshes and sou'-westers. Like the children, they too wore high rubber boots.

The children took a look at them as they passed. The man was tall and well built, with shaggy eyebrows and a determined mouth. The boy was about sixteen, also tall and well built. He was not a bad-looking boy, but he had rather a sullen expression.

'Good morning,' said the man, and nodded. 'Good morning,' chorused the children, politely. The man looked them over keenly, and then he and the boy went on.

'Wonder who they are?' said George. 'Mother didn't say there were any new people here.'

'Just walked over from the next village, I expect,' said Dick.

They went on for some way. 'We'll walk to the coast-guard's cottage and then go back,' said Julian. 'Hi, Tim, don't go so near the cliff!'

The coastguard lived in a little whitewashed cottage on the cliff, facing the sea. Two other cottages stood beside it, also whitewashed. The children knew the coastguard

220

well. He was a red-faced, barrel-shaped man, fond of joking.

He was nowhere to be seen when they came to his cottage. Then they heard his enormous voice singing a sea-shanty in the little shed behind. They went to find him.

'Hallo, coastguard,' said Anne.

He looked up and grinned at the children. He was busy making something. 'Hallo to you!' he said. 'So you're back again are you? Bad pennies, the lot of you – always turning up when you're not wanted!'

'What are you making?' asked Anne.

'A windmill for my young grandson,' said the coastguard, showing it to Anne. He was very clever at making toys.

'Oh, it's *lovely*,' said Anne, taking it in her hands. 'Does the windmill part go round – oh yes – it's super, coastguard!'

'I've been making quite a bit of money out of my toys,' said the old fellow, proudly. 'I've got some new neighbours in the next cottage – man and a boy – and the man's been buying all the toys I make. Seems to have a lot of nephews and nieces! He gives me good prices too.'

'Oh – would that be the man and the boy we met, I wonder?' said Dick. 'Both tall, and well built – and the man had shaggy eyebrows.'

'That's right,' said the coastguard, trimming a bit of his windmill. 'Mr Curton and his son. They came here some weeks ago. You ought to get to know the son, Master Julian. He's about your age, I should think. Must be pretty lonely for him up here!'

'Doesn't he go to any school?' asked Julian.

'No. He's been ill, so his father said. Got to have plenty of sea-air and that sort of thing. Not a bad sort of boy. He comes and helps me with my toys sometimes. And he likes to mess about with my telescope.'

221

'I do too,' said George. 'I love looking through your telescope. Can I look through now? I'd like to see if I can spot Kirrin Island.'

'Well, you won't see much this weather,' said the coastguard. 'You wait a few minutes. See that break in the clouds? Well, it'll clear in a few minutes, and you'll be able to see your island easily. That's a funny thing your father's built there, Miss. Part of his work, I suppose.'

'Yes,' said George. 'Oh Timmy – look what he's done, coastguard – he's upset that tin of paint. Bad boy, Timmy!'

'It's not my tin,' said the coastguard. 'It's a tin belonging to that young fellow next door. I told you he comes in to help me sometimes. He brought in that tin to help paint a little dolls' house I made for his father.'

'Oh dear,' said George, in dismay. 'Do you think he'll be cross when he knows Timmy spilt it?'

'Shouldn't think so,' said the coastguard. 'He's a queer boy though – quiet and a bit sulky. Not a bad boy, but doesn't seem very friendly like.'

George tried to clear up the mess of paint. Timmy had some on his paws, and made a little pattern of green paw-marks as he pattered about the shed.

'I'll tell the boy I'm sorry, if I meet him on the way back,' she said. 'Timmy if you dare to go near any more tins of paint you shan't sleep on my bed tonight.'

'The weather's a bit clearer now,' said Dick. 'Can we have a squint through the telescope, coastguard?'

'Let *me* see my island first,' said George at once. She tilted the telescope in the direction of Kirrin Island. She looked through it earnestly, and a smile came over her face.

'Yes, I can see it clearly. There's the tower Father has had built. I can even see the glass room quite clearly, and there's nobody in it. No sign of Father anywhere.'

Everyone had a turn at looking through the telescope. It

222

was fascinating to see the island appearing so close. On a clear day it would be even easier to see all the details. 'I can see a rabbit scampering,' said Anne, when her turn came.

'Don't you let that dog of yours squint through the telescope then,' said the coastguard at once. 'He'll try to get down it after that rabbit!'

Timmy cocked his ears up at the mention of the word rabbit. He looked all round and sniffed. No, there was no rabbit. Then why did people mention them?

'We'd better go now,' said Julian. 'We'll be up here again sometime, and we'll come and see what toys you've done. Thanks for letting us look through the telescope.'

'You're welcome!' said the old fellow. 'You're not likely to wear it out through looking! Come along any time you want to use it.'

They said good-bye and went off, Timmy capering round them. 'Couldn't we see Kirrin Island well!' said Anne. 'I wished I could see where your father was, George. Wouldn't it be fun if we spotted him just coming out of his hiding-place?'

The four children had discussed this problem a good deal since they had left the island. It puzzled them very much indeed. How did it happen that George's father knew a hiding-place that they didn't know? Why, they had been over every inch of the island! It must be quite a big hiding-place too, if he had got all his stuff for his experiments with him. According to George's mother, there had been quite a lot of this, to say nothing of stores of food.

'If Father knew a place I didn't know, and never told me about it, I think he's jolly mean,' George said half a dozen times. 'I do really. It's *my* island!'

'Well, he'll probably tell you when he's finished the work he's on,' said Julian. 'Then you'll know. We can all go and explore it then, wherever it is.'

After they left the coastguard's cottage they turned their steps home. They made their way along the cliff, and then saw the boy they had met before. He was standing on the path looking out to sea. The man was not with him.

He turned as they came up and gave them a pale kind of smile. 'Hallo! Been up to see the coastguard?'

'Yes,' said Julian. 'Nice old fellow, isn't he?'

'I say,' said George, 'I'm so sorry but my dog upset a tin

of green paint, and the coastguard said it was yours. Can I pay you for it, please?'

'Goodness, no!' said the boy. 'I don't mind. There wasn't much of it left anyway. That's a nice dog of yours.'

'Yes, he is,' said George, warmly. 'Best dog in the world. I've had him for years, but he's still as young as ever. Do you like dogs?'

'Oh yes,' said the boy, but he made no move to pat Timmy or fuss him, as most people did. And Timmy did not run round the boy and sniff at him as he usually did when he met anyone new. He just stood by George, his tail neither up nor down.

'That's an interesting little island,' said the boy, pointing to Kirrin. 'I wish I could go there.'

'It's *my* island,' said George, proudly. 'My very own.'

'Really?' said the boy, politely. 'Could you let me go over one day then?'

'Well – not just at present,' said George. 'You see, my father's there – working – he's a scientist.'

'Really?' said the boy again. 'Er – has he got some new experiment on hand, then?'

'Yes,' said George.

'Ah – and that queer tower is something to do with it, I suppose,' said the boy, looking interested for the first time. 'When will his experiment be finished?'

'What's that to do with you?' said Dick, suddenly. The others stared at him in surprise. Dick sounded rather rude, and it was not like him.

'Oh nothing!' said the boy, hastily. 'I only thought that if his work will soon be finished, perhaps your brother would take me over to his island!'

George couldn't help feeling pleased. This boy thought *she* was a boy! George was always gracious to people who made the mistake of thinking she was a boy.

'Of *course* I'll take you!' she said. 'It shouldn't be long before I do – the experiment is nearly done.'

225

7

A little squabble

A sound made them turn. It was the boy's father coming up. He nodded to the children. 'Making friends?' he said, amiably. 'That's right. My boy's pretty lonely here. I hope you'll come up and see us some time. Finished your conversation, son?'

'Yes,' said the boy. 'This boy here says that island is his, and he's going to take me over it when his father has finished his work there – and that won't be long.'

'And do you know the way through all those wicked rocks?' said the man. '*I* shouldn't care to try it. I was talking to the fishermen the other day, and not one of them appeared to know the way!'

This was rather astonishing. Some of the fishermen *did* know it. Then the children remembered that the men had all been forbidden to take anyone to the island while Uncle Quentin was at work there. It was clear that they had pretended not to know the way, in loyalty to their orders.

'Did you want to go to the island then?' asked Dick, suddenly.

'Oh no! But my boy here would love to go,' said the man. '*I* don't want to be seasick, bobbing up and down on those waves near the island. I'm a poor sailor. I never go on the sea if I can help it!'

'Well, we must go,' said Julian. 'We've got to do some shopping for my aunt. Good-bye!'

'Come and see us as soon as you can,' said the man. 'I've a fine television set that Martin here would like to show you. Any afternoon you like!'

'Oh thanks!' said George. She seldom saw television. 'We'll come!'

They parted, and the four children and Timmy went on down the cliff-path.

'Whatever made you sound so rude, Dick?' said George. 'The way you said "What's that to do with you?" sounded quite insulting.'

'Well – I just felt suspicious, that's all,' said Dick. 'That boy seemed to be so jolly interested in the island and in your father's work, and when it would be finished.'

'Why shouldn't he be?' demanded George. 'Everyone in the village is interested. They all know about the tower. And all the boy wanted to know was when he could go to my island – that's why he asked when Father's work would be finished. I liked him.'

'You only liked him because he was ass enough to think you were a boy,' said Dick. 'Jolly girlish-looking boy you are, that's all I can say.'

George flared up at once. 'Don't be mean! I'm *not* girlish-looking. I've far more freckles than you have, for one thing, and better eyebrows. *And* I can make my voice go deep.'

'You're just silly,' said Dick, in disgust. 'As if freckles are boyish! Girls have them just as much as boys. I don't believe that boy thought you were a boy at all. He was just sucking up to you. He must have heard how much you like playing at being what you aren't.'

227

George walked up to Dick with such a furious look on her face that Julian hastily put himself in between them. 'Now, no brawls,' he said. 'You're both too old to begin slapping each other like kids in the nursery. Let me tell you, you're both behaving like babies, not like boys *or* girls!'

Anne was looking on with scared eyes. George didn't go off the deep end like this usually. And it *was* funny of Dick to have spoken so rudely to the boy on the cliff. Timmy gave a sudden little whine. His tail was down, and he looked very miserable.

'Oh George – Timmy can't *bear* you to quarrel with Dick!' said Anne. 'Look at him! He's just miserable!'

'He didn't like that boy a bit,' said Dick. 'That was another thing I thought was funny. If Timmy doesn't like a person, *I* don't like him either.'

'Timmy doesn't *always* rush round new people,' said George. 'He didn't growl or snarl, anyway. All right, all right, Julian; I'm not going to start brawling. But I do think Dick is being silly. Making a mountain out of a molehill – just because someone was interested in Kirrin Island and Father's work, and just because Timmy didn't caper all round him. He was such a solemn sort of boy that I'm not surprised Timmy wasn't all over him. He probably knew the boy wouldn't like it. Timmy's clever like that.'

'Oh, do stop,' said Dick. 'I give in – gracefully! I may be making a fuss. Probably am. I couldn't help my feelings, though.'

Anne gave a sigh of relief. The squabble was over. She hoped it wouldn't crop up again. George had been very touchy since she had been home. If only Uncle Quentin would hurry up and finish his work, and they could all go to the island as much as they liked, things would be all right.

'I'd rather like to see that television set,' said George.

'We might go up some afternoon.

'Right,' said Julian. 'But on the whole, I think it would be best if we steered clear of any talk about your father's work. Not that we know much. Still, we do know that once before there were people after one of his theories. The secrets of the scentists are very, very important these days, you know, George. Scientists are VIP!'

'What's VIP?' asked Anne.

'Very Important People, baby!' said Julian, with a laugh. 'What did you think it meant? Violet, Indigo, Purple? I guess those are the colours Uncle Quentin would go if he knew anyone was trying to snoop into his secrets!'

Everyone laughed, even George. She looked affectionately at Julian. He was always so sensible and good-tempered. She really would go by what he said.

The day passed swiftly. The weather cleared and the sun came out strongly. The air smelt of gorse and primroses and the salt of the sea. Lovely! They went shopping for Aunt Fanny, and stopped to talk with James, the fisher-boy.

'Your father's got the island, I see,' he said to George with a grin. 'Bad luck, Miss. You'll not be going over there so often. And nobody else will, either, so I've heard.'

'That's right,' said George. 'Nobody is allowed to go over there for some time. Did you help to take some of the stuff over, James?'

'Yes. I know the way, you see, because I've been with you,' said James. 'Well, Miss, how did you find your boat when you went across yesterday? I got her all ship-shape for you, didn't I?'

'Yes, you did, James,' said George, warmly. 'You made her look beautiful. You must come across to the island with us next time we go.'

'Thanks,' said James, his ready grin showing all his

white teeth. 'Like to leave Timmy with me for a week or two? See how he wants to stay!'

George laughed. She knew James was only joking. He was very fond of Timmy, though, and Timmy adored James. He was now pushing himself hard against the fisher-boy's knees, and trying to put his nose into his brown hand. Timmy had never forgotten the time when James looked after him so well.

The evening came, and the bay was softly blue. Little white horses flecked it here and there. The four gazed across to Kirrin Island. It always looked so lovely at this time of the evening.

The glass top of the tower winked and blinked in the sun. It looked almost as if someone was signalling. But there was no one in the little glass room. As the children watched they heard a faint rumbling sound, and suddenly the top of the tower was ablaze with a curious glare.

'Look! That's what happened yesterday!' said Julian, in excitement. 'Your father's at work all right, George. I do wonder what he's doing!'

Then there came a throbbing sound, almost like the noise of an aeroplane, and once more the glass top of the tower shone and blazed, as the wires became full of some curious power.

'Weird,' said Dick. 'A bit frightening too. Where's your father at this very moment, I wonder, George. How I'd like to know!'

'I bet he's forgotten all about meals again,' said George. 'Didn't he wolf our sandwiches – he must have been starving. I wish he'd let Mother go over there and look after him.'

Her mother came in at that moment. 'Did you hear the noise?' she said. 'I suppose that was your father at work again. Oh dear, I hope he doesn't blow himself up one of these days!'

'Aunt Fanny, can I stay up till half past ten tonight?'

230

asked Anne, hopefully. 'To see Uncle Quentin's signal, you know?'

'Good gracious, no!' said her aunt. 'No one needs to stay up. I am quite capable of watching for it myself!'

'Oh Aunt Fanny! Surely I and Dick can stay up!' said Julian. 'After all, we're not in bed till ten at school.'

'Yes – but this is *half past* ten, and you wouldn't even be in bed then,' said his aunt. 'There's no reason why you shouldn't lie in bed and watch for it though, if you want to – providing you haven't fallen asleep!'

'Oh yes – I can do that,' said Julian. 'My window looks across to Kirrin Island. Six flashes with a lantern? I shall count them carefully.'

So the four went to bed at the usual time. Anne was asleep long before half past ten, and George was so drowsy that she could not make herself get up and go into the boys' room. But Dick and Julian were both wide awake. They lay in their beds and looked out of the window. There was no moon, but the sky was clear, and the stars shone down, giving a faint light. The sea looked very black. There was no sign of Kirrin Island. It was lost in the darkness of the night.

'Almost half past ten,' said Julian, looking at his watch which had luminous hands. 'Now then, Uncle Quentin, what about it?'

Almost as if his uncle was answering him, a light shone out in the glass top of the tower. It was a clear, small light, like the light of a lantern.

Julian began to count. 'One flash.' There was a pause. 'Two flashes.' Another pause 'Three ... four ... five ...six!'

The flashes stopped. Julian snuggled down into bed. 'Well, that's that. Uncle Quentin's all right. I say, it's weird to think of him climbing that spiral stairway right to the top of the tower, in the dark of night, isn't it? – just to mess about with those wires.'

231

'Mmmmm,' said Dick sleepily. 'I'd rather he did it,
than I! You can be a scientist if you like, Ju – but *I* don't
want to climb towers in the dead of night on a lonely
island. I'd like Timmy there, at least!'

Someone knocked on their door and it opened. Julian
sat up at once. It was Aunt Fanny.

'Oh Julian dear – did you see the flashes? I forgot to count them. Were there six?'

'Oh yes, Aunt Fanny! I'd have rushed down to tell you if anything was wrong. Uncle's all right. Don't you worry!'

'I wish I'd told him to do an *extra* flash to tell me if he's had some of that nice soup,' said his aunt. 'Well, good night, Julian. Sleep well!'

8

Down in the quarry

The next day dawned bright and sunny. The four tore down to breakfast, full of high spirits. 'Can we bathe? Aunt Fanny, it's *really* warm enough! Oh do say we can!'

'Of course not! Whoever heard of bathing in April!' said Aunt Fanny. 'Why, the sea is terribly cold. Do you want to be in bed for the rest of the holiday with a chill?'

'Well, let's go for a walk on the moors at the back of Kirrin Cottage,' said George. 'Timmy would love that. Wouldn't you, Tim?'

'Woof,' said Timmy, thumping his tail hard on the ground.

'Take your lunch with you if you like,' said her mother. 'I'll pack some for you.'

'You'll be glad to be rid of us for a little while, I expect, Aunt Fanny,' said Dick, with a grin. 'I know what we'll do. We'll go to the old quarry and look for prehistoric weapons! We've got a jolly good museum at school, and I'd like to take back some stone arrowheads or something like that.'

234

They all liked hunting for things. It would be fun to go to the old quarry, and it would be lovely and warm in the hollow there.

'I hope we shan't find a poor dead sheep there, as we once did,' said Anne, with a shudder. 'Poor thing! It must have fallen down and baa-ed for help for ages.'

'Of course we shan't,' said Julian. 'We shall find stacks of primroses and violets though, growing down the sides of the quarry. They are always early there because it's sheltered from every wind.'

'I should love to have bunches of primroses,' said his aunt. 'Nice big ones! Enough to put all over the house.'

'Well, while the boys are looking for arrow-heads we'll look for primroses,' said Anne, pleased. 'I like picking flowers.'

'And Timmy, of course, will hunt for rabbits, and will hope to bring home enough for you to decorate the larder from top to bottom,' said Dick, solemnly. Timmy looked thrilled and gave an excited little woof.

They waited for Uncle Quentin's signal at half past ten. It came – six flashes of a mirror in the sun. The flashes were quite blinding.

'Nice little bit of heliographing!' said Dick. 'Good morning and good-bye, Uncle! We'll watch for you tonight. Now, everybody ready?'

'Yes! Come on, Tim! Who's got the sandwiches? I say, isn't the sun hot!'

Off they all went. It was going to be a really lovely day!

The quarry was not really very far – only about a quarter of a mile. The children went for a walk beforehand, for Timmy's sake. Then they made for the quarry.

It was a queer place. At some time or other it had been deeply quarried for stone, and then left to itself. Now the sides were covered with small bushes and grass and plants of all kinds. In the sandy places heather grew.

235

The sides were very steep, and as few people came there, there were no paths to follow. It was like a huge rough bowl, irregular in places, and full of colour now where primroses opened their pale petals to the sky. Violets grew there by the thousand, both white and purple. Cowslips were opening too, the earliest anywhere.

'Oh, it's lovely!' said Anne, stopping at the top and looking down. 'Simply super! I never in my life saw so many primroses – nor such huge ones!'

'Be careful how you go, Anne,' said Julian. 'These sides are very steep. If you lose your footing you'll roll right down to the bottom – and find yourself with a broken arm or leg!'

'I'll be careful,' said Anne. 'I'll throw my basket down to the bottom, so that I can have two hands to cling to bushes with, if I want to. I shall be able to fill that basket cramful of primroses and violets!'

She flung the basket down, and it bounced all the way to the bottom of the quarry. The children climbed down to where they wanted to go – the girls to a great patch of big primroses, the boys to a place where they thought they might find stone weapons.

'Hallo!' said a voice, suddenly, from much lower down. The four stopped in surprise, and Timmy growled.

'Why – it's you!' said George, recognizing the boy they had met the day before.

'Yes. I don't know if you know my name. It's Martin Curton,' said the boy.

Julian told him their names too. 'We've come to picnic here,' he said. 'And to see if we can find stone weapons. What have you come for?'

'Oh – to see if I can find stone weapons too,' said the boy.

'Have you found any?' asked George.

'No. Not yet.'

'Well, you won't find any just there,' said Dick. 'Not in heather! You want to come over here, where the ground is bare and gravelly.'

Dick was trying to be friendly, to make up for the day before. Martin came over and began to scrape about with the boys. They had trowels with them, but he had only his hands.

'Isn't it hot down here?' called Anne. 'I'm going to take off my coat.'

Timmy had his head and shoulders down a rabbit-hole. He was scraping violently, sending up heaps of soil behind him in a shower.

'Don't go near Timmy unless you want to be buried in earth!' said Dick. 'Hey, Timmy – is a rabbit really worth all that hard work?'

Apparently it was, for Timmy, panting loudly, went on digging for all he was worth. A stone flew high in the air and hit Julian. He rubbed his cheek. Then he looked at the stone that lay beside him. He gave a shout. 'Look at this – a jolly fine arrow-head! Thanks, Timmy, old fellow. Very good of you to go digging for me. What about a hammer-head next?'

The others came to see the stone arrow-head. Anne thought she would never have known what it was – but Julian and Dick exclaimed over it in admiration.

'Jolly good specimen,' said Dick. 'See how it's been shaped, George? To think that this was used thousands of years ago to kill the enemies of a cave-man!' Martin did not say much. He just looked at the arrow-head, which certainly was a very fine unspoilt specimen, and then turned away. Dick thought he was a queer fellow. A bit dull and boring. He wondered if they ought to ask him to their picnic. He didn't want to in the least.

But George did! 'Are you having a picnic here too?' she said. Martin shook his head.

'No. I've not brought any sandwiches.'

237

'Well, we've plenty. Stay and have some with us when we eat them,' said George, generously.

'Thanks. It's very nice of you,' said the boy. 'And will you come and see my television set this afternoon in return! I'd like you to.'

'Yes, we will,' said George. 'It would be something to do! Oh Anne – just look at those violets! I've never seen such big white ones before. Won't Mother be pleased?'

The boys went deeper down, scraping about with their trowels in any likely place. They came to where a shelf of stone projected out a good way. It would be a nice place to have their lunch. The stone would be warm to sit on, and was flat enough to take ginger-beer bottles and cups in safety.

At half past twelve they all had their lunch. They were very hungry. Martin shared their sandwiches, and became quite friendly over them.

'Best sandwiches I've ever tasted,' he said. 'I do like those sardine ones. Does your mother make them for you? I wish I had a mother. Mine died ages ago.'

There was a sympathetic silence. The four could not think of any worse thing to happen to a boy or girl. They offered Martin the nicest buns, and the biggest piece of cake immediately.

'I saw your father flashing his signals last night,' said Martin, munching a bun.

Dick looked up at once. 'How do you know he was signalling?' he asked. 'Who told you?'

'Nobody,' said the boy. 'I just saw the six flashes, and I thought it must be George's father.' He looked surprised at Dick's sharp tone. Julian gave Dick a nudge, to warn him not to go off the deep end again.

George scowled at Dick. 'I suppose you saw my father signalling this morning too,' she said to Martin. 'I bet scores of people saw the flashes. He just heliographs with a

238

mirror at half past ten to signal that he's all right – and flashes a lantern at the same time at night.'

Now it was Dick's turn to scowl at George. Why give away all this information? It wasn't necessary. Dick felt sure she was doing it just to pay him out for his sharp question. He tried to change the subject.

'Where do you go to school?' he asked.

'I don't,' said the boy. 'I've been ill.'

'Well, where did you go to school before you were ill?' asked Dick.

I – I had a tutor,' said Martin. 'I didn't go to school.'

'Bad luck!' said Julian. He thought it must be terrible not to go to school and have all the fun, the work and the games of school-life. He looked curiously at Martin. Was he one of these rather stupid boys who did no good at school, but had to have a tutor at home? Still he didn't *look* stupid. He just looked rather sullen and dull.

Timmy was sitting on the warm stone with the others. He had his share of the sandwiches, but had to be rationed, as Martin had to have some too.

He was funny with Martin. He took absolutely no notice of him at all. Martin might not have been there!

And Martin took no notice of Timmy. He did not talk to him, or pat him. Anne was sure he didn't really like dogs, as he had said. How could anyone be with Timmy and not give him even *one* pat?

Timmy did not even look at Martin, but sat with his back to him, leaning against George. It was really rather amusing, if it wasn't so odd. After all, George was talking in a friendly way to Martin; they were all sharing their food with him – and Timmy behaved as if Martin simply wasn't there at all!

Anne was just about to remark on Timmy's odd behaviour when he yawned, shook himself, and leapt down from the rock. 'He's going rabbiting again,' said Julian.

'Hey, Tim – find me another arrow-head will you, old fellow?'

Timmy wagged his tail. He disappeared under the shelf of rock, and there came the sound of digging. A shower of stones and soil flew into the air.

The children lay back on the stone and felt sleepy. They talked for some minutes, and then Anne felt her eyes closing. She was awakened by George's voice.

'Where's Timmy? Timmy! Timmy! Come here! Where have you got to?'

But no Timmy came. There was not even an answering bark. 'Oh blow, said George. 'Now he's gone down some extra-deep rabbit hole, I suppose. I must get him. Timmy! Wherever are you?'

9

George makes a discovery – and loses her temper

George slipped down from the rock. She peered under it. There was a large opening there, scattered with stones that Timmy had loosened in his digging.

'Surely you haven't at last found a rabbit hole big enough to go down!' said George. 'TIMMY! Where are you?'

Not a bark, not a whine came from the hole. George wriggled under the shelf of rock, and peered down the burrow. Timmy had certainly made it very big. George called up to Julian.

'Julian! Throw me down your trowel, will you?'

The trowel landed by her foot. George took it and began to make the hole bigger. It might be big enough for Timmy, but it wasn't big enough for her!

She dug hard and soon got very hot. She crawled out and looked over on to the rock to see if she could get one of the others to help her. They were all asleep.

'Lazy things!' thought George, quite forgetting that she too would have been dozing if she hadn't wondered where Timmy had gone.

She slipped down under the rock again and began to dig hard with her trowel. Soon she had made the hole big enough to get through. She was surprised to find quite a large passage, once she had made the entrance big enough to take her. She could crawl along on hands and knees!

'I say – I wonder if this is just some animal's runway – or leads somewhere!' thought George. 'TIMMY! Where *are* you?'

From somewhere deep in the quarry side there came a faint whine. George felt thankful. So Timmy *was* there, after all. She crawled along, and then quite suddenly the tunnel became high and wide and she realized that she must be in a passage. It was perfectly dark, so she could not see anything, she could only feel.

Then she heard the sound of pattering feet, and Timmy pressed affectionately against her legs, whining. 'Oh Timmy – you gave me a bit of a fright!' said George. 'Where have you been? Is this a real passage – or just a tunnel in the quarry, made by the old miners, and now used by animals?'

'Woof,' said Timmy, and pulled at George's jeans to make her go back to the daylight.

'All right, I'm coming!' said George. 'Don't imagine I want to wander alone in the dark! I only came to look for you.'

She made her way back to the shelf of rock. By this time Dick was awake, and wondered where George had gone. He waited a few minutes, blinking up into the deep blue sky, and then sat up.

242

'George!' There was no answer. So, in his turn Dick slipped down from the rock and looked around. And, to his very great astonishment he saw first Timmy, and then George on hands and knees, appearing out of the hole under the rock. He stared open-mouthed, and George began to giggle.

'It's all right. I've only been rabbiting with Timmy!'

She stood beside him, shaking and brushing soil from her jersey and trousers. 'There's a passage behind the entrance to the hole under the rock,' she said. 'At first it's just a narrow tunnel, like an animal's hole – then it gets wider – and then it becomes a proper high wide passage! I couldn't see if it went on, of course, because it was dark. Timmy was a long way in.'

'Good gracious!' said Dick. 'It sounds exciting.'

'Let's explore it, shall we?' said George. 'I expect Julian's got a torch.'

'No,' said Dick. 'We won't explore today.'

The others were now awake, and listening with interest. 'Is it a secret passage?' said Anne, thrilled. 'Oh do let's explore it!'

'No, not today,' said Dick again. He looked at Julian. Julian guessed that Dick did not want Martin to share this secret. Why should he? He was not a real friend of theirs, and they had only just got to know him. He nodded back to Dick.

'No, we won't explore today. Anyway, it may be nothing – just an old tunnel made by the quarrymen.'

Martin was listening with great interest. He went and looked into the hole. 'I wish we could explore,' he said. 'Maybe we could plan to meet again with torches and see if there really is a passage there.'

Julian looked at his watch. 'Nearly two o'clock. Well, Martin, if we're going to see that half past two programme of yours, we'd better be getting on.'

Carrying baskets of primroses and violets, the girls

began to climb up the steep side of the quarry. Julian took Anne's basket from her, afraid she might slip and fall. Soon they were all at the top. The air felt quite cool there after the warmth of the quarry.

They made their way to the cliff path and before long were passing the coastguard's cottage. He was out in his garden, and he waved to them.

They went in the gateway of the next-door cottage. Martin pushed the door open. His father was sitting at the window of the room inside, reading. He got up with a broad, welcoming smile.

'Well, well, well! This *is* nice! Come along in, do. Yes, the dog as well. I don't mind dogs a bit. I like them.'

It seemed rather a crowd in the small room. They all shook hands politely. Martin explained hurriedly that he had brought the children to see a television programme.

'A good idea,' said Mr Curton, still beaming. Anne stared at his great eyebrows. They were very long and thick. She wondered why he didn't have them trimmed – but perhaps he liked them like that. They made him look very fierce, she thought.

The four looked round the little room. There was a television set standing at the far end, on a table. There was also a magnificent wireless – and something else that made the boys stare with interest.

'Hallo! You've got a transmitting set, as well as a receiving set,' said Julian.

'Yes,' said Mr Curton. 'It's a hobby of mine. I made that set.'

'Well! You must be brainy!' said Dick.

'What's a transmitting set?' asked Anne. 'I haven't heard of one before.'

'Oh, it just means a set to send out messages by wireless – like police-cars have, when they send back messages to the police stations,' said Dick. 'This is a very powerful one, though.'

244

Martin was fiddling about with the television switches. Then the programme began.

It was great fun seeing the television programme. When it was over Mr Curton asked them to stay to tea.

'Now don't say no,' he said. 'I'll ring up and ask your aunt, if you like, if you're afraid she might be worried.'

'Well – if you'd do that, sir,' said Julian. 'I think she *would* wonder where we'd gone!'

Mr Curton rang up Aunt Fanny. Yes, it was quite all right for them to stay, but they mustn't be too late back. So they settled down to an unexpectedly good tea. Martin was not very talkative, but Mr Curton made up for it. He laughed and joked and was altogether very good company.

The talk came round to Kirrin Island. Mr Curton said how beautiful it looked each evening. George looked pleased.

'Yes,' she said. '*I* always think that. I do wish Father hadn't chosen this particular time to work on my island. I'd planned to go and stay there.'

'I suppose you know every inch of it!' said Mr Curton.

'Oh yes!' said George. 'We all do. There are dungeons there, you know – real dungeons that go deep down – where we once found gold ingots.'

'Yes – I remember reading about that,' said Mr Curton. 'That must have been exciting. Fancy *finding* the dungeons too! And there's an old well too you once got down, isn't there?'

'Yes,' said Anne, remembering. 'And there is a cave where we once lived – it's got an entrance through the roof, as well as from the sea.'

'And I suppose your father is conducting his marvellous experiments down in the dungeons?' said Mr Curton. 'Well, what a strange place to work in!'

'No – we don't . . .' began George, when she got a kick on the ankle from Dick. She screwed up her face in pain. It had been a very sharp kick indeed.

'What were you going to say?' said Mr Curton, looking surprised.

'Er – I was just going to say that – er – er – we don't know which place Father has chosen,' said George, keeping her legs well out of the way of Dick's feet.

Timmy gave a sudden sharp whine. George looked down at him in surprise. He was looking up at Dick, with a very hurt expression.

'What's the matter, Timmy!' said George anxiously.

'He's finding the room too hot, I think,' said Dick. 'Better take him out, George.'

246

George, feeling quite anxious, took him out. Dick joined her. She scowled at him. 'What did you want to kick me for like that? I shall have a frightful bruise.'

'You know jolly well why I did,' said Dick. 'Giving away everything like that! Can't you see the chap's very interested in your father being on the island? There may be nothing in it at all, but you might at least keep your mouth shut. Just like a girl, can't help blabbing. I had to stop you somehow. I don't mind telling you I trod jolly hard on poor old Timmy's tail too, to make him yelp, so that you'd stop talking!'

'Oh – you beast!' said George, indignantly. 'How *could* you hurt Timmy?'

'I didn't want to. It was a shame,' said Dick, stopping to fondle Timmy's ears. 'Poor old Tim. I didn't want to hurt you, old fellow.'

'I'm going home,' said George, her face scarlet with anger. 'I hate you for talking to me like that – telling me I blab like a girl – and stamping on poor Timmy's tail. You can go back and say I'm taking Timmy home.'

'Right,' said Dick. 'And a jolly good thing too. The less you talk to Mr Curton the better. *I'm* going back to find out exactly what he is and what he does. I'm getting jolly suspicious. You'd better go before you give anything else away!'

Almost choking with rage, George went off with Timmy. Dick went back to make her apologies. Julian and Anne, sure that something was up, felt most uncomfortable. They rose to go, but to their surprise, Dick became very talkative and appeared to be suddenly very much interested in Mr Curton and what he did.

But at last they said good-bye and went. 'Come again, do,' said Mr Curton, beaming at the three of them. 'And tell the other boy – what's his name, George – that I hope his dog is quite all right again now. Such a nice, well-behaved dog! Well good-bye! See you again soon, I hope!'

10

A surprising signal

'What's up with George?' demanded Julian, as soon as they were safely out of earshot. 'I know you kicked her at tea-time, for talking too much about the island – that was idiotic of her – but why has she gone home in a huff?'

Dick told them how he had trodden on poor Timmy's tail to make him whine, so that George would turn her attention to him and stop talking. Julian laughed, but Anne was indignant.

'That was *horrid* of you, Dick.'

'Yes, it was,' said Dick. 'But I couldn't think of any other way to head George off the island. I really honestly thought she was giving away to that fellow all the things he badly wanted to know. But now I think he wanted to know them for quite another reason.'

'What do you mean?' said Julian puzzled.

'Well, I thought at first he must be after Uncle Quentin's secret, whatever it is,' said Dick, 'and that was why he wanted to know all the ins and outs of everything. But now that he's told me he's a journalist – that's a man who writes for the newspapers, Anne – I think after all he only wants the information so that he can use it for his paper, and make a splash when Uncle has finished his work.'

'Yes, I think that too,' said Julian thoughtfully; 'in fact, I'm pretty sure of it. Well, there's no harm in that but I don't see why we should sit there and be pumped all the time. He could easily say, "Look here, I'd be obliged if you'd spill the beans about Kirrin Island – I want to use it in a newspaper story." But he didn't say that.'

'No. So I was suspicious,' said Dick. 'But I see now he'd want all sorts of tit-bits about Kirrin Island to put in his newspaper, whatever it is. Blow! Now I shall have to explain to George I was wrong – and she really is in a temper!'

'Let's take the road to Kirrin Village and go to get some bones for Timmy at the butcher's,' said Julian. 'A sort of apology to Tim!'

This seemed a good idea. They bought two large meaty bones at the butcher's, and then went to Kirrin Cottage. George was up in her bedroom with Timmy. The three went up to find her.

She was sitting on the floor with a book. She looked up sulkily as they came in.

'George, sorry I was such a beast,' said Dick. 'I did it in a good cause, if you only knew it. But I've discovered that Mr Curton isn't a spy, seeking out your father's secret – he's only a journalist, smelling out a story for his paper! Look – I've brought these for Timmy – I apologize to him too.'

George was in a very bad temper, but she tried to respond to Dick's friendliness. She gave him a small smile.

'All right. Thanks for the bones. Don't talk to me tonight anybody. I feel mad, but I'll get over it.'

They left her sitting on the floor. It was always best to leave George severely alone when she was in one of her tempers. As long as Timmy was with her, she was all right, and he certainly would not leave her while she was cross and unhappy.

George did not come down to supper. Dick explained. 'We had a bit of a row, Aunt Fanny, but we've made it up. George still feels sore about it though. Shall I take her supper up?'

'No, I will,' said Anne, and she took up a tray of food.

'I'm not hungry,' said George, so Anne prepared to take it away again. 'Well, you can leave it,' said George hurriedly. 'I expect Timmy will like it.'

So Anne, with a secret smile to herself left the tray. All the dishes were empty by the time she climbed the stairs to fetch the tray again!

'Dear me – Timmy *was* hungry!' she said to George, and her cousin smiled sheepishly. 'Aren't you coming down now? We're going to play monopoly.'

'No thanks. You leave me alone this evening, and I'll be all right tomorrow,' said George. 'Really I will.'

So Julian, Dick, Anne and Aunt Fanny played monopoly without George. They went up to bed at the usual time and found George in bed, fast asleep, with Timmy curled up on her toes.

'I'll look out for Uncle Quentin's signal,' said Julian, as he got into bed. 'Gosh, it's a dark night tonight.'

He lay in bed and looked out of the window towards Kirrin Island. Then, at exactly half past ten, the six flashes came – flash, flash, flash, through the darkness. Julian buried his head in his pillow. Now for a good sleep!

He was awakened by a throbbing noise some time later. He sat up and looked out of the window, expecting to see the top of the tower ablaze with light, as it sometimes was when his uncle conducted a special experiment. But nothing happened. There was no flare of light. The throbbing died away and Julian lay down again.

'I saw Uncle's signals all right last night, Aunt Fanny,' he said next morning. 'Did you?'

250

'Yes,' said his aunt. 'Julian, do you think you would watch for them this morning, dear? I have to go and see the vicar about something, and I don't believe I should be able to see the tower from the vicarage.'

'Yes, of course I will, Aunt Fanny,' said Julian. 'What's the time now? Half past nine. Right. I'll write some letters sitting by the window in my room – and at half past ten I'll watch for the signals.'

He wrote his letters interrupted first by Dick, then by George, Anne and Timmy, who wanted him to go on the beach with them. George had quite recovered herself now, and was trying to be specially nice to make up for yesterday's temper.

'I'll come at half past ten,' said Julian. 'After I've seen the signals from the tower. They're due in ten minutes.'

At half past ten he looked at the glass top of the tower. Ah – there was the first signal, blazing brightly as the sun caught the mirror held by his uncle in the tower.

'One flash,' counted Julian. 'Two – three – four – five – six. He's all right.'

He was just about to turn away when another flash caught his eyes. 'Seven!' Then another came. Eight. Nine. Ten. Eleven. Twelve.

'How queer,' said Julian. 'Why twelve flashes? Hallo here we go again!'

Another six flashes came from the tower, then no more at all. Julian wished he had a telescope, then he could see right into the tower! He sat and thought for a moment, puzzled. Then he heard the others come pounding up the stairs. They burst into the room.

'Julian! Father flashed eighteen times instead of six!'

'Did you count them, Ju?'

'Why did he do that? Is he in danger of some sort?'

'No. If he was he'd flash the SOS signal,' said Julian.

'He doesn't know Morse!' said George.

'Well, I expect he just wants to let us know that he needs something,' said Julian. 'We must go over today and find out what it is. More food perhaps.'

So, when Aunt Fanny came home they suggested they should all go over to the island. Aunt Fanny was pleased.

'Oh yes! That would be nice. I expect your uncle wants a message sent off somewhere. We'll go this morning.'

George flew off to tell James she wanted her boat. Aunt Fanny packed up plenty of food with Joanna's help. Then they set off to Kirrin Island in George's boat.

As they rounded the low wall of rocks and came into the little cove, they saw Uncle Quentin waiting for them. He waved his hand, and helped to pull in the boat when it ran gently on to the sand.

'We saw your treble signal,' said Aunt Fanny. 'Did you want something, dear?'

'Yes, I did,' said Uncle Quentin. 'What's that you've got in your basket, Fanny? More of those delicious sandwiches. I'll have some!'

'Oh Quentin – haven't you been having your meals properly again?' said Aunt Fanny. 'What about that lovely soup?'

'What soup?' said Uncle Quentin, looking surprised. 'I wish I'd known about it. I could have done with some last night.'

'But *Quentin!* I told you about it before,' said Aunt Fanny. 'It will be bad by now. You must pour it away. Now don't forget – pour it away! Where is it? Perhaps I had better pour it away myself.'

'No. I'll do it,' said Uncle Quentin. 'Let's sit down and have our lunch.'

It was much too early for lunch, but Aunt Fanny at once sat down and began to unpack the food. The children were always ready for a meal at any time, so they didn't in the least mind lunch being so early.

'Well, dear – how is your work getting on?' asked Aunt

Fanny, watching her husband devour sandwich after sandwich. She began to wonder if he had had anything at all to eat since she had left him two days ago.

'Oh very well indeed,' said her husband. 'Couldn't be better. Just got to a most tricky and interesting point. I'll have another sandwich, please.'

'Why did you signal eighteen times, Uncle Quentin?' asked Anne.

'Ah, well – it's difficult to explain, really,' said her uncle. 'The fact is – I can't help feeling there's somebody else on this island besides myself!'

'*Quentin!* What in the world do you mean?' cried Aunt Fanny, in alarm. She looked over her shoulder as if she half expected to see somebody there. All the children stared in amazement at Uncle Quentin.

He took another sandwich. 'Yes, I know it sounds mad. Nobody else could possibly have got here. But I know there *is* someone!'

'Oh don't Uncle!' said Anne, with a shiver. 'It sounds horrid. And you're all alone at night too!'

'Ah, that's just it! I wouldn't mind a bit if I *was* all alone at night!' said her uncle. 'What worries me is that I don't think I *shall* be all alone.'

'Uncle, what makes you think there's somebody here?' asked Julian.

'Well, when I had finished the experiment I was doing last night – about half past three in the early morning it would be – but pitch dark, of course,' said Uncle Quentin, 'I came into the open for a breath of fresh air. And I could swear I heard somebody cough – yes, cough twice!'

'Good gracious!' said Aunt Fanny, startled. 'But Quentin – you might have been mistaken. You do imagine things sometimes, you know, when you're tired.'

'Yes, I know,' said her husband. 'But I couldn't imagine *this*, could I?'

He put his hand into his pocket and took something out.

He showed it to the others. It was a cigarette end, quite crisp and fresh.

'Now, I don't smoke cigarettes. Nor do any of you! Well then – who smoked that cigarette? And how did he come here? No one would bring him by boat – and that's the only way here.'

There was a silence. Anne felt scared. George stared at her father, puzzled. Who could be here? And why? And how had they got there?

'Well, Quentin – what are you going to do?' said his wife. 'What would be best?'

'I'll be all right if George will give her consent to something,' said Uncle Quentin. 'I want Timmy here, George! Will you leave him behind with me?'

11

George makes a hard choice

There was a horrified silence. George stared at her father in complete dismay. Everyone waited to see what she would say.

'But Father – Timmy and I have never been separated once,' she said at last, in a pleading voice. 'I do see you want him to guard you – and you *can* have him – but I'll have to stay here too!'

'Oh no!' said her father at once. 'You can't possibly stay, George. That's out of the question. As for never being separated from Timmy, well surely you wouldn't mind that for once? If it was to ensure my safety?'

George swallowed hard. This was the most difficult decision she had ever had to make in her life. Leave Timmy behind on the island – where there was some unknown hidden enemy, likely to harm him if he possibly could!

And yet there was Father too – he might be in danger if there was no one to guard him.

'I shall just *have* to stay here, Father,' she said. 'I can't leave Timmy behind unless I stay too. It's no good.'

Her father began to lose his temper. He was like George – he wanted his own way, and if he didn't have it he was going to make a fuss!

'If I'd asked Julian or Dick or Anne this same thing, and they'd had a dog, they would all have said yes, at once!' he raged. 'But you, George, you must always make things difficult if you can! You and that dog – anyone would think he was worth a thousand pounds!'

'He's worth much more than that to me,' said George, in a trembling voice. Timmy crept nearer to her and pushed his nose into her hand. She held his collar as if she would not let him go for a moment.

'Yes. That dog's worth more to you than your father or mother or anyone,' said her father, in disgust.

'No, Quentin, I can't have you saying things like that,' said his wife, firmly. 'That's just silly. A mother and father are quite different from a dog – they're loved in different ways. But you are perfectly right, of course – Timmy *must* stay behind with you – and I shall certainly not allow George to stay with him. I'm not going to have *both* of you exposed to danger. It's bad enough to worry about *you*, as it is.'

George looked at her mother in dismay.

'Mother! Do tell father I must stay here with Timmy.'

'Certainly not,' said her mother. 'Now George, be unselfish. If it were left to Tim to decide, you know perfectly well that he would stay here – and stay *without* you. He would say to himself, "I'm needed here – my eyes are needed to spy out enemies, my ears to hear a quiet footfall – and maybe my teeth to protect my master. I shall be parted from George for a few days – but she, like me, is big enough to put up with that!" That's what Timmy would say, George, if it were left to him.'

Everyone had been listening to this unexpected speech with great attention. It was about the only one that could persuade George to give in willingly!

She looked at Timmy. He looked back at her, wagging his tail. Then he did an extraordinary thing – he got up, walked over to George's father, and lay down beside him, looking at George as if to say 'There you are! Now you know what *I* think is right!'

'You see?' said her mother. 'He agrees with me. You've always said that Timmy was a good dog, and this proves it. He knows what his duty is. You ought to be proud of him.'

'I am,' said George, in a choky voice. She got up and walked off. 'All right,' she said over her shoulder. 'I'll leave him on the island with Father. I'll come back in a minute.'

Anne got up to go after poor George, but Julian pulled her down again. 'Leave her alone! She'll be all right. Good old Timmy – you know what's right and what's wrong, don't you? Good dog, splendid dog!'

Timmy wagged his tail. He did not attempt to follow George. No – he meant to stay by her father now, even though he would much rather be with his mistress. He was sorry that George was unhappy – but sometimes it was better to do a hard thing and be unhappy about it, than try to be happy without doing it.

'Oh Quentin dear, I don't like this business of you being here and somebody else spying on you,' said his wife, 'I really don't. How long will you be before you've finished your work?'

'A few days more,' said her husband. He looked at Timmy admiringly. 'That dog might almost have known what you were saying, Fanny, just now. It was remarkable the way he walked straight over to me.'

257

'He's a very clever dog,' said Anne warmly. 'Aren't you, Tim? You'll be quite safe with him, Uncle Quentin. He's terribly fierce when he wants to be!'

'Yes. I shouldn't care to have him leaping at *my* throat,' said her uncle. 'He's so big and powerful. Are there any more pieces of cake?'

'Quentin, it's really too bad of you to go without your meals,' said his wife. 'It's no good telling me you haven't, because you wouldn't be as ravenous as this if you had had your food regularly.'

Her husband took no notice of what she was saying. He was looking up at his tower. 'Do you ever see those wires at the top blaze out?' he asked. 'Wonderful sight, isn't it?'

'Uncle, you're not inventing a new atom bomb, or anything are you?' asked Anne.

Her uncle looked at her scornfully. 'I wouldn't waste my time inventing things that will be used to kill and maim people! No – I'm inventing something that will be of the greatest use to mankind. You wait and see!'

George came back. 'Father,' she said, 'I'm leaving Timmy behind for you – but please will you do something for me?'

'What?' asked her father. 'No silly conditions now! I shall feed Timmy regularly, and look after him, if that's what you want to ask me. I may forget my own meals, but you ought to know me well enough to know I shouldn't neglect any animal dependent on me.'

'Yes – I know, Father,' said George, looking a bit doubtful all the same. 'What I wanted to ask you was this – when you go up in the tower to signal each morning, will you please take Timmy with you? I shall be up at the coastguard's cottage, looking through his telescope at the glass room in the tower – and I shall be able to see Timmy then. If I catch just a glimpse of him each day and know he's all right, I shan't worry so much.'

'Very well,' said her father. 'But I don't suppose for a

258

moment that Timmy will be able to climb up the spiral stairway.'

'Oh, he can, Father – he's been up it once already,' said George.

'Good heavens!' said her father. 'Has the dog been up there too? All right, George – I promise I'll take him up with me each morning that I signal, and get him to wag his tail at you. There! Will that satisfy you?'

'Yes. Thank you,' said George. 'And you'll give him a few kind words and a pat occasionally, Father, won't you . . . and . . .?'

'And put his bib on for him at meal-times, I suppose, and clean his teeth for him at night!' said her father, looking cross again. 'I shall treat Timmy like a proper grown-up dog, a friend of mine, George – and believe me, that's the way he wants me to treat him. Isn't it, Timmy? You like all those frills to be kept for your mistress, don't you, not for me?'

'Woof,' said Timmy, and thumped his tail. The children looked at him admiringly. He really was a very sensible clever dog. He seemed somehow much more grown-up than George.

'Uncle, if anything goes wrong, or you want help or anything, flash eighteen times again,' said Julian. 'You ought to be all right with Timmy. He's better than a dozen policemen – but you never know.'

'Right. Eighteen flashes if I want you over here for anything,' said his uncle. 'I'll remember. Now you'd better all go. It's time I got on with my work.'

'You'll pour that soup away, won't you, Quentin?' said his wife, anxiously. 'You don't want to make yourself ill by eating bad soup. It must be green by now! It would be so like you to forget all about it while it was fresh and good – and only remember when it was bad!'

'What a thing to say!' said her husband, getting up. 'Anyone would think I was five years old, without a brain in my head, the way you talk to me!'

'You've plenty of brains dear, we all know that,' said his wife. 'But you don't seem very old sometimes! Now look after yourself – and keep Timmy by you all the time.'

'Father won't need to bother about *that*,' said George. 'Timmy will keep by *him*! You're on guard, Timmy, aren't you? And you know what *that* means!'

'Woof,' said Timmy, solemnly. He went with them all to the boat, but he did not attempt to get in. He stood by George's father and watched the boat bob away over the water. 'Good-bye, Timmy!' shouted George, in a funny fierce voice. 'Look after yourself!'

Her father waved, and Timmy wagged his tail. George

took one of the pairs of oars from Dick and began to row furiously, her face red with the hard work.

Julian looked at her in amusement. It was hard work for him, too, to keep up with the furious rowing, but he didn't say anything. He knew all this fury in rowing was George's way of hiding her grief at parting with Timmy. Funny old George! She was always so intense about things – furiously happy or furiously unhappy, in the seventh heaven of delight or down in the very depths of despair or anger.

Everyone talked hard so that George would think they were not noticing her feelings at parting with Timmy. The talk, of course, was mostly about the unknown man on the island. It seemed very mysterious indeed that he should suddenly have arrived.

'How did he get there? I'm sure not one of the fishermen would have taken him,' said Dick. 'He must have gone at night, of course, and I doubt if there is anyone but George who would know the way in the dark – or even dare to try and find it. These rocks are so close together, and so near the surface; one yard out of the right course and any boat would have a hole in the bottom!'

'No one could reach the island by swimming from the shore,' said Anne. 'It's too far, and the sea is too rough over these rocks. I honestly do wonder if there *is* anyone on the island after all. Perhaps that cigarette end was an old one.'

'It didn't look it,' said Julian. 'Well, it just beats me how anyone got there!'

He fell into thought, puzzling out all the possible and impossible ways. Then he gave an exclamation. The others looked at him.

'I've just thought – would it be possible for an aeroplane to parachute anyone down on the island? I did hear a throbbing noise one night – was it last night? It must have been a plane's engine, of course! *Could* anyone be dropped on the island?'

261

'Easily,' said Dick. 'I believe you've hit on the explanation, Ju! Good for you! But I say – whoever it is must be in deadly earnest, to risk being dropped on a small island like that in the dark of night!'

In deadly earnest! That didn't sound at all nice. A little shiver went down Anne's back. 'I *am* glad Timmy's there,' she said. And everyone felt the same – yes even George!

12

The old map again

It was only about half past one when they arrived back, because they had had lunch so very early, and had not stayed long on the island. Joanna was most surprised to see them.

'Well, here you are again!' she said. 'I hope you don't all want another lunch, because there's nothing in the house till I go to the butcher's!'

'Oh no, Joanna – we've had our picnic lunch,' said her mistress, 'and it was a good thing we packed so much, because the master ate quite half of the lunch! He still hasn't had that nice soup we made for him. Now it will be bad of course.'

'Oh, the men! They're as bad as children!' said Joanna.

'*Well!*' said George. 'Do you really think any of *us* would let your good soup go bad, Joanna? You know jolly well we'd probably eat it up before we ought to!'

'That's true – I wouldn't accuse any of you four – or Timmy either – of playing about with your food,' said

263

Joanna. 'You make good work of it, the lot of you. But where is Timmy?'

'I left him behind to look after Father,' said George. Joanna stared at her in surprise. She knew how passionately fond of Timmy George was.

'You're a very good girl – sometimes!' she said. 'See now – if you're still hungry because your father has eaten most of your lunch, you go and look in the biscuit tin. I made you some of your favourite ginger biscuits this morning. You go and find them.'

That was always Joanna's way! If she thought anyone was upset, she offered them her best and freshest food. George went off to find the biscuits.

'You're a kind soul, Joanna,' said George's mother. 'I'm so thankful we left Timmy there. I feel happier about the master now.'

'What shall we do this afternoon?' said Dick, when they had finished munching the delicious ginger biscuits. 'I say, aren't these good? You know, I do think good cooks deserve some kind of decoration, just as much as good soldiers or scientists, or writers. I should give Joanna the OBCBE.'

'Whatever's that?' said Julian.

'Order of the Best Cooks of the British Empire,' said Dick grinning. 'What did you think it was? "Oh Be Careful Before Eating"?'

'You really are an absolute donkey,' said Julian. 'Now, what *shall* we do this afternoon?'

'Go and explore the passage in the quarry,' said George.

Julian cocked an eye at the window. 'It's about to pour with rain,' he said. 'I don't think that clambering up and down the steep sides of that quarry in the wet would be very easy. No – we'll leave that till a fine day.'

'I'll tell you what we'll do,' said Anne suddenly. 'Do you remember that old map of Kirrin Castle we once found in

264

a box? It had plans of the castle in it – a plan of the dungeons, and of the ground floor, and of the top part. Well, let's have it out and study it! Now we know there is another hiding-place somewhere, we might be able to trace it on that old map. It's sure to be on it somewhere – but perhaps we didn't notice it before!'

The others looked at her, thrilled. 'Now that really is a brilliant idea of yours, Anne,' said Julian, and Anne glowed with pleasure at his praise. 'A very fine idea indeed. Just the thing for a wet afternoon. Where's the map? I suppose you've got it somewhere safe, George?'

'Oh yes,' said George. 'It's still in that old wooden box, inside the tin lining. I'll get it.'

She disappeared upstairs and came down again with the map. It was made of thick parchment, and was yellow with age. She laid it out on the table. The others bent over it, eager to look at it once more.

'Do you remember how frightfully excited we were when we first found the box?' said Dick.

'Yes, and we couldn't open it, so we threw it out of the top window down to the ground below, hoping it would burst open!' said George.

'And the crash woke up Uncle Quentin,' said Anne, with a giggle. 'And he came out and got the box and wouldn't let us have it!'

'Oh dear yes – and poor Julian had to wait till Uncle Quentin was asleep, and creep in and get the box to see what was in it!' finished Dick. 'And we found this map – and how we pored over it!'

They all pored over it again. It was in three parts, as Anne had said – a plan of the dungeons, a plan of the ground floor and a plan of the top part.

'It's no good bothering about the top part of the castle,' said Dick. 'It's all fallen down and ruined. There's practically none of it left except for that one tower.'

'I say!' said Julian, suddenly putting his finger on a

certain spot in the map, 'do you remember there were *two* entrances to the dungeons? One that seemed to start somewhere about that little stone room – and the other that started where we did at last find the entrance? Well – we never found the other entrance, did we?'

'No! We didn't!' said George, in excitement. She pushed Julian's finger away from the map. 'Look – there are steps shown here – somewhere where that little room is – so there *must* be an entrance there! Here's the *other* flight of steps – the ones we did find, near the well.'

'I remember that we hunted pretty hard for the entrance in the little room,' said Dick. 'We scraped away the weeds from every single stone, and gave it up at last. Then we found the other entrance, and forgot all about this one.'

'And *I* think Father has found the entrance we *didn't* find!' said George, triumphantly. 'It leads underground, obviously. Whether or not it joins up with the dungeons we know I can't make out from this map. It's a bit blurred here. But it's quite plain that there *is* an entrance here, with stone steps leading underground somewhere! See, there's some sort of passage or tunnel marked, leading from the steps. Goodness knows where it goes, it's so smeared.'

'It joins up with the dungeons, I expect,' said Julian. 'We never explored the whole of them, you know – they're so vast and weird. If we explored the whole place, we should probably come across the stone steps leading from somewhere near that little room. Still, they may be ruined or fallen in now.'

'No, they can't be,' said George. 'I'm perfectly *sure* that's the entrance Father has found. And I'll tell you something that seems to prove it, too.'

'What?' said everyone.

'Well, do you remember the other day when we first went to see Father?' said George. 'He didn't let us stay long, and he came to see us off at the boat. Well, we tried to

266

see where he went, but we couldn't – but Dick said he saw the jackdaws rising up in a flock, as if they had been suddenly disturbed – and he wondered if Father had gone somewhere in that direction.'

Julian whistled. 'Yes – the jackdaws build in the tower, which is by the little room – and anyone going into the room would disturb them. I believe you're right, George.'

'It's been puzzling me awfully where Uncle Quentin could be doing his work,' said Dick. 'I simply could *not* solve the mystery – but now I think we have!'

'I wonder how Father found his hiding-place,' said George, thoughtfully. 'I still think it was mean of him not to tell me.'

'There must have been some reason,' said Dick, sensibly. 'Don't start brooding again!'

'I'm not,' said George. 'I'm puzzled, that's all. I wish we could take the boat and go over to the island at once, and explore!'

'Yes. I bet we'd find the entrance all right now,' said Dick. 'Your father is sure to have left some trace of where it is – a stone a bit cleaner than the rest – or weeds scraped off – or something.'

'Do you suppose the unknown enemy on the island knows Uncle Quentin's hiding-place?' said Anne, suddenly. 'Oh, I do hope he doesn't! He could so easily shut him in if he did.'

'Well, he hasn't gone there to shut Uncle up – he's gone there to steal his secret, or find it out,' said Julian. 'Golly, I'm thankful he's got Timmy. Timmy could tackle a dozen enemies.'

'Not if they had guns,' said George, in a small voice. There was a silence. It was not a nice thought to think of Timmy at the wrong end of a gun. This had happened once or twice before in their adventures, and they didn't want to think of it happening again.

'Well, it's no good thinking silly things like that,' said Dick, getting up. 'We've had a jolly interesting half-hour. I think we've solved *that* mystery. But I suppose we shan't know for certain till your father's finished his experiment, George, and left the island – then we can go over and have a good snoop round.'

'It's still raining,' said Anne, looking out of the window. 'But it's a bit clearer. It looks as if the sun will be out soon. Let's go for a walk.'

'I shall go up to the coastguard's cottage,' said George, at once. 'I want to look through his telescope to see if I can just get a glimpse of Timmy.'

'Try the field-glasses,' suggested Julian. 'Go up to the top of the house with them.'

'Yes, I will,' said George. 'Thanks for the idea.'

She fetched the field-glasses, where they hung in the hall, and took them out of their leather case. She ran upstairs with them. But she soon came down again, looking disappointed.

'The house isn't high enough for me to see much of the island properly. I can see the glass top of the tower easily, of course – but the telescope would show it much better. It's more powerful. I think I'll go up and have a squint. You don't need to come if you don't want to.' She put the glasses back into their case.

'Oh, we'll all come and have a squint for old Timmy dog,' said Dick, getting up. 'And I don't mind telling you what we'll see!'

'What?' said George, in surprise.

'We'll see Timmy having a perfectly wonderful time, chasing every single rabbit on the island!' said Dick with a grin. 'My word – you needn't worry about Timmy not having his food regularly! He'll have rabbit for breakfast, rabbit for dinner, rabbit for tea – and rain-water from his favourite pool. Not a bad life for old Timmy!'

'You know perfectly well he'll do nothing of the sort,'

268

said George. 'He'll keep close to Father and not think of rabbits once!'

'You don't know Timmy if you think that,' said Dick dodging out of George's way. She was turning red with exasperation. 'I bet that's why he wanted to stay. *Just* for the rabbits!'

George threw a book at him. It crashed to the floor. Anne giggled. 'Oh stop it, you two. We'll never get out. Come on Ju – we won't wait for the squabblers!'

13

Afternoon with Martin

By the time they reached the coastguard's cottage the sun was out. It was a real April day, with sudden showers and then the sun sweeping out, smiling. Everything glittered, especially the sea. It was wet underfoot, but the children had on their rubber boots.

They looked for the coastguard. As usual he was in his shed, singing and hammering.

'Good-day to you,' he said, beaming all over his red face. 'I was wondering when you'd come and see me again. How do you like this railway station I'm making?'

'It's better than any I've ever seen in the shops,' said Anne in great admiration. The coastguard certainly had made it well, down to the smallest detail.

He nodded his head towards some small wooden figures of porters and guards and passengers. 'Those are waiting to be painted,' he said. 'That boy Martin said he'd come in and do them for me – very handy with his paints he is, a proper artist – but he's had an accident.'

'*Has* he? What happened?' said Julian.

'I don't quite know. He was half-carried home this morning by his father,' said the coastguard. 'Must have slipped and fallen somewhere. I went out to ask, but Mr Curton was in a hurry to get the boy on a couch. Why don't you go in and ask after him? He's a queer sort of boy – but he's not a bad boy.'

'Yes, we will go and ask,' said Julian. 'I say, coast-guard – would you mind if we looked through your telescope again?'

'Now you go and look at all you want to!' said the old fellow. 'I tell you, you won't wear it out by looking! I saw the signal from your father's tower last night, Miss George – just happened to be looking that way. He went on flashing for a long time, didn't he?'

'Yes,' said George. 'Thank you. I'll go and have a look now.'

She went to the telescope and trained it on her island. But no matter where she looked she could not see Timmy, or her father. They must be down in his workroom,

271

wherever it was. She looked at the glass room in the top of the tower. That was empty too, of course. She sighed. It would have been nice to see Timmy.

The others had a look through as well. But nobody saw Timmy. It was plain that he was keeping close to his master — a proper little guard!

'Well – shall we go in and see what's happened to Martin?' said Julian, when they had finished with the telescope. 'It's just about to pour with rain again – another April shower! We could wait next door till it's over.'

'Right, Let's go,' said Dick. He looked at George. 'Don't be afraid I shall be rude, George. Now that I know Mr Curton is a journalist, I shan't bother about him.'

'All the same – I'm not "blabbing" any more,' said George, with a grin. 'I see your point now – even if it doesn't matter, I still shan't "blab" any more.'

'Good for you!' said Dick, pleased. 'Spoken like a boy!'

'Ass!' said George, but she was pleased all the same.

They went through the front gateway of the next cottage. As they filed in, they heard an angry voice.

'Well, you can't! Always wanting to mess about with a brush and paint. I thought I'd knocked that idea out of your head. You lie still and get that ankle better. Spraining it just when I want your help!'

Anne stopped, feeling frightened. It was Mr Curton's voice they could hear through the open window. He was giving Martin a good talking to about something, that was plain. The others stopped too, wondering whether to go in or not.

Then they heard a bang, and saw Mr Curton leaving the cottage from the back entrance. He walked rapidly down the garden, and made for the path, that led to the back of the cliff. There was a road there that went to the village.

'Good. He's gone. *And* he didn't see us!' said Dick. 'Who

272

would have thought that such a genial, smiling fellow could have such a rough brutal voice when he loses his temper? Come on – let's pop in and see poor Martin while there's a chance.'

They knocked on the door. 'It's us!' called Julian, cheerfully. 'Can we come in?'

'Oh yes!' shouted Martin from indoors, sounding pleased. Julian opened the door and they all went in.

'I say! We heard you'd had an accident,' said Julian. 'What's up? Are you hurt much?'

'No. It's just that I twisted my ankle, and it was so painful to walk on that I had to be half-carried up here,' said Martin. 'Silly thing to do!'

'Oh – it'll soon be right if it's just a twist,' said Dick. 'I've often done that. The thing is to walk on it as soon as you can. Where were you when you fell?'

Martin went suddenly red, to everyone's surprise. 'Well – I was walking on the edge of the quarry with my father – and I slipped and rolled a good way down,' he said.

There was a silence. Then George spoke. 'I say,' she said, 'I hope you didn't go and give away our little secret to your father? I mean – it's not so much fun when grown-ups share a secret. They want to go snooping about themselves – and it's much more fun to discover things by ourselves. You didn't tell him about that hole under the shelf of rock, did you?'

Martin hesitated. 'I'm afraid I did,' he said at last. 'I didn't think it would matter. I'm sorry.'

'Blow!' said Dick. 'That was our own little discovery. We wanted to go and explore it this afternoon, but we thought it would be so wet we'd fall down the steep slope.'

Julian looked at Martin sharply. 'I suppose that's what happened to *you*?' he said. 'You tried clambering down and slipped!'

'Yes,' said Martin. 'I'm really sorry if you thought it

was your secret. I just mentioned it to my father out of interest – you know – something to say – and he wanted to go down and see for himself.'

'I suppose journalists are always like that,' said Dick. 'Wanting to be on the spot if there's anything to be ferreted out. It's their job. All right, Martin – forget it. But do try and head your father off the quarry. We *would* like to do a bit of exploring, before he butts in. Though there may be nothing to be found at all!'

There was a pause. Nobody knew quite what to say. Martin was rather difficult to talk to. He didn't talk like any ordinary boy – he never made a joke, or said anything silly.

'Aren't you bored, lying here?' said Anne feeling sorry for him.

'Yes, awfully. I wanted my father to go in and ask the coastguard to bring in some little figures I said I'd paint for him,' said Martin. 'But he wouldn't let me. You know I simply love painting – even doing a little thing like that – painting clothes on toy porters and guards – so long as I can have a brush in my hand and colours to choose from!'

This was the longest speech Martin had ever made to the four children! His face lost its dull, bored look as he spoke, and became bright and cheerful.

'O – you want to be an artist, I suppose?' said Anne. 'I would like that too!'

'Anne! you can't even draw a cat that looks like one!' said Dick, scornfully. 'And when you drew a cow I thought it was an elephant.'

Martin smiled at Anne's indignant face. 'I'll show you some of my pictures,' he said. 'I have to keep them hidden away, because my father can't bear me to want to be an artist!'

'Don't get up if you don't want to,' said Julian. 'I'll get them for you.'

'It's all right. If it's good for me to try and walk, I will,'

274

said Martin, and got off the couch. He put his right foot gingerly to the floor and then stood up. 'Not so bad after all!' he said. He limped across the room to a bookcase. He put his hand behind the second row of books and brought out a cardboard case, big and flat. He took it to the table. He opened it and spread out some pictures.

'Gracious!' said Anne. 'They're *beautiful*! Did you really do these?'

They were queer pictures for a boy to draw, for they were of flowers and trees, birds and butterflies – all drawn and coloured most perfectly, every detail put in lovingly.

Julian looked at them in surprise. This boy was certainly gifted. Why, these drawings were as good as any he had ever seen in exhibitions! He picked a few up and took them to the window.

'Do you mean to say your father doesn't think these are good – doesn't think it's worth while to let you train as an artist?' he said, in surprise.

'He hates my pictures,' said Martin, bitterly. 'I ran away from school, and went to an art-school to train – but he found me and forbade me to think of drawing any more. He thinks it's a weak, feeble thing for a man to do. So I only do it in secret now.'

The children looked at Martin with sympathy. It seemed an awful thing to them that a boy who had no mother, should have a father who hated the thing his son most loved. No wonder he always looked dull and miserable and sullen!

'It's very bad luck,' said Julian at last. 'I wish we could do something to help.'

'Well – get me those figures and the paint tins from the coastguard,' said Martin, eagerly. 'Will you? Father won't be back till six. I'll have time to do them. And do stay and have tea with me. It's so dull up here. I hate it.'

'Yes, I'll get the things for you,' said Julian. 'I can't for the life of me see why you shouldn't have something to

amuse yourself with if you want to. And we'll ring up my
aunt and tell her we're staying here to tea – so long as we
don't eat everything you've got!'

'Oh, that's all right,' said Martin, looking very cheerful
indeed. 'There's plenty of food in the house. My father has
an enormous appetite. I say, thanks most awfully.'

Julian rang up his aunt. The girls and Dick went to fetch
the figures and the paint from the coastguard. They
brought them back and arranged them on a table beside

Martin. His eyes brightened at once. He seemed quite different.

'This is grand,' he said. 'Now I can get on! It's a silly little job, this, but it will help the old man next door, and I'm always happy when I'm messing about with a brush and paints!'

Martin was very, very clever at painting the little figures. He was quick and deft, and Anne sat watching him, quite fascinated. George went to hunt in the larder for the tea-things. There was certainly plenty of food! She cut some bread and butter, found some new honey, brought out a huge chocolate cake and some ginger buns, and put the kettle on to boil.

'I say, this is really grand,' said Martin again. 'I wish my father wasn't coming back till eight. By the way – where's the dog? I thought he always went everywhere with you! Where's Timmy?'

14

A shock for George

Dick looked at George. He didn't think it would matter telling Martin where Timmy was, so long as George didn't give the *reason* why he had been left on the island.

But George was going to hold her tongue now. She looked at Martin and spoke quite airily. 'Oh, Timmy? We left him behind today. He's all right.'

'Gone out shopping with your mother, I suppose, hoping for a visit to the butcher's!' said Martin. This was the first joke he had ever made to the children, and though it was rather a feeble one they laughed heartily. Martin looked pleased. He began to try and think of another little joke, while his deft hands put reds and blues and greens on the little wooden figures.

They all had a huge tea. Then, when the clock said a quarter to six the girls carried the painted figures carefully back to the coastguard, who was delighted with them. Dick took back the little tins of paint, and the brush stuck in a jar of turpentine.

'Well now, he's clever that boy, isn't he?' said the

278

coastguard, eyeing the figures in delight. 'Looks sort of miserable and sulky – but he's not a bad sort of boy!'

'I'll just have one more squint through your telescope,' said George, 'before it gets too dark.'

She tilted it towards her island. But once more there was no sign of Timmy, or of her father either. She looked for some time, and then went to join the others. She shook her head as they raised their eyebrows inquiringly.

The girls washed up the tea-things, and cleared away neatly. Nobody felt as if they wanted to wait and see Mr Curton. They didn't feel as if they liked him very much, now they knew how hard he was on Martin.

'Thanks for a lovely afternoon,' said Martin, limping to the door with them. 'I enjoyed my spot of painting, to say nothing of your company.'

'You stick out for your painting,' said Julian. 'If it's the thing you've *got* to do, and you know it, you must go all out for it. See?'

'Yes,' said Martin, and his face went sullen again. 'But there are things that make it difficult – things I can't very well tell you. Oh well – never mind! I dare say it will all come right one day, and I'll be a famous artist with pictures in the academy!'

'Come on, quickly,' said Dick, in a low voice to Julian. 'There's his father coming back!'

They hurried off down the cliff-path, seeing Mr Curton out of the corner of their eyes, coming up the other path.

'Horrid man!' said Anne. 'Forbidding Martin to do what he really longs to do. And he seemed so nice and jolly and all-over-us, didn't he?'

'Very all-over-us,' said Dick, smiling at Anne's new word. 'But there are a lot of people like that – one thing at home and quite another outside!'

'I hope Mr Curton hasn't been trying to explore that passage in the side of the quarry,' said George, looking back, and watching the man walk up to his back door. 'It would be too bad if he butted in and spoilt our fun. I mean – there may be nothing to discover at all – but it will be fun even finding there *is* nothing.'

'Very involved!' said Dick, with a grin. 'But I gather what you mean. I say, that was a good tea, wasn't it?'

'Yes,' said George, looking all round her in an absent-minded manner.

'What's up?' said Dick. 'What are you looking like that for?'

'Oh – how silly of me – I was just looking for Timmy,' said George. 'You know, I'm so used to him always being at my heels or somewhere near that I just can't get used to him not being here.'

'Yes, I feel a bit like that too,' said Julian. 'As if there was something missing all the time. Good old Tim! We shall miss him awfully, all of us – but you most of all, George.'

'Yes. Especially on my bed at night,' said George. 'I shan't be able to go to sleep for ages and ages.'

'I'll wrap a cushion up in a rug and plonk it down on your feet when you're in bed,' said Dick. 'Then it will feel like Timmy!'

'It won't! Don't be silly,' said George, rather crossly. 'And anyway it wouldn't *smell* like him. He's got a lovely smell.'

'Yes, a Timmy-smell,' agreed Anne. 'I like it too.'

The evening went very quickly, playing the endless game of monopoly again. Julian lay in bed later, watching for his uncle's signal. Needless to say, George was at the window too! They waited for half past ten.

'Now!' said Julian. And just as he spoke there came the first flash from the lantern in the tower.

'One,' counted George, 'two – three – four – five – six!' She waited anxiously to see if there were any more, but there weren't.

280

'Now you can go to bed in peace,' said Julian to George. 'Your father is all right, and that means that Timmy is all right too. Probably he has remembered to give Timmy a good supper and has had some himself as well!'

'Well, Timmy would soon remind him, if he forgot to feed him, that's one thing,' said George, slipping out of the room. 'Good night, Dick; good night, Ju! See you in the morning.'

And back she went to her own bed and snuggled down under the sheets. It was queer not to have Timmy on her feet. She tossed about for a while, missing him, and then fell asleep quite suddenly. She dreamed of her island. She was there with Timmy – and they were discovering ingots of gold down in the dungeon. What a lovely dream!

Next morning dawned bright and sunny again. The April sky was as blue as the forget-me-nots coming out in the garden. George gazed out of the dining-room window at breakfast time wondering if Timmy was running about her island.

'Dreaming about Tim?' said Julian, with a laugh. 'Never mind – you'll soon see him, George. Another hour or so and you'll feast your eyes on him through the coastguard's telescope!'

'Do you really think you'll be able to make out Tim, if he's in the tower with your father at half past ten?' asked her mother. 'I shouldn't have thought you would be able to.'

'Yes, I shall, Mother,' said George. 'It's a very powerful telescope, you know. I'll just go up and make my bed, then I'll go up the cliff-path. Anyone else coming?'

'I want Anne to help me with some turning out,' said her mother. 'I'm looking out some old clothes to give to the vicar's wife for her jumble sale. You don't mind helping me, Anne, do you?'

'No, I'd like to,' said Anne at once. 'What are the boys going to do?'

'I think I must do a bit of my holiday work this morning,' said Julian, with a sigh. 'I don't want to – but I've kept on putting it off. You'd better do some too, Dick. You know what you are – you'll leave it all to the last day if you're not careful!'

'All right. I'll do some too,' said Dick. 'You won't mind scooting up to the coastguard's cottage alone, will you, George?'

'Not a bit,' said George. 'I'll come back just after half past ten, as soon as I've spotted Timmy and Father.'

She disappeared to make her bed. Julian and Dick went to fetch some books. Anne went to make her bed too, and then came down to help her aunt. In a few minutes George yelled good-bye and rushed out of the house.

'What a hurricane!' said her mother. 'It seems as if George never walks if she can possibly run. Now Anne – put the clothes in three piles – the very old – the not so old – and the quite nice.'

Just before half past ten Julian went up to his window to watch for the signal from his uncle. He waited patiently. A few seconds after the half-hour the flashes came – one, two, three, four, five, six – good! Now George would settle down for the day. Perhaps they could go to the quarry in the afternoon. Julian went back to his books and was soon buried in them, with Dick grunting by his side.

At about five minutes to eleven there was the sound of running feet and panting breath. George appeared at the door of the sitting-room where the two boys were doing their work. They looked up.

George was red in the face, and her hair was wind-blown. She fought to get her breath enough to speak. 'Julian! Dick! Something's happened – Timmy wasn't there!'

'What do you mean?' said Julian in surprise. George slumped down on a chair, still panting. The boys could see that she was trembling too.

'It's serious, Julian! I tell you Timmy wasn't in the tower when the signals came!'

'Well – it only means that your absent-minded father forgot to take him up with him,' said Julian, in his most sensible voice. 'What *did* you see?'

'I had my eye glued to the telescope,' said George, 'and suddenly I saw someone come into the little glass room at the top. I looked for Timmy, of course, at once – but I tell you, he wasn't there! The six flashes came, the man disappeared – and that was all. No Timmy! Oh I do feel so dreadfully worried, Julian.'

'Well, don't be,' said Julian, soothingly. 'Honestly, I'm sure that's what happened. Your father forgot about Timmy. Anyway, if you saw *him*, obviously things are all right.'

'I'm not thinking about Father!' cried George. 'He must be all right if he flashed his signals – I'm thinking about Timmy. Why, even if Father forgot to take him, he'd go with him. You know that!'

'Your father might have shut the door at the bottom and prevented Timmy from going up,' said Dick.

'He might,' said George, frowning. She hadn't thought of that. 'Oh dear – now I shall worry all day long. *Why* didn't I stay with Timmy? What shall I do now?'

'Wait till tomorrow morning,' said Dick. 'Then probably you'll see old Tim all right.'

'Tomorrow morning! Why, that's *ages* away!' said poor George. She put her head in her hands and groaned. 'Oh, nobody understands how much I love Timmy. You would perhaps if you had a dog of your own, Julian. It's an awful feeling, really. Oh Timmy, are you all right?'

'Of course he's all right,' said Julian, impatiently. 'Do pull yourself together, George.'

'I *feel* as if something's wrong,' said George, looking obstinate. 'Julian – I think I'd better go across to the island.'

283

'No,' said Julian at once. 'Don't be idiotic, George. Nothing is wrong, except that your father's been forgetful. He's sent his OK signal. That's enough! You're not to go and create a scene over there with him. That would be disgraceful!'

'Well – I'll try and be patient,' said George, unexpectedly meek. She got up, looking worried. Julian spoke in a kinder voice.

'Cheer up, old thing! You do like to go off the deep end, don't you?'

284

15

In the middle of the night

George did not moan any more about her worries. She went about with an anxious look in her blue eyes, but she had the sense not to tell her mother how worried she was at not seeing Timmy in the glass room, when her father signalled.

She mentioned it, of course, but her mother took the same view as Julian did. 'There! I knew he'd forget to take Timmy up! He's so very forgetful when he's at work.'

The children decided to go to the quarry that afternoon and explore the tunnel under the shelf of rock. So they set off after their lunch. But when they came to the quarry, they did not dare to climb down the steep sides. The heavy rain of the day before had made them far too dangerous.

'Look,' said Julian, pointing to where the bushes and smaller plants were ripped up and crushed. 'I bet that's where old Martin fell down yesterday! He might have broken his neck!'

'Yes. I vote we don't attempt to go down till it's as dry as it was the other day,' said Dick.

It was very disappointing. They had brought torches, and a rope, and had looked forward to a little excitement. 'Well, what shall we do?' asked Julian.

'I'm going back home,' said George, unexpectedly. 'I'm tired. You others go for a walk.'

Anne looked at George. She did seem rather pale. 'I'll come back with you, George,' said Anne slipping her hand through her cousin's arm. But George shook it off.

'No thanks, Anne. I want to be alone.'

'Well – we'll go over to the cliff then,' said George. 'It'll be nice and blowy up there. See you later, George!'

They went off. George turned and sped back to Kirrin Cottage. Her mother was out. Joanna was upstairs in her bedroom. George went to the larder and took several things from it. She bundled them into a bag and then fled out of the house.

She found James the fisher-boy. 'James! You're not to tell a soul. I'm going over to Kirrin Island tonight – because I'm worried about Timmy. We left him there. Have my boat ready at ten o'clock.'

James was always ready to do anything in the world for George. He nodded and asked no questions at all. 'Right, Miss. It'll be ready. Anything you want put in it?'

'Yes, this bag,' said George. 'Now don't split on me, James. I'll be back tomorrow if I find Tim's all right.'

She fled back to the house. She hoped Joanna would not notice the things she had taken from the larder shelf.

'I can't help it if what I'm doing is wrong,' she kept whispering to herself. 'I know something isn't right with Timmy. And I'm not at all sure about Father, either. He *wouldn't* have forgotten his solemn promise to me about taking Timmy up with him. I'll have to go across to the island. I can't help it if it's wrong!'

The others wondered what was up with George when they came back from their walk. She was so fidgety and restless. They had tea and then did some gardening for

Aunt Fanny. George did some too, but her thoughts were far away, and twice her mother had to stop her pulling up seedlings instead of weeds.

Bedtime came. The girls got into bed at about a quarter to ten. Anne was tired and fell asleep at once. As soon as George heard her regular breathing she crept quietly out of bed and dressed again. She pulled on her warmest jersey, got her raincoat, rubber boots and a thick rug, and tiptoed downstairs.

Out of the side door she went and into the night. There was a bit of a moon in the sky, so it was not as dark as usual. George was glad. She would be able to see her way through the rocks a little now – though she was sure she could guide the boat even in the dark!

James was waiting for her. Her boat was ready. 'Everything's in,' said James. 'I'll push off. Now you be careful, Miss – and if you do scrape a rock, row like anything in case she fills and sinks. Ready?'

Off went George, hearing the lap-lap of the water against the sides of the boat. She heaved a sigh of relief, and began to row strongly away from the shore. She frowned as she rowed. Had she brought everything she might want? Two torches. Plenty of food. A tin-opener. Something to drink. A rug to wrap herself in tonight.

Back at Kirrin Cottage Julian lay in bed watching for his uncle's signal. Half past ten. Now for the signal. Ah, here they were! One – two – three – four – five – six! Good. Six and no more!

He wondered why George hadn't come into his and Dick's room to watch for them. She had last night. He got up, padded to the door of George's room and put his head in 'George!' he said softly. 'It's OK. Your father's signals have just come again.'

There was no reply. Julian heard regular breathing and turned to go back to bed. The girls must be asleep already! Well, George couldn't really be worrying much about

Timmy now, then! Julian got into his bed and soon fell asleep himself. He had no idea that George's bed was empty – no idea that even now George was battling with the waves that guarded Kirrin Island!

It was more difficult than she had expected, for the moon did not really give very much light, and had an annoying way of going behind a cloud just when she badly needed every scrap of light she could get. But, deftly and cleverly, she managed to make her way through the

288

passage between the hidden rocks. Thank goodness the tide was high so that most of them were well below the surface!

At last she swung her boat into the little cove. Here the water was perfectly calm. Panting a little, George pulled her boat up as far as she could. Then she stood in the darkness and thought hard.

What was she going to do? She did not know where her father's hiding-place was – but she felt certain the entrance to it must be somewhere in or near the little stone room. Should she make her way to that?

Yes, she would. It would be the only place to shelter in for the night, anyway. She would put on her torch when she got there, and hunt round for any likely entrance to the hiding-place. If she found it, she would go in – and what a surprise she would give her father! If old Timmy was there he would go mad with delight.

She took the heavy bag, draped the rug over her arm, and set off. She did not dare to put on her torch yet, in case the unknown enemy was lurking near. After all, her father had heard him cough at night!

George was not frightened. She did not even think about being frightened. All her thoughts were set on finding Timmy and making sure he was safe.

She came to the little stone room. It was pitch-dark in there, of course – not even the faint light of the moon pierced into its blackness. George had to put on her torch.

She put down her bundle by the wall at the back, near the old fireplace recess. She draped the rug over it and sat down to have a rest, switching off her torch.

After a while she got up cautiously and switched on her torch again. She began to search for the hiding-place. Where *could* the entrance be? She flashed her torch on to every flagstone in the floor of the room. But not one looked as if it had been moved or lifted. There was nothing to show where there might be an entrance underground.

She moved round the walls, examining those too in the light of her torch. No – there was no sign that a hidden way lay behind any of those stones either. It was most tantalising. If she only knew!

She went to wrap the rug round her, and to sit and think. It was cold now. She was shivering, as she sat there in the dark, trying to puzzle out where the hidden entrance could be.

And then she heard a sound! She jumped and then stiffened all over, holding her breath painfully. What was it?

There was a curious grating noise. Then a slight thud. It came from the recess where people long ago had built their big log fires! George sat perfectly still, straining her eyes and ears.

She saw a beam of light in the fireplace recess. Then she heard a man's cough!

Was it her father? He had a cough at times. She listened hard. The beam of light grew brighter. Then she heard another noise – it sounded as if someone had jumped down from somewhere! And then – a voice!

'Come on!'

It was not her father's voice! George grew cold with fear then. Not her father's voice! Then what had happened to him – and to Timmy?

Someone else jumped down into the recess, grumbling. 'I'm not used to this crawling about!'

That wasn't her father's voice either. So there were *two* unknown enemies! Not one. And they knew her father's secret workroom. George felt almost faint with horror. Whatever had happened to him and Timmy?

The men walked out of the little stone room without seeing George at all. She guessed they were going to the tower. How long would they be? Long enough for her to search for the place they had appeared from?

She strained her ears again. She heard their footsteps

going into the great yard. She tiptoed to the doorway and looked out. Yes – there was the light of their torch near the tower! If they were going up, there would be plenty of time to look round.

She went back into the little stone room. Her hands were trembling and she found it difficult to switch on her torch. She went to the fireplace recess and flashed the light in it.

She gave a gasp! Half way up the recess at the back was a black opening! She flashed the light up there. Evidently there was a movable stone half way up that swung back and revealed an entrance behind. An entrance to what? Were there steps such as were shown in the old map?

Feeling quite breathless, George stood on tip-toe and flashed her light into the hole. Yes – there were steps! They went down into the wall at the back. She remembered that the little stone room backed on to one of the immensely thick old walls still left.

She stood there, uncertain what to do. Had she better go down and see if she could find Timmy and her father? But if she did, she might be made a prisoner too. On the other hand, if she stayed outside, and the men came back and shut up the entrance, she might not be able to open it. She would be worse off than ever!

'I'll go down!' she suddenly decided. 'But I'd better take my bag and the rug, in case the men come back and see them. I don't want them to know I'm on the island if I can help it! I could hide them somewhere down there, I expect. I wonder if this entrance leads to the dungeons.'

She lifted up the rug and the bag and pushed them into the hole. She heard the bag roll down the steps, the tins inside making a muffled noise.

Then she climbed up herself. Gracious, what a long dark flight of steps! Wherever did they lead to?

16

Down to the caves

George went cautiously down the stone steps. They were
steep and narrow. 'I should think they run right down in
the middle of the stone wall,' thought George 'Goodness,
here's a narrow bit!'

It was so narrow that she had to go sideways. 'A fat man
would never get through there!' she thought to herself.
'Hallo – the steps have ended!'

She had got the rug round her shoulders, and had
picked up her bag on the way down. In her other hand she
held her torch. It was terribly dark and quiet down there.
George did not feel scared because she was hoping to see
Timmy at any moment. No one could feel afraid with
Timmy just round the corner, ready to welcome them!

She stood at the bottom of the steps, her torch showing
her a narrow tunnel. It curved sharply to the left. 'Now
will it join the dungeons from here?' she wondered, trying
to get her sense of direction to help her. 'They can't be far
off. But there's no sign of them at the moment.'

She went down the narrow tunnel. Once the roof came

down so low she almost had to crawl. She flashed her torch on it. She saw black rock there, which had evidently been too hard to be removed by the tunnel-builders long ago.

The tunnel went on and on and on. George was puzzled. Surely by now she must have gone by all the dungeons! Why – she must be heading towards the shore of the island! How very queer! Didn't this tunnel join the dungeons then? A little further and she would be under the bed of the sea itself.

The tunnel took a deep slope downwards. More steps appeared, cut roughly from rock. George climbed down them cautiously. Where in the world was she going?

At the bottom of the steps the tunnel seemed to be cut out of solid rock – or else it was a natural passage, not made by man at all. George didn't know. Her torch showed her black, rocky walls and roof, and her feet stumbled over an irregular rocky path. How she longed for Timmy beside her!

'I must be very deep down,' she thought, pausing to flash her torch round her once more. 'Very deep down and very far from the castle! Good gracious – whatever's that awful noise?'

She listened. She heard a muffled booming and moaning. Was it her father doing one of his experiments? The noise went on and on, a deep, never-ending boom.

'Why – I believe it's the sea!' said George, amazed. She stood and listened again. 'Yes – it *is* the sea – over my head! I'm under the rocky bed of Kirrin Bay!'

And now poor George did feel a bit scared! She thought of the great waves surging above her, she thought of the restless, moving water scouring the rocky bed over her head, and felt frightened in case the sea should find a way to leak down into her narrow tunnel!

'Now don't be silly,' she told herself sternly. 'This tunnel has been here under the sea-bed for hundreds of years – why should it suddenly become unsafe just when *you* are in it, George?'

Talking to herself like this, to keep up her spirits, she went on again. It was very queer indeed to think she was walking under the sea. So this was where her father was at work! Under the sea itself.

And then George suddenly remembered something he had said to them all, the first time they had visited him on the island. What was it now? 'Oh yes! He said he had to have water *above* and *around* him!' said George. '*Now* I see what he meant! His workroom is somewhere down here – so the sea-water is *above* him – and it's all *round* the tower, because it's built on an island!'

Water above and water around – so that was why her father had chosen Kirrin Island for his experiment. How had he found the secret passage under the sea, though? 'Why, even I didn't know of that,' said George. 'Hallo – what am I coming to?'

She stopped. The passage had suddenly widened out into an enormous dark cave, whose roof was unexpectedly high, lost in dark shadows. George stared round. She saw queer things there that she didn't understand at all – wires, glass boxes, little machines that seemed to be at work without a sound, whose centres were alive with queer, gleaming, shivering light.

Sudden sparks shot up now and again, and when that happened a funny smell crept round the cave. 'How weird all this is!' thought George. 'However can Father understand all these machines and things! I wonder where he is. I do hope those men haven't made him prisoner somewhere!'

From this queer Aladdin's cave another tunnel led. George switched on her torch again and went into it. It was much like the other one, but the roof was higher.

She came to another cave, smaller this time, and crammed with wires of all kinds. There was a curious humming

294

sound here, like thousands of bees in a hive. George half-expected to see some flying round.

'It must be these wires making the noise,' she said. There was nobody in the cave at all, but it led into another one, and George hoped that soon she would find Timmy and her father.

She went into the next cave, which was perfectly empty and very cold. She shivered. Then down another passage, and into a small cave. The first thing she saw beyond this tiny cave was a light!

A light! Then perhaps she was coming to the cave her father must be in! She flashed her torch round the little cave she was now standing in and saw tins of food, bottles of beer, tins of sweets, and a pile of clothes of some sort. Ah, this was where her father kept his stores. She went on to the next cave. wondering why Timmy had not heard her and come to greet her.

She looked cautiously into the cave where the light came from. Sitting at a table, his head in his hands, perfectly still, was her father! There was no sign of Timmy.

'Father!' said George. The man at the table jumped violently and turned round. He stared at George as if he really could not believe his eyes. Then he turned back again, and buried his face in his hands.

'*Father*!' said George again, quite frightened because he did not say anything to her.

He looked round again, and this time he got up. He stared at George once more, and then sat down heavily. George ran to him. 'What's the matter? Oh Father, what's the matter? Where's Timmy?'

'George! Is it *really* you, George? I thought I must be dreaming when I looked up and saw you!' said her father. 'How did you get here? Good gracious, it's impossible that you should be here!'

'Father are you all right? What's happened – and where's Timmy?' said George, urgently. She looked all round, but could see no sign of him. Her heart went cold. Surely nothing awful had happened to Timmy?

'Did you see two men?' asked her father. 'Where were they?'

'Oh Father – we keep asking each other questions and

not answering them!' said George. 'Tell me first – where is Timmy?'

'I don't know,' said her father. 'Did those two men go to the tower?'

'Yes,' said George. 'Father, what's happened?'

'Well, if they've gone to the tower, we've got about an hour in peace,' said her father. 'Now listen to me, George, very carefully. This is terribly important.'

'I'm listening,' said George. 'But do hurry up and tell me about Timmy.'

'These two men were parachuted down on to the island, to try and find out my secret,' said her father. 'I'll tell you what my experiments are for, George – they are to find a way of replacing all coal, coke and oil – an idea to give the world all the heat and power it wants, and to do away with mines and miners.'

'Good gracious!' said George. 'It would be one of the most wonderful things the world has ever known.'

'Yes,' said her father. 'And I should *give* it to the whole world – it shall not be in the power of any one country, or collection of men. It shall be a gift to the whole of mankind – but, George, there are men who want my secret for themselves, so that they may make colossal fortunes out of it.'

'How hateful!' cried George. 'Go on, Father – how did they hear of it?'

'Well, I was at work on this idea with some of my colleagues, my fellow-workers,' said her father. 'And one of them betrayed us, and went to some powerful business men to tell them of my idea. So when I knew this I decided to come away in secret and finish my experiments by myself. Then nobody could betray me.'

'And you came here!' said George. 'To my island.'

'Yes – because I needed water over me and water around me,' said her father. 'Quite by chance I looked at a copy of that old map, and thought that if the passage shown there – the one leading from the little stone room, I mean – if the passage there *really* did lead under the sea, as it seemed to show, that would be the ideal place to finish my experiments.'

'Oh Father – and I made such a fuss!' said George, ashamed now, to remember how cross she had been.

'Did you?' said her father, as if he had forgotten all about that. 'Well, I got all my stuff and came here. And now these fellows have found me, and got hold of me!'

'Poor Father! Can't I help?' said George. 'I could go back and bring help over here, couldn't I?'

'Yes, you could!' said her father. 'But you mustn't let those men see you, George.'

'I'll do anything you want me to, Father, anything!' said George. 'But first do tell me what's happened to Timmy?'

298

'Well, he kept by me all the time,' said her father. 'Really, he's a wonderful dog, George. And then, this morning, just as I was coming out of the entrance in that little room to go up into the tower with Timmy to signal, the two men pounced on me and forced me back here.'

'But what happened to Timmy?' asked George, impatiently. Would her father *never* tell her what she wanted to know?

'He flew at the men, of course,' said her father. 'But somehow or other one of them lassoed him with a noose of rope and caught him. They pulled the rope so right round his neck that he almost choked.'

'Oh poor, poor Timmy,' said George, and the tears ran down her cheeks. 'Is he – do you think – he's all right, Father?'

'Yes. From what I heard the men saying afterwards I think they've taken him to some cave and shut him in there,' said her father. 'Anyway, I saw one of them getting some dog-biscuits out of a bag this evening – so that looks as if he's alive and kicking – and hungry!'

George heaved a great sigh of relief. So long as Timmy was alive and all right! She took a few steps towards what she thought must be another cave. 'I'm going to find Timmy, Father,' she said. 'I *must* find him!'

17

Timmy at last

'No, George!' called her father sharply. 'Come back.
There is something very important I want to say. Come
here!'

George went over to him, filled with impatience to get to
Timmy, wherever he was. She *must* find him!

'Now listen,' said her father. 'I have a book in which I
have made all my notes of this great experiment. The men
haven't found it! I want you to take it safely to the
mainland, George. Don't let it out of your sight! If the men
get hold of it they would have all the information they
needed!'

'But don't they know everything just by looking at your
wires and machines and things?' asked George.

'They know a very great deal,' said her father, 'and
they've found out a lot more since they've been here – but
not quite enough. I daren't destroy my book of notes,
because if anything should happen to me, my great idea
would be completely lost. So, George, I must entrust it to

you and you must take it to an address I will give you, and hand it to the person there.'

'It's an awful responsibility,' said George, a little scared of handling a book which meant so much, not only to her father, but possibly to the whole of the world. 'But I'll do my best, Father. I'll hide in one of the caves till the men come back, and then I'll slip back up the passage to the hidden entrance, get out, go to my boat and row back to the mainland. Then I'll deliver your book of notes without fail, and get help sent over here to you.'

'Good girl,' said her father, and gave her a hug. 'Honestly, George, you do behave as bravely as any boy. I'm proud of you.'

George thought that was the nicest thing her father had ever said to her. She smiled at him. 'Well, Father, I'll go and see if I can find Timmy now. I simply must see that he's all right before I go to hide in one of the other caves.'

'Very well,' said her father. 'The man who took the biscuits went in that direction – still further under the sea, George. Oh – by the way – how is it you're here, in the middle of the night?'

It seemed to strike her father for the first time that George also might have a story to tell. But George felt that she really couldn't waste any more time – she *must* find Timmy!

'I'll tell you later, Father,' she said. 'Oh – where's that book of notes?'

Her father rose and went to the back of the cave. He took a box and stood on it. He ran his hand along a dark ridge of rock, and felt about until he had found what he wanted.

He brought down a slim book, whose pages were of very thin paper. He opened the book and George saw many beautifully drawn diagrams, and pages of notes in her father's small neat handwriting.

'Here you are,' said her father, handing her the book, 'do

301

the best you can. If anything happens to me, this book will still enable my fellow-workers to give my idea to the world. If I come through this all right, I shall be glad to have the book, because it will mean I shall not have to work out all my experiments again.'

George took the precious book. She stuffed it into her macintosh pocket, which was a big one. 'I'll keep it safe, Father. Now I must go and find Timmy, or those two men will be back before I can hide in one of the other caves.'

She left her father's cave and went into the next one. There was nothing there at all. Then on she went down a passage that twisted and turned in the rock.

And then she heard a sound she longed to hear. A whine! Yes, really a whine!

'Timmy!' shouted George, eagerly. 'Oh Timmy! I'm coming!'

Timmy's whine stopped suddenly. Then he barked joyously. 'Woof, woof, woof, woof!' George almost fell as she tried to run down the narrow tunnel. Her torch showed her a big boulder that seemed to be blocking up a small cave in the side of the tunnel. Behind the boulder Timmy barked, and scraped frantically!

George tugged at the stone with all her strength. 'Timmy!' she panted. 'Timmy! I'll get you out! I'm coming! Oh, Timmy!'

The stone moved a little. George tugged again. It was almost too heavy for her to move at all, but despair made her stronger than she had ever been in her life. The stone quite suddenly swung to one side, and George just got one of her feet out of its way in time, or it would have been crushed.

Timmy squeezed out of the space left. He flung himself on George, who fell on the ground with her arms tight round him. He licked her face and whined, and she buried her nose in his thick fur in joy. 'Timmy! What have they done to you? Timmy, I came as soon as I could!'

302

Timmy whined again and again in joy, and tried to paw and lick George as if he couldn't have enough of her. It would have been difficult to say which of the two was the happier.

At last George pushed Timmy away firmly. 'Timmy we've got work to do! We've got to escape from here and get across to the mainland and bring help.'

'Woof,' said Timmy. George stood up and flashed her torch into the tiny cave where Timmy had been. She saw that there was a bowl of water there and some biscuits. The men had not ill-treated him, then, except to lasso him and half-choke him when they caught him. She felt round his neck tenderly, but except for a swollen ridge there, he seemed none the worse.

'Now hurry up – we'll go back to Father's cave – and then find another cave beyond his to hide in till the two men come back from the tower. Then we'll creep out into the little stone room and row back to the mainland,' said George. 'I've got a very, very important book here in my pocket, Timmy.'

Timmy growled suddenly, and the hairs on the back of his neck rose up. George stiffened, and stood listening.

A stern voice came down the passage. 'I don't know who you are or where you've come from – but if you have dared to let that dog loose he'll be shot! And, to show you that I mean what I say, here's something to let you know I've a revolver!'

Then there came a deafening crash, as the man pulled the trigger, and a bullet hit the roof somewhere in the passage. Timmy and George almost jumped out of their skins. Timmy would have leapt up the passage at once, but George had her hand on his collar. She was very frightened, and tried hard to think what was best to do.

The echoes of the shot went on and on. It was horrid. Timmy stopped growling, and George stayed absolutely still.

'Well?' said the voice, 'did you hear what I said? If that dog is loose, he'll be shot. I'm not having my plans spoilt now. And you, whoever you are, will please come up the tunnel and let me see you. But I warn you – if the dog's with you, that's the end of him!'

'Timmy! Timmy, run away and hide somewhere!' whispered George suddenly. And then she remembered something else that filled her with despair. She had her father's precious book of notes with her – in her pocket! Suppose the man found it on her? It would break her father's heart to know that his wonderful secret had been stolen from him after all.

George hurriedly took the thin, flat little book from her pocket. She pushed it at Timmy. 'Put it in your mouth. Take it with you, Tim. And go and hide till it's safe to come. Quick! Go, Timmy, go! I'll be all right.'

To her great relief Timmy, with the book in his mouth, turned and disappeared down the tunnel that led further under the sea. How she hoped he would find a safe hiding place! The tunnel must end soon – but maybe before it did, Timmy would settle down in some dark corner and wait for her to call him again.

'Will you come up the passage or not?' shouted the voice angrily. 'You'll be sorry if I have to come and fetch you – because I shall shoot all the way along!' 'I'm coming!' called George, in a small voice, and she went up the passage. She soon saw a beam of light, and in a moment she was in the flash of a powerful torch. There was a surprised exclamation.

'Good heavens! A boy! What are *you* doing here, and where did you come from?'

George's short curly hair made the man with the torch think she was a boy, and George did not tell him he was wrong. The man held a revolver, but he let it drop as he saw George.

'I only came to rescue my dog, and to find my father,' said George, in a meek voice.

'Well, you can't move that heavy stone!' said the man. 'A kid like you wouldn't have the strength. And you can't rescue your father either! We've got him prisoner, as you no doubt saw.'

'Yes,' said George, delighted to think that the man was sure she had not been strong enough to move the big stone. She wasn't going to say a word about Timmy! If the man thought he was still shut up in that tiny cave, well and good!

Then she heard her father's voice, anxiously calling from somewhere beyond the man. 'George! Is that you? Are you all right?'

'Yes, Father!' shouted back George, hoping that he would not ask anything about Timmy. The man beckoned her to come to him. Then he pushed her in front of him and they walked to her father's cave.

'I've brought your boy back,' said the man. 'Silly little idiot – thinking he could set that savage dog free! We've got him penned up in a cave with a big boulder in front!'

Another man came in from the opposite end of the cave. He was amazed to see George. The other man explained.

'When I got down here, I heard a noise out beyond this cave, the dog barking and someone talking to him – and found this kid there, trying to set the dog free. I'd have shot the dog, of course, if he *had* been freed.'

'But – how did this boy get here?' asked the other man, still amazed.

'Maybe *he* can tell us that!' said the other. And then, for the first time, George's father heard how George had got there and why.

She told them how she had watched for Timmy in the glass room of the tower and hadn't seen him – and that had worried her and made her suspicious. So she had come across to the island in her boat at night, and had seen where the men came from. She had gone down the tunnel, and kept on till she came to the cave, where she had found her father.

The three men listened in silence. 'Well, you're a tiresome nuisance,' one of the men said to George, 'but my word, you're a son to be proud of. It's not many boys would have been brave enough to run so much risk for anyone.'

'Yes. I'm really proud of you, George,' said her father. He looked at her anxiously. She knew what he was thinking – what about his precious book? Had she been sensible enough to hide it? She did not dare to let him know anything while the men were there.

'Now, this complicates matters,' said the other man, looking at George. 'If you don't go back home you'll soon be missed, and there will be all kinds of search-parties going on – and maybe someone will send over to the island here to tell your father you have disappeared! We don't want anyone here at present – not till we know what we want to know!'

He turned to George's father. 'If you will tell us what we want to know, and give us all your notes, we will set you free, give us whatever sum of money you ask us for, and disappear ourselves.'

'And if I still say I won't?' said George's father.

'Then I am afraid we shall blow up the whole of your machines and the tower – and possibly you will never be found again because you will be buried down here,' said the man, in a voice that was suddenly very hard.

There was a dead silence. George looked at her father. 'You couldn't do a thing like that,' he said at last. 'You would gain nothing by it at all!'

'It's all or nothing with us,' said the man. 'All or nothing. Make up your mind. We'll give you till half past ten tomorrow morning – about seven hours. Then either you tell us everything, or we blow the island sky-high!'

They went out of the cave and left George and her father together. Only seven hours! And then, perhaps, the end of Kirrin Island!

18

Half past four in the morning

As soon as the men were out of earshot, George's father spoke in a low voice.

'It's no good. I'll have to let them have my book of notes. I can't risk having you buried down here, George. I don't mind anything for myself – workers of my sort have to be ready to take risks all their lives – but it's different now you're here!'

'Father, I haven't got the book of notes,' whispered George, thankfully. 'I gave them to Timmy. I *did* manage to get that stone away from the entrance to his little prison – though the men think I didn't! I gave the book to Timmy and told him to go and hide till I fetched him.'

'Fine work, George!' said her father. 'Well – perhaps if you got Timmy now and brought him here – he could deal with these two men before they suspect he is free! He is quite capable of getting them both down on the ground at once.'

308

'Oh yes! It's your only chance,' said George. 'I'll go and get him now. I'll go a little way along the passage and whistle. Father – why didn't *you* go and try and rescue Timmy?'

'I didn't want to leave my book,' said her father. 'I dared not take it with me, in case the men came after me and found it. They've been looking in all the caves for it. I couldn't bear to leave it here, and go and look for the dog. I was sure he was all right, when I saw the men taking biscuits out of the bag. Now do go, George, and whistle to Timmy. The men may be back at any moment.'

George took her torch and went into the passage that led to the little cave where Timmy had been. She whistled loudly, and then waited. But no Timmy came. She whistled again, and then went farther along the passage. Still no Timmy.

She called him loudly. 'TIMMY! TIMMY! COME HERE!' But Timmy did not come. There was no sound of scampering feet, no joyful bark.

'Oh bother!' thought George. 'I hope he hasn't gone so far away that he can't hear me. I'll go a little farther.'

So she made her way along the tunnel, past the cave where Timmy had been, and then on down the tunnel again. Still no Timmy.

George rounded a corner and then saw that the tunnel split into three. Three different passages, all dark, silent and cold. Oh dear! She didn't in the least know which to take. She took the one on the left.

But that also split into three a little way on! George stopped. 'I shall get absolutely lost in this maze of passages under the sea if I go on,' she thought. 'I simply daren't. It's too frightening. TIMMY! TIMMY!'

Her voice went echoing along the passage and sounded very queer indeed. She retraced her steps and went right back to her father's cave, feeling miserable.

'Father, there's no sign of Timmy at all. He must have

gone along one of the passages and got lost! Oh dear, this is awful. There are lots of tunnels beyond this cave. It seems as if the whole rocky bed of the sea is mined with tunnels!' George sat down and looked very downhearted.

'Quite likely,' said her father. 'Well – that's a perfectly good plan gone wrong. We must try and think of another.'

'I do wonder what Julian and the others will think when they wake up and find me gone,' said George, suddenly. 'They might even come and try to find me here.'

'That wouldn't be much good,' said her father. 'These men will simply come down here and wait, and nobody will know where we are. The others don't know of the entrance in the little stone room, do they?'

'No,' said George. 'If they came over here I'm sure they'd never find it! We've looked before. And that would mean they'd be blown up with the island. Father, this is simply dreadful.'

'If only we knew where Timmy was!' said her father, 'or if we could get a message to Julian to tell him not to come. What's the time? My word, it's half past three in the early morning! I suppose Julian and the others are fast asleep.'

Julian *was* fast asleep. So was Anne. Dick was in a deep sleep as well, so nobody guessed that George's bed was empty.

But, about half past four Anne awoke, feeling very hot. 'I really must open the window!' she thought. 'I'm boiling!'

She got up and went to the window. She opened it, and stood looking out. The stars were out and the bay shone faintly.

'George,' whispered Anne. 'Are you awake?'

She listened for a reply. But none came. Then she listened more intently. Why, she couldn't even hear George's breathing! Surely George was there?

She felt over George's bed. It was flat and empty. She

310

switched on the light and looked at it. George's pyjamas were still on the bed. Her clothes were gone.

'George has gone to the island!' said Anne, in a fright. 'All in the dark by herself!'

She went to the boys' room. She felt about Julian's bed for his shoulder, and shook him hard. He woke up with a jump. 'What is it? What's up?'

'Julian! George is gone. Her bed's not been slept in,' whispered Anne. Her whisper awoke Dick, and soon both boys were sitting up wide awake.

'Blow! I might have guessed she'd do a fool thing like that,' said Julian. 'In the middle of the night too – and all those dangerous rocks to row round. *Now* what are we going to do about it? I *told* her she wasn't to go to the island – Timmy would be quite all right! I expect Uncle Quentin forgot to take him up to the tower with him yesterday, that's all. She might have waited till half past ten this morning – then she would probably have seen him.'

'Well – we can't do anything now, I suppose, can we?' said Anne, anxiously.

'Not a thing,' said Julian. 'I've no doubt she's safely on Kirrin Island by now, making a fuss of Timmy, and having a good old row with Uncle Quentin. Really George is the limit!'

They talked for half an hour and then Julian looked at his watch. 'Five o'clock. We'd better try and get a bit more sleep. Aunt Fanny will be worried in the morning when she hears of George's latest escapade!'

Anne went back to her room. She got into bed and fell asleep. Julian could not sleep – he kept thinking of George and wondering where exactly she was. Wouldn't he give her a talking-to when she came back!

He suddenly heard a peculiar noise downstairs. What-ever could it be? It sounded like someone climbing in at a window. Was there one open? Yes, the window of the little wash-place might be open. Crash! What in the world was that? It couldn't be a burglar – no burglar would be foolish enough to make such a noise.

There was a sound on the stairs, and then the bedroom door was pushed open. In alarm Julian put out his hand to switch on the light, but before he could do something heavy jumped right on top of him!

He yelled and Dick woke up with a jump. He put on the light – then Julian saw what was on his bed – Timmy!

'Timmy! How did you get here? Where's George! Timmy, is it really you?'

'Timmy!' echoed Dick, amazed. 'Has George brought him back then? Is she here too?'

Anne came in, wakened by the noise. 'Why, *Timmy*! Oh Julian, is George back too, then?'

'No, apparently not,' said Julian, puzzled. 'I say, Tim, what's this you've got in your mouth? Drop it, old chap, drop it!'

Timmy dropped it. Julian picked it up from the bed. 'It's a book of notes – all in Uncle's handwriting! What *does* this mean? How did Timmy get hold of it – and why did he bring it here? It's most extraordinary!'

Nobody could imagine why Timmy had suddenly appeared with the book of notes – and no George.

'It's very queer,' said Julian. 'There's something I don't understand here. Let's go and wake Aunt Fanny.'

So they went and woke her up, telling her all they knew. She was very worried indeed to hear that George was gone. She picked up the book of notes and knew at once that it was very important.

'I must put this into the safe,' she said. 'I know this is valuable. How *did* Timmy get hold of it?'

Timmy was acting queerly. He kept pawing at Julian and whining. He had been very pleased to see everyone, but he seemed to have something on his mind.

'What is it, old boy?' asked Dick. 'How did you get here? You didn't swim, because you're not wet. If you came in a boat, it must have been with George – and yet you've left her behind!'

'*I* think something's happened to George,' said Anne, suddenly. 'I think Timmy keeps pawing you to tell you to go with him and find her. Perhaps she brought him back in the boat, and then was terribly tired and fell asleep on the beach or something. We ought to go and see.'

'Yes, I think we ought,' said Julian. 'Aunt Fanny, would you like to wake Joanna and get something hot ready, in case we find George is tired out and cold? We'll go down to the beach and look. It will soon be daylight now. The eastern sky is just beginning to show its first light.'

'Well go and dress then,' said Aunt Fanny, still looking very worried indeed. 'Oh, what a dreadful family I've got – always in some scrape or other!'

The three children began to dress. Timmy watched them, waiting patiently till they were ready. Then they all went downstairs and out of doors. Julian turned towards the beach, but Timmy stood still. He pawed at Dick and then ran a few steps in the opposite direction.

'Why – he doesn't *want* us to go the beach! He wants us to go another way!' cried Julian, in surprise. 'All right, Timmy – you lead the way and we'll follow!'

19

A meeting with Martin

Timmy ran round the house and made for the moor behind. It was most extraordinary. Wherever was he going?

'This is awfully queer,' said Julian. 'I'm sure George can't be anywhere in this direction.'

Timmy went on swiftly, occasionally turning his head to make sure everyone was following him. He led the way to the quarry!

'The quarry! Did George come here then?' said Dick. 'But why?'

The dog disappeared down into the middle of the quarry, slipping and sliding down the steep sides as he went. The others followed as best they could. Luckily it was not as slippery as before, and they reached the bottom without accident.

Timmy went straight to the shelf of rock and disappeared underneath it. They heard him give a short sharp bark as if to say 'Come on! This is the way! Hurry up!'

'He's gone into the tunnel under there,' said Dick. 'Where we thought we might explore and didn't. There must be a passage or something there, then. But is George there?'

'I'll go first,' said Julian, and wriggled through the hole. He was soon in the wider bit and then came out into the part where he could almost stand. He walked a little way in the dark, hearing Timmy bark impatiently now and then. But in a moment or two Julian stopped.

'It's no good trying to follow you in the dark, Timmy!' he called. 'We'll have to go back and get torches. I can't see a foot in front of me!'

Dick was just wriggling through the first part of the hole. Julian called to him to go back.

'It's too dark,' he said. 'We must go and get torches. If George for some reason is up this passage, she must have had an accident, and we'd better get a rope, and some brandy.'

Anne began to cry. She didn't like the idea of George lying hurt in that dark passage. Julian put his arm round her as soon as he was in the open air again. He helped her up the sides of the quarry, followed by Dick.

'Now don't worry. We'll get her all right. But it beats me why she went there – and I still can't imagine how Tim and she came from the island, if they are here, instead of on the beach!'

'Look – there's Martin!' suddenly said Dick in surprise. So there was! He was standing at the top of the quarry, and seemed just as surprised to see them as they were to see him!

'You're up early,' called Dick. 'And goodness me – are you going gardening or something? Why the spades?'

Martin looked sheepish and didn't seem to know what to say. Julian suddenly walked up to him and caught hold of his shoulder. 'Look here, Martin! There's some funny business going on here! What are you going to do with

316

those spades? Have you seen George? Do you know where she is, or anything about her? Come on, tell me!'

Martin shook his shoulder away from Julian's grip looking extremely surprised.

'George? No! What's happened to him?'

'George isn't a him – she's a her,' said Anne, still crying. 'She's disappeared. We thought she'd gone to the island to find her dog – and Timmy suddenly appeared at Kirrin Cottage, and brought us here!'

'So it looks as if George might be somewhere near here,'

said Julian. 'And I want to know if you've seen her or know anything of her whereabouts?'

'No, Julian. I swear I don't!' said Martin.

'Well, tell me what you're doing here so early in the morning, with spades,' said Julian, roughly. 'Who are you waiting for? Your father?'

'Yes,' said Martin.

'And what are you going to do?' asked Dick. 'Going exploring up the hole there?'

'Yes,' said Martin again, sullen and worried. 'No harm in that, is there?'

'It's all – very – queer!' said Julian, eyeing him and speaking slowly and loudly. 'But – let me tell you this – *we're* going exploring – not you! If there's anything queer up that hole, *we'll* find it! We shall not allow you or your father to get through the hole. So go and find him and tell him that!'

Martin didn't move. He went very white, and stared at Julian miserably. Anne went up to him, tears still on her face and put her hand on his arm.

'Martin, what is it? Why do you look like that? What's the mystery?'

And then, to the dismay and horror of everyone, Martin turned away with a noise that sounded very like a sob! He stood with his back to them, his shoulder shaking.

'Good gracious! What *is* up?' said Julian, in exasperation. 'Pull yourself together, Martin! Tell us what's worrying you.'

'Everything, everything!' said Martin, in a muffled voice. Then he swung round to face them. 'You don't know what it is to have no mother and no father – nobody who cares about you – and then . . .'

'But you *have* got a father!' said Dick at once.

'I haven't. He's not my father, that man. He's only my guardian, but he makes me call him father whenever we're on a job together.'

318

'A job? What sort of job?' said Julian.

'Oh any kind – all beastly,' said Martin. 'Snooping round and finding things out about people, and then getting money from them if we promise to say nothing – and receiving stolen goods and selling them – and helping people like the men who are after your uncle's secret . . .'

'*Oho!*' said Dick at once. 'Now we're coming to it. I *thought* you and Mr Curton were both suspiciously interested in Kirrin Island. What's this present job, then?'

'My guardian will half-kill me for telling all this,' said Martin. 'But, you see, they're planning to blow up the island – and it's about the worst thing I've ever been mixed up in – and I know your uncle is there – and perhaps George too now, you say. I can't go on with it!'

A few more tears ran down his cheeks. It was awful to see a boy crying like that, and the three felt sorry for Martin now. They were also full of horror when they heard him say that the island was to be blown up!

'How do you know this?' asked Julian.

'Well, Mr Curton's got a wireless receiver and transmitter as you know,' explained Martin, 'and so have the fellows on the island – the ones who are after your uncle's secret – so they can easily keep in touch with one another. They mean to get the secret if they can – if not they are going to blow the whole place sky-high so that *nobody* can get the secret. But they can't get away by boat because they don't know the way through those rocks . . .'

'Well, how will they get away then?' demanded Julian.

'We feel sure this hole that Timmy found the other day, leads down to the sea, and under the sea-bed to Kirrin Island,' said Martin. 'Yes, I know it sounds too mad to be true – but Mr Curton's got an old map which clearly shows there was once a passage under the sea-bed. If there is – well, the fellows across on the island can escape down it, after making all preparations for the island to be blown up. See?'

'Yes,' said Julian, taking a long breath. 'I *do* see. I see it all very clearly now. I see something else too! *Timmy* has found his way from the island, using that same passage you have just told us about – and *that's* why he's led us back here – to take us to the island and rescue Uncle Quentin and George.'

There was a deep silence. Martin stared at the ground. Dick and Julian thought hard. Anne sobbed a little. It all seemed quite unbelievable to her. Then Julian put his hand on Martin's arm.

'Martin! You did right to tell us. We may be able to prevent something dreadful. But you must help. We may need those spades of yours – and I expect you've got torches too. We haven't. We don't want to waste time going back and getting them – so will you come with us and help us? Will you lend us those spades and torches?'

'Would you trust me?' said Martin, in a low voice. 'Yes, I want to come and help you. And if we get in now, my guardian won't be able to follow, because he won't have a torch. We can get to the island and bring your uncle and George safely back.'

'Good for you!' said Dick. 'Well, come on then. We've been talking far too long. Come on down again, Ju. Hand him a spade and torch, Martin.'

'Anne you're not to come,' said Julian to his little sister. 'You're to go back and tell Aunt Fanny what's happened. Will you do that?'

'Yes. I don't want to come,' said Anne. 'I'll go back now. Do be careful, Julian!'

She climbed down with the boys and then stood and watched till all three had disappeared into the hole. Timmy, who had been waiting impatiently during the talking, barking now and again, was glad to find that at last they were going to make a move. He ran ahead in the tunnel, his eyes gleaming green every time he turned to see if they were following.

320

Anne began to climb up the steep side of the quarry again. Then, thinking she heard a cough, she stopped and crouched under a bush. She peered through the leaves and saw Mr Curton. Then she heard his voice.

'Martin! Where on earth are you?'

So he had come to look for Martin and go up the tunnel with him! Anne hardly dared to breathe. Mr Curton called again and again, then made an impatient noise and began to climb down the side of the quarry.

Suddenly he slipped! He clutched at a bush as he passed, but it gave way. He rolled quite near Anne, and caught sight of her. He looked astonished, but then his look became one of fear as he rolled more and more quickly to the bottom of the deep quarry. Anne heard him give a deep groan as at last he came to a stop.

Anne peered down in fright. Mr Curton was sitting up, holding one of his legs and groaning. He looked up to see if he could spy Anne.

'Anne!' he called. 'I've broken my leg, I think. Can you fetch help? What are you doing here so early? Have you seen Martin?'

Anne did not answer. If he had broken his leg, then he couldn't go after the others! And Anne could get away quickly. She climbed carefully, afraid of rolling down to the bottom, and having to lie beside the horrid Mr Curton.

'Anne! Have you seen Martin? Look for him and get help for me, will you?' shouted Mr Curton, and then groaned again.

Anne climbed to the top of the quarry and looked down. She cupped her hands round her mouth and shouted loudly:

'You're a very wicked man. I shan't fetch help for you. I simply can't *bear* you!'

And, having got all that off her chest, the little girl shot off at top speed over the moor.

'I must tell Aunt Fanny. She'll know what to do! Oh I hope the others are safe. What shall we do if the island blows up? I'm glad, glad, glad I told Mr Curton he was a very wicked man.'

And on she ran, panting. Aunt Fanny would know what to do!

322

20

Everything boils up!

Meanwhile the three boys and Timmy were having a strange journey underground. Timmy led the way without faltering, stopping every now and again for the others to catch up with him.

The tunnel at first had a very low roof and the boys had to walk along in a stooping position, which was very tiring indeed. But after a bit the roof became higher and Julian, flashing his torch round, saw that the walls and floor, instead of being made of soil, were now made of rock. He tried to reckon out where they were.

'We've come practically straight towards the cliff,' he said to Dick. 'That's allowing for a few turns and twists. The tunnel has sloped down so steeply the last few hundred yards that I think we must be very far underground indeed.'

It was not until the boys heard the curious booming noise that George had heard in the caves, that they knew they must be under the rocky bed of the sea. They were

323

walking under the sea to Kirrin Island. How strange, how unbelievably astonishing!

'It's like a peculiarly vivid dream,' said Julian. 'I'm not sure I like it very much! All right Tim – we're coming. Hallo – what's this?'

They all stopped. Julian flashed his torch ahead and saw a pile of fallen rocks. Timmy had managed to squeeze himself through a hole in them and go through to the other side, but the boys couldn't.

'This is where the spades come in, Martin!' said Dick, cheerfully. 'Take a hand!'

By dint of pushing and shovelling, the boys at last managed to move the pile of fallen rocks enough to make a way past. 'Thank goodness for the spades!' said Julian.

They went on, and were soon very glad of the spades again, to move another heap of rock. Timmy barked impatiently when they kept him waiting. He was very anxious to get back to George.

Soon they came to where the tunnel forked into two. But Timmy took the right-hand passage without hesitation, and when that one forked into three, he again chose one without stopping to think for a moment.

'Marvellous, isn't he?' said Julian. 'All done by smell! He's been this way once, so he knows it again. We should be completely lost under here if we came by ourselves.'

Martin was not enjoying this adventure at all. He said very little, but laboured on after the others. Dick guessed he was worrying about what was going to happen when the adventure was over. Poor Martin. All he wanted to do was to draw – and instead of that he had been dragged into one horrible job after another, and used as a cat's-paw by his evil guardian.

'Do you think we're anywhere near the island?' said Dick, at last. 'I'm getting tired of this!'

'Yes, we must be,' said Julian. 'In fact I think we'd

better be as quiet as we can, in case we come suddenly on the enemy!'

So, without speaking again, they went as quietly as they could – and then suddenly they saw a faint light ahead of them. Julian put out his hand to stop the others.

They were nearing the cave where George's father had his books and papers – where George had found him the night before. Timmy stood in front of them, listening too. He was not going to run headlong into danger!

They heard voices, and listened intently to see whose they were. 'George's – and Uncle Quentin's,' said Julian at last. And as if Timmy had also satisfied himself that those were indeed the two voices, the dog ran ahead and went into the lighted cave, barking joyfully.

'Timmy!' came George's voice, and they heard something overturn as she sprang up. 'Where have you been?'

'Woof,' said Timmy, trying to explain. 'Woof!'

And then Julian and Dick ran into the cave followed by Martin! Uncle Quentin and George stared in the very greatest amazement.

'Julian! Dick! And *Martin*! How did *you* get here?' cried George, while Timmy jumped and capered round her.

'I'll explain,' said Julian. 'It was Timmy that fetched us!' And he related the whole story of how Timmy had come into Kirrin Cottage in the early morning and had jumped on his bed, and all that had happened since.

And then, in their turn, Uncle Quentin and George told all that had happened to *them*!

'Where are the two men?' asked Julian.

'Somewhere on the island,' said George. 'I went scouting after them some time ago, and followed them up to where they get out into the little stone room. I think they're there until half past ten, when they'll go up and signal, so that people will think everything is all right.'

'Well, what are our plans?' said Julian. 'Will you come

back down the passage under the sea with us? Or what shall we do?'

'Better not do that,' said Martin, quickly. 'My guardian may be coming – and he's in touch with other men. If he wonders where I am, and thinks something is up, he may call in two or three others, and we might meet them making their way up the passage.'·

They did not know, of course, that Mr Curton was even then lying with a broken leg at the bottom of the quarry. Uncle Quentin considered.

'I've been given seven hours to say whether or not I will give the fellows my secret,' he said. 'That time will be up just after half past ten. Then the men will come down again to see me. I think between us we ought to be able to capture them – especially as we've got Timmy with us!'

'Yes – that's a good idea,' said Julian. 'We could hide somewhere till they come – and then set Timmy on them before they suspect anything!'

Almost before he had finished these words the light in the cave went out! Then a voice spoke out of the blackness.

'Keep still! One movement and I'll shoot.'

George gasped. What was happening? Had the men come back unexpectedly? Oh, why hadn't Timmy given them warning? She had been fondling his ears, so probably he had been unable to hear anything!

She held Timmy's collar, afraid that he would fly at the man in the darkness and be shot. The voice spoke again.

'Will you or will you not give us your secret?'

'Not,' said Uncle Quentin in a low voice.

'You will have this whole island, and all your work blown up then, and yourself too and the others?'

'Yes! You can do what you like!' suddenly yelled George. 'You'll be blown up yourself too. You'll never be able to get away in a boat – you'll go on the rocks!'

The man in the darkness laughed. 'We shall be safe,' he said. 'Now keep at the back of the cave. I have you covered with my revolver.'

They all crouched at the back. Timmy growled, but George made him stop at once. She did not know if the men knew he was free or not.

Quiet footsteps passed across the cave in the darkness. George listened, straining her ears. Two pairs of footsteps! Both men were passing through the cave. She knew where they were going! They were going to escape by the undersea passage – and leave the island to be blown up behind them!

As soon as the footsteps had died away, George switched on her torch. 'Father! Those men are escaping now, down the sea-tunnel. We must escape too – but not that way, My boat is on the shore. Let's get there quickly and get away before there's any explosion.'

'Yes, come along,' said her father. 'But if only I could get up into my tower, I could stop any wicked plan of theirs! They mean to use the power there. I know – but if I could get up to the glass room, I could undo all their plans!'

'Oh do be quick then, Father!' cried George, getting in quite a panic now. 'Save my island if you can!'

They all made their way through the cave up to the passage that led to the stone flight of steps from the little stone room. And there they had a shock!

The stone could not be opened from the inside! The men had altered the mechanism so that it could now only be opened from the outside.

In vain Uncle Quentin swung the lever to and fro. Nothing happened. The stone would not move.

'It's only from outside it can be opened,' he said in despair. 'We're trapped!'

They sat down on the stone steps in a row, one above the other. They were cold, hungry and miserable. What could they do now? Make their way back to the cave, and then go on down the under-sea tunnel?

'I don't want to do that,' said Uncle Quentin. 'I'm so afraid that if there is an explosion, it may crack the rocky bed of the sea, which is the roof of the tunnel – and then water would pour in. It wouldn't be pleasant if we happened to be there at that moment.'

'Oh no. Don't let's be trapped like that,' said George with a shudder. 'I couldn't bear it.'

328

'Perhaps I could get something to explode this stone away,' said her father, after a while. 'I've got plenty of stuff if only I've time to put it together.'

'Listen!' said Julian, suddenly. 'I can hear something outside this wall. Sh!'

They all listened intently. Timmy whined and scratched at the stone that would not move.

'It's voices!' cried Dick. 'Lots of them. Who can it be?'

'Be *quiet*,' said Julian, fiercely. 'We *must* find out!'

'I know, I know!' said George, suddenly. 'It's the fishermen who have come over in their boats! *That's* why the men didn't wait till half past ten! *That's* why they've gone in such a hurry! They saw the fisherboats coming!'

'Then Anne must have brought them!' cried Dick. 'She must have run home to Aunt Fanny, told her everything and given the news to the fishermen – and they've come to rescue us! Anne! ANNE! WE'RE HERE!'

Timmy began to bark deafeningly. The others encouraged him, because they felt certain that Timmy's bark was louder than their shouts!

'WOOF! WOOF! WOOF!'

Anne heard the barking and the shouting as soon as she ran into the little stone room. 'Where are you? Where are you?' she yelled.

'HERE! HERE! MOVE THE STONE!' yelled Julian, shouting so loudly that everyone near him jumped violently.

'Move aside, Miss – I can see which stone it is,' said a man's deep voice. It was one of the fishermen. He felt round and about the stone in the recess, sure it was the right one because it was cleaner than the others through being used as an entrance.

Suddenly he touched the right place, and found a tiny iron spike. He pulled it down – and the lever swung back behind it, and pulled the stone aside!

Everyone hurried out, one on top of the other! The six

fishermen standing in the little room stared in astonishment. Aunt Fanny was there too, and Anne. Aunt Fanny ran to her husband as soon as he appeared – but to her surprise he pushed her away quite roughly.

He ran out of the room, and hurried to the tower. Was he in time to save the island and everyone on it? Oh hurry, hurry!

21

The end of the adventure

'Where's he gone?' said Aunt Fanny, quite hurt. Nobody answered. Julian, George and Martin were watching the tower with anxious intensity. If only Uncle Quentin would appear at the top. Ah – there he was!

He had taken up with him a big stone. As everyone watched he smashed the glass round the tower with stone. Crash! Crash! Crash!

The wires that ran through the glass were broken and split as the glass crashed into pieces. No power could race through them now. Uncle Quentin leaned out of the broken glass room and shouted exultantly.

'It's all right! I was in time! I've destroyed the power that might have blown up the island – you're safe!'

George found that her knees were suddenly shaking. She had to sit down on the floor. Timmy came and licked her face wonderingly. Then he too sat down.

'What's he doing, smashing the tower up?' asked a burly fisherman. 'I don't understand all this.'

Uncle Quentin came down the tower and rejoined them. 'Another ten minutes and I should have been too late,' he said. 'Thank goodness, Anne, you all arrived when you did.'

'I ran all the way home, told Aunt Fanny, and we got the fishermen to come over as soon as they could get out their boats,' explained Anne. 'We couldn't think of any other way of rescuing you. Where are the wicked men?'

'Trying to escape down the under-sea tunnel,' said Julian. 'Oh – you don't know about that, Anne!' And he told her, while the fishermen listened open-mouthed.

'Look here,' said Uncle Quentin, when he had finished. 'As the boats are here, the men might as well take all my gear back with them. I've finished my job here. I shan't want the island any more.'

'Oh! Then *we* can have it!' said George, delighted. 'And there's plenty of the holidays left. We'll help to bring up what you want, Father.'

'We ought to get back as quickly as we can, so as to catch those fellows at the other end of the tunnel, sir,' said one of the fishermen.

'Yes. We ought,' said Aunt Fanny.

'Gracious! They'll find Mr Curton there with a broken leg,' said Anne, suddenly remembering.

The others looked at her in surprise. This was the first they had heard of Mr Curton being in the quarry. Anne explained.

'And I told him he was a very wicked man,' she ended triumphantly.

'Quite right,' said Uncle Quentin, with a laugh. 'Well, perhaps we'd better get my gear another time.'

'Oh, two of us can see to that for you now,' said the burly fisherman. 'Miss George here, she's got her boat in the cove, and you've got yours, sir. The others can go back with you, if you like – and Tom and me, we'll fix up your things and bring them across to the mainland later on. Save us coming over again, sir.'

'Right,' said Uncle Quentin, pleased. 'You do that then. It's down in the caves through that tunnel behind the stone.'

They all went down to the cove. It was a beautiful day and the sea was very calm, except just round the island where the waters were always rough. Soon the boats were being sailed or rowed to the mainland.

'The adventure is over!' said Anne. 'How queer – I didn't think it was one while it was happening – but now I see it was!'

'Another to add to our long list of adventures,' said Julian. 'Cheer up, Martin – don't look so blue. Whatever happens, we'll see you don't come out badly over this. You helped us, and you threw in your lot with us. We'll see that you don't suffer – won't we, Uncle Quentin? We'd never have got through those falls of rock if we hadn't had Martin and his spades!'

'Well – thanks,' said Martin. 'If you can get me away from my guardian – and never let me see him again – I'll be happy!'

'It's quite likely that Mr Curton will be put somewhere safe where he won't be able to see his friends for quite a long time,' said Uncle Quentin dryly. 'So I don't think you need worry.'

As soon as the boats reached shore, Julian, Dick, Timmy and Uncle Quentin went off to the quarry to see if Mr Curton was still there – and to wait for the other two men to come out of the tunnel!

Mr Curton was there all right, still groaning and calling for help. Uncle Quentin spoke to him sternly.

'We know your part in this matter, Curton. You will be dealt with by the police. They will be along in a short while.'

Timmy sniffed round Mr Curton, and then walked

away, nose in air, as if to say 'What a nasty bit of work!' The others arranged themselves at the mouth of the hole and waited.

But nobody came. An hour went by – two hours. Still nobody. 'I'm glad Martin and Anne didn't come,' said Uncle Quentin. 'I do wish we'd brought sandwiches.'

At that moment the police arrived, scrambling down the steep sides of the quarry. The police doctor was with them and he saw to Mr Curton's leg. Then, with the help of the others, he got the man to the top with great difficulty.

'Julian, go back and get sandwiches,' said Uncle Quentin at last. 'It looks as if we've got a long wait!'

Julian went back, and was soon down the quarry with neat packets of ham sandwiches and a thermos of hot coffee. The two policemen who were still left offered to stay and watch, if Uncle Quentin wanted to go home.

'Dear me, no!' he said. 'I want to see the faces of these two fellows when they come out. It's going to be one of the nicest moments of my life! The island is not blown up. My secret is safe. My book is safe. My work is finished. And I just want to tell these things to my two dear friends!'

'You know, Father, I believe they've lost their way underground,' said George. 'Julian said there were many different passages. Timmy took the boys through the right ones, of course – but they would have been quite lost if they hadn't had him with them!'

Her father's face fell at the thought of the men being lost underground. He did so badly want to see their dismayed faces when they arrived in the quarry!

'We could send Timmy in,' said Julian. 'He would soon find them and bring them out. Wouldn't you, Tim?'

'Woof,' said Timmy, agreeing.

'Oh yes – that's a good idea,' said George. 'They won't hurt him if they think he can show them the way out! Go in in, Timmy. Find them boy; find them! Bring them here!'

'Woof,' said Timmy, obligingly, and disappeared under the shelf of rock.

Everyone waited, munching sandwiches and sipping coffee. And then they heard Timmy's bark again, from underground!

There was a panting noise, then a scraping sound as

somebody came wriggling out from under the rock. He stood up – and then he saw the silent group watching him. He gasped.

'Good morning, Johnson,' said Uncle Quentin, in an amiable voice. 'How are you?'

Johnson went white. He sat down on the nearby heather. 'You win!' he said.

'I do,' said Uncle Quentin. 'In fact, I win handsomely. Your little plan went wrong. My secret is still safe – and next year it will be given to the whole world!'

There was another scraping sound and the second man arrived. He stood up too – and then he saw the quietly watching group.

'Good morning, Peters,' said Uncle Quentin. 'So nice to see you again. How did you like your underground walk? We found it better to come by sea.'

Peters looked at Johnson, and he too sat down suddenly. 'What's happened?' he said to Johnson.

'It's all up,' said Johnson. Then Timmy appeared, wagging his tail, and went to George.

'I bet they were glad when Timmy came up to them!' said Julian.

Johnson looked at him. 'Yes. We were lost in those hateful tunnels. Curton said he'd come to meet us, but he never came.'

'No. He's probably in the prison hospital by now, with a broken leg,' said Uncle Quentin. 'Well, constable – do your duty.'

Both men were at once arrested. Then the whole company made their way back over the moor. The two men were put into a police car and driven off. The rest of the company went into Kirrin Cottage to have a good meal.

'I'm most terribly hungry,' said George. 'Joanna, have you got anything nice for breakfast?'

'Not much,' said Joanna, from the kitchen. 'Only bacon and eggs and mushrooms!'

336

'Ooooh!' said Anne, 'Joanna, you shall have the OBCBE!'

'And what may that be?' cried Joanna, but Anne couldn't remember.

'It's a decoration!' she cried.

'Well, I'm not a Christmas tree!' shouted back Joanna. 'You come and help with the breakfast!'

It was a very jolly breakfast that the seven of them – no eight, for Timmy must certainly be counted – sat down to. Martin, now that he was free of his guardian, became quite a different boy.

The children made plans for him. 'You can stay with the coastguard, because he likes you – he kept on and on saying you weren't a bad boy! And you can come and play with us and go to the island. And Uncle Quentin will see if he can get you into an art-school. He says you deserve a reward for helping to save his wonderful secret!'

Martin glowed with pleasure. It seemed as if a load had fallen away from his shoulders. 'I've never had a chance till now,' he said, 'I'll make good. You see if I don't!'

'Mother! Can we go and stay on Kirrin Island and watch the tower being taken down tomorrow?' begged George. 'Do say yes! And can we stay there a whole week? We can sleep in that little room as we did before.'

'Well – I suppose you can!' said her mother, smiling at George's eager face. 'I'd rather like to have your father to myself for a few days and feed him up a bit.'

'Oh – that reminds me, Fanny,' said her husband, suddenly. 'I tried some soup you left for me, the night before last. And my dear, it was horrible! Quite bad!'

'Oh *Quentin*! I told you to pour it away! You know I did,' said his wife, distressed. 'It must have been completely bad. You really are dreadful.'

They all finished their breakfast at last, and went out into the garden. They looked across Kirrin Bay to Kirrin Island. It looked lovely in the morning sun.

'We've had a lot of adventures together,' said Julian. 'More than most children. They *have* been exciting, haven't they?'

Yes – they have, but now we must say good-bye to the Five, and to Kirrin Island too. Good-bye, Julian, Dick, George, Anne – and Timmy. But only Timmy hears our good-bye, for he has such sharp ears.

Enid Blyton's

FIVE GO OFF TO CAMP

ILLUSTRATED BY JOLYNE KNOX

CONTENTS

CONTENTS

1
Holiday time

'Two jolly fine tents, four groundsheets, four sleeping-bags – I say, what about Timmy? Isn't he going to have a sleeping-bag too?' said Dick, with a grin.

The other three children laughed, and Timmy, the dog, thumped his tail hard on the ground.

'Look at him,' said George. 'He's laughing, too! He's got his mouth stretched wide open.'

They all looked at Timmy. He really did look as if a wide grin stretched his hairy mouth from side to side.

'He's a darling,' said Anne, hugging him. 'Best dog in the world, aren't you, Timmy?'

'Woof!' said Timmy, agreeing. He gave Anne a wet lick on her nose.

The four children, Julian, tall and strong for his age, Dick, George and Anne were busy planning a camping holiday. George was a girl, not a boy, but she would never answer to her real name, Georgina. With her freckled face and short, curly hair she really did look more like a boy than a girl.

343

'It's absolutely wizard, being allowed to go on a camping holiday all by ourselves,' said Dick. 'I never thought our parents would allow it, after the terrific adventure we had last summer, when we went off in caravans.'

'Well – we shan't be *quite* all by ourselves,' said Anne. 'Don't forget we've got Mr Luffy to keep an eye on us. He'll be camping quite near.'

'Pooh! Old Luffy!' said Dick, with a laugh. 'He won't know if we're there or not. So long as he can study his precious moorland insects, he won't bother about us.'

'Well, if it hadn't been that he was going to camp, too, we wouldn't have been allowed to go,' said Anne. 'I heard Daddy say so.'

Mr Luffy was a master at the boys' school, an elderly, dreamy fellow with a passion for studying all kinds of insect-life. Anne avoided him when he carried about boxes of insect specimens, because sometimes they escaped and came crawling out. The boys liked him and thought him fun, but the idea of Mr Luffy keeping an eye on them struck them as very comical.

'It's more likely we'll have to keep an eye on *him*,' said Julian. 'He's the sort of chap whose tent will always be falling down on top of him, or he'll run out of water, or sit down on his bag of eggs. Old Luffy seems to live in the world of insects, not in our world!'

'Well, he can go and live in the world of insects if he likes, so long as he doesn't interfere with *us*,' said George, who hated interfering people. 'This sounds as if it will be a super holiday – living in tents on the high moors, away from everybody, doing exactly what we like, when we like and how we like.'

'Woof!' said Timmy, thumping his tail again.

'That means he's going to do as *he* likes, too,' said Anne. 'You're going to chase hundreds of rabbits, aren't you, Timmy, and bark madly at anyone who dares to come within two miles of us!'

344

'Now be quiet a minute, Anne!' said Dick, picking up his list again. 'We really must check down our list and find out if we've got every single thing we want. Where did I get to – oh, four sleeping-bags.'

'Yes, and you wanted to know if Timmy was to have one,' said Anne, with a giggle.

'Of course he won't,' said George. 'He'll sleep where he always does – won't you, Timmy? On my feet.'

'Couldn't we get him just a *small* sleeping-bag?' asked Anne. 'He'd look sweet with his head poking out of the top.'

'Timmy hates looking sweet,' said George. 'Go on, Dick. I'll tie my hanky round Anne's mouth if she interrupts again.'

Dick went on down his list. It was a very interesting one. Things like cooking-stoves, canvas buckets, enamel plates and drinking-cups were on it and each item seemed to

345

need a lot of discussion. The four children enjoyed themselves very much.

'You know, it's almost as much fun planning a holiday
like this as having it,' said Dick. 'Well – I shouldn't think
we've forgotten a thing, have we?'

'No. We've probably thought of too much!' said Julian.
'Well, old Luffy says he'll take all our things on the trailer
behind his car, so we'll be all right. I shouldn't like to carry
them ourselves!'

'Oh, I wish next week would come!' said Anne. 'Why is
it that the time seems so long when you're waiting for
something nice to happen, and so short when something
nice *is* happening?'

'Yes – it seems the wrong way round, doesn't it?' said
Dick, with a grin. 'Anyone got the map? I'd like to take
another squint at the spot where we're going.'

Julian produced a map from his pocket. He opened it
and the four children sprawled round it. The map showed
a vast and lonely stretch of moorland, with very few
houses indeed.

'Just a few small farms, that's all,' said Julian pointing
to one or two. 'They can't get much of a living out of such
poor land, though. See, that's about the place where we're
going – just there – and on the opposite slope is a small
farm where we shall get milk, eggs and butter when we
need them. Luffy's been there before. He says it's a rather
small farm, but jolly useful to campers.'

'These moors are awfully high, aren't they?' said
George. 'I guess they'll be freezing cold in the winter.'

'They are,' said Julian. 'And they may be jolly windy
and cold in the summer, too, so Luffy says we'd better take
sweaters and things. He says in the winter they are
covered with snow for months. The sheep have to be dug
out when they get lost.'

Dick's finger followed a small winding road that made
its way over the wild stretch of moorland. 'That's the road

we go,' he said. 'And I suppose we strike off here, look, where a cart-track is shown. That would go to the farm. We shall have to carry our stuff from wherever Luffy parks his car, and take it to our camping-place.'

'Not too near Luffy, I hope,' said George.

'Oh, no. He's agreed to keep an eye on us, but he'll forget all about us once he's settled down in his own tent,' said Julian. 'He will, really. Two chaps I know once went out in his car with him for a day's run, and he came back without them in the evening. He'd forgotten he had them with him, and had left them wandering somewhere miles and miles away.'

'Good old Luffy,' said Dick. 'That's the sort of fellow we want! He won't come sprinting up to ask if we've cleaned our teeth or if we've got our warm jerseys on!'

The others laughed, and Timmy stretched his doggy mouth into a grin again. His tongue hung out happily. It was good to have all four of his friends with him again, and to hear them planning a holiday. Timmy went to school with George and Anne in term time, and he missed the two boys very much. But he belonged to George, and would not dream of leaving her. It was a good thing that George's school allowed pets, or George would certainly not have gone!

Julian folded up the map again. 'I hope all the things we've ordered will come in good time,' he said. 'We've got about six days to wait. I'd better keep on reminding Luffy that we're going with him, or he's quite likely to start without us!'

It was difficult to have to wait so long now that every-thing was planned. Parcels came from various stores and were eagerly opened. The sleeping-bags were fine.

'Super!' said Anne.

'Smashing!' said George, crawling into hers. 'Look! I can lace it up at the neck – and it's got a hood thing to come right over my head. Golly, it's warm! I shan't mind the coldest night if I'm sleeping in this. I vote we sleep in them tonight.'

'What? In our bedrooms?' said Anne.

'Yes. Why not? Just to get used to them,' said George, who felt that a sleeping-bag was a hundred times better than an ordinary bed.

So that night all four slept on the floor of their bedrooms in their sleeping-bags, and voted them very comfortable and as warm as toast.

'The only thing is, Timmy kept wanting to come right inside mine,' said George, 'and honestly there isn't enough room. Besides, he'd be cooked.'

'Well, he seemed to spend half the night on my tummy,' grumbled Julian. 'I shall jolly well keep the bedroom door shut if Timmy's going to spend the night flopping on everyone's bag in turn.'

'I don't mind the flopping, so much as the frightful habit he's got of turning himself round and round and round before he flops down,' complained Dick. 'He did that on me last night. Silly habit of his.'

'He can't help it,' said George at once. 'It's a habit that wild dogs had centuries and centuries ago – they slept in reeds and rushes, and they got into the way of turning themselves round and round in them, to trample them down and make themselves a good sleeping-place. And our dogs go on turning themselves round now, before they go to sleep, even though there aren't any rushes to trample down.'

'Well! I wish Timmy would forget his doggy ancestors were wild dogs with rushy beds, and just remember he's a nice tame dog with a basket of his own,' said Dick. 'You should see my tummy today! It's all printed over with his foot-marks.'

'Fibber!' said Anne. 'You do exaggerate, Dick. Oh, I do wish Tuesday would come. I'm tired of waiting.'

'It'll come all right,' said Julian. And so, it did, of

348

course. It dawned bright and sunny, with a sky that was a deep blue, flecked with tiny white clouds.

'Good-weather clouds,' said Julian, pleased. 'Now let's hope old Luffy has remembered it's today we're starting off. He's due here at ten o'clock. We're taking sandwiches for the whole party. Mother thought we'd better, in case Luffy forgot his. If he's remembered them it won't matter, because we're sure to be able to eat them ourselves. And there's always Timmy to finish things up!'

Timmy was as excited as the four children. He always knew when something nice was going to happen. His tail was on the wag the whole time, his tongue hung out, and he panted as if he had been running a race. He kept getting under everyone's feet, but nobody minded.

Mr Luffy arrived half an hour late, just when everyone was beginning to feel he had forgotten to come. He was at the wheel of his big old car, beaming. All the children knew him quite well, because he lived not far away and often came to play bridge with their father and mother.

'Hallo, hallo!' he cried. 'All ready, I see! Good for you! Pile the things on the trailer, will you? Mine are there too but there's plenty of room. I've got sandwiches for everyone, by the way. My wife said I'd better bring plenty.'

'We'll have a fine feast today then,' said Dick, helping Julian to carry out the folded-up tents and sleeping-bags, while the girls followed with the smaller things. Soon everything was on the trailer and Julian made them safe with ropes.

They said good-bye to the watching grown-ups and climbed excitedly into the car. Mr Luffy started up his engine and put the lever into first gear with a frightful noise.

'Good-bye!' called all the grown-ups, and Julian's mother added a last word. 'DON'T get into any awful adventure this time!'

'Of course they won't!' called back Mr Luffy cheerfully.

'I'll see to that. There are no adventures to be found on a wild and deserted moor. Good-bye!'

Off they went, waving madly, and shouting good-bye all the way down the road. 'Good-bye! Good-byeeeeee! Hurrah, we're off at last!'

The car raced down the road, the trailer bumping madly after it. The holiday had begun!

2

Up on the moors

Mr Luffy was not a good driver. He went too fast, especially round the corners, and many times Julian looked behind at the trailer in alarm, afraid that every-thing would suddenly leap off it at some sharp bend.

He saw the bundle of sleeping-bags jump high into the air, but fortunately they remained on the trailer. He touched Mr Luffy on the shoulder.

'Sir! Could you go a bit slower, please! The trailer will be empty by the time we arrive, if the luggage leaps about on it much more.'

'My word! I forgot we had a trailer,' said Mr Luffy, slowing down at once. 'Remind me if I go over thirty-five miles an hour, will you? Last time I took the trailer with me, I arrived with only half the goods on it. I don't want that to happen again.'

Julian certainly hoped it wouldn't. He kept a sharp eye on the speedometer, and when it veered towards forty he tapped Mr Luffy on the arm.

Mr Luffy looked supremely happy. He didn't like term

time, but he loved holidays. Term time interfered with the study of his beloved insect-world. Now he was off with four nice children he liked, for a holiday on a moorland he knew was alive with bees, beetles, butterflies and every other kind of insect he wanted. He looked forward to teaching the four children quite a lot. They would have been horrified if they guessed this, but they didn't.

He was an odd-looking fellow. He had very untidy, shaggy eyebrows over kind and gentle brown eyes that always reminded Dick of a monkey's. He had a rather large nose, which looked fiercer than it was because, unexpectedly, it had quite a forest of hairs growing out of the nostrils. He had an untidy moustache, and a round chin with a surprising dimple in the middle of it.

His ears always fascinated Anne. They were large and turned rather forward, and Mr Luffy could waggle the right one if he wanted to. To his great sorrow he had never been able to waggle the left one. His hair was thick and untidy, and his clothes always looked loose, comfortable and rather too big for him.

The children liked him. They couldn't help it. He was so odd and gentle and untidy and forgetful – and yet sometimes unexpectedly fierce. Julian had often told them the story of Tom Killin the bully.

Mr Luffy had once found Tom bullying a small new boy in the cloakroom, dragging him round and round it by his belt. With a roar like an angry bull, Mr Luffy had pounced on the big bully, got him by the belt, lifted him up and stuck him firmly on a peg in the cloakroom.

'There you stay till you get someone to lift you down!' Mr Luffy had thundered, 'I can get hold of a belt too, as you can see!'

And then he had stalked out of the cloakroom with the small, terrified boy beside him, leaving the bully hung up high on the peg, quite unable to free himself. And there he

352

had to stay, because not one of the boys who came pouring in from a game of football would lift him down.

'And, if the peg hadn't given way under his weight, he'd be stuck up there still,' Julian had said with a grin. 'Good old Luffy! You'd never think he could be fierce like that, would you?'

Anne loved that story. Mr Luffy became quite a hero to her after that. She was pleased to sit next to him in the car, and chatter about all kinds of things. The other three were squashed at the back with Timmy on their feet. George firmly prevented him from climbing up on her knee because it was so hot. So he contented himself with trying to stand up with his paws on the window-ledge and his nose over the side.

They stopped about half past twelve for lunch. Mr Luffy had indeed provided sandwiches for everyone. And remarkably fine ones they were too, made the evening before by Mrs Luffy.

'Cucumber, dipped in vinegar! Ham and lettuce! Egg! Sardine! Oooh, Mr Luffy, your sandwiches are much nicer than ours,' said Anne, beginning on two together, one cucumber and the other ham and lettuce.

They were all very hungry. Timmy had a bit from everyone, usually the last bite, and watched each sandwich eagerly till his turn came. Mr Luffy didn't seem to understand that Timmy had to have the last bite of any sandwich, so Timmy simply took it out of his hand, much to his surprise.

'A clever dog,' he said, and patted him. 'Knows what he wants and takes it. Very clever.'

That pleased George, of course. She thought that Timmy was the cleverest dog in the world, and indeed it did seem like it at times. He understood every word she said to him, every pat, every stroke, every gesture. He would be much, much better at keeping an eye on the four children and guarding them than forgetful Mr Luffy.

They drank ginger-beer and then ate some ripe plums. Timmy wouldn't have any plums, but he licked up some spilt ginger-beer. Then he snuffled up a few odd crumbs and went to drink at a little stream nearby.

The party set off again in the car. Anne fell asleep. Dick gave an enormous yawn and fell asleep too. George wasn't sleepy, nor was Timmy, but Julian was. He didn't dare to take his eye off the speedometer, though, because Mr Luffy seemed to be very much inclined to speed along too fast again, after his good lunch.

'We won't stop for tea till we get there,' said Mr Luffy suddenly, and Dick woke up with a jump at the sound of his booming voice. 'We should be there about half past five. Look, you can see the moorland in the distance now – all ablaze with heather!'

Everybody looked ahead, except Anne, who was still fast asleep. Rising up to the left for miles upon miles was the heather-covered moorland, a lovely sight to see. It looked wild and lonely and beautiful, blazing with heather, and shading off into a purple-blue in the distance.

'We take this road to the left, and then we're on the moors,' said Mr Luffy, swinging violently to the left, and making the luggage in the trailer jump high again. 'Here we go.'

The car climbed the high moorland road steadily. It passed one or two small houses, and in the distance the children could see little farms in clearings. Sheep dotted the moorland, and some of them stood staring at the car as it drove by.

'We've got about twenty miles to go, I should think,' said Mr Luffy, jamming on his brakes suddenly to avoid two large sheep in the middle of the road. 'I wish these creatures wouldn't choose the centre of the road to gossip in. Hi, get on there! Let me pass!'

Timmy yelped and tried to get out of the car. The sheep

hurriedly decided to move, and the car went on. Anne was thoroughly awake by now, having been almost jerked out of her seat by the sudden stop.

'What a shame to wake you!' said Mr Luffy, gazing down at her kindly, and almost running into a ditch by the side of the road. 'We're nearly there, Anne.'

They climbed steadily, and the wind grew a little cold. All around the children the moors stretched for mile upon mile, never-ending. Little streams sometimes splashed right down to the roadway, and ran beside it.

'We can drink the water in these streams,' said Mr Luffy. 'Crystal clear, and cold as ice! There's one quite near where we're going to camp.'

That was good news. Julian thought of the big canvas buckets they had brought. He didn't particularly want to carry those for miles. If there was a stream near their camping place it would be easy to get the buckets filled with washing-water.

The road forked into two. To the right was a good road, leading on and on. To the left it became not much more than a cart-track. 'That's the one we take,' said Mr Luffy, and the car jerked and jolted over it. He was forced to go slowly, and the children had time to see every little thing they passed.

'I shall leave the car here,' said Mr Luffy, bringing it to a standstill beside a great rock that stood up bare and grey out of the moor. 'It will be sheltered from the worst winds and rain. I thought we'd camp over yonder.'

There was a little slope just there, backed by some enormous gorse bushes. Thick heather grew everywhere. Julian nodded. It was a good place for camping. Those thick gorse bushes would provide fine shelter from the winds.

'Right, sir,' he said. 'Shall we have tea first, or unpack now?'

'Tea first,' said Mr Luffy. 'I've brought a very good

little stove for boiling and cooking things. Better than a wood fire. That makes kettles and saucepans so black.'

'We've got a stove, too,' said Anne. She scrambled out of the car and looked all round. 'It's lovely here – all heather and wind and sun! Is that the farm over there – the one we shall go to for eggs and things?'

She pointed to a tiny farmhouse on the hill opposite. It stood in a small clearing. In a field behind it were three or four cows and a horse. A small orchard stood at the side, and a vegetable garden lay in front. It seemed odd to see such a trim little place in the midst of the moorland.

'That's Olly's Farm,' said Mr Luffy. 'It's changed hands, I believe, since I was here three years ago. I hope the new people are nice. Now – did we leave something to eat for our tea?'

They had, because Anne had wisely put away a good many sandwiches and bits of cake for tea-time. They sat in the heather, with bees humming all round them, and munched solidly for fifteen minutes. Timmy waited patiently for his bits, watching the bees that hummed round him. There were thousands of them.

'And now I suppose we'd better put up our tents,' said Julian. 'Come on, Dick – let's unpack the trailer. Mr Luffy, we don't intend to camp on top of you, sir, because you won't want four noisy children too near. Where would you like your tent put?'

Mr Luffy was about to say that he would like to have the four children and Timmy quite close, when it suddenly occurred to him that perhaps they might not want him too near. They might want to make a noise, or play silly games, and if he were near it would stop them enjoying themselves in their own way.

So he made up his mind not to be too close. 'I'll pitch my tent down there, where that old gorse bush is,' he said. 'And if you'd like to put yours up here, where there's a

356

half-circle of gorse bushes keeping off the wind, you'd be well sheltered. And we shan't interfere with one another at all.'

'Right, sir,' said Julian, and he and Dick began to tackle the tents. It was fun. Timmy got under everyone's feet as usual, and ran off with an important rope, but nobody minded.

By the time that dusk came creeping up the heather-covered moorland, all three tents were up, the ground-sheets were put down, and the sleeping-bags unrolled on them, two in each of the children's tents, and one in Mr Luffy's.

'I'm going to turn in,' said Mr Luffy. 'My eyes are almost shut. Good night all of you. Sleep well!'

He disappeared into the dusk. Anne yawned widely, and that set the others off too. 'Come on – let's turn in, too,' said Julian. 'We'll have a bar of chocolate each, and a few biscuits. We can eat those in our sleeping-bags. Good-night, girls. Won't it be grand to wake up tomorrow morning?'

He and Dick disappeared into their tent. The girls crawled into theirs with Timmy. They undressed, and got into their warm, soft sleeping-bags.

'This is super!' said George, pushing Timmy to one side. 'I never felt so cosy in my life. *Don't* do that, Timmy. Don't you know the difference between my feet and my middle? That's better.'

'Good night,' said Anne, sleepily. 'Look, George, you can see the stars shining through the opening of the tent. Don't they look enormous?'

But George didn't care whether they were enormous or not. She was fast asleep, tired out with the day's run. Timmy cocked one ear when he heard Anne's voice, and gave a little grunt. That was his way of saying good night. Then he put his head down and slept.

'Our first night of camping,' thought Anne, happily. 'I

357

shan't go to sleep. I shall lie awake and look at the stars and smell that heathery smell.'

But she didn't. In half a second she was sound asleep, too!

3

Anne's volcano

Julian awoke first in the morning. He heard a strange and lonely sound floating overhead. 'Coor-lie! Coor-lie!'

He sat up and wondered where he was and who was calling. Of course! He was in his tent with Dick – they were camping on the moors. And that wild cry overhead came from a curlew, the bird of the moorlands.

He yawned and lay down again. It was early in the morning. The sun put its warm fingers in at his tent opening, and he felt the warmth on his sleeping-bag. He felt lazy and snug and contented. He also felt hungry, which was a nuisance. He glanced at his watch.

Half past six. He really was too warm and comfortable to get up yet. He put out his hand to see if there was any chocolate left from the night before, and found a little piece. He put it into his mouth and lay there contentedly, listening to more curlews, and watching the sun climb a little higher.

He fell asleep again, and was awakened by Timmy busily licking his face. He sat up with a start. The girls were peering in at his tent, grinning. They were fully dressed already.

'Wake up, lazy!' said Anne. 'We sent Timmy in to get you up. It's half past seven. We've been up for ages.'

'It's a simply heavenly morning,' said George. 'Going to be a frightfully hot day. Do get up. We're going to find the stream and wash in it. It seems silly to lug heavy buckets of water to and fro for washing, if the stream's nearby.'

Dick awoke too. He and Julian decided to go and take a bathe in the stream. They wandered out into the sunny morning, feeling very happy and very hungry. The girls were just coming back from the stream.

'It's over there,' said Anne, pointing. 'Timmy, go with them and show them. It's a lovely little brown stream, awfully cold, and it's got ferns along its banks. We've left the bucket there. Bring it back full, will you?'

'What do you want us to do that for, if you've already washed?' asked Dick.

'We want water for washing-up the dishes,' said Anne. 'I suddenly remembered we'd need water for that. I say, do you think we ought to wake up Mr Luffy? There's no sign of him yet.'

'No, let him sleep,' said Julian. 'He's probably tired out with driving the car so slowly! We can easily save him some breakfast. What are we going to have?'

'We've unpacked some bacon rashers and tomatoes,' said Anne, who was a very good little housewife and loved cooking. 'How do you light the stove, Julian?'

'George knows,' said Julian. 'I say, did we pack a frying-pan?'

'Yes. I packed it myself,' said Anne. 'Do go and bathe if you're going to. Breakfast will be ready before you are!'

Timmy gravely trotted off with the boys and showed them the stream. Julian and Dick at once lay down in the clear brown bed, and kicked wildly. Timmy leapt in too, and there were yells and shrieks.

'Well – I should think we've woken up old Luffy now!' said Dick, rubbing himself down with a rough towel. 'How lovely and cold that was. The trouble is it's made me feel twice as hungry!'

'Doesn't that frying bacon smell good?' said Julian, sniffing the air. They walked back to the girls. There was still no sign of Mr Luffy. He must indeed sleep very soundly!

They sat down in the heather and began their breakfast. Anne had fried big rounds of bread in the fat, and the boys told her she was the best cook in the world. She was very pleased.

'I shall look after the food side for you,' she said. 'But George must help with the preparing of the meals and washing-up. See, George?'

George didn't see. She hated doing all the things that girls had to do, such as making beds and washing-up. She looked sulky.

'Look at old George! Why bother about the washing-up when there's Timmy only too pleased to use his tongue to wash every plate?' said Dick.

Everyone laughed, even George. 'All right,' she said, 'I'll help of course. Only let's use as few plates as possible, then there won't be much washing-up. Is there any more fried bread, Anne?'

'No. But there are some biscuits in that tin,' said Anne. 'I say, boys, who's going to go to the farm each day for milk and things? I expect they can let us have bread, too, and fruit.'

'Oh, one or other of us will go,' said Dick. 'Anne, hadn't you better fry something for old Luffy now? I'll go and wake him. Half the day will be gone if he doesn't get up now.'

'I'll go and make a noise like an earwig outside his tent,'

361

said Julian, getting up. 'He might not wake with all our yells and shouts, but he'd certainly wake at the call of a friendly earwig!'

He went down to the tent. He cleared his throat and called politely: 'Are you awake yet, sir?'

There was no answer. Julian called again. Then, puzzled, he went to the tent opening. The flap was closed. He pulled it aside and looked in.

The tent was empty! There was nobody there at all.

'What's up, Ju?' called Dick.

'He's not here,' said Julian. 'Where can he be?'

There was a silence. For a panic-stricken moment Anne thought one of their queer adventures was beginning. Then Dick called out again: 'Is his bug-tin gone? You know, the tin box with straps that he takes with him when he goes insect-hunting? And what about his clothes?'

Julian inspected the inside of the tent again. 'Okay!' he called, much to everyone's relief. 'His clothes are gone, and so has his bug-tin. He must have slipped out early before we were awake. I bet he's forgotten all about us and breakfast and everything!'

'That would be just like him,' said Dick. 'Well, we're not his keepers. He can do as he likes! If he doesn't want breakfast, he needn't have any. He'll come back when he's finished his hunting, I suppose.'

'Anne! Can you get on with the doings if Dick and I go to the farmhouse and see what food they've got?' asked Julian. 'The time's getting on, and if we're going for a walk or anything today, we don't want to start too late.'

'Right,' said Anne. 'You go too, George. I can manage everything nicely, now that the boys have brought me a bucketful of water. Take Timmy. He wants a walk.'

George was only too pleased to get out of the washing-up. She and the boys, with Timmy trotting in front, set off to the farmhouse. Anne got on with her jobs, humming

362

softly to herself in the sunshine. She soon finished them, and then looked to see if the others were coming back. There was no sign of them, or of Mr Luffy either.

'I'll go for a walk on my own,' thought Anne. 'I'll follow that little stream uphill and see where it begins. That would be fun. I can't possibly lose my way if I keep by the water.'

She set off in the sunshine and came to the little brown stream that gurgled down the hill. She scrambled through the heather beside it, following its course uphill. She liked all the little green ferns and the cushions of velvety moss that edged it. She tasted the water – it was cold and sweet and clean.

Feeling very happy all by herself, Anne walked on and on. She came at last to a big mound of a hill-top. The little stream began there, half-way up the mound. It came gurgling out of the heathery hillside, edged with moss, and made its chattering way far down the hill.

'So that's where you begin, is it?' said Anne. She flung herself down on the heather, hot with her climb. It was nice there, with the sun on her face, and the sound of the trickling water nearby.

She lay listening to the humming bees and the water. And then she heard another sound. She took no notice of it at all at first.

Then she sat up, frightened. 'The noise is underground! Deep, deep underground! It rumbles and roars. Oh, what is going to happen? Is there going to be an earthquake!'

The rumbling seemed to come nearer and nearer. Anne didn't even dare to get up and run. She sat there and trembled.

Then there came an unearthly shriek, and not far off a most astonishing thing happened. A great cloud of white smoke came right out of the ground and hung in the air before the wind blew it away. Anne was simply horrified. It was so sudden, so very unexpected on this quiet hillside.

The rumbling noise went on for a while and then gradually faded away.

Anne leapt to her feet in a panic. She fled down the hill, screaming loudly: 'It's a volcano! Help! Help! I've been sitting on a volcano. It's going to burst, it's sending out smoke. Help, help, it's a VOLCANO!'

She tore down the hillside, caught her foot on a tuft of heather and went rolling over and over, sobbing. She came to rest at last, and then heard an anxious voice calling:

'Who's that? What's the matter?'

It was Mr Luffy's voice. Anne screamed to him in relief. 'Mr Luffy! Come and save me! There's a volcano here!'

There was such terror in her voice that Mr Luffy came racing to her at once. He sat down beside the trembling girl and put his arm round her. 'Whatever's the matter?' he said. 'What's frightened you?'

Anne told him again. 'Up there – do you see? That's a volcano, Mr Luffy. It trembled and rumbled and then it shot up clouds of smoke. Oh quick, before it sends out red hot cinders!'

'Now, now!' said Mr Luffy, and to Anne's surprise and relief he actually laughed. 'Do you mean to tell me you don't know what that was?'

'No, I don't,' said Anne.

'Well,' said Mr Luffy, 'under this big moor run two or three long tunnels to take trains from one valley to another. Didn't you know? They make the rumbling noise you heard, and the sudden smoke you saw was the smoke sent up by a train below. There are big vent-holes here and there in the moor for the smoke to escape from.'

'Oh, good gracious me!' said Anne, going rather red. 'I didn't even *know* there were trains under here. What an extraordinary thing! I really did think I was sitting on a volcano, Mr Luffy. You won't tell the others will you. They would laugh at me dreadfully.'

364

'I won't say a word,' said Mr Luffy. 'And now I think we'll go back. Have you had breakfast? I'm terribly hungry. I went out early after a rather rare butterfly I saw flying by my tent.'

'We've had breakfast *ages* ago,' said Anne. 'But if you like to come back with me now I'll cook you some bacon, Mr Luffy. And some tomatoes and fried bread.'

'Aha! It sounds good,' said Mr Luffy. 'Now – not a word about volcanoes. That's our secret.'

And off they went to the tents, where the others were wondering what in the world had become of Anne. Little did they know she had been 'sitting on a volcano!'

4

Spook-trains

The boys and George were full of talk about the farm. 'It's a nice little place,' said Julian, sitting down while Anne began to cook breakfast for Mr Luffy. 'Pretty farmhouse, nice little dairy, well-kept sheds. And even a grand piano in the drawing-room.'

'Gracious! You wouldn't think they'd make enough money to buy a thing like that, would you?' said Anne, turning over the bacon in the pan.

'The farmer's got a fine new car,' went on Julian. 'Brand new. Must have cost him a pretty penny. His boy showed it to us. And he showed us some jolly good new farm machinery too.'

'Very interesting,' said Mr Luffy. 'I wonder how they make their money, farming that bit of land? The last people were hard-working folk, but they certainly couldn't have afforded a new car or a grand piano.'

'And you should have seen the lorries they've got!' said Dick. 'Beauties! Old army ones, I should think. The boy said his father's going to use them for carting things from the farm to the market.'

'What things?' said Mr Luffy, looking across at the little farmhouse. 'I shouldn't have thought they needed an army of lorries for that! An old farm wagon would carry all *their* produce.'

'Well – that's what he told us,' said Dick. 'Everything certainly looked very prosperous, I must say. He must be a jolly good farmer.'

'We got eggs and butter and fruit, and even some bacon,' said George. 'The boy's mother didn't seem worried about how much we had, and she hardly charged us anything. We didn't see the farmer.'

Mr Luffy was now eating his breakfast. He was certainly very hungry. He brushed away the flies that hung round his head, and when one settled on his right ear he waggled it violently. The fly flew off in surprise.

'Oh, do that again!' begged Anne. 'How do you do it? Do you think if I practised hard for weeks I could make my ear move?'

'No, I don't think so,' said Mr Luffy, finishing his breakfast. 'Well, I've got some writing to do now. What are you going to do? Go for a walk?'

'We might as well take a picnic lunch and go off somewhere,' said Julian. 'How about it?'

'Yes,' said Dick. 'Can you pack us dinner and tea, Anne? We'll help. What about hard-boiled eggs?'

It wasn't long before they had a picnic meal packed in greaseproof paper.

'You won't get lost, will you?' said Mr Luffy.

'Oh no, sir,' said Julian, with a laugh. 'I've got a compass, anyway, and a jolly good bump of locality, too. I usually know the way to go. We'll see you this evening, when we get back.'

'*You* won't get lost, Mr Luffy, will you?' asked Anne, looking worried.

'Don't be cheeky, Anne,' said Dick, rather horrified at Anne's question. But she really meant it. Mr Luffy was so absent-minded that she could quite well picture him wandering off and not being able to find his way back.

He smiled at her. 'No,' he said. 'I know my way about here all right – I know every stream and path and er – volcano!'

Anne giggled. The others stared at Mr Luffy, wondering what in the world he meant, but neither he nor Anne told them. They said good-bye and set off.

'It's heavenly walking today,' said Anne. 'Shall we follow a path if we find one or not?'

'Might as well,' said Julian. 'It'll be a bit tiring scrambling through heather all the day.'

So when they did unexpectedly come across a path they followed it. 'It's just a shepherd's path, I expect,' said Dick. 'I bet it's a lonely job, looking after sheep up on these desolate heathery hills.'

They went on for some way, enjoying the stretches of bright heather, the lizards that darted quickly away from their feet and the hosts of butterflies of all kinds that hovered and fluttered. Anne loved the little blue ones best and made up her mind to ask Mr Luffy what all their names were.

They had their lunch on a hill-top overlooking a vast stretch of heather, with grey-white blobs in it here and there – the sheep that wandered everywhere.

And, in the very middle of the meal, Anne heard the same rumbling she had heard before – and then, not far off, out spouted some white smoke from the ground. George went quite pale. Timmy leapt to his feet, growling and barking, his tail down. The boys roared with laughter.

'It's all right, Anne and George. It's only the trains underground here. We knew they ran under the moors and we thought we'd see what you did when you first heard them rumbling, and saw the smoke.'

'I'm not a bit frightened,' said Anne, and the boys

looked at her, astonished. It was George who was the scared one! Usually it was quite the other way round.

George got back her colour and laughed. She called Timmy. 'It's all right, Tim. Come here. You know what trains are, don't you?'

The children discussed the trains. It really did seem queer to think of trains in those hollowed-out tunnels down below the moors – the people in them, reading their newspapers and talking – down in tunnels where the sun never shone at all.

'Come on,' said Julian, at last. 'Let's go on. We'll walk to the top of the next slope, amd then I think we ought to turn back.'

They found a little path that Julian said must be a rabbit-path, because it was so narrow, and set off, chattering and laughing. They climbed through the heather to the top of the next slope. And at the top they got quite a surprise.

Down in the valley below was a silent and deserted stretch of railway lines! They appeared out of the black hole of a tunnel-mouth, ran for about half a mile, and then ended in what seemed to be a kind of railway yard.

'Look at that,' said Julian. 'Old derelict lines – not used any more, I should think. I suppose that tunnel's out of date, too.'

'Let's go down and have a squint,' said Dick. 'Come on! We've got plenty of time, and we can easily go back a shorter way.'

They set off down the hill to the lines. They arrived some way from the tunnel-mouth, and followed the lines to the deserted railway yard. There seemed to be nobody about at all.

'Look,' said Dick, 'there are some old wagons on that set of lines over there. They look as if they haven't been used for a hundred years. Let's give them a shove and set them going!'

370

'Oh, no!' said Anne, afraid. But the two boys and George, who had always longed to play about with real railway trucks, ran over to where three or four stood on the lines. Dick and Julian shoved hard at one. It moved. It ran a little way and crashed into the buffers of another. It made a terrific noise in the silent yard.

A door flew open in a tiny hut at the side of the yard, and a terrifying figure came out. It was a one-legged man, with a wooden peg for his other leg, two great arms that might

371

quite well belong to a gorilla, and a face as red as a tomato, except where grey whiskers grew.

He opened his mouth and the children expected a loud and angry yell. Instead out came a husky, hoarse whisper:

'What you doing? Ain't it bad enough to hear spook-trains a-running at night, without hearing them in the daytime, too?'

The four children stared at him. They thought he must be quite mad. He came nearer to them, and his wooden leg tip-tapped queerly. He swung his great arms loosely. He peered at the children as if he could hardly see them.

'I've bruck me glasses,' he said, and to their astonishment and dismay two tears ran down his cheeks. 'Poor old Wooden-Leg Sam, he's bruck his glasses. Nobody cares about Wooden-Leg Sam now, nobody at all.'

There didn't seem anything to say to all this. Anne felt sorry for the queer old man, but she kept well behind Julian.

Sam peered at them again. 'Ain't you got no tongues in your 'eads? Am I seeing things again, or are you there?'

'We're here and we're real,' said Julian. 'We happened to see this old railway yard and we came down to have a look at it. Who are you?'

'I've telled you – I'm Wooden-Leg Sam,' said the old man impatiently. 'The watchman, see? Though what there is to watch here, beats me. Does they think I'm a-going to watch for them spook-trains? Well, I'm not. Not me, Sam Wooden-Leg. I've seed many queer things in my life, yes, and bin scared by them too, and I'm not watching for any spook-trains no more.'

The children listened curiously. 'What spook-trains?' asked Julian.

Wooden-Leg Sam came closer. He looked all round as if he thought there might be someone listening, and then spoke in a hoarser whisper than usual.

'Spook-trains, I tell 'ee. Trains what come outa that

tunnel by nights all by theirselves, and go back all by theirselves. Nobody in them. One night they'll come for old Sam Wooden-Leg – but, ee, I'm smart, I am. I lock myself into my hut and get under the bed. And I blows my candle out so those spook-trains don't know I'm there.'

Anne shivered. She pulled at Julian's hand. 'Julian! Let's go. I don't like it. It sounds all queer and horrid. What does he mean?'

The old man seemed suddenly to change his mood. He picked up a large cinder and threw it at Dick, hitting him on the head. 'You clear out! I'm watchman here, ain't I? And what did They tell me? They told me to chase away anyone that came. Clear out, I tell you!'

In terror Anne fled away. Timmy growled and would have leapt at the queer old watchman, but George had her hand on his collar. Dick rubbed his head where the cinder had hit him.

'We're going,' he said, soothingly to Sam. It was plain that the old fellow was queer in his mind. 'We didn't mean to trespass. You look after your spook-trains. We won't interfere with you!'

The boys and George turned away, and caught up with Anne. 'What did he mean?' she asked, scared. 'What are spook-trains? Trains that aren't real? Does he really see them at night?'

'He just imagines them,' said Julian. 'I expect being there all alone in that deserted old railway yard has made him think queer things. Don't worry, Anne. There are no such things as spook-trains.'

'But he spoke as if there were,' said Anne, 'he did really. I'd hate to see a spook-train. Wouldn't you Ju?'

'No. I'd *love* to see one,' said Julian, and he turned to Dick. 'Wouldn't you, Dick? Shall we come one night and watch? Just to see?'

5

Back at camp again

The children and Timmy left the deserted railway yard behind them and climbed up the heathery slope to find their way back to their camping-place. The boys could not stop talking about Wooden-Leg Sam and the queer things he said.

'It's a funny business altogether,' said Julian. 'I wonder why that yard isn't used any more – and where that tunnel leads to – and if trains ever do run there.'

'I expect there's quite an ordinary explanation,' said Dick. 'It's just that Wooden-Leg Sam made it all seem so queer. If there had been a proper watchman we shouldn't have thought there was anything queer about it at all.'

'Perhaps the boy at the farm would know,' said Julian. 'We'll ask him tomorrow. I'm afraid there aren't any spook-trains really – but, gosh, I'd love to go and watch for one, if there were any.'

'I wish you wouldn't talk like that,' said Anne, unhappily. 'You know, it makes me feel as if you want another adventure. And I don't.'

374

'Well, there won't be any adventure, so don't worry,' said Dick, comfortingly. 'And, anyway, if there was an adventure you could always go and hold old Luffy's hand. He wouldn't see an adventure if it was right under his nose. You'd be quite safe with him.'

'Look – who's that up there?' said George, seeing Timmy prick up his ears, and then hearing him give a little growl.

'Shepherd or something, I should think,' said Julian. He shouted out cheerfully. 'Good afternoon! Nice day it's been!'

The old man on the path just above them nodded his head. He was either a shepherd or farm labourer of some sort. He waited for them to come up.

'You see any of my sheep down along there?' he asked them. 'Got a cross on them in red they have.'

'No. There aren't any down there,' said Julian. 'But there are some further along the hill. We've been down to the railway yard and we'd have seen any sheep on the slope below.'

Don't you go down there,' said the old shepherd, his faded blue eyes looking into Julian's. 'That's a bad place, that is.'

'Well, we've been hearing about spook-trains!' said Julian, with a laugh. 'Is that what you mean?'

'Ay. There's trains that nobody knows of a-running out of that tunnel,' said the shepherd. 'Many's the time I've heard them when I've been up here of a night with my sheep. That tunnel's not been used for thirty years – but the trains, they still come out of it, just as they used to.'

'How do you know? Have you seen them?' asked Julian, a cold shiver creeping down his spine quite suddenly.

'No. I've only heard them,' said the old man. 'Choo, choo, they go, and they jangle and clank. But they don't whistle no more. Old Wooden-Leg Sam, he reckons they's spook-trains, with nobody to drive them and nobody to tend them. Don't you go down to that place. It's bad and skeery.'

Julian caught sight of Anne's scared face. He laughed loudly. 'What a tale! I don't believe in spook-trains – and neither do you, shepherd. Dick, have you got the tea in your bag? Let's find a nice place and have some sandwiches and cake. Will you join us, shepherd?'

'No, thankee kindly,' said the old man, moving off. 'I be after my sheep. Always wandering they are, and they keep me wandering, too. Good day, sir, and don't ee go down to that bad place.'

Julian found a good spot out of sight of 'that bad place', and they all sat down. 'All a lot of nonsense,' said Julian, who wanted Anne to feel happier again. 'We can easily ask the farmer's boy about it tomorrow. I expect it's all a silly tale made up by that old one-legged fellow, and passed on to the shepherd.'

'I expect so,' said Dick. 'You noticed that the shepherd had never actually *seen* the trains, Julian? Only heard them. Well, sound travels far at night, and I expect what he heard was simply the rumblings of the trains that go underground here. There's one going somewhere now! I can feel the ground trembling!'

They all could. It was a queer feeling. The rumbling stopped at last and they sat and ate their tea, watching Timmy scraping at a rabbit-hole and trying his hardest to get down it. He covered them with sandy soil as he burrowed, and nothing would stop him. He seemed to have gone completely deaf.

'Look here, if we don't get Timmy out of that hole now he'll be gone down so far that we'll have to drag him out by his tail,' said Julian, getting up. 'Timmy! TIM-MY! The rabbit's miles away. Come on out.'

It took both George and Julian to get him out. He was most indignant. He looked at them as if to say: '*Well*, what spoil-sports! Almost got him and you drag me out!'

376

He shook himself, and bits of grit and sand flew out of his hair. He took a step towards the hole again, but George caught hold of his tail. 'No, Timmy. Home now!'

'He's looking for a spook-train,' said Dick, and that made everyone laugh, even Anne.

They set off back to the camping-place, pleasantly tired, with Timmy following rather sulkily at their heels. When they at last got back they saw Mr Luffy sitting waiting for them. The blue smoke from his pipe curled up into the air.

'Hallo, hallo!' he said, and his brown eyes looked up at them from under his shaggy eyebrows. 'I was beginning to wonder if you'd got lost. Still, I suppose that dog of yours would always bring you back.'

Timmy wagged his tail politely. 'Woof,' he agreed, and went to drink out of the bucket of water. Anne stopped him just in time.

'No, Timmy! You're not to drink out of our washing-up water. There's yours, in the dish over there.'

Timmy went to his dish and lapped. He thought Anne was very fussy. Anne asked Mr Luffy if he would like any supper.

'We're not having a proper supper,' she said. 'We had tea so late. But I'll cook you something if you like, Mr Luffy.'

'Very kind of you. But I've had an enormous tea,' said Mr Luffy. 'I've brought up a fruit cake for you, from my own larder. Shall we share it for supper? And I've got a bottle of lime juice, too, which will taste grand with some of the stream water.'

The boys went off to get some fresh stream water for drinking. Anne got out some plates and cut slices of the cake.

'Well,' said Mr Luffy. 'Had a nice walk?'

'Yes,' said Anne, 'except that we met a queer one-legged man who told us he saw spook-trains.'

377

Mr Luffy laughed. 'Well, well! He must be a cousin of a little girl I know who thought she was sitting on a volcano.'

Anne giggled. 'You're not to tease me. No, honestly, Mr Luffy, this old man was a watchman at a sort of old railway yard – not used now – and he said when the spook-trains came, he blew out his light and got under his bed so that they shouldn't get him.'

'Poor old fellow,' said Mr Luffy. 'I hope he didn't frighten you.'

'He did a bit,' said Anne. 'And he threw a cinder at Dick and hit him on the head. Tomorrow we're going to the farm to ask the boy there if he's heard of the spook-trains, too. We met an old shepherd who said he'd heard them but not seen them.'

'Well, well – it all sounds most interesting,' said Mr Luffy. 'But these exciting stories usually have a very tame explanation, you know. Now would you like to see what I found today? A very rare and interesting little beetle.'

He opened a small square tin and showed a shiny beetle to Anne. It had green feelers and a red fiery spot near its tail-end. It was a lovely little thing.

'Now that's much more exciting to me than half a dozen spook-trains,' he told Anne. 'Spook-trains won't keep me awake at night – but thinking of this little beetle-fellow here certainly will.'

'I don't very much like beetles,' said Anne. 'But this one certainly is pretty. Do you really like hunting about all day for insects, and watching them, Mr Luffy?'

'Yes, very much,' said Mr Luffy. 'Ah, here come the boys with the water. Now we'll hand the cake round, shall we? Where's George? Oh, there she is, changing her shoes.'

George had a blister, and she had been putting a strip of plaster on her heel. She came up when the boys arrived and the cake was handed round. They sat in a circle,

378

munching, while the sun gradually went down in a blaze of red.

'Nice day tomorrow again,' said Julian. 'What shall we do?'

'We'll have to go to the farm first,' said Dick. 'The farmer's wife said she'd let us have some more bread if we turned up in the morning. And we could do with more eggs if we can get them. We took eight hard-boiled ones with us today and we've only one or two left. And who's eaten all the tomatoes, I'd like to know?'

'All of you,' said Anne at once. 'You're perfect pigs over the tomatoes.'

'I'm afraid I'm one of the pigs,' apologized Mr Luffy. 'I think you fried me six for my breakfast, Anne.'

'That's all right,' said Anne. 'You didn't have as many as the others, even so! We can easily get some more.'

It was pleasant sitting there, eating and talking, and drinking lime juice and stream water. They were all tired, and it was nice to think of the cosy sleeping-bags. Timmy lifted his head and gave a vast yawn, showing an enormous amount of teeth.

'Timmy! I could see right down to your tail then!' said George. 'Do shut your mouth up. You've made us all yawn.'

So he had. Even Mr Luffy was yawning. He got up. 'Well, I'm going to turn in,' he said. 'Good night. We'll make plans tomorrow morning. I'll bring up some breakfast for you, if you like. I've got some tins of sardines.'

'Oh, thanks,' said Anne. 'And there's some of this cake left. I hope you won't think that's too funny a breakfast, Mr Luffy – sardines and fruit cake?'

'Not a bit. It sounds a most sensible meal,' came Mr Luffy's voice from down the hillside. 'Good night!'

The children sat there a few minutes longer. The sun went right out of sight. The wind grew a little chilly. Timmy yawned enormously again.

'Come on,' said Julian. 'Time we turned in. Thank goodness Timmy didn't come into our tent and walk all over me last night. Good night, girls. It's going to be a heavenly night – but as I shall be asleep in about two shakes of a duck's tail, I shan't see much of it!'

The girls went into their tent. They were soon in their sleeping-bags. Just before they went to sleep Anne felt the slight shivering of the earth that meant a train was running underground somewhere. She could hear no rumbling sound. She fell asleep thinking of it.

The boys were not asleep. They, too, had felt the trembling of the earth beneath them, and it had reminded them of the old railway yard.

'Funny about those spook-trains, Dick,' said Julian, sleepily. 'Wonder if there *is* anything in it.'

'No. How could there be?' said Dick. 'All the same we'll go to the farm tomorrow and have a chat with that boy. He lives on the Moors and he ought to know the truth.'

'The real truth is that Wooden-Leg Sam is potty, and imagines all he says, and that the old shepherd, like all country people, is ready to believe in anything strange,' said Julian.

'I expect you're right,' said Dick. 'Oh my goodness, what's that?'

A dark shape stood looking in at the tent-flap. It gave a little whine.

'Oh, it's you, Timmy. Would you mind *not* coming and pretending you're a spook-train or something?' said Dick. 'And if you dare to put so much as half a paw on my middle, I'll scare you down the hill with a roar like a man-eating tiger. Go away.'

Timmy put a paw on Julian. Julian yelled out to George. 'George! Call this dog of yours, will you? He's just about to turn himself round twenty times on my middle, and curl himself up for the night.'

There was no answer from George. Timmy, feeling that

he was not wanted, disappeared. He went back to George and curled himself up on her feet. He put his nose down on his paws and slept.

'Spooky Timmy,' murmured Julian, re-arranging himself. 'Timmy spooky – no, I mean – oh dear, what do I mean?'

'Shut up,' said Dick. 'What with you and Timmy messing about, I can't get – to – sleep!' But he could and he did – almost before he had finished speaking. Silence fell on the little camp, and nobody noticed when the next train rumbled underground – not even Timmy!

6

Day at the farm

The next day the children were up very early, as early as Mr Luffy, and they all had breakfast together. Mr Luffy had a map of the moorlands, and he studied it carefully after breakfast.

'I think I'll go off for the whole day,' he said to Julian, who was sitting beside him. 'See that little valley marked here – Crowleg Vale – well, I have heard that there are some of the rarest beetles in Britain to be found there. I think I'll take my gear and go along. What are you four going to do?'

'Five,' said George at once. 'You've forgotten Timmy.'

'So I have. I beg his pardon,' said Mr Luffy, solemnly. 'Well – what are you going to do?'

'We'll go over to the farm and get some more food,' said Julian. 'And ask that farm-boy if he's heard the tale of the spook-trains. And perhaps look round the farm and get to know the animals there. I always like a farm.'

'Right,' said Mr Luffy, beginning to light his pipe.

'Don't worry about me if I'm not back till dusk. When I'm bug-hunting I lose count of the time.'

'You're sure you won't get lost?' said Anne, anxiously. She didn't really feel that Mr Luffy could take proper care of himself.

'Oh yes. My right ear always warns me if I'm losing my way,' said Mr Luffy. 'It waggles hard.'

He waggled it at Anne and she laughed. 'I wish you'd tell me how you do that,' she said. 'I'm sure you know. You can't think how thrilled the girls at school would be if I learnt that trick. They'd think it was super.'

Mr Luffy grinned and got up. 'Well, so long,' he said. 'I'm off before Anne makes me give her a lesson in ear-waggles.'

He went off down the slope to his own tent. George and Anne washed-up, while the boys tightened some tent ropes that had come loose, and generally tidied up.

'I suppose it's quite all right leaving everything un-guarded like this,' said Anne, anxiously.

'Well, we did yesterday,' said Dick. 'And who's likely to come and take anything up here in this wild and lonely spot, I'd like to know? You don't imagine a spook-train will come along and bundle everything into its luggage-van, do you, Anne?'

Anne giggled. 'Don't be silly. I just wondered if we ought to leave Timmy on guard, that's all.'

'Leave Timmy!' said George, amazed. 'You don't really think I'd leave Timmy behind every time we go off anywhere, Anne? Don't be an idiot.'

'No, I didn't really think you would,' said Anne. 'Well, I suppose nobody will come along here. Throw over that tea-cloth, George, if you've finished with it.'

Soon the tea-cloths were hanging over the gorse bushes to dry in the sun. Everything was put away neatly in the tents. Mr Luffy had called a loud good-bye and gone. Now the five were ready to go off to the farm.

Anne took a basket, and gave one to Julian too. 'To bring back the food,' said she. 'Are you ready to go now?'

They set off over the heather, their knees brushing through the honeyed flowers, and sending scores of busy bees into the air. It was a lovely day again, and the children felt free and happy.

They came to the trim little farm. Men were at work in the fields, but Julian did not think they were very industrious. He looked about for the farm-boy.

The boy came out of a shed and whistled to them. 'Hallo! You come for some more eggs? I've collected quite a lot for you.'

He stared at Anne. 'You didn't come yesterday. What's your name?'

'Anne,' said Anne. 'What's yours?'

'Jock,' said the boy, with a grin. He was rather a nice boy, Anne thought, with straw-coloured hair, blue eyes, and rather a red face which looked very good-tempered.

'Where's your mother?' said Julian. 'Can we get some bread and other things from her today? We ate an awful lot of our food yesterday, and we want to stock up our larder again!'

'She's busy just now in the dairy,' said Jock. 'Are you in a hurry? Come and see my pups.'

They all walked off with him to a shed. In there, right at the end, was a big box lined with straw. A collie dog lay there with five lovely little puppies. She growled at Timmy fiercely, and he backed hurriedly out of the shed. He had met fierce mother-dogs before, and he didn't like them!

The four children exclaimed over the fat little puppies, and Anne took one out very gently. It cuddled into her arms and made funny little whining noises.

'I wish it was mine,' said Anne. 'I should call it Cuddle.'

'What a frightful name for a dog,' said George scornfully. 'Just the kind of silly name you *would* think of, Anne.

384

Let me hold it. Are they all yours, Jock?'

'Yes,' said Jock, proudly. 'The mother's mine, you see. Her name's Biddy.'

Biddy pricked up her ears at her name and looked up at Jock out of bright, alert eyes. He fondled her silky head.

'I've had her for four years,' he said. 'When we were at Owl Farm, old Farmer Burrows gave her to me when she was eight weeks old.'

'Oh – were you at another farm before this one, then?' asked Anne. 'Have you always lived on a farm? Aren't you lucky!'

'I've only lived on two,' said Jock. 'Owl Farm and this one. Mum and I had to leave Owl Farm when Dad died, and we went to live in a town for a year. I hated that. I was glad when we came here.'

'But I thought your father was here!' said Dick, puzzled.

'That's my stepfather,' said Jock. 'He's no farmer, though!' He looked round and lowered his voice. 'He doesn't know much about farming. It's my mother that tells the men what to do. Still, he gives her plenty of money to do everything well, and we've got fine machinery and wagons and things. Like to see the dairy? It's slap up-to-date and Mum loves working in it.'

Jock took the four children to the shining, spotless dairy. His mother was at work there with a girl. She nodded and smiled at the children. 'Good morning! Hungry again? I'll pack you up plenty of food when I've finished in the dairy. Would you like to stay and have dinner with my Jock? He's lonely enough here in the holidays, with no other boy to keep him company.'

'Oh, *yes* – do let's!' cried Anne, in delight. 'I'd like that. Can we, Ju?'

'Yes. Thank you very much, Mrs – er – Mrs . . .' said Julian.

'I'm Mrs Andrews,' said Jock's mother. 'But Jock is Jock Robins – he's the son of my first husband, a farmer. Well, stay to dinner all of you, and I'll see if I can give you a meal that will keep you going for the rest of the day!'

This sounded good. The four children felt thrilled, and Timmy wagged his tail hard. He liked Mrs Andrews.

'Come on,' said Jock, joyfully. 'I'll take you all round the farm, into every corner. It's not very big, but we're going to make it the best little farm on the moorlands. My stepfather doesn't seem to take much interest in the work of the farm, but he's jolly generous when it comes to handing out money to Mum to buy everything she wants.'

It certainly seemed to the children that the machinery on the farm was absolutely up-to-date. They examined the combine, they went into the little cowshed and admired the clean stone floor with white brick walls, they climbed into the red-painted wagons, and they wished they could try the two motor-tractors that stood side by side in a barn.

'You've got plenty of men here to work the farm,' said

Julian. 'I shouldn't have thought there was enough for so many to do on this small place.'

'They're not good workers,' said Jock, his face creasing into frowns. 'Mum's always getting wild with them. They just don't know what to do. Dad gives her plenty of men to work the farm, but he always chooses the wrong ones!' They don't seem to like farm-work, and they're always running off to the nearest town whenever they can. There's only one good fellow and he's old. See him over there? His name's Will.'

The children looked at Will. He was working in the little vegetable garden, an old fellow with a shrivelled face, a tiny nose and a pair of very blue eyes. They liked the look of him.

'Yes. He *looks* like a farm-worker,' said Julian. 'The others don't.'

'He won't work with them,' said Jock. 'He just says rude things to them, and calls them ninnies and idjits.'

'What's an idjit?' asked Anne.

'An idiot, silly,' said Dick. He walked up to old Will. 'Good morning,' he said. 'You're very busy. There's always a lot to do on a farm, isn't there?'

The old fellow looked at Dick out of his very blue eyes, and went on with his work. 'Plenny to do and plenny of folkses to do it, and not much done,' he said, in a croaking kind of voice. 'Never thought as I'd be put to work with ninnies and idjits. No, that I didn't Ninnies and Idjits!'

'There! What did I tell you?' said Jock, with a grin. 'He's always calling the other men that, so we just have to let him work right away from them. Still, I must say he's about right – most of the fellows here don't know the first thing about work on a farm. I wish my stepfather would let us have a few proper workers instead of these fellows.'

'Where's your stepfather?' said Julian, thinking he must be rather peculiar to pour money into a little moorland farm like this, and yet choose the wrong kind of workers.

'He's away for the day,' said Jock. 'Thank goodness!' he added, with a sideways look at the others.

'Why? Don't you like him?' asked Dick.

'He's all right,' said Jock. 'But he's not a farmer, though he makes out he's always wanted to be – and what's more he doesn't like me one bit. I try to like him for Mum's sake. But I'm always glad when he's out of the way.'

'Your mother's nice,' said George.

'Oh, yes – Mum's grand,' said Jock. 'You don't know what it means to her to have a little farm of her own again, and to be able to run it with the proper machinery and all.'

They came to a large barn. The door was locked. 'I told you what was in here before,' said Jock. 'Lorries! You can peek through that hole here at them. Don't know why my stepfather wanted to buy up so many, but I suppose he got them cheap – he loves to get things cheap and sell them dear! He did say they'd be useful on the farm, to take goods to the market.'

'Yes – you told us that when we were here yesterday,' said Dick. 'But you've got heaps of wagons for that!'

'Yes. I reckon they weren't bought for the farm at all, but for holding here till prices went high and he could make a lot of money,' said Jock, lowering his voice. 'I don't tell Mum that. So long as she gets what she wants for the farm, I'm going to hold my tongue.'

The children were very interested in all this. They wished they could see Mr Andrews. He must be a queer sort of fellow, they thought. Anne tried to imagine what he was like.

'Big and tall and dark and frowny,' she thought. 'Rather frightening and impatient, and he certainly won't like children. People like that never do.'

They spent a very pleasant morning poking about the little farm. They went back to see Biddy the collie and her pups. Timmy stood patiently outside the shed, with his tail down. He didn't like George to take so much interest in other dogs.

A bell rang loudly. 'Good! Dinner!' said Jock. 'We'd better wash. We're all filthy. Hope you feel hungry, because I guess Mum's got a super dinner for us.'

'I feel terribly hungry,' said Anne. 'It seems ages since we had breakfast. I've almost forgotten it!'

They all felt the same. They went into the farmhouse and were surprised to find a very nice little bathroom to wash in. Mrs Andrews was there, putting out a clean roller towel.

'Fine little bathroom, isn't it?' she said. 'My husband had it put in for me. First proper bathroom I've ever had!'

A glorious smell rose up from the kitchen downstairs. 'Come on!' said Jock, seizing the soap. 'Let's hurry. We'll be down in a minute, Mum!'

And they were. Nobody was going to dawdle over washing when a grand meal lay waiting for them downstairs!

7

Mr Andrews comes home

They all sat down to dinner. There was a big meat-pie, a cold ham, salad, potatoes in their jackets, and home-made pickles. It really was difficult to know what to choose.

'Have some of both,' said Mrs Andrews, cutting the meat-pie. 'Begin with the pie and go on with the ham. That's the best of living on a farm, you know – you do get plenty to eat.'

After the first course there were plums and thick cream, or jam tarts and the same cream. Everyone tucked in hungrily.

'I've never had such a lovely dinner in my life,' said Anne, at last. 'I wish I could eat some more but I can't. It was super, Mrs Andrews.'

'Smashing,' said Dick. That was his favourite word these holidays. 'Absolutely smashing.'

'Woof,' said Timmy, agreeing. He had had a fine plateful of meaty bones, biscuits and gravy, and he had licked up every crumb and every drop. Now he felt he would like to have a snooze in the sun and not do a thing for the rest of the day.

The children felt rather like that, too. Mrs Andrews handed them a chocolate each and sent them out of doors. 'You go and have a rest now,' she said. 'Talk to Jock. He doesn't get enough company of his own age in the holidays. You can stay on to tea, if you like.'

'Oh, thanks,' said everyone, although they all felt that they wouldn't even be able to manage a biscuit. But it was so pleasant at the farm that they felt they would like to stay as long as they could.

'May we borrow one of Biddy's puppies to have with us?' asked Anne.

'If Biddy doesn't mind,' said Mrs Andrews, beginning to clear away. 'And if Timmy doesn't eat it up!'

'Timmy wouldn't dream of it!' said George at once. 'You go and get the puppy, Anne. We'll find a nice place in the sun.'

Anne went off to get the puppy. Biddy didn't seem to mind a bit. Anne cuddled the fat little thing against her, and went off to the others, feeling very happy. The boys had found a fine place against a haystack, and sat leaning against it, the sun shining down warmly on them.

'Those men of yours seem to take a jolly good lunch-hour off,' said Julian, not seeing any of them about.

Jock gave a snort. 'They're bone lazy. I'd sack the lot if I were my stepfather. Mum's told him how badly the men work, but he doesn't say a word to them. I've given up bothering. I don't pay their wages – if I did, I'd sack the whole lot!'

'Let's ask Jock about the spook-trains,' said George, fondling Timmy's ears. 'It would be fun to talk about them.'

'Spook-trains? Whatever are they?' asked Jock, his eyes wide with surprise. 'Never heard of them!'

'Haven't you really?' asked Dick. 'Well, you don't live very far from them, Jock!'

'Tell me about them,' said Jock. 'Spook-trains – no, I've never heard of one of those.'

'Well, I'll tell you what we know,' said Julian. 'Actually we thought you'd be able to tell us much more about them than we know ourselves.'

He began to tell Jock about their visit to the deserted railway yard, and Wooden-Leg Sam, and his peculiar behaviour. Jock listened, enthralled.

'Coo!' I wish I'd been with you. Let's all go there together, shall we?' he said. 'This was quite an adventure you had, wasn't it? You know, I've never had a single adventure in all my life, not even a little one. Have you?'

The four children looked at one another, and Timmy looked at George. Adventures! What didn't they know about them? They had had so many.

'Yes. We've had heaps of adventures – real ones – smashing ones,' said Dick. 'We've been down in dungeons, we've been lost in caves, we've found secret passages, we've looked for treasure – well, I can't tell you what we've done! It would take too long.'

'No, it wouldn't,' said Jock eagerly. 'You tell me. Go on. Did you all have the adventures? Little Anne, here, too?'

'Yes, all of us,' said George. 'And Timmy as well. He rescued us heaps of times from danger. Didn't you, Tim?'

'Woof, woof,' said Timmy, and thumped his tail against the hay.

They began to tell Jock about their many adventures. He was a very, very good listener. His eyes almost fell out of his head, and he went brick-red whenever they came to an exciting part.

'My word!' he said at last. 'I've never heard such things in my life before. Aren't you lucky? You just go about

392

having adventures all the time, don't you? I *say* – do you think you'll have one here, these hols?'

Julian laughed. 'No. Whatever kind of adventure would there be on these lonely moorlands? Why, you yourself have lived here for three years, and haven't even had a tiny adventure.'

Jocked sighed. 'That's true. I haven't.' Then his eyes brightened again. 'But see here – what about those spook-trains you've been asking me about? Perhaps you'll have an adventure with those?'

'Oh, no, I don't want to,' said Anne, in a horrified voice. 'An adventure with spook-trains would be simply horrid.'

'I'd like to go down to that old railway yard with you and see Wooden-Leg Sam,' said Jock longingly. 'Why, that would be a real adventure to me, you know – just talking to a queer old man like that, and wondering if he was suddenly going to throw cinders at us. Take me with you next time you go.'

'Well – I don't know that we meant to go again,' said Julian. 'There's really nothing much in his story except imagination – the old watchman's gone queer in the head through being alone there so much, guarding a yard where nothing and nobody ever comes. He's just re-membering the trains that used to go in and out before the line was given up.'

'But the shepherd said the same as Sam,' said Jock. 'I *say* – what about going down there one night and watch-ing for a spook-train!'

'NO!' said Anne, in horror.

'You needn't come,' said Jock. 'Just us three boys.'

'And me,' said George at once. 'I'm as good as any boy, and I'm not going to be left out. Timmy's coming, too.'

'Oh, please don't make these awful plans,' begged poor Anne. 'You'll *make* an adventure come, if you go on like this.'

Nobody took the least notice of her. Julian looked at

393

Jock's excited face. 'Well,' he said, 'if we do go there again, we'll tell you. And if we think we'll go watching for spook-trains, we'll take you with us.'

Jock looked as if he could hug Julian. 'That's wizard of you,' he said. 'Thanks most frightfully. Spook-trains! I *say*, just suppose we really did see one! Who'd be driving it? Where would it come from?'

'Out of the tunnel, Wooden-Leg Sam says,' said Dick. 'But I don't see how we'd spot it, except by the noise it made, because apparently the spook-trains only arrive in the dark of the night. Never in the daytime. We wouldn't *see* much, even if we were there.'

It was such an exciting subject to Jock that he persisted in talking about it all the afternoon. Anne got tired of listening, and went to sleep with Biddy's puppy in her arms. Timmy curled up by George and went to sleep too. He wanted to go for a walk, but he could see that there was no hope with all this talking going on.

It was tea-time before any of them had expected it. The bell rang, and Jock looked most surprised.

'Tea! Would you believe it? Well, I *have* had an exciting afternoon talking about all this. And look here, if you don't make up your minds to go spook-train hunting I'll jolly well go off by myself. If only I could have an adventure like the kind you've had, I'd be happy.'

They went in to tea, after waking Anne up with difficulty. She took the puppy back to Biddy, who received it gladly and licked it all over.

Julian was surprised to find that he was quite hungry again. 'Well,' he said, as he sat down at the table. 'I didn't imagine I'd feel hungry again for a week – but I do. What a wizard tea, Mrs Andrews. Isn't Jock lucky, to have meals like this always!'

There were home-made scones with new honey. There were slices of bread thickly spread with butter, and new-made cream cheese to go with it. There was sticky brown

394

gingerbread, hot from the oven, and a big solid fruit cake that looked almost like a plum pudding when it was cut, it was so black.

'Oh dear! I wish now I hadn't had so much dinner,' sighed Anne. 'I don't feel hungry enough to eat a bit of everything and I would so like to!'

Mrs Andrews laughed. 'You eat what you can, and I'll give you some to take away, too,' she said. 'You can have some cream cheese, and the scones and honey – and some of the bread I made this morning. And maybe you'd like a slab of the gingerbread. I made plenty.'

'Oh, thanks,' said Julian. 'We'll be all right tomorrow with all that. You're a marvellous cook, Mrs Andrews. I wish I lived on your farm.'

There was the sound of a car coming slowly up the rough track to the farmhouse, and Mrs Andrews looked up. 'That's Mr Andrews come back,' she said. 'My husband, you know, Jock's stepfather.'

Julian thought she looked a little worried. Perhaps Mr Andrews didn't like children and wouldn't be pleased to see them sitting round his table when he came home tired.

'Would you like us to go, Mrs Andrews?' he asked politely. 'Perhaps Mr Andrews would like a bit of peace for his meal when he comes in – and we're rather a crowd, aren't we?'

Jock's mother shook her head. 'No, you can stay. I'll get him a meal in the other room if he'd like it.'

Mr Andrews came in. He wasn't in the least like Anne or the others had imagined him to be. He was a short, dark little man, with a weak face and a nose much too big for it. He looked harassed and bad-tempered, and stopped short when he saw the five children.

'Hallo, dear,' said Mrs Andrews. 'Jock's got his friends here today. Would you like a bit of tea in your room? I can easily put a tray there.'

'Well,' said Mr Andrews, smiling a watery kind of smile, 'Perhaps it would be best. I've had a worrying kind of day, and not much to eat.'

'I'll get you a tray of ham and pickles and bread,' said his wife. 'It won't take a minute. You go and wash.'

Mr Andrews went out. Anne was surprised that he seemed so small and looked rather stupid. She had imagined someone big and burly, strong and clever, who was always going about doing grand deals and making a lot of money. Well, he must be cleverer than he looked, to make enough money to give Mrs Andrews all she needed for her farm.

Mrs Andrews bustled about with this and that, laying a tray with a snow-white cloth, and plates of food. Mr Andrews could be heard in the bathroom, splashing as he washed. Then he came downstairs and put his head in at the door. 'My meal ready?' he asked. 'Well, Jock – had a good day?'

'Yes, thanks,' said Jock, as his stepfather took the tray from his mother and turned to go. 'We went all round the farm this morning – and we talked and talked this afternoon. And oh, I say – do you know anything about spook-trains, sir?'

Mr Andrews was just going out of the door. He turned in surprise. 'Spook-trains? What are you talking about?'

'Well, Julian says there's an old deserted railway yard a good way from here, and spook-trains are supposed to come out of the tunnel there in the dark of night,' said Jock. 'Have you heard of them?'

Mr Andrews stood stock still, his eyes on his stepson. He looked dismayed and shocked. Then he came back into the room and kicked the door shut behind him.

'I'll have my tea here after all,' he said. 'Well, to think you've heard of those spook-trains! I've been careful not to mention them to your mother or to you, Jock, for fear of scaring you!'

396

'Gee!' said Dick. 'Are they really true then? They can't be.'

'You tell me all you know, and how you know about it,' said Mr Andrews, sitting down at the table with his tray. 'Go on. Don't miss out a thing. I want to hear everything.'

Julian hesitated. 'Oh – there's nothing really to tell, sir – just a lot of nonsense.'

'You tell it me!' almost shouted Mr Andrews. 'Then I'll tell *you* a few things. And I tell you, you won't go near that old railway yard again – no, that you won't!'

8

A lazy evening

The five children and Mrs Andrews stared in surprise at Mr Andrews, when he shouted at them. He repeated some of his words again.

'Go on! You tell me all you know. And then I'll tell *you*!'

Julian decided to tell, very shortly, what had happened at the old railway yard, and what Wooden-Leg Sam had said. He made the tale sound rather bald and dull. Mr Andrews listened to it with the greatest interest, never once taking his eyes off Julian.

Then he sat back and drank a whole cup of strong tea at one gulp. The children waited for him to speak, wondering what he had to say.

'Now,' he said, making his voice sound important and impressive, 'you listen to me. Don't any of you ever go down to that yard again. It's a bad place.'

'Why?' asked Julian. 'What do you mean – a bad place?'

'Things have happened there – years and years ago,' said Mr Andrews. 'Bad things. Accidents. It was all shut up after that and the tunnel wasn't used any more. See? Nobody was allowed to go there, and nobody did, because they were scared. They knew it was a bad place, where bad things happen.'

Anne felt frightened. 'But Mr Andrews – you don't mean there really are spook-trains, do you?' she asked, her face rather pale.

Mr Andrews pursed up his lips and nodded very solemnly indeed. 'That's just what I do mean. Spook-trains come and go. Nobody knows why. But it's bad luck to be there when they come. They might take you away, see?'

Julian laughed. 'Oh – not as bad as that, sir, surely! Anyway, you're frightening Anne, so let's change the subject. I don't believe in spook-trains.'

But Mr Andrews didn't seem to want to stop talking about the trains. 'Wooden-Leg Sam was right to hide himself when they come along,' he said. 'I don't know how he manages to stay on in a bad place like that. Never knowing when a train is going to come creeping out of that tunnel in the darkness.'

Julian was not going to have Anne frightened any more. He got up from the table and turned to Mrs Andrews.

'Thank you very much for a lovely day and lovely food!' he said. 'We must go now. Come along, Anne.'

'Wait a minute,' said Mr Andrews. 'I just want to warn you all very solemnly that you mustn't go down to that railway yard. You hear me, Jock? You might never come back. Old Wooden-Leg Sam's mad, and well he may be, with spook-trains coming along in the dead of night. It's a bad and dangerous place. You're not to go near it!'

'Well – thank you for the warning, sir,' said Julian, politely, suddenly disliking the small man with the big nose very much indeed. 'We'll be going. Good-bye, Mrs Andrews. Good-bye, Jock. Come along tomorrow and have a picnic with us, will you?'

'Oh, thanks! Yes, I will,' said Jock. 'But wait a minute – aren't you going to take any food with you?'

'Yes, of course they are,' said Mrs Andrews, getting up from her chair. She had been listening to the conversation with a look of puzzled wonder on her face. She went out into the scullery, where there was a big, cold larder. Julian followed her. He carried the two baskets.

'I'll give you plenty,' said Mrs Andrews, putting loaves, butter, and cream cheese into the baskets. 'I know what appetites you youngsters get. Now don't you be too scared at what my husband's just been saying – I saw that little Anne was frightened. I've never heard of the spook-trains, and I've been here for three years. I don't reckon there's much in the tale, you know, for all my husband's so set on warning you not to go down to the yard.'

Julian said nothing. He thought that Mr Andrews had behaved rather queerly about the whole story. Was he one of the kind of people who believed in all sorts of silly things and got scared himself? He looked weak enough! Julian found himself wondering how a nice woman like Mrs Andrews could have married such a poor specimen of a man. Still, he was a generous fellow, judging by all Jock had said, and perhaps Jock's mother felt grateful to him for giving her the farm and the money to run it with. That must be it.

Julian thanked Mrs Andrews, and insisted on paying her, though she would have given him the food for nothing. She came into the kitchen with him and he saw that the others had already gone outside. Only Mr Andrews was left, eating ham and pickles.

'Good-bye, sir,' said Julian politely.

'Good-bye. And you remember what I've told you, boy,' said Mr Andrews. 'Bad luck comes to people who see the spook-trains – yes, terrible bad luck. You keep away from them.'

Julian gave a polite smile and went out. It was evening

now and the sun was setting behind the moorland hills, though it still had a long way to go before it disappeared. He caught up with the others. Jock was with them.

'I'm just coming half-way with you,' said Jock. 'I say! My stepfather was pretty scary about those trains, wasn't he?'

'I felt pretty scary too, when he was warning us about them,' said Anne. 'I shan't go down to that yard again, ever. Will you, George?'

'If the boys did, I would,' said George, who didn't look very much as if she wanted to, all the same.

'*Are* you going to the yard again?' asked Jock, eagerly. 'I'm not scared. Not a bit. It would be an adventure to go and watch for a spook-train.'

'We might go,' said Julian. 'We'll take you with us, if we do. But the girls aren't to come.'

'Well, I like that!' said George angrily. 'As if you could leave me behind! When have I been scared of anything? I'm as brave as any of you.'

'Yes. I know. You can come as soon as we find out it's all a silly story,' said Julian.

'I shall come whenever you go,' flashed back George. 'Don't you dare to leave me out. I'll never speak to you again if you do.'

Jock looked most surprised at this sudden flare-up of temper from George. He didn't know how fierce she could be!

'I don't see why George shouldn't come,' he said. 'I bet she'd be every bit as good as a boy. I thought she was one when I first saw her.'

George gave him one of her sweetest smiles. He couldn't have said anything she liked better! But Julian would not change his mind.

'I mean what I say. The girls won't come if we do go, so that's that. For one thing, Anne certainly wouldn't want

401

to come, and if George came without her she'd be left all alone up at the camp. She wouldn't like that.'

'She could have Mr Luffy's company,' said George, looking sulky again.

'Idiot! As if we'd want to tell Mr Luffy we were going off exploring deserted railway yards watched over by a mad, one-legged fellow who swears there are spook-trains!' said Julian. 'He'd stop us going. You know what grown-ups are. Or he'd come with us, which would be worse.'

'Yes. He'd see moths all the time, not spook-trains,' said Dick, with a grin.

'I'd better go back now,' said Jock. 'It's been a grand day. I'll come up tomorrow and picnic with you. Good-bye.'

They called good-bye to Jock, and went on their way to the camp. It was quite nice to see it again, waiting for them, the two tents flapping a little in the breeze. Anne pushed her way through the tent-flap, anxious to see that everything was untouched.

Inside the tent it was very hot. Anne decided to put the food they had brought under the bottom of the big gorse bush. It would be cooler there. She was soon busy about her little jobs. The boys went down to see if Mr Luffy was back, but he wasn't.

'Anne! We're going to bathe in the stream!' they called. 'We feel hot and dirty. Are you coming? George is coming too.'

'No, I won't come,' Anne called back. 'I've got lots of things to do.'

The boys grinned at one another. Anne did so enjoy 'playing house'. So they left her to it, and went to the stream, from which yells and howls and shrieks soon came. The water was colder than they expected, and nobody liked to lie down in it – but everyone was well and truly splashed, and the icy-cold drops falling on their hot bodies made them squeal and yell. Timmy didn't in the least mind the iciness of the water. He rolled over and over in it, enjoying himself.

'Look at him, showing off!' said Dick. 'Aha, Timmy, if I could bathe in a fur coat like you, I wouldn't mind the cold water either.'

'Woof,' said Timmy, and climbed up the shallow bank. He shook himself violently and thousands of icy-cold silvery drops flew from him and landed on the three shivering children. They yelled and chased him away.

It was a pleasant, lazy evening. Mr Luffy didn't appear

at all. Anne got a light meal of bread and cream cheese and a piece of gingerbread. Nobody felt like facing another big meal that day. They lay in the heather and talked comfortably.

'This is the kind of holiday I like,' said Dick.

'So do I,' said Anne. 'Except for the spook-trains. That's spoilt it a bit for me.'

'Don't be silly, Anne,' said George. 'If they are not real it's just a silly story, and if they are real, well, it might be an adventure.'

There was a little silence. 'Are we going down to the yard again?' asked Dick lazily.

'Yes, I think so,' said Julian. 'I'm not going to be scared off it by weird warnings from Pa Andrews.'

'Then I vote we go one night and wait to see if a spook-train does come along,' said Dick.

'I shall come too,' said George.

'No, you won't,' said Julian. 'You'll stay with Anne.'

George said nothing, but everyone could feel mutiny in the air.

'Do we tell Mr Luffy, or don't we?' said Dick.

'You know we've said we wouldn't,' said Julian. He yawned. 'I'm getting sleepy. And the sun has gone, so it will soon be dark. I wonder where old Luffy is?'

'Do you think I'd better wait up and see if he wants something to eat?' said Anne, anxiously.

'No. Not unless you want to keep awake till midnight!' said Julian. 'He'll have got some food down in his tent. He'll be all right. I'm going to turn in. Coming, Dick?'

The boys were soon in their sleeping-bags. The girls lay in the heather for a little while longer, listening to the lonely-sounding cry of the curlews going home in the dusk. Then they, too, went into their own tent.

Once safely in their sleeping-bags, the two boys felt suddenly wide awake. They began to talk in low voices.

'Shall we take Jock down to see the yard in the day-

404

time? Or shall we go one night and watch for the Train from Nowhere?' said Julian.

'I vote we go and watch at night,' said Dick. 'We'll never see a spook-train in the daytime. Wooden-Leg Sam is an interesting old chap, especially when he chucks cinders about – but I don't know that I like him enough to go and visit him again!'

'Well – if Jock badly wants to go and have a snoop round tomorrow morning when he comes, we'd better take him,' said Julian. 'We can always go one night, too, if we want to.'

'Right. We'll wait and see what Jock says,' said Dick. They talked a little longer and then felt sleepy. Dick was just dropping off when he heard something coming wriggling through the heather. A head was stuck through the opening of the tent.

'If you dare to come in, I'll smack your silly face,' said Dick, thinking it was Timmy. 'I know what you want, you perfect pest – you want to flop down on my tummy. You just turn yourself round and go away! Do you hear?'

The head in the opening moved a little but didn't go away. Dick raised himself up on one elbow.

'Put one paw inside my tent and you'll be sent rolling down the hill!' he said. 'I love you very much in the daytime, but I'm not fond of you at night – not when I'm in a sleeping-bag anyway. Scoot!'

The head made a peculiar apologetic sound. Then it spoke. 'Er – you're awake, I see. Are all of you all right – the girls too? I'm only just back.'

'Gosh! It's Mr Luffy,' said Dick, filled with horror. 'I say, sir – I'm most awfully sorry – I thought you were Timmy, come to flop himself down on top of me, like he often does. So sorry, sir.'

'Don't mention it!' said the shadowy head with a chuckle. 'Glad you're all right. See you tomorrow!'

9

Night visitor

Mr Luffy slept very late the next morning and nobody liked to disturb him. The girls yelled with laughter when they heard how Dick had spoken to him the night before, thinking he was Timmy the dog.

'He was very decent about it,' said Dick. 'Seemed to think it was quite amusing. I hope he'll still think so this morning!'

They were all sitting eating their breakfast – ham, tomatoes, and the bread Mrs Andrews had given them the day before. Timmy collected the bits as usual, and wondered if George would let him have a lick of the cream cheese she was now putting on her bread. Timmy loved cheese. He looked at the lump in the dish and sighed all over George. He could easily eat that in one mouthful! How he wished he could.

'I wonder what time Jock will come up,' said George. 'If he came up pretty soon, we could go for a nice long walk over the moors, and picnic somewhere. Jock ought to know some fine walks.'

'Yes. We'll mess about till he comes, and then tell him he's to be our guide and take us to the nicest walk he knows,' said Anne. 'Oh Timmy, you beast – you've taken my nice lump of cream cheese right out of my fingers!'

'Well, you were waving it about under his nose, so what could you expect?' said George. 'He thought you were giving it to him.'

'Well, he shan't have any more, It's too precious,' said Anne. 'Oh, dear – I wish we didn't eat so much. We keep bringing in stacks of food, and it hardly lasts any time.'

'I bet Jock will bring some more,' said Dick. 'He's a sensible sort of fellow. Did you get a peep into that enormous larder of his mother's? It's like a great cave, goes right back into the wall, with dozens of stone shelves – and all filled with food. No wonder Jock's tubby.'

'Is he? I never noticed,' said Anne. 'Is that him whistling?'

It wasn't. It was a curlew, very high up. 'Too early for him yet,' said Julian. 'Shall we help you to clear up, Anne?'

'No. That's my job and George's,' said Anne firmly. 'You go down and see if Mr Luffy is awake. He can have a bit of ham and a few tomatoes, if he likes.'

They went down to Mr Luffy's tent. He was awake, sitting at the entrance, eating some kind of breakfast. He waved a sandwich at them.

'Hallo, there! I'm late this morning. I had a job getting back. I went much too far. Sorry I woke you up last night, Dick.'

'You didn't. I wasn't asleep,' said Dick, going rather red. 'Did you have a good day, Mr Luffy?'

'Bit disappointing. Didn't find quite all the creatures I'd hoped,' said Mr Luffy. 'What about you? Did you have a good day?'

'Fine,' said Dick, and described it. Mr Luffy seemed

very interested in everything, even in Mr Andrews's rather frightening warning about the railway yard.

'Silly chap he sounds,' said Mr Luffy, shaking the crumbs off his front. 'All the same – I should keep away from the yard, if I were you. Stories don't get about for nothing, you know. No smoke without fire!'

'Why, sir – surely *you* don't believe there's anything spooky about the trains there?' said Dick, in surprise.

'Oh, no – I doubt if there *are* any trains,' said Mr Luffy. 'But when a place has got a bad name it's usually best to keep away from it.'

'I suppose so, sir,' said Dick and Julian together. Then they hastily changed the subject, afraid that Mr Luffy, like Mr Andrews, might also be going to forbid them to visit the railway yard. And the more they were warned about it and forbidden to go, the more they felt that they really must!

'Well, we must get back,' said Dick. 'We're expecting Jock – that's the boy at the farm – to come up for the day, and we thought we'd go out walking and take our food with us. Are you going out, too, sir?'

'Not today,' said Mr Luffy. 'My legs are tired and stiff with so much scrambling about yesterday, and I want to mount some of the specimens I found. Also I'd like to meet your farm friend – what's his name – Jock?'

'Yes, sir,' said Julian. 'Right. We'll bring him along as soon as he comes, then off we'll go. You'll be left in peace all day!'

But Jock didn't come. The children waited for him all the morning and he didn't turn up. They held up their lunch until they were too hungry to wait any longer, and then they had it on the heather in front of their tents.

'Funny,' said Julian. 'He knows where the camp is, because we pointed it out to him when he came half-way home with us yesterday. Perhaps he'll come this afternoon.'

408

But he didn't come in the afternoon either, nor did he come after tea. Julian debated whether or not to go and see what was up, but decided against it. There must be some good reason why Jock hadn't come, and Mrs Andrews wouldn't want them all visiting her two days running.

It was a disappointing day. They didn't like to leave the tents and go for even a short stroll in case Jock came. Mr Luffy was busy all day long with his specimens. He was sorry Jock had disappointed them. 'He'll come tomorrow,' he said. 'Have you got enough food? There's some in that tin over there if you want it.'

'Oh, no, thank you, sir,' said Julian. 'We've plenty really. We're going to have a game of cards. Like to join us?'

'Yes, I think I will,' said Mr Luffy, getting up and stretching himself. 'Can you play rummy?'

They could – and they beat poor Mr Luffy handsomely, because he couldn't play at all. He blamed his luck on his bad cards, but he enjoyed the game immensely. He said the only thing that really put him off was the way that Timmy stood behind him and breathed down his neck all the time.

'I kept feeling certain that Timmy thought he knew how to play my cards better than I could,' he complained. 'And whenever I did something wrong, he breathed down my neck harder than usual.'

Everyone laughed, and George privately thought that Timmy would probably play very much better than Mr Luffy if only he could hold the cards.

Jock didn't come at all. They put the cards away when they could no longer see them, and Mr Luffy announced that he was going to bed. 'It was very late when I got back last night,' he said. 'I really must have an early night.'

The others thought they would go to bed too. The thought of their cosy sleeping-bags was always a nice one when darkness came on.

409

The girls crept into their bags and Timmy flopped down on George. The boys were in their bags about the same time and Dick gave a loud yawn.

'Good night, Ju,' he said, and fell fast asleep. Julian was soon asleep too. In fact, everyone was sound asleep when Timmy gave a little growl. It was such a small growl that neither of the girls heard it, and certainly Dick and Julian didn't, away in their tent.

Timmy raised his head and listened intently. Then he gave another small growl. He listened again. Finally he got up, shook himself, still without waking George, and stalked out of the tent, his ears cocked and his tail up. He had heard somebody or something, and although he thought it was all right, he was going to make sure.

Dick was sound asleep when he felt something brushing against the outside of his tent. He awoke at once and sat up. He looked at the tent opening. A shadow appeared there and looked in.

Was it Timmy? Was it Mr Luffy? He mustn't make a mistake this time. He waited for the shadow to speak. But it didn't. It just stayed there as if it were listening for some movement inside the tent. Dick didn't like it.

'Timmy!' he said at last, in a low voice.

Then the shadow spoke: 'Dick? Or is it Julian? It's Jock here. I've got Timmy beside me. Can I come in?'

'*Jock*!' said Dick, in surprise. 'Whatever have you come at this time of night for? And why didn't you come today? We waited ages for you.'

'Yes. I know. I'm awfully sorry,' said Jock's voice, and the boy wriggled himself into the tent. Dick poked Julian awake.

'Julian! Here's Jock – and Timmy. Get off me, Timmy. Here, Jock, see if you can squeeze inside my sleeping-bag – there's room for us both, I think.'

'Oh, thanks,' said Jock, and squeezed inside with difficulty. 'How warm it is! I say, I'm terribly sorry I didn't

410

come today – but my stepfather suddenly announced he wanted me to go somewhere with him for the whole day. Can't think why. He doesn't bother about me as a rule.'

'That was mean of him, seeing that he knew you were to come on a picnic with us,' said Julian. 'Was it something important?'

'No. Not at all,' said Jock. 'He drove off to Endersfield – that's about forty miles away – parked me in the public library there, saying he'd be back in a few minutes – and he didn't come back till past tea-time! I had some sand-wiches with me, luckily. I felt pretty angry about it, I can tell you.'

'Never mind. Come tomorrow instead,' said Dick.

'I can't,' said Jock in despair. 'He's gone and arranged for me to meet the son of some friend of his – a boy called Cecil Dearlove – what a name! I'm to spend the day with this frightful boy. The worst of it is Mum's quite pleased about it. She never thinks my stepfather takes enough notice of me – good thing he doesn't, *I* think.'

'Oh blow – so you won't be able to come tomorrow either,' said Julian. 'Well – what about the next day?'

'It should be all right,' said Jock. 'But I've a feeling I'll have dear love of a Cecil planked on me for the day – to show him the cows and the puppies, dear pet! Ugh! When I could be with you four and Timmy.'

'It's bad luck,' said Julian. 'It really is.'

'I thought I'd better come and tell you,' said Jock. 'It's the first chance I've had, creeping up here tonight. I've brought some more food for you, by the way. I guessed you'd want some. I feel down in the dumps about that adventure – you know, going to see the railway yard. I was going to ask you to take me today.'

'Well – if you can't come tomorrow either – and perhaps not the next day – what about going one night?' said Dick. 'Would you like to come up tomorrow night, about this time? We won't tell the girls. We'll just go off by ourselves, we three boys – and watch!'

Jock was too thrilled to say a word. He let out a deep breath of joy. Dick laughed.

'Don't get too thrilled. We probably shan't see a thing. Bring a torch if you've got one. Come to our tent and jerk my toe. I'll probably be awake, but if I'm not, that'll wake me all right! And don't say a word to anyone of course.'

'Rather not,' said Jock, overjoyed. 'Well – I suppose I'd better be going. It was pretty weird coming over the

412

moorland in the dark. There's no moon, and the stars don't give much light. I've left the food outside the tent. Better look out that Timmy doesn't get it.'

'Right. Thanks awfully,' said Julian. Jock got out of Dick's sleeping-bag and went backwards out of the tent, with Timmy obligingly licking his nose all the way. Jock then found the bag of food and rolled it in to Julian, who put it safely under the groundsheet.

'Good night,' said Jock, in a low voice, and they heard him scrambling over the heather. Timmy went with him, pleased at this unexpected visitor, and the chance of a midnight walk. Jock was glad to have the dog's company. Timmy went right to the farm with him and then bounded back over the moorland to the camping-place, longing to pounce on the rabbits he could smell here and there, but wanting to get back to George.

In the morning Anne was amazed to find the food in her 'larder' under the gorse bush. Julian had popped it there to surprise her. 'Look at this!' she cried, in astonishment. 'Meat-pies – more tomatoes – eggs, wherever did they come from?'

'Spook-train bought them in the night,' said Dick, with a grin.

'Volcano shot them up into the air,' said Mr Luffy, who was also there. Anne threw a tea-cloth at him.

'Tell me how it came here,' she demanded. 'I was worried about what to give you all for breakfast – and now there's more than we can possibly eat. Who put it there? George, do you know?'

But George didn't. She glanced at the smiling faces of the two boys. 'I bet Jock was here last night,' she said to them. 'Wasn't he?' And to herself she said: 'Yes – and somehow I think they've planned something together. You won't trick *me*, Dick and Julian. I'll be on the lookout from now on! Wherever you go, I go too!'

10

Hunt for a spook-train

That day passed pleasantly enough. The children, Timmy, and Mr Luffy all went off to a pool high up on the moorlands. It was called 'The Green Pool' because of its cucumber-green colour. Mr Luffy explained that some curious chemicals found there caused the water to look green.

'I hope we shan't come out looking green, too,' said Dick, getting into his bathing trunks. 'Are you going to bathe, Mr Luffy?'

Mr Luffy was. The children expected him to be a very poor swimmer and to splash about at the edge and do very little – but to their surprise he was magnificent in the water, and could swim faster even than Julian.

They had great fun, and when they were tired they came out to bask in the sun. The high road ran alongside the green pool, and the children watched a herd of sheep being driven along, then a car or two came by, and finally a big army lorry. A boy sat beside the driver, and to the children's surprise he waved wildly at them.

414

'Who was that?' said Julian astonished. 'Surely he doesn't know us?'

George's sharp eye had seen who it was. 'It was Jock! Sitting beside the driver. And, look, here comes his step-father's fine new car. Jock's preferred to go with the lorry-driver instead of his stepfather! I don't blame him, either!'

The bright new car came by, driven by Mr Andrews. He didn't glance at the children by the wayside, but drove steadily on after the lorry.

'Going to market, I suppose,' said Dick, lying back again. 'Wonder what they're taking?'

'So do I,' said Mr Luffy. 'He must sell his farm produce at very high prices to be able to buy that fine car and all the machinery and gear you've told me about. Clever fellow, Mr Andrews!'

'He doesn't look at all clever,' said Anne. 'He looks rather a weak, feeble sort of man, really, Mr Luffy. I can't even imagine him being clever enough to beat anyone down, or get the better of them.'

'Very interesting,' said Mr Luffy. 'Well, what about another dip before we have our dinner?'

It was a very nice day, and Mr Luffy was very good company. He could make fine jokes very solemnly indeed, and only the fact that his ear waggled violently showed the others that he too, was enjoying the joke. His right ear seemed to love to join in the joke, even if Mr Luffy's face was as solemn as Timmy's.

They arrived home at the camp about tea-time and Anne got a fine tea ready. They took it down to eat in front of Mr Luffy's tent. As the evening came on Julian and Dick felt excitement rising in them. In the daytime neither of them really believed a word about the 'spook-trains', but as the sun sank and long shadows crept down the hills they felt pleasantly thrilled. Would they really see anything exciting that night?

It was a very dark night at first, because clouds lay across the sky and hid even the stars. The boys said good night to the girls and snuggled down into their sleeping-bags. They watched the sky through the tent opening.

Gradually the big clouds thinned out. A few stars appeared. The clouds thinned still more and fled away in rags. Soon the whole sky was bright with pin-points of light, and a hundred thousand stars looked down on the moorlands.

'We shall have a bit of starlight to see by,' whispered

416

Julian. 'That's good. I don't want to stumble about over the heather and break my ankle in rabbit-holes in the pitch darkness. Nor do I want to use my torch on the way to the yard in case it's seen.'

'It's going to be fun!' Dick whispered back. 'I hope Jock comes. It will be maddening if he doesn't.'

He did come. There was a scrambling over the heather and once again a shadow appeared at the tent opening.

'Julian! Dick! I've come. Are you ready?'

It was Jock's voice, of course. Dick's thumb pressed the switch of his torch and for a moment its light fell on Jock's red, excited face, and then was switched off again.

'Hallo, Jock! So you were able to come,' said Dick. 'I say, was that you in the lorry this morning, going by the green pool?'

'Yes. Did you see me? I saw you and waved like mad,' said Jock. 'I wanted to stop the lorry and get down and speak to you, but the driver's an awful bad-tempered sort of fellow. He wouldn't hear of stopping. Said my step-father would be wild with him if he did. Did you see *him* – my stepfather, I mean? He was in his car behind.'

'Were you off to market or something?' asked Julian.

'I expect that's where the lorry was going,' said Jock. 'It was empty, so I suppose my stepfather was going to pick up something there. I came back in the car. The lorry was supposed to come later.'

'How did you like Cecil Dearlove?' asked Dick, grinning in the darkness.

'Awful! Worse than his name,' groaned Jock. 'Wanted me to play soldiers all the time! The frightful thing is I've got to have him at the farm for the day tomorrow. Another day gone west. What shall I do with him?'

'Roll him in the pig-sty,' suggested Dick. 'Or put him with Biddy's puppies and let him sleep there. Tell him to play soldiers with them.'

Jock chuckled. 'I wish I could. The worst of it is Mum is

awfully pleased that my stepfather's got this Cecil boy for me to be friends with. Don't let's talk about it. Are you ready to start off?'

'Yes,' said Julian, and began to scramble quietly out of his bag. 'We didn't tell the girls. Anne doesn't want to come, and I don't want George to leave Anne by herself. Now, let's be very, very quiet till we're out of hearing.'

Dick got out of his bag too. The boys had not undressed that night, except for their coats, so all they had to do was to slip these on, and then crawl out of the tent.

'Which is the way – over there?' whispered Jock. Julian took his arm and guided him. He hoped he wouldn't lose his way in the starlit darkness. The moorland looked so different at night!

'If we make for that hill you can dimly see over there against the starlit sky, we should be going in the right direction,' said Julian. So on they went, keeping towards the dark hill that rose up to the west.

It seemed very much farther to the railway yard at night than in the daytime. The three boys stumbled along, sometimes almost falling as their feet caught in tufts of heather. They were glad when they found some sort of path they could keep on.

'This is about where we met the shepherd,' said Dick, in a low voice. He didn't know why he spoke so quietly. He just felt as if he must. 'I'm sure we can't be very far off now.'

They went on for some way, and then Julian pulled Dick by the arm. 'Look,' he said. 'Down there, I believe that's the old yard. You can see the lines gleaming faintly here and there.'

They stood on the heathery slope above the old yard, straining their eyes. Soon they could make out dim shapes. Yes, it was the railway yard all right.

Jock clutched Julian's sleeve. 'Look – there's a light down there! Do you see it?'

418

The boys looked – and, sure enough, down in the yard towards the other side of it, was a small yellow light. They stared at it.

'Oh – I think I know what it is,' said Dick, at last. 'It's the light in the watchman's little hut – old Wooden-Leg Sam's candle. Don't you think so, Ju?'

'Yes. You're right,' said Julian. 'I tell you what we'll do – we'll creep right down into the yard, and go over to the hut. We'll peep inside and see if old Sam is there. Then we'll hide somewhere about – and wait for the spook-train to come!'

They crept down the slope. Their eyes had got used to the starlight by now, and they were beginning to see fairly well. They got right down to the yard, where their feet made a noise on some cinders there.

They stopped. 'Someone will hear us if we make a row like this,' whispered Julian.

'Who will?' whispered back Dick. 'There's no one here except old Sam in his hut?'

'How do you know there isn't?' said Julian. 'Good heavens, Jock, don't make such a row with your feet!'

They stood there, debating what was the best thing to do.' We'd better walk right round the edge of the yard,' said Julian at once. 'As far as I remember, the grass has grown there. We'll walk on that.'

So they made their way to the edge of the yard. Sure enough, there was grass there, and they walked on it without a sound. They went slowly and softly to where the light shone dimly in Sam's little hut.

The window was high and small. It was just about at the level of their heads, and the three boys cautiously eased themselves along to it and looked in.

Wooden-Leg Sam was there. He sat sprawled in a chair, smoking a pipe. He was reading a newspaper, squinting painfully as he did so. He obviously had not had his 'bruck' glasses mended yet. On a chair beside him was

419

his wooden leg. He had unstrapped it, and there it lay.

'He's not expecting the spook-train tonight, or he wouldn't have taken off his wooden leg,' whispered Dick.

The candlelight flickered and shadows jumped about the tiny hut. It was a poor, ill-furnished little place, dirty and untidy. A cup without saucer or handle stood on the table, and a tin kettle boiled on a rusty stove.

Sam put down his paper and rubbed his eyes. He muttered something. The boys could not hear it, but they felt certain it was something about his 'bruck' glasses.

420

'Are there many lines in this yard?' whispered Jock, tired of looking in at old Sam. 'Where do they go to?'

'About half a mile or so up there is a tunnel,' said Julian, pointing past Jock. 'The lines come from there and run here, where they break up in many pairs – for shunting and so on, in the old days, I suppose, when this place was used.'

'Let's go up the lines to the tunnel,' said Jock. 'Come on. There's nothing to be seen here. Let's walk up to the tunnel.'

'All right,' said Julian. 'We may as well. I don't expect we'll see much up there either! I think these spook-trains are all a tall story of old Sam's!'

They left the little hut with its forlorn candlelight, and made their way round the yard again. Then they followed the single-track line away from the yard and up towards the tunnel. It didn't seem to matter walking on cinders now, and making a noise. They walked along, talking in low voices.

And then things began to happen! A far-off muffled noise came rumbling out of the tunnel, which was now so near that the boys could see its black mouth. Julian heard it first. He stood still and clutched Dick.

'I say! Listen! Can you here that?'

The others listened. 'Yes,' said Dick. 'But it's only a train going through one of the underground tunnels – the noise is echoing out through this one.'

'It isn't. That noise is made by a train coming through this tunnel!' said Julian. The noise grew louder and louder. A clanking made itself heard too. The boys stepped off the lines and crouched together by the side, waiting, hardly daring to breathe.

Could it be the spook-train? They watched for the light of an engine-lamp to appear like a fiery eye in the tunnel. But none came. It was darker than night in there! But the noise came nearer and nearer and nearer. Could there be the noise of a train without a train? Julian's heart began to beat twice as fast, and Dick and Jock found themselves clutching one another without knowing it.

The noise grew thunderous, and then out from the tunnel came something long and black, with a dull glow in front that passed quickly and was gone. The noise deafened the boys, and then the clanking and rumbling grew less as the train, or whatever it was, passed by. The ground trembled and then was still.

'Well, there you are,' said Julian, in a rather trembly voice. 'The spook-train – without a light or a signal! Where's it gone? To the yard, do you think?'

'Shall we go and see?' asked Dick. 'I didn't see anyone in the cab, even in the glow of what must have been the fire there – but there must be *someone* driving it! I say, what a weird thing, isn't it? It *sounded* real enough, anyway.'

'We'll go to the yard,' said Jock, who, of the three, seemed the least affected. 'Come on.'

They made their way very slowly – and then Dick gave a sharp cry. 'Blow! I've twisted my ankle. Half a minute!'

He sank down to the ground in great pain. It was only a sharp twist, not a sprain, but for a few minutes Dick could do nothing but groan. The others dared not leave him. Julian knelt by him, offering to rub the ankle, but Dick wouldn't let him touch it. Jock stood by anxiously.

It took about twenty minutes for Dick's ankle to be strong enough for him to stand on again. With the help of the others he got to his feet and tested his ankle. 'It's all right, I think. I can walk on it – slowly. Now we'll go to the yard and see what's happening!'

But even as they started to walk slowly back, they heard a noise coming up the lines from the far-away yard, 'Rumble, rumble, rumble, jangle, clank!'

'It's coming back again!' said Julian. 'Stand still. Watch! It'll be going back into the tunnel!'

They stood still and watched and listened. Again the

422

noise came nearer and grew thunderous. They saw the glow of what might be the fire in the cab, and then it passed. The train disappeared into the blackness of the tunnel mouth and they heard the echo of its rumblings for some time.

'Well, there you are! There *is* a spook-train!' said Julian, trying to laugh, though he felt a good deal shaken. 'It came and it went – where from or where to, nobody knows! But – we've heard it and seen it, in the darkness of the night. And jolly creepy it was, too!'

11

Mostly about Jock

The three boys stood rather close together, glad to feel each other in the darkness. They couldn't believe that they had found what they had come looking for so doubtfully! What kind of a train was this that had come rumbling out of the tunnel so mysteriously, and then, after a pause at the yard, had gone just as mysteriously back again?

'If only I hadn't twisted my ankle, we could have followed the train down the lines to the yard, and have gone quite close to it there,' groaned Dick. 'What an ass I am, messing things up at the most exciting moment!'

'You couldn't help it,' said Jock. 'I *say*! We've seen the spook-train! I can hardly believe it. Does it go all by itself, with nobody to drive it? Is it a real train?'

'Judging by the noise it made, it's real all right,' said Julian. 'And it shot out smoke, too. All the same – it's jolly queer. I can't say I like it much.'

'Let's go and see what's happened to Wooden-Leg Sam,' said Dick. 'I bet he's under his bed!'

They made their way slowly back to the yard, Dick limping a little, though his ankle was practically all right again. When they came to the yard they looked towards Sam's hut. The light was there no longer.

'He's blown it out and got under the bed!' said Dick. 'Poor Sam! It really must be terrifying for him. Let's go and peep into his hut.'

They went over to it and tried to see in at the window. But there was nothing to be seen. The hut was in complete darkness. Then suddenly a little flare flashed out somewhere near the floor.

'Look – there's Sam! He's lighting a match,' said Julian. 'See – he's peeping out from under the bed. He looks scared stiff. Let's tap on the window and ask him if he's all right.'

But that was quite the wrong thing to do! As soon as Julian tapped sharply on the window, Sam gave an anguished yell and retired hurriedly under the bed again, his wavering match-light going out.

'It's come for to take me!' they heard him wailing. 'It's come for to take me! And me with my wooden leg off too.'

'We're only frightening the poor old fellow,' said Dick. 'Come on. Let's leave him. He'll have a fit or something if we call out to him. He honestly thinks the spook-train's come to get him.'

They wandered round the dark yard for a few minutes, but there was nothing to find out in the darkness. No more rumbling came to their ears. The spook-train was evidently not going to run again that night.

'Let's go back,' said Julian. 'That really was exciting! Honestly, my hair stood on end when that train came puffing out of the tunnel. Where on earth did it come from? And what's the reason for it?'

They gave it up, and began to walk back to the camp. They scrambled through the heather, tired but excited. 'Shall we tell the girls we've seen the train?' said Dick.

425

'No,' said Julian. 'It would only scare Anne, and George would be furious if she knew we'd gone without her. We'll wait and see if we discover anything more before we say anything, either to the girls or to old Luffy.'

'Right,' said Dick. 'You'll hold your tongue, too, won't you, Jock?'

'Course,' said Jock, scornfully. 'Who would I tell? My stepfather? Not likely! How furious he'd be if he knew we'd all pooh-poohed his warnings and gone down to see the spook-train after all!'

He suddenly felt something warm against his legs, and gave a startled cry: 'What's this? Get away!'

But the warm thing turned out to be Timmy, who had come to meet the three boys. He pressed against each of them in turn and whined a little.

'He says, "Why didn't you take me with you?" ' said Dick. 'Sorry, old thing, but we couldn't. George would never have spoken to us again if we'd taken you, and left her behind! How would you have liked spook-trains, Timmy? Would you have run into a corner somewhere and hidden?'

'Woof,' said Timmy, scornfully. As if he would be afraid of anything!

They reached their camping-place and began to speak in whispers. 'Good-bye, Jock. Come up tomorrow if you can. Hope you don't have that Cecil boy to cope with!'

'Good-bye! See you soon,' whispered Jock, and disappeared into the darkness, with Timmy at his heels. Another chance of a midnight walk? Good, thought Timmy, just what he'd like! It was hot in the tent, and a scamper in the cool night air would be fine.

Timmy growled softly when they came near to Olly's Farm, and stood still, the hackles on his neck rising up a little. Jock put his hand on the dog's head and stopped.

'What's the matter, old boy? Burglars or something?'

He strained his eyes in the darkness. Big clouds now

426

covered the stars and there was no light at all to see by. Jock made out a dim light in one of the barns. He crept over to it to see what it was. It went out as he came near, and then he heard the sound of footsteps, the quiet closing of the barn door, and the click of a padlock as it was locked.

Jock crept nearer – too near, for whoever it was must have heard him and swung round, lashing out with his arm. He caught Jock on the shoulder, and the boy over-balanced. He almost fell, and the man who had struck him clutched hold of him. A flash-light was put on and he blinked in the sudden light.

'It's you, Jock!' said an astonished voice, rough and impatient. 'What are you doing out here at this time of night?'

'Well, what are *you* doing?' demanded Jock, wriggling free. He switched on his own torch and let the light fall on the man who had caught him. It was Peters, one of the farm men, the one in whose lorry he had ridden that very day.

'What's it to do with you?' said Peters, angrily. 'I had a breakdown, and I've only just got back. Look here – you're fully dressed! Where have you been at this time of night? Did you hear me come in and get up to see what was happening?'

'You never know!' said Jock cheekily. He wasn't going to say anything that might make Peters suspicious of him. 'You just never know!'

'Is that Biddy?' said Peters, seeing a dark shadow slinking away. 'Do you mean to say you've been out with Biddy? What in the world have you been doing?'

Jock thanked his lucky stars that Peters hadn't spotted it was Timmy, not Biddy. He moved off without saying another word. Let Peters think what he liked! It was bad luck, though, that Peters had had a breakdown and come in late. If the man told his stepfather he'd seen Jock, fully

427

dressed in the middle of the night, there'd be questions asked by both his mother and his stepfather, and Jock, who was a truthful boy, would find things very difficult to explain.

He scuttled off to bed, climbing up the pear-tree outside

his window, and dropping quietly into his room. He opened his door softly to hear if anyone was awake in the house, but all was dark and silent.

'Blow Peters!' thought Jock. 'If he splits on me, I'm for it!'

He got into bed, pondered over the curious happenings of the night for a few minutes, and then slid into an uneasy sleep, in which spook-trains, Peters, and Timmy kept doing most peculiar things. He was glad to awake in the bright, sunny morning and find his mother shaking him.

'Get up, Jock! You're very late. Whatever's made you so sleepy? We're half-way through breakfast!'

Peters, apparently, didn't say anything to Jock's step-father about seeing Jock in the night. Jock was very thankful. He began to plan how to slip off to the others at the camp. He'd take them some food! That would be a fine excuse.

'Mum, can I take a basket of stuff to the campers?' he said, after breakfast. 'They must be running short now.'

'Well – that boy is coming,' said his mother. 'What's his name – Cecil something? Your stepfather says he's such a nice boy. You did enjoy your day with him yesterday, didn't you?'

Jock would have said quite a lot of uncomplimentary things about dear Cecil if his stepfather had not been there, sitting by the window reading the paper. As it was, he shrugged his shoulders and made a face, hoping that his mother would understand his feelings. She did.

'What time is Cecil coming?' she said. 'Perhaps there's time for you to run to the camp with a basket.'

'I don't want him running off up there,' said Mr Andrews, suddenly butting into the conversation, and putting down his newspaper. 'Cecil may be here at any minute – and I know what Jock is! He'd start talking to those kids and forget all about coming back. Cecil's father is a great friend of mine, and Jock's got to be polite to him,

429

and be here to welcome him. There's to be no running off to that camp today.'

Jock looked sulky. Why must his stepfather suddenly interfere in his plans like this? Rushing him off to the town, making him take Cecil for a friend! Just when some other children had come into his rather lonely life and livened it up, too! It was maddening.

'Perhaps I can go up to the camp myself with some food,' said his mother, comfortingly. 'Or maybe the children will come down for some.'

Jock was still sulky. He stalked out into the yard and went to look for Biddy. She was with her pups who were now trying to crawl round the shed after her. Jock hoped the campers would come to fetch food themselves that day. Then at least he would get a word with them.

Cecil arrived by car. He was about the same age as Jock, though he was small for twelve years old. He had curly hair which was too long, and his grey flannel suit was very, very clean and well-pressed.

'Hallo!' he called to Jock. 'I've come. What shall we play at? Soldiers?'

'No. Red Indians,' said Jock, who had suddenly remembered his old Red Indian head-dress with masses of feathers round it, and a trail of them falling down the back. He rushed indoors, grinning. He changed into the whole suit, and put on his head-dress. He took his paint-box and hurriedly painted a frightful pattern of red, blue and green on his face. He found his tomahawk and went downstairs. He would play at Red Indians, and scalp that annoying Pale-Face!

Cecil was wandering round by himself. To his enormous horror, as he turned a corner, a most terrifying figure rose up from behind a wall, gave a horrible yell and pounced on him, waving what looked like a dangerous chopper.

Cecil turned and fled, howling loudly, with Jock leaping

430

madly after him, whooping for all he was worth, and thoroughly enjoying himself. He had had to play at soldiers all the day before with dear Cecil. He didn't see why Cecil shouldn't play Red Indians all day with him today!

Just at that moment, the four campers arrived to fetch food, with Timmy running beside them. They stopped in amazement at the sight of Cecil running like the wind, howling dismally, and a fully-dressed and painted Red Indian leaping fiercely after him.

Jock saw them, did a comical war-dance all round them, much to Timmy's amazement, yelled dramatically, pretended to cut off Timmy's tail and then tore after the vanishing Cecil.

The children began to laugh helplessly. 'Oh dear!' said Anne, with tears of laughter in her eyes, 'that must be Cecil he's after. I suppose this is Jock's revenge for having to play soldiers all day with him yesterday. Look, there they go round the pig-sty. Poor Cecil. He really thinks he's going to be scalped!'

Cecil disappeared into the farm kitchen, sobbing, and Mrs Andrews ran to comfort him. Jock made off back to the others, grinning all over his war-painted face.

'Hallo,' he said. 'I'm just having a nice quiet time with dear Cecil. I'm so glad to see you. I wanted to come over, but my stepfather said I wasn't to – I must play with Cecil. Isn't he frightful?'

'Awful,' everyone agreed.

'I say – will your mother be wild with you for frightening Cecil like that? Perhaps we'd better not ask her for any food yet?' said Julian.

'Yes – you'd better wait a bit,' said Jock, leading them to the sunny side of the haystack they had rested by before. 'Hallo, Timmy! Did you get back all right last night?'

Jock had completely forgotten that the girls didn't know of the happenings of the night before. Both Anne and

431

George at once pricked up their ears. Julian frowned at Jock, and Dick gave him a secret nudge.

'What's up?' said George, seeing all this by-play. 'What happened last night?'

'Oh, I just came up to have little night-talk with the boys – and Timmy walked back with me,' said Jock, airily. 'Hope you didn't mind him coming, George.'

George flushed an angry red. 'You're keeping something from me,' she said to the boys. 'Yes, you are. I know you are. I believe you went off to the railway yard last night! Did you?'

There was an awkward silence. Julian shot an annoyed look at poor Jock, who could have kicked himself.

'Go on – tell me,' persisted George, an angry frown on her forehead. 'You beasts! You did go! And you never woke me up to go with you! Oh, I do think you're mean!'

'Did you see anything?' said Anne, her eyes going from one boy to another. Each of the girls sensed that there had been some kind of adventure in the night.

'Well,' began Julian. And then there was an interruption. Cecil came round the haystack, his eyes red with crying. He glared at Jock.

'Your father wants you,' he said. 'You're to go at once. You're a beast, and I want to go home. Can't you hear your father yelling for you? He's got a stick – but I'm not sorry for you! I hope he whacks you hard!'

432

12

George loses her temper

Jock made a face at Cecil and got up. He went slowly off round the haystack, and the others listened in silence for whacks and yells. But none came.

'He frightened me,' said Cecil, sitting down by the others.

'Poor icle ting,' said Dick at once.

'Darling baby,' said George.

'Mother's pet,' said Julian. Cecil glared at them all. He got up again, very red.

'If I didn't know my manners, I'd smack your faces,' he said, and marched off hurriedly, before his own could be smacked.

The four sat in silence. They were sorry for Jock. George was angry and sulky because she knew the others had gone off without her the night before. Anne was worried.

They all sat there for about ten minutes. Then round the haystack came Jock's mother, looking distressed. She carried a big basket of food.

433

The children all stood up politely. 'Good morning, Mrs Andrews,' said Julian.

'I'm sorry I can't ask you to stop today,' said Mrs Andrews. 'But Jock has really behaved very foolishly. I wouldn't let Mr Andrews give him a hiding because it would only make Jock hate his stepfather, and that would never do. So I've sent him up to bed for the day. You won't be able to see him, I'm afraid. Here is some food for you to take. Oh, dear – I'm really very sorry about all this. I can't think what came over Jock to behave in such a way. It's not a bit like him.'

Cecil's face appeared round the haystack, looking rather smug. Julian grinned to himself.

'Would you like us to take Cecil for a nice long walk over the moors?' he said. 'We can climb hills and jump over streams and scramble through the heather. It would make such a nice day for him.'

Cecil's face immediately disappeared.

'Well,' said Mrs Andrews, 'that really would be very kind of you. Now that Jock's been sent upstairs for the day there's no one for Cecil to play with. But I'm afraid he's a bit of a mother's boy, you know. You'll have to go carefully with him. Cecil! Cecil! Where are you? Come and make friends with these children.'

But Cecil had gone. There was no answer at all. He didn't want to make friends with 'these children'. He knew better than that! Mrs Andrews went in search of him, but he had completely disappeared.

The four children were not at all surprised. Julian, Dick and Anne grinned at one another. George stood with her back to them, still sulky.

Mrs Andrews came back again, out of breath. 'I can't find him,' she said. 'Never mind. I'll find something for him to do when he appears again.'

'Yes. Perhaps you've got some beads for him to thread? Or a nice easy jigsaw puzzle to do?' said Julian, very politely. The others giggled. A smile appeared on Mrs Andrews's face.

'Bad boy!' she said. 'Oh dear – poor Jock. Well's it's his own fault. Now good-bye, I must get on with my work.'

She ran off to the dairy. The children looked round the haystack. Mr Andrews was getting into his car. He would soon be gone. They waited a few minutes till they heard the car set off down the rough cart-track.

'That's Jock's bedroom – where the pear-tree is,' said Julian. 'Let's just have a word with him before we go. It's a shame.'

They went across the farmyard and stood under the pear-tree – all except George, who stayed behind the haystack with the food, frowning. Julian called up to the window above: 'Jock!'

A head came out, the face still painted terrifyingly in streaks and circles. 'Hallo! He didn't whack me. Mum wouldn't let him. All the same, I'd rather he had – it's awful being stuck up here this sunny day. Where's dear Cecil?'

'I don't know. Probably in the darkest corner of one of the barns,' said Julian. 'Jock, if things are difficult in the daytime, come up at night. We've got to see you somehow.'

'Right,' said Jock. 'How do I look? Like a real Red Indian?'

'You look frightful,' grinned Julian. 'I wonder old Timmy knew you.'

'Where's George?' asked Jock.

'Sulking behind the haystack,' said Dick. 'We shall have an awful day with her now. You let the cat properly out of the bag, you idjit!'

'Yes. I'm a ninny and an idjit,' said Jock, and Anne giggled. 'Look – there's Cecil. You might tell him to beware of the bull, will you?'

'Is there a bull?' said Anne, looking alarmed.

'No. But that's no reason why he shouldn't beware of one,' grinned Jock. 'So long! Have a nice day!'

The three left him, and strolled over to Cecil, who had just appeared out of a dark little shed. He made a face at them, and stood ready to run to the dairy where Mrs Andrews was busy.

Julian suddenly clutched Dick and pointed behind Cecil. 'The bull! Beware of the bull!' he yelled suddenly.

Dick entered into the joke. 'The bull's loose! Look out! Beware of the bull!' he shouted.

Anne gave a shriek. It all sounded so real that, although she knew it was a joke, she felt half-scared. 'The bull!' she cried.

Cecil turned green. His legs shook. 'W-w-w-where is it?' he stammered.

'Look out behind you!' yelled Julian, pointing. Poor Cecil, convinced that a large bull was about to pounce on him from behind, gave an anguished cry and tore on tottering legs to the dairy. He threw himself against Mrs Andrews.

'Save me, save me! The bull's chasing me.'

'But there's no bull here,' said Mrs Andrews, in surprise. 'Really, Cecil! Was it a pig after you, or something?'

Helpless with laughter, the three children made their way back to George. They tried to tell her about the make-believe bull, but she turned away and wouldn't listen. Julian shrugged his shoulders. Best to leave George to herself when she was in one of her rages! She didn't lose her temper as often as she used to, but when she did she was very trying indeed.

They went back to the camp with the basket of food. Timmy followed soberly. He knew something was wrong with George and he was unhappy. His tail was down, and he looked miserable. George wouldn't even pat him.

When they got back to the camp, George flared up.

'How dare you go off without me when I told you I

meant to come? Fancy taking Jock and not letting me go! I think you're absolute beasts. I never really thought you'd do a thing like that, you and Dick.'

'Don't be silly, George,' said Julian. 'I told you we didn't mean to let you and Anne go. I'll tell you all that happened – and it's pretty thrilling!'

'What? Tell me quickly!' begged Anne, but George obstinately turned away her head as if she was not interested.

Julian began to relate all the curious happenings of the night. Anne listened breathlessly. George was listening too, though she pretended not to. She was very angry and very hurt.

'Well, there you are,' said Julian, when he had finished. 'If that's what people mean by spook-trains, there was one puffing in and out of that tunnel all right! I felt pretty scared, I can tell you. Sorry you weren't there too, George – but I didn't want to leave Anne alone.'

George was not accepting any apologies. She still looked furious.

'I suppose Timmy went with you,' she said. 'I think that was horrid of him – to go without waking me, when he knew I'd like to be with you on the adventure.'

'Oh, don't be so silly,' said Dick, in disgust. 'Fancy being angry with old Tim, too! You're making him miserable. And anyway, he *didn't* come with us. He just came to meet us when we got back, and then went off to keep Jock company on his way back to the farm.'

'Oh,' said George, and she reached out her hand to pat Timmy, who was filled with delight. 'At least Timmy was loyal to me then. That's something.'

There was a silence. Nobody ever knew quite how to treat George when she was in one of her moods. It was really best to leave her to herself, but they couldn't very well go off and leave the camp just because George was there, cross and sulky.

Anne took hold of George's arm. She was miserable when George behaved like this. 'George,' she began. 'There's no need to be cross with me, too. *I* haven't done anything!'

'If you weren't such a little coward, too afraid to go with us, I'd have been able to go too,' said George unkindly, dragging her arm away.

Julian was disgusted. He saw Anne's hurt face and was angry with George.

'Shut up, George,' he said. 'You're behaving like a girl, for all you think you're as good as a boy! Saying catty things like that! I'm astonished at you.'

George was ashamed of herself, but she was too proud to say so. She glared at Julian.

'And *I'm* astonished at *you*,' she said. 'After all the adventures we've had together, you try to keep me out of this one. But you *will* let me come next time, won't you, Julian?'

'What! After your frightful behaviour today?' said Julian, who could be just as obstinate as George when he wanted to. 'Certainly not. This is my adventure and Dick's – and perhaps Jock's. Not yours or Anne's.'

He got up and stalked down the hill with Dick. George sat pulling bits of heather off the stems, looking mutinous and angry. Anne blinked back tears. She hated this sort of thing. She got up to get dinner ready. Perhaps after a good meal they would all feel better.

Mr Luffy was sitting outside his tent, reading. He had already seen the children that morning. He looked up, smiling.

'Hallo! Come to talk to me?'

'Yes,' said Julian, an idea uncurling itself in his mind. 'Could I have a look at that map of yours, Mr Luffy? The big one you've got showing every mile of these moorlands?'

'Of course. It's in the tent somewhere,' said Mr Luffy.

438

The boys found it and opened it. Dick at once guessed why Julian wanted it. Mr Luffy went on reading.

'It shows the railways that run under the moorlands too, doesn't it?' said Julian. Mr Luffy nodded.

'Yes. There are quite a few lines. I suppose it was easier to tunnel under the moors from valley to valley rather than make a permanent way over the top of them. In any case, a railway over the moors would probably be completely snowed up in the winter-time.'

The boys bent their heads over the big map; it showed the railways as dotted lines when they went underground, but by long black lines when they appeared in the open air, in the various valleys.

They found exactly where they were. Then Julian's finger ran down the map a little and came to where a small line showed itself at the end of a dotted line.

He looked at Dick, who nodded. Yes – that showed where the tunnel was, out of which the 'spook-train' had come, and the lines to the deserted yard. Julian's finger went back from the yard to the tunnel, where the dotted lines began. His finger traced the dotted lines a little way till they became whole lines again. That was where the train came out into another valley!

Then his finger showed where the tunnel that led from the yard appeared to join up with another one, that also ran for some distance before coming out into yet another valley. The boys looked at one another in silence.

Mr Luffy suddenly spotted a day-flying moth and got up to follow it. The boys took the chance of talking to one another.

'The spook-train either runs through its own tunnel to the valley beyond – or it turns off into this fork and runs along to the other valley,' said Julian, in a low voice. 'I tell you what we'll do, Dick. We'll get Mr Luffy to run us down to the nearest town to buy something – and we'll slip along to the station there and see if we can't make a few inquiries about these two tunnels. We may find out something.'

'Good idea,' said Dick, as Mr Luffy came back. 'I say, sir, are you very busy today? Could you possibly run us down to the nearest town after dinner?'

'Certainly, certainly,' said Mr Luffy, amiably. The boys looked at one another in delight. *Now* they might find out something! But they wouldn't take George with them. No – they would punish her for her bad temper by leaving her behind!

440

13

A thrilling plan

Anne called them to dinner. 'Come along!' she cried. 'I've got it all ready. Tell Mr Luffy there's plenty for him, too.'

Mr Luffy came along willingly. He thought Anne was a marvellous little camp-housekeeper. He looked approvingly at the spread set out on a white cloth on the ground.

'Hm! Salad. Hard-boiled eggs. Slices of tongue. And what's this – apple-pie! My goodness! Don't tell me you cooked that here, Anne.'

Anne laughed. 'No. All this came from the farm, of course. Except the lime juice and water.'

George ate with the others, but said hardly a word. She was brooding over her wrongs, and Mr Luffy looked at her several times, puzzled.

'Are you quite well, George?' he said, suddenly. George went red.

'Yes, thank you,' she said, and tried to be more herself, though she couldn't raise a smile at all. Mr Luffy watched her, and was relieved to see that she ate as much as the others. Probably had some sort of row, he guessed correctly. Well, it would blow over! He knew better than to interfere.

They finished lunch and drank all the lime juice. It was a hot day and they were very thirsty indeed. Timmy emptied all his dish of water and went and gazed longingly into the canvas bucket of washing-water. But he was too well-behaved to drink it, now that he knew he mustn't. Anne laughed, and poured some more water into his dish.

'Well,' said Mr Luffy, beginning to fill his old brown pipe, 'if anyone wants to come into town with me this afternoon, I'll be starting in fifteen minutes.'

'I'll come!' said Anne, at once. 'It won't take George and me long to wash-up these things. Will you come too, George?'

'No,' said George, and the boys heaved a sigh of relief. They had guessed she wouldn't want to come with them — but, if she'd known what they were going to try and find out, she would have come all right!

'I'm going for a walk with Timmy,' said George, when all the washing-up had been done.

'All right,' said Anne, who secretly thought that George would be much better left on her own to work off her ill-feelings that afternoon. 'See you later.'

George and Timmy set off. The others went with Mr Luffy to where his car was parked beside the great rock. They got in.

'Hi! The trailer's fastened to it,' called Julian. 'Wait a bit. Let me get out and undo it. We don't want to take an empty trailer bumping along behind us for miles.'

'Dear me. I always forget to undo the trailer,' said Mr Luffy, vexed. 'The times I take it along without meaning to!'

The children winked at one another. Dear old Luffy! He was always doing things like that. No wonder his wife fussed round him like an old hen with one foolish chicken when he was at home.

442

They went off in the car, jolting over the rough road till they came to the smooth highway. They stopped in the centre of the town. Mr Luffy said he would meet them for tea at five o'clock at the hotel opposite the parking-place.

The three of them set off together, leaving Mr Luffy to go to the library and browse there. It seemed funny to be without George. Anne didn't much like it, and said so.

'Well, we don't like going off without George either,' said Julian. 'But honestly, she can't behave like that and get away with it. I thought she'd grown out of that sort of thing.'

'Well, you know how she adores an adventure,' said Anne. 'Oh dear – if I hadn't felt so scared you'd have taken me along, and George would have gone too. It's quite true what she said about me being a coward.'

'You're not,' said Dick. 'You can't help being scared of things sometimes – after all, you're the youngest of us – but being scared doesn't make you a coward. I've known you to be as brave as any of us when you've been scared stiff!'

'Where are we going?' asked Anne. The boys told her, and her eyes sparkled.

'Oh – are we going to find out where the spook-train comes from? It might come from one of two valleys then, judging from the map.'

'Yes. The tunnels aren't really very long ones,' said Julian. 'Not more than a mile, I should think. We thought we'd make some inquiries at the station and see if there's anyone who knows anything about the old railway yard and the tunnel beyond. We shan't say a word about the spook-train, of course.'

They walked into the station. They went up to a railway plan and studied it. It didn't tell them much. Julian turned to a young porter who was wheeling some luggage along.

'I say! Could you help us? We're camping up on the

443

moorlands, and we're quite near a deserted railway yard with lines that run into an old tunnel. Why isn't the yard used any more?'

'Don't know,' said the boy. 'Ee should ask old Tucky there – see him? He knows all the tunnels under the moors like he knows the back of his hand. Worked in them all when he was a boy.'

'Thanks,' said Dick, pleased. They went over to where an old whiskered porter was sitting in the sun, enjoying a rest till the next train came in.

444

'Excuse me,' said Julian politely. 'I've been told that you know all about the moorland tunnels like the back of your hand. They must be very, very interesting.'

'Me feyther and me grandfeyther built they tunnels,' said the old porter, looking up at the children out of small faded eyes that watered in the strong sunlight. 'And I've bin guard on all the trains that ran through they.'

He mumbled a long string of names, going through all the list of tunnels in his mind. The children waited patiently till he had finished.

'There's a tunnel near where we're camping on the moorlands,' said Julian, getting a word in at last. 'We're not far from Olly's Farm. We came across an old deserted railway yard, with lines that led into a tunnel. Do you know it?'

'Oh ay, that's an old tunnel,' said Tucky, nodding his grey head, on which his porter's cap sat all crooked. 'Hasn't been used for many a long year. Nor the yard either. Weren't enough traffic there, fur as I remember. Shut up the yard they did. Tunnel baint used no more.'

The boys exchanged glances. So it wasn't used any more! Well, they knew better.

'The tunnel joins another, doesn't it?' said Julian. The porter, pleased at their interest in the old tunnels he knew so well, got up and went into an office behind. He came out with a dirty, much-used map, which he spread out on his knee. His black finger-nail pointed to a mark on the map.

'That's the yard, see? It was called Olly's Yard, after the farm. Them's the lines to the tunnel. Here's the tunnel. It runs right through to Kilty Vale – there 'tis. And here's where it used to join the tunnel to Roker's Vale. But that were bricked up years ago. Summat happened there – the roof fell in, I think it was – and the company decided not to use the tunnel to Roker's Vale at all.'

The children listened with the utmost interest. Julian reasoned things out in his mind. If that spook-train came from anywhere then it must come from Kilty Vale, because that was the only place the lines went to now, since the way to Roker's Vale had been bricked up where the tunnels joined.

'I suppose no trains run through the tunnel from Kilty Vale to Olly's Yard now, then?' he said.

Tucky snorted. 'Didn't I tell 'ee it's not bin used for years? The yard at Kilty Vale's been turned into summat else, though the lines are still there. There's bin no engine through that tunnel since I were a young man.'

This was all very, very interesting. Julian bought old Tucky a packet of cigarettes which gave him such pleasant shock that he wanted to tell the children everything all over again. He even gave them the old map.

'Oh, thanks,' said Julian, delighted to have it. He looked at the others. 'This'll be jolly useful!' he said, and they nodded.

They left the pleased old man and went out into the town. They found a little park and sat down on a seat. They were longing to discuss all that Tucky had told them.

'It's jolly queer,' said Dick. 'No trains run there now – the tunnel's not been used for ages – and Olly's Yard must have been derelict for years.'

'And yet – there appear to be trains that come and go!' said Julian.

'Then – they *must* be spook-trains,' said Anne, her eyes wide and puzzled. 'Julian – they must be, mustn't they?'

'Looks like it,' said Julian. 'It's most mysterious. I can't understand it.'

'Ju,' said Dick, suddenly. 'I know what we'll do! We'll wait one night again till we see the spook-train come out of the tunnel to the yard. Then one of us can sprint off to the *other* end of the tunnel – it's only about a mile long – and wait for it to come out the other side! Then we'll find out

446

why a train still runs from Kilty Vale to Olly's Yard through that old tunnel.'

'Jolly good idea,' said Julian, thrilled. 'What about tonight? If Jock comes, he can go, too. If he doesn't, just you and I will go. *Not* George.'

They all felt excited. Anne wondered if she would be brave enough to go too, but she knew that when the night came she wouldn't feel half as brave as she did now! No, she wouldn't go. There was really no need for her to join in this adventure at present. It hadn't even turned out to be a proper one yet – it was only an unsolved mystery!

George hadn't come back from her walk when they reached the camp. They waited for her, and at last she appeared with Timmy, looking tired out.

'Sorry I was an ass this morning,' she said at once. 'I've walked my temper off! Don't know what came over me.'

'That's all right,' said Julian amiably. 'Forget it.'

They were all very glad that George had recovered her temper, for she was a very prickly person indeed when she was angry. She was rather subdued and said nothing at all about spook-trains or tunnels. So they said nothing either.

The night was fine and clear. Stars shone out brilliantly again in the sky. The children said good night to Mr Luffy at ten o'clock and got into their sleeping-bags. Julian and Dick did not mean to go exploring till midnight, so they lay and talked quietly.

About eleven o'clock they heard somebody moving cautiously outside. They wondered if it was Jock, but he did not call out to them. Who could it be?

Then Julian saw a familiar head outlined against the starlit sky. It was George. But what in the world was she doing? He couldn't make it out at all. Whatever it was, she wasn't making any noise over it, and she obviously thought the boys were asleep. Julian gave a nice little snore or two just to let her go on thinking so.

At last she disappeared. Julian waited a few minutes

448

and then put his head cautiously out of the tent opening. He felt about, and his fingers brushed against some string. He grinned to himself and got back into the tent.

'I've found out what George was doing,' he whispered. 'She's put string across the entrance of our tent, and I bet it runs to her tent – and she's tied it to her big toe or something, so that if we go out without her she'll feel the pull of the string when we go through it – and wake up and follow us!'

'Good old George,' chuckled Dick. 'Well, she'll be unlucky. We'll squeeze out under the sides of the tent!'

Which was what they did do at about a minute past twelve! They didn't disturb George's string at all. They were out on the heather and away down the slope while George was sleeping soundly in her tent beside Anne, waiting for the pull on her toe which didn't come. Poor George!

The boys arrived at the deserted railway yard and looked to see if Wooden-Leg Sam's candle was alight. It was. So the spook-train hadn't come along *that* night, yet.

They were just scrambling down to the yard when they heard the train coming. There was the same rumbling noise as before, muffled by the tunnel – and then out of the tunnel, again with no lamps, came the spook-train, clanking on its way to the yard!

'Quick, Dick! You sprint off to the tunnel opening and watch for the train to go back in again. And I'll find my way across the moor to the other end of the tunnel. There was a path marked on that old map, and I'll follow that!' Julian's words tumbled over each other in his excitement. 'I'll jolly well watch for the spook-train to complete its journey, and see if it vanishes into thin air or what!'

And off he went to find the path that led over the moors to the other end of the tunnel. He meant to see what happened the other end if he had to run all the way!

14

Jock comes to camp

Julian found the path quite by chance and went along it as fast as he could. He used his torch, for he did not think he would meet anyone out on such a lonely way at that time of night. The path was very much overgrown, but he could follow it fairly easily, even running at times.

'If that spook-train stops about twenty minutes in the yard again, as it did before, it will give me just about time to reach the other end of the tunnel,' panted Julian. 'I'll be at Kilty's Yard before it comes.'

It seemed a very long way. But at last the path led downwards, and some way below him Julian could see what might be a railway yard. Then he saw that big sheds were built there – or what looked like big sheds in the starlight.

He remembered what the old porter had said. Kilty's Yard was used for something else now – maybe the lines had been taken up. Maybe even the tunnel had been stopped up, too. He slipped quickly down the path and came into what had once been the old railway yard. Big buildings loomed up on every side. Julian thought they must be workshops of some kind. He switched his torch on and off very quickly, but the short flash had shown him what he was looking for – two pairs of railway lines. They were old and rusty, but he knew they must lead to the tunnel.

He followed them closely, right up to the black mouth of the dark tunnel. He couldn't see inside at all. He switched his torch on and off quickly. Yes – the lines led right inside the tunnel. Julian stopped and wondered what to do.

'I'll sneak into the tunnel a little way and see if it's bricked up anywhere,' he thought. So in he went, walking between one pair of lines. He put on his torch, certain that no one would see its light and challenge him to say what he was doing out so late at night.

The tunnel stretched before him, a great yawning hole, disappearing into deep blackness. It was certainly not bricked up. Julian saw a little niche in the brickwork of the tunnel and decided to crouch in it. It was one of the niches made for workmen to stand in when trains went by in the old days.

Julian crouched down in the dirty old niche and waited. He glanced at the luminous face of his watch. He had been twenty minutes getting here. Maybe the train would be along in a few minutes. He would be very, very close to it! Julian couldn't help wishing that Dick was with him. It was so eerie waiting there in the dark for a mysterious train that apparently belonged to no one and came and went from nowhere to nowhere!

He waited and he waited. Once he thought he heard a rumble far away down the tunnel, and he held his breath, feeling certain that the train was coming. But it didn't come. Julian waited for half an hour and still the train had not appeared. What had happened to it?

'I'll wait another ten minutes and then I'm going,' Julian decided. 'I've had about enough of hiding in a dark, dirty tunnel waiting for a train that doesn't come! Maybe it has decided to stay in Olly's Yard for the night.'

After ten minutes he gave it up. He left the tunnel, went into Kilty's Yard and then up the path to the moors. He hurried along it, eager to see if Dick was at the other end of the tunnel. Surely he would wait there till Julian came back!

Dick was there, tired and impatient. When he saw a quick flash from Julian's torch he answered it with his own. The two boys joined company thankfully.

'You *have* been ages!' said Dick, reproachfully. 'What happened? The spook-train went back into the tunnel ages and ages ago. It only stayed about twenty minutes in the yard again.'

'Went back into the tunnel!' exclaimed Julian. 'Did it really? Well, it never came out the other side! I waited for ages. I never even heard it – though I did hear a very faint rumble once, or thought I did.'

The boys fell silent, puzzled and mystified. What sort of a train was this that puffed out of a tunnel at dead of night, and went back again, but didn't appear out of the other end?

'I suppose the entrance to that second tunnel the porter told us about *is* really bricked up?' said Julian at last. 'If it wasn't, the train could go down there, of course.'

'Yes. That's the only solution, if the train's a real one and not a spook one,' agreed Dick. 'Well, we can't go exploring the tunnels now – let's wait and do it in the day-time. I've had enough tonight!'

Julian had had enough too. In silence the two boys went back to camp. They quite forgot the string in front of their tent, and scrambled right through it. They got into the sleeping-bags thankfully.

The string, fastened to George's big toe through a hole she had cut in her sleeping-bag, pulled hard, and George woke up with a jump. Timmy was awake, having heard

452

the boys come back. He licked George when she sat up.

George had not undressed properly. She slipped quickly out of her bag and crawled out of her tent. Now she would catch the two boys going off secretly and follow them!

But there was no sign or sound of them anywhere around. She crawled silently to their tent. Both boys had fallen asleep immediately, tired out with their midnight trip. Julian snored a little, and Dick breathed so deeply that George could quite well hear him as she crouched outside, listening. She was very puzzled. Someone had pulled at her toe – so somebody must have scrambled through that string. After listening for a few minutes, she gave it up and went back to her tent.

In the morning, George was furious! Julian and Dick related their night's adventure, and George could hardly believe that once again they had gone without her – and that they had managed to get away without disturbing the string! Dick saw George's face and couldn't help laughing.

'Sorry, old thing. We discovered your little trick and avoided it when we set out – but blessed if we didn't forget all about it coming back. We must have given your toe a frightful tug. Did we? I suppose you *did* tie the other end of the string to your toe?'

George looked as if she could throw all the breakfast things at him. Fortunately for everyone, Jock arrived at that moment. He didn't wear his usual beaming smile but seemed rather subdued.

'Hallo, Jock!' said Julian. 'Just in time for a spot of breakfast. Sit down and join us.'

'I can't,' said Jock. 'I've only a few minutes. Listen. Isn't it rotten – I'm to go away and stay with my step-father's sister for two weeks! Two weeks! You'll be gone when I come back, won't you?'

'Yes. But, Jock – *why* have you got to go away?' said Dick, surprised. 'Has there been a row or something?'

453

'I don't know,' said Jock. 'Mum won't say, but she looks pretty miserable. My stepfather's in a frightful temper. It's my opinion they want me out of the way for some reason. I don't know this sister of my stepfather's very well – only met her once – but she's pretty awful.'

'Well – come over here and stay with us, if they want to get rid of you,' said Julian, sorry for Jock. Jock's face brightened.

'I *say* – that's a fine idea!' he said.

'Smashing,' agreed Dick. 'Well, I don't see what's to stop you. If they want to get rid of you, it can't matter where you go for a fortnight. We'd love to have you.'

'Right. I'll come,' said Jock. 'I'll not say a word about it, though, to my stepfather. I'll let Mum into the secret. She was going to take me away today, but I'll just tell her I'm coming to you instead. I don't think she'll split on me, and I hope she'll square things with my step-aunt.'

Jock's face beamed again now. The others beamed back, even George, and Timmy wagged his tail. It would be nice to have Jock – and what a lot they had to tell him.

He went off to break the news to his mother, while the others washed up and cleared things away. George became sulky again when Jock was gone. She simply could not or would not realize that Julian meant what he said!

When they began to discuss everything that had happened the night before, George refused to listen. 'I'm not going to bother about your stupid spook-trains any more,' she said. 'You wouldn't let me join you when I wanted to, and now I shan't take any interest in the matter.'

And she walked off with Timmy, not saying where she was going.

'Well – let her go,' said Julian, exasperated and cross. 'What does she expect me to do? Climb down and say we'll let her come the next night we go?'

'We said we'd go in the daytime,' said Dick. 'She could

454

come then, because if Anne doesn't want to come it won't matter leaving her here alone in the daytime.'

'You're right,' said Julian. 'Let's call her back and tell her.' But by that time George was out of hearing.

'She's taken sandwiches,' said Anne. 'She means to be gone all day. Isn't she an idiot?'

Jock came back after a time, with two rugs and an extra jersey and more food. 'I had hard work to persuade Mum,' he said. 'But she said yes at last. Though mind you, I'd have come anyhow! I'm not going to be shoved about by my stepfather just out of spite. I *say* – isn't this sport! I never thought I'd be camping out with you. If there isn't room in your tent for me, Julian, I can sleep out on the heather.'

'There'll be room,' said Julian. 'Hallo, Mr Luffy! You've been out early!'

Mr Luffy came up and glanced at Jock. 'Ah, is this your friend from the farm? How do you do? Come to spend a few days with us? I see you have an armful of rugs!'

'Yes. Jock's coming to camp a bit with us,' said Julian. 'Look at all the food he's brought. Enough to stand a siege!'

'It is indeed,' said Mr Luffy. 'Well, I'm going to go through some of my specimens this morning. What are you going to do?'

'Oh, mess about till lunchtime,' said Julian. 'Then we might go for a walk.'

Mr Luffy went back to his tent and they could hear him whistling softly as he set to work. Suddenly Jock sat up straight and looked alarmed.

'What's the matter?' asked Dick. Then he heard what Jock had heard. A shrill whistle blown loudly by somebody some way off.

'That's my stepfather's whistle,' said Jock. 'He's whistling for me. Mum must have told him, or else he's found out I've come over here.'

455

'Quick – let's scoot away and hide,' said Anne. 'If you're not here he can't take you back! Come on! Maybe he'll get tired of looking for you, and go.'

Nobody could think of a better idea, and certainly nobody wanted to face a furious Mr Andrews. All four shot down the slope and made their way to where the heather was high and thick. They burrowed into it and lay still, hidden by some high bracken.

Mr Andrews's voice could soon be heard, shouting for Jock, but no Jock appeared. Mr Andrews came out by Mr Luffy's tent. Mr Luffy, surprised at the shouting, put his head out of his tent to see what it was all about. He didn't like the look of Mr Andrews at all.

'Where's Jock?' Mr Andrews demanded, scowling at him.

'I really do not know,' said Mr Luffy.

'He's got to come back,' said Mr Andrews, roughly. 'I won't have him hanging about here with those kids.'

'What's wrong with them?' inquired Mr Luffy. 'I must say I find them very well-behaved and pleasant-mannered.'

Mr Andrews stared at Mr Luffy, and put him down as a silly, harmless old fellow who would probably help him to get Jock back if he went about it the right way.

'Now look here,' said Mr Andrews. 'I don't know who you are, but you must be a friend of the children's. And if so, then I'd better warn you they're running into danger. See?'

'Really? In what way?' asked Mr Luffy, mildly and disbelievingly.

'Well, there's bad and dangerous places about these moorlands,' said Mr Andrews. 'Very bad. I know them. And those children have been messing about in them. See? And if Jock comes here, he'll start messing about too, and I don't want him to get into any danger. It would break his mother's heart.'

'Quite,' said Mr Luffy.

'Well, will you talk to him and send him back?' said Mr Andrews. 'That railway yard now – that's a most danger-ous place. And folks do say that there's spook-trains there. I wouldn't want Jock to be mixed up in anything of that sort.'

457

'Quite,' said Mr Luffy again, looking closely at Mr Andrews. 'You seem very concerned about this – er – railway yard.'

'Me? Oh, no,' said Mr Andrews. 'Never been near the horrible place. I wouldn't want to see spook-trains – make me run a mile! – It's just that I don't want Jock to get into danger. I'd be most obliged if you'd talk to him and send him home, when they all come back from wherever they are.'

'Quite,' said Mr Luffy again, most irritatingly. Mr Andrews gazed at Mr Luffy's bland face and suddenly wished he could smack it. 'Quite, quite, quite!' Gr-r-r-r-r-r!

He turned and went away. When he had gone for some time, and was a small speck in the distance, Mr Luffy called loudly.

'He's gone! Please send Jock here so that I can – er – address a few words to him.'

Four children appeared from their heathery hiding-place. Jock went over to Mr Luffy, looking mutinous.

'I just wanted to say,' said Mr Luffy, 'that I quite understand why you want to be away from your step-father, and that I consider it's no business of mine where you go in order to get away from him!'

Jock grinned. 'Oh, thanks awfully,' he said. 'I thought you were going to send me back!' He rushed over to the others. 'It's all right,' he said. 'I'm going to stay, and, I say – what about going and exploring down that tunnel after lunch? We *might* find that spook-train then!'

'Good idea!' said Julian. 'We will! Poor old George – she'll miss that little adventure too!'

15

George has an adventure

George had gone off with one fixed idea in her mind. She was going to find out something about that mysterious tunnel! She thought she would walk over the moorlands to Kilty's Yard, and see what she could see there. Maybe she could walk right back through the tunnel itself!

She soon came to Olly's Yard. There it lay below her, with Wooden-Leg Sam pottering about. She went down to speak to him. He didn't see or hear her coming and jumped violently when she called to him.

He swung round, squinting at her fiercely. 'You clear off!' he shouted. 'I've been told to keep you children outa here, see? Do you want me to lose my job?'

'Who told you to keep us out?' asked George, puzzled as to who could have known they had been in the yard.

'*He* did, see?' said the old man. He rubbed his eyes, and then peered at George short-sightedly again. 'Bruck me glasses,' he said.

'Who's "he" – the person who told you to keep us out?' said George.

But the old watchman seemed to have one of his sudden queer changes of temper again. He bent down and picked up a large cinder. He was about to fling it at George when Timmy gave a loud and menacing growl. Sam dropped his arm.

'You clear out,' he said. 'You don't want to get a poor old man like me into trouble, do you? You look a nice kind boy you do. You wouldn't get Wooden-Leg Sam into trouble, would you?'

George turned to go. She decided to take the path that led to the tunnel and peep inside. But when she got there there was nothing to see. She didn't feel that she wanted to walk all alone inside that dark mouth, so she took the path that Julian had taken the night before, over the top of the tunnel. But she left it half-way to look at a curious bump that jutted up from the heather just there.

She scraped away at the heather and found something hard beneath. She pulled at it but it would not give. Timmy, thinking she was obligingly digging for rabbits, came to help. He scrambled below the heather – and then he suddenly gave a bark of fright and disappeared!

George screamed: 'Timmy! What have you done? Where are you?'

To her enormous relief she heard Timmy's bark some way down. Where *could* he be? She called again, and once more Timmy barked.

George tugged at the tufts of heather, and then suddenly she saw what the curious mound was. It was a built-up vent-hole for the old tunnel – a place where the smoke came curling out in the days when trains ran there often. It had been barred across with iron, but the bars had rusted and fallen in, and heather had grown thickly over them.

'Oh, Timmy – you must have fallen down the vent,' said George, anxiously. 'But not very far down. Wait a bit and I'll see what I can do. If only the others were here to help!'

But they weren't, and George had to work all by herself to try and get down to the broken bars. It took her a very long time, but at last she had them exposed, and saw where Timmy had fallen down.

He kept giving short little barks, as if to say: 'It's all right. I can wait. I'm not hurt!'

George had to sit down and take a rest after her efforts. She was hungry, but she said to herself that she would *not* eat till she had somehow got down to Timmy, and found out where he was. Soon she began her task again.

She climbed down through the fallen-in vent. It was very difficult, and she was terrified of the rusty old iron bars breaking off under her weight. But they didn't.

Once down in the vent she discovered steps made of great iron nails projecting out. Some of them had thin rungs across. There had evidently once been a ladder up to the top of the vent. Most of the rungs had gone, but the iron nails that supported them still stood in the brick walls of the old round vent. She heard Timmy give a little bark. He was quite near her now.

Cautiously she went down the great hole. Her foot touched Timmy. He had fallen on a collection of broken iron bars, which, caught in part of the old iron ladder, stuck out from it, and made a rough landing-place for the dog to fall on.

'Oh, Timmy,' said George, horrified. 'However am I going to get you out of here? This hole goes right down into the tunnel.'

She couldn't possibly pull Timmy up the hole. It was equally impossible to get him down. He could never climb down the iron ladder, especially as it had so many rungs missing.

George was in despair. 'Oh, Timmy! Why did I lose my temper and walk out on the others to do some exploring all by myself? Don't fall, Timmy. You'll break your legs if you do.'

461

Timmy had no intention of falling. He was frightened, but so far his curious landing-place felt firm. He kept quite still.

'Listen, Tim,' said George, at last. 'The only thing I can think of is to climb down round it somehow and see how far it is to the tunnel itself. There might even be someone there to help! No, that's silly. There can't be. But I might find an old rope – anything – that I could use to help you down with. Oh, dear, what a horrible nightmare!'

George gave Timmy a reassuring pat, and then began to feel about for the iron rungs with her feet. Further down they were all there, and it was easy to climb lower and lower. She was soon down in the tunnel itself. She had her torch with her and switched it on. Then she nearly gave a scream of horror.

Just near to her was a silent train! She could almost touch the engine. Was it – could it be – the spook-train itself? George stared at it, breathing fast.

It looked very, very old and out-of-date. It was smaller than the trains she was used to – the engine was smaller and so were the trucks. The funnel was longer and the wheels were different from those of ordinary trains. George stared at the silent train by the light of her torch, her mind in a muddle. She really didn't know *what* to think!

It *must* be the spook-train! It had come from this tunnel the night before, and had gone back again – and it hadn't run all the way through to Kilty's Yard, because Julian had watched for it, and it hadn't come out there. No – it had run here, to the middle of the dark tunnel, and there it stood, waiting for night so that it might run again.

George shivered. The train belonged to years and years ago! Who drove it at night? Did anybody? Or did it run along without a driver, remembering its old days and old ways? No – that was silly. Trains didn't think or remember. George shook herself and remembered Timmy.

462

And just at that very moment, poor Timmy lost his foot-hold on the iron bars, and fell! He had stretched out to listen for George, his foot had slipped – and now he was hurtling down the vent! He gave a mournful howl.

He struck against part of the ladder and that stopped his headlong fall for a moment. But down he went again, scrabbling as he fell, trying to get hold of something to save himself.

George heard him howl and knew he was falling. She was so horror-stricken that she simply couldn't move. She stood there at the bottom of the vent like a statue, not even breathing.

Timmy fell with a thump beside her, and a groan was jerked out of him. In a trice George was down by him on her knees. 'Timmy! Are you hurt? Are you alive? Oh, Timmy, say something!'

'Woof,' said Timmy, and got up rather unsteadily on his four legs. He had fallen on a pile of the softest soot! The smoke of many, many years had sooted the walls of the vent, and the weather had sent it down to the bottom, until quite a pile had collected at one side. Timmy had fallen plump in the middle of it, and almost buried himself. He shook himself violently, and soot flew out all over George.

She didn't know or care. She hugged him, and her face and clothes grew as black as soot! She felt about and found the soft pile that had saved Timmy from being hurt.

'It's soot! I came down the other side of the vent, so I didn't know the soot was there. Oh, Timmy, what a bit of luck for you! I thought you'd be killed – or at least badly hurt,' said George.

He licked her sooty nose and didn't like the taste of it.

George stood up. She didn't like the idea of climbing up that horrid vent again – and, anyway, Timmy couldn't. The only thing to do was to walk out of the tunnel. She wouldn't have fancied walking through the tunnel before, in case she met the spook-train – but here it was, close beside her, and she had been so concerned about Timmy that she had quite forgotten it.

Timmy went over to the engine and smelt the wheels. Then he jumped up into the cab. Somehow the sight of

464

Timmy doing that took away all George's fear. If Timmy could jump up into the spook-train, there couldn't be much for her to be afraid of!

She decided to examine the trucks. There were four of them, all covered trucks. Shining her torch, she climbed up into one of them, pulling Timmy up behind her. She expected to find it quite empty, unloaded many, many years ago by long-forgotten railwaymen.

But it was loaded with boxes! George was surprised. Why did a spook-train run about with boxes in it? She shone her torch on to one – and then quickly switched it out!

She had heard a noise in the tunnel. She crouched down in the truck, put her hand on Timmy's collar, and listened. Timmy listened, too, the hackles rising on his neck.

It was a clanging noise. Then there came a bang. Then a light shone out, and the tunnel was suddenly as bright as day!

The light came from a great lamp in the side of the tunnel. George peeped cautiously out through a crack in the truck. She saw that this place must be where the tunnel forked. One fork went on to Kilty's Yard – but surely the other fork was supposed to be bricked up? George followed the lines with her eyes. One set went on down the tunnel to Kilty's Yard, the other set ran straight into a great wall, which was built across the second tunnel, that once led to Roker's Yard.

'Yes – it *is* bricked up, just as the old porter told Julian,' said George to herself. And then she stared in the greatest amazement, clutching the side of the truck, hardly believing her eyes.

Part of the wall was opening before her! Before her very eyes, a great mass of it slid back in the centre of the wall – back and back – until a queer-shaped opening, about the size of the train itself, showed in the thick wall. George gasped. Whatever could be happening?

A man came through the opening. George felt sure she had seen him before somewhere. He came up to the engine of the train and swung himself into the cab.

There were all sorts of sounds then from the cab. What was the man doing? Starting the fire to run the train? George did not dare to try and see. She was trembling now, and Timmy pressed himself against her to comfort her.

Then came another set of noises – steam noises. The man must be going to start the engine moving. Smoke came from the funnel. More noises, and some clanks and clangs.

It suddenly occurred to George that the man might be going to take the train through that little opening in the bricked-up wall. Then – supposing he shut the wall up again – George would be a prisoner! She would be in the truck, hidden behind that wall, and the wall would be closed so that she couldn't escape.

'I must get out before it's too late,' thought George, in a panic. 'I only hope the man doesn't see me!'

But just as she was about to try and get out, the engine gave a loud 'choo-choo', and began to move backwards! It ran down the lines a little way, then forward again, and this time its wheels were on the set of lines that led to the second tunnel, where the small opening now showed so clearly in the wall.

George didn't dare to get out of the moving train. So there she crouched as the engine steamed quickly to the hole in the wall that stretched right across the other tunnel. That hole just fitted it! It must have been made for it, thought George, as the train moved through it.

The train went right through and came out in another tunnel. Here there was a bright light, too. George peered out through the crack. There was more than a tunnel here! What looked like vast caves stretched away on each side of the tunnel, and men lounged about in them. Who on earth

466

were they, and what were they doing with that old train?

There was a curious noise at the back of the train. The hole in the stout brick wall closed up once more! Now there was no way in or out. 'It's like the Open-Sesame trick in Ali Baba and the Forty Thieves,' thought George. 'And, like Ali Baba, I'm in the cave – and don't know the way to get myself out! Thank goodness Timmy is with me!'

The train was now at a standstill. Behind it was the thick wall – and then George saw that in front of it was a thick wall, too! This tunnel must be bricked up in two places – and in between was this extraordinary cavern, or whatever it was. George puzzled her head over the strange place, but couldn't make head or tail of it.

'Well! Whatever would the others say if they knew you and I were actually in the spook-train itself, tucked away in its hiding-place where nobody in the world can find it?' whispered George to Timmy. 'What are we to do, Timmy?'

Timmy wagged his tail cautiously. He didn't understand all this. He wanted to lie low for a bit and see how things turned out.

'We'll wait till the men have gone away, Timmy,' whispered George. 'That is, if they ever do! Then we'll get out and see if we can manage that Open-Sesame entrance and get away. We'd better tell Mr Luffy about all this. There's something very queer and very mysterious here – and we've fallen headlong into it!'

16

In the tunnel again

Jock was really enjoying himself at the camp. He had a picnic lunch with the others, and ate as much as they did, looking very happy. Mr Luffy joined them, and Jock beamed at him, feeling that he was a real friend.

'Where's George?' asked Mr Luffy.

'Gone off by herself,' said Julian.

'Have you quarrelled, by any chance?' said Mr Luffy.

'A bit,' said Julian. 'We have to let George get over it by herself, Mr Luffy. She's like that.'

'Where's she gone?' said Mr Luffy, helping himself to a tomato. 'Why isn't she back to dinner?'

'She's taken hers with her,' said Anne. 'I feel a bit worried about her, somehow. I hope she's all right.'

Mr Luffy looked alarmed. 'I feel a bit worried myself,' he said. 'Still, she's got Timmy with her.'

'We're going off on a bit of exploring,' said Julian, when they had all finished eating. 'What are *you* going to do, Mr Luffy?'

'I think I'll come with you,' said Mr Luffy, unexpectedly. The children's hearts sank. They couldn't possibly go exploring for spook-trains in the tunnel if Mr Luffy was with them.

'Well – I don't think it will be very interesting for you, sir,' said Julian, rather feebly. However, Mr Luffy took the hint and realised he wasn't wanted that afternoon.

'Right,' he said. 'In that case I'll stay here and mess about.'

The children sighed with relief. Anne cleared up, with Jock helping her, and then they called good-bye to Mr Luffy and set off, taking their tea with them.

Jock was full of excitement. He was so pleased to be with the others, and he kept thinking of sleeping in the camp that night – what fun it would be! Good old Mr Luffy, taking his side like that. He bounded after the others joyfully as they went off to the old railway yard.

Wooden-Leg Sam was pottering about there as usual. They waved to him, but he didn't wave back. Instead he shook his fist at them and tried to bawl in his husky voice: 'You clear out! Trespassing, that's what you are. Don't you come down here or I'll chase you!'

'Well, we won't go down then,' said Dick, with a grin. 'Poor old man – thinking of chasing us with that wooden leg of his. We won't give him the chance. We'll just walk along here, climb down the lines and walk up them to the tunnel.'

Which is what they did, much to the rage of poor Sam. He yelled till his voice gave out, but they took no notice, and walked quickly up the lines. The mouth of the tunnel looked very round and black as they came near.

'Now we'll jolly well walk right through this tunnel and see where that spook-train is that came out of it the other night,' said Julian. 'It didn't come out the other end, so it *must* be somewhere in the middle of the tunnel.'

'If it's a real spook-train, it might completely disappear,' said Anne, not liking the look of the dark tunnel at all. The others laughed.

'It won't have disappeared,' said Dick. 'We shall come across it somewhere, and we'll examine it thoroughly and try and find out exactly what it is, and why it comes and goes in such a mysterious manner.'

They walked into the black tunnel, and switched on their torches, which made little gleaming paths in front of them. They walked up the middle of one pair of lines, Julian in front keeping a sharp look-out for anything in the shape of a train!

The lines ran on and on. The children's voices sounded queer and echoing in the long tunnel. Anne kept close to Dick, and half wished she hadn't come. Then she remembered that George had called her a coward, and she put up her head, determined not to show that she was scared.

Jock talked almost without stopping. 'I've never done anything like this in my life. I call this a proper adventure, hunting for spook-trains in a dark tunnel. It makes me feel nice and shivery all over. I do hope we find the train. It simply *must* be here somewhere!'

They walked on and on and on. But there was no sign of any train. They came to where the tunnel forked into the second one, that used to run to Roker's Vale. Julian flashed his torch on the enormous brick wall that stretched across the second tunnel.

'Yes, it's well and truly bricked up,' he said. 'So that only leaves this tunnel to explore. Come on.'

They went on again, little knowing that George and Timmy were behind that brick wall, hidden in a truck of the spook-train itself! They walked on and on down the lines, and found nothing interesting at all.

They saw a little round circle of bright light some way in front of them. 'See that?' said Julian. 'That must be the end of this tunnel – the opening that goes into Kilty's

470

Yard. Well – if the train isn't between here and Kilty's Yard, it's gone!'

In silence they walked down the rest of the tunnel, and came out into the open air. Workshops were built all over Kilty's Yard. The entrance to the tunnel was weed-grown and neglected. Weeds grew even across the lines there.

'Well, no train has been out of this tunnel here for years,' said Julian, looking at the thick weeds. 'The wheels would have chopped the weeds to bits.'

'It's extraordinary,' said Dick, puzzled. 'We've been right through the tunnel – and there's no train there at all – yet we know it goes in and out of it. What's happened to it?'

'It *is* a spook-train,' said Jock, his face red with excitement. 'Must be. It only exists at night, and then comes out on its lines, like it used to do scores of years ago.'

'I don't like thinking that,' said Anne, troubled. 'It's a horrid thought.'

'What are we going to do now?' Julian. 'We seem to have come to a blank. No train – nothing to see – empty tunnel. What a dull end to an adventure.'

471

'Let's walk back all the way again,' said Jock – he wanted to squeeze as much out of this adventure as he could. 'I know we shan't see the train this time any more than we did the last time – but you never know!'

'I'm not coming through that tunnel again,' said Anne. 'I want to be out in the sun. I'll walk over the top of the tunnel, along the path there that Julian took the other night – and you three can walk back, and meet me at the other end.'

'Right,' said Julian and the three boys disappeared into the dark tunnel. Anne ran up the path that led alongside the top of it. How good it was to be in the open air again! That horrid tunnel! She ran along gaily, glad to be out in the sun.

She got to the other end of the tunnel quite quickly, and sat down on the path above the yard to wait for the others. She looked for Wooden-Leg Sam. He was nowhere to be seen. Perhaps he was in his little hut.

She hadn't been there for more than two minutes when something surprising happened. A car came bumping slowly down the rough track to the yard! Anne sat up and watched. A man got out – and Anne's eyes almost fell out of her head. Why, it was – surely it was Mr Andrews, Jock's stepfather!

He went over to Sam's hut and threw open the door. Anne could hear the sound of voices. Then she heard another noise – the sound of a heavy lorry coming. She saw it come cautiously down the steep, rough track. It ran into an old tumble-down shed and stayed there. Then three men came out and Anne stared at them. Where had she seen them before?

'Of course! They're the farm labourers at Jock's farm!' she thought. 'But what are they doing here? How very queer!'

Mr Andrews joined the men and, to Anne's dismay, they began to walk up the lines to the tunnel! Her heart

472

almost stopped. Goodness, Julian, Dick and Jock were still in that tunnel, walking through it. They would bump right into Mr Andrews and his men – and then what would happen? Mr Andrews had warned them against going there, and had ordered Jock not to go.

Anne stared at the four men walking into the far-off mouth of the tunnel. What could she do? How could she warn the boys? She couldn't! She would just have to stay there and wait for them to come out – probably chased by a furious Mr Andrews and the other men. Oh dear, dear – if they were caught they would probably all get an awful whacking! What *could* she do?

'I can only wait,' thought poor Anne. 'There's nothing else to do. Oh, do come, Julian, Dick and Jock. I daren't do anything but wait for you.'

She waited and waited. It was now long past tea-time. Julian had the tea, so there was nothing for Anne to eat. Nobody came out of the tunnel. Not a sound was heard. Anne at last decided to go down and ask Wooden-Leg Sam a few questions. So, rather afraid, the little girl set off down to the yard.

Sam was in his hut, drinking cocoa, and looking very sour. Something had evidently gone wrong. When he saw Anne's shadow across the doorway he got up at once, shaking his fist.

'What, you children again! Didn't you go into that there tunnel this afternoon, and didn't I go up and telephone to Mr Andrews to come and catch you all, poking your noses in all the time? How did you get out of that tunnel? Are the others with you? Didn't Mr Andrews catch you, eh?'

Anne listened to all this in horror. So old Sam had actually managed to telephone Mr Andrews, and tell tales of them – so that Jock's stepfather and his men had come to catch them. This was worse than ever.

'You come in here,' said Sam suddenly, and he darted

473

his big arm at her. 'Come on. I don't know where the others are, but I'll get one of you!'

Anne gave a scream and ran away at top speed. Wooden-Leg Sam went after her for a few yards and then gave it up. He bent down and picked up a handful of cinders. A shower of them fell all round Anne, and made her run faster than ever.

She tore up the path to the heather, and was soon on the moors again, panting and sobbing. 'Oh, Julian! Oh, Dick! What's happened to you? Oh, where's George? If only she would come home, she'd be brave enough to look for them, but I'm not. I must tell Mr Luffy. He'll know what to do!'

She ran on and on, her feet catching continually in the tufts of thick heather. She kept falling over and scrambling up again. She now had only one idea in her mind – to find Mr Luffy and tell him every single thing! Yes, she would tell him about the spook-trains and all. There was something queer and important about the whole thing now, and she wanted a grown-up's help.

She staggered on and on. 'Mr Luffy! Oh, Mr Luffy, where are you? MR LUFFY!'

But no Mr Luffy answered her. She came round the gorse bushes she thought were the ones sheltering the camp – but, alas, the camp was not there. Anne had lost her way!

'I'm lost,' said Anne, the tears running down her cheeks. 'But I mustn't get scared. I must try to find the right path now. Oh, dear, I'm quite lost! Mr LUFFY!'

Poor Anne. She stumbled on blindly, hoping to come to the camp, calling every now and again. 'Mr Luffy. Can you hear me? MR LUFFFFFFFY!'

474

17

An amazing find

In the meantime, what had happened to the three boys walking back through the tunnel? They had gone slowly along examining the lines to see if a train could have possibly run along them recently. Few weeds grew in the dark airless tunnel, so they could not tell by those.

But, when they came about half-way, Julian noticed an interesting thing. 'Look,' he said, flashing his torch on to the lines before and behind them. 'See that? The lines are black and rusty behind us now – but here this pair of lines is quite bright – as if they had been used a lot.'

He was right. Behind them stretched black and rusty lines, sometimes buckled in places – but in front of them, stretching to the mouth of the tunnel leading to Olly's Yard, the lines were bright, as if train-wheels had run along them.

'That's queer,' said Dick. 'Looks as if the spook-train ran only from here to Olly's Yard and back. But why? And where in the world is it now? It's vanished into thin air!'

Julian was as puzzled as Dick. Where *could* a train be if it was not in the tunnel? It had obviously run to the middle of the tunnel, and then stopped – but where had it gone now?

'Let's go to the mouth of the tunnel and see if the lines are bright all the way,' said Julian at last. 'We can't discover much here – unless the train suddenly materialises in front of us!'

They went on down the tunnel, their torches flashing on the lines in front of them. They walked earnestly as they went. They didn't see four men waiting for them, four men who crouched in a little niche at the side of the tunnel, waiting there in the dark.

'Well,' said Julian, 'I think –' and then he stopped, because four dark figures suddenly pounced on the three boys and held them fast. Julian gave a shout and struggled, but the man who had hold of him was far too strong to escape from. Their torches were flung to the ground. Julian's broke, and the other two torches lay there, their beams shining on the feet of the struggling company.

It didn't take more than twenty seconds to make each boy a captive, his arms behind his back. Julian tried to kick, but his captor twisted his arm so fiercely that he groaned in pain and stopped his kicking.

'Look here! What's all this about?' demanded Dick. 'Who are you, and what do you think you're doing? We're only three boys exploring an old tunnel. What's the harm in that?'

'Take them all away,' said a voice that everyone recognised at once.

'Mr Andrews! Is it you?' cried Julian. 'Set us free. You know us – the boys at the camp. And Jock's here too. What do you think you're doing?'

Mr Andrews didn't answer, but he gave poor Jock a box on the right ear that almost sent him to the ground.

Their captors turned them about, and led them roughly up the tunnel, towards the middle. Nobody had a torch so

476

it was all done in the darkness and the three boys stumbled badly, though the men seemed sure-footed enough.

They came to a halt after a time. Mr Andrews left them and Julian heard him go off somewhere to the left. Then there came a curious noise – a bang, a clank, and then a sliding, grating sound. What could be happening? Julian strained his eyes in the darkness, but he could see nothing at all.

He didn't know that Mr Andrews was opening the bricked-up wall through which the train had gone. He didn't know that he and the others were being pushed out of the first tunnel into the other one, through the curious hole in the wall. The three boys were shoved along in the darkness, not daring to protest.

Now they were in the curious place between the two walls which were built right across the place where the second tunnel forked from the first one. The place where the spook-train stood in silence – the place where George was, still hidden in one of the trucks with Timmy! But nobody knew that, of course; not even Mr Andrews guessed that a girl and a dog were listening in a truck nearby!

He put on a torch and flashed it in the faces of the three boys, who, although they were not showing any fear, felt rather scared all the same. This was so weird and un-expected, and they had no idea where they were at all.

'You were warned not to go down to that yard,' said the voice of one of the men. 'You were told it was a bad and dangerous place. So it is. And you've got to suffer for not taking heed of the warning! You'll be tied up and left here till we've finished our business. Maybe that'll be three days, maybe it'll be three weeks!'

'Look here – you can't keep us prisoner for all that time!' said Julian, alarmed. 'Why, there will be search parties out for us all over the place! They will be sure to find us.'

'Oh, no they won't,' said the voice. 'Nobody will find you here. Now, Peters – tie 'em up!'

Peters tied the three boys up. They had their legs tied, and their arms too, and were set down roughly against a wall. Julian protested again.

'What are you doing this for? We're quite harmless. We don't know a thing about your business, whatever it is.'

'We're not taking any chances,' said the voice. It was not Mr Andrews's voice, but a firm, strong one, full of determination and a large amount of annoyance.

'What about Mum?' said Jock suddenly, to his stepfather. 'She'll be worried.'

'Well, let her be worried,' said the voice again, answering before Mr Andrews could say a word. 'It's your own fault. You were warned.'

The feet of the four men moved away. Then there came the same noises again as the boys had heard before. They were made by the hole in the wall closing up, but the boys didn't know that. They couldn't imagine what they were. The noises stopped and there was dead silence. There was also pitch darkness. The three boys strained their ears, and felt sure that the men had gone.

'Well! The brutes! Whatever are they up to?' said Julian in a low voice, trying to loosen the ropes round his hands.

'They've got some secret to hide,' said Dick. 'Gosh, they've tied my feet so tightly that the rope is cutting into my flesh.'

'What's going to happen?' came Jock's scared voice. This adventure didn't seem quite so grand to him now.

'Sh!' said Julian suddenly. 'I can hear something!'

They all lay and listened. What was it they could hear.

'It's – it's a dog whining,' said Dick, suddenly.

It was. It was Timmy in the truck with George. He had heard the voices of the boys he knew, and he wanted to get to them. But George, not sure yet that the men had gone, still had her hand on his collar. Her heart beat for joy to

478

think she was alone no longer. The three boys – and
Anne, too, perhaps – were there, in the same queer place
as she and Timmy were.

The boys listened hard. The whining came again.
Then, George let go her hold of Timmy's collar, and he
leapt headlong out of the truck. His feet pattered eagerly
over the ground. He went straight to the boys in the
darkness, and Julian felt a wet tongue licking his face. A
warm body pressed against him, and a little bark told him
who it was.

'Timmy! I say, Dick – it's Timmy!' cried Julian, in joy. 'Where did he come from? Timmy, is it really you?'

'Woof,' said Timmy, and licked Dick next and then Jock.

'Where's George then?' wondered Dick.

'Here,' said a voice, and out of the truck scrambled George, switching on her torch as she did so. She went over the boys. 'Whatever's happened? How did you come here? Were you captured or something!'

'Yes,' said Julian. 'But, George – where are we? And what are *you* doing here too? It's like a peculiar dream!'

'I'll cut your ropes first, before I stop to explain anything,' said George, and she took out her sharp knife. In a few moments she had cut the boys' bonds, and they all sat up, rubbing their sore ankles and wrists, groaning.

'Thanks, George! Now I feel fine,' said Julian, getting up. 'Where *are* we? Gracious, is that an engine there? What's it doing here?'

'That, Julian, is the spook-train!' said George, with a laugh. 'Yes, it is, really.'

'But we walked all the way down the tunnel and out of the other end, without finding it,' said Julian puzzled. 'It's most mysterious.'

'Listen, Ju,' said George. 'You know where that second tunnel is bricked up, don't you? Well, there's a way in through the wall – a whole bit of it moves back in a sort of Open-Sesame manner! The spook-train can run in through the hole, on the rails. Once it's beyond the wall it stops, and the hole is closed up again.'

George switched her torch round to show the astonished boys the wall through which they had come. Then she swung her torch to the big wall opposite. 'See that?' she said. 'There are *two* walls across this second tunnel, with a big space in between – where the spook-train hides! Clever, isn't it?'

'It would be, if I could see any sense in it,' said Julian.

480

'But I can't. Why should anyone mess about with a silly spook-train at night?'

'That's what we've got to find out,' said George. 'And now's our chance. Look, Julian – look at all the caves stretching out on either side of the tunnel here. They would make wonderful hiding-places!'

'What for?' said Dick. 'I can't make head or tail of this!'

George swung her torch on the three boys and then asked a sudden question: 'I say – where's Anne?'

'Anne! She didn't want to come back with us through the tunnel, so she ran over the moorlands to meet us at the other end, by Olly's Yard,' said Julian. 'She'll be worried stiff, won't she, when we don't turn up. I only hope she doesn't come wandering up the tunnel to meet us – she'll run into those men if she does.'

Everyone felt worried. Anne hated the tunnel and she would be very frightened if people pounced on her in the darkness. Julian turned to George.

'Swing your torch round and let's see these caves. There doesn't seem to be anyone here now. We could have a snoop round.'

George swung her torch round, and Julian saw vast and apparently fathomless caves stretching out on either side, cut out of the sides of the tunnel. Jock saw something else. By the light of the torch he caught sight of a switch on the wall. Perhaps it opened the hole in the wall.

He crossed to it and pulled it down. Immediately the place was flooded with a bright light. It was a lightswitch he had found. They all blinked in the sudden glare.

'That's better,' said Julian, pleased. 'Good for you, Jock! Now we can see what we're doing.'

He looked at the spook-train standing silently near them on its rails. It certainly looked very old and forgotten – as if it belonged to the last century, not to this.

'It's quite a museum piece,' said Julian, with interest.

481

'So that's what we heard puffing in and out of the tunnel at night – old Spooky!'

'I hid in that truck there,' said George, pointing, and she told them her own adventure. The boys could hardly believe she had actually puffed into this secret place, hidden on the spook-train itself!

'Come on – now let's look at these caves,' said Dick. They went over to the nearest one. It was packed with crates and boxes of all kinds. Julian pulled one open and whistled.

'All black market stuff, I imagine. Look here – crates of tea – crates of whisky and brandy – boxes and boxes of stuff – goodness knows what! This is a real black market hiding-place!'

The boys explored a little further. The caves were piled high with valuable stuff, worth thousands of pounds.

'All stolen, I suppose,' said Dick. 'But what do they *do* with it? I mean – how do they dispose of it? They bring it here in the train, of course, and hide it – but they must have some way of getting rid of it.'

'Would they repack it on the train and run it back to the yard when they had enough lorries to take it away?' said Julian.

'No!' said Dick. 'Of course not. Let me see – they steal it – pile it on to lorries at night, take it somewhere temporarily . . .'

'Yes – to my mother's farm!' said Jock, in a scared voice. 'All those lorries there in the barn – that's what they're used for! And they come down to Olly's Yard at night and the stuff is loaded in secret on the old train that comes puffing out to meet them – and then it's taken back here and hidden!'

'Wheeeee-ew!' Julian whistled. 'You're right, Jock! That's just what happens. What a cunning plot – to use a perfectly honest little farm as a hiding-place – to stock the farm with black-market men for labourers – no wonder

482

they are such bad workers – and to wait for dark nights to run the stuff down to the yard and load it on the train!'

'Your stepfather must make a lot of money at this game,' said Dick to Jock.

'Yes. That's why he can afford to pour money into the farm,' said Jock, miserably. 'Poor Mum. This will break her heart. All the same, I don't think my stepfather's the chief one in this. There's somebody behind him.'

'Yes,' said Julian, thinking of the mean little Mr Andrews, with his big nose and weak chin. 'There probably is. Now – I've thought of something else. If this stuff is got rid of in any other way except down the tunnel it came up, there must somewhere be a way out of these caves!'

'I believe you're right,' said George. 'And if there is – we'll find it! And what's more, we'll escape that way!'

'Come on!' said Julian, and he switched off the glaring light. 'Your torch will give enough light now. We'll try this cave first. Keep your eyes open, all of you!'

18

A way of escape

The four children and Timmy went into the big cave. They made their way round piles of boxes, chests and crates, marvelling at the amount the men must have stolen from time to time.

'These aren't man-made caves,' said Julian. 'They're natural. I expect the roof did perhaps fall in where the two tunnels met, and the entrance between them was actually blocked up.'

'But were *two* walls built then?' said Dick.

'Oh, no. We can't guess how it was that this black market hiding-place came into existence,' said Julian, 'but it might perhaps have been known there were caves here – and when someone came prospecting along the tunnel one day, maybe they even found an old train buried under a roof-fall or something like that.'

'And resurrected it, and built another wall secretly for a hiding-place – and used the train for their own purposes!' said Dick. 'Made that secret entrance, too. How ingenious!'

'Or it's possible the place was built during the last war,' said Julian. 'Maybe secret experiments were carried on here – and given up afterwards. The place might have

484

been discovered by the black marketeers then, and used in this clever way. We can't tell!'

They had wandered for a good way in the cave by now, without finding anything of interest beyond the boxes and chests of all kinds of goods. Then they came to where a pile was very neatly arranged, with numbers chalked on boxes that were built up one on top of another. Julian halted.

'Now this looks as if these boxes were about to be shifted off somewhere,' he said. 'All put in order and numbered. Surely the exit must be somewhere here?'

He took George's torch from her and flashed it all round. Then he found what he wanted. The beam of light shone steadily on a strong roughly-made wooden door, set in the wall of the cave. They went over to it in excitement.

'This is what we want!' said Julian. 'I bet this is the exit to some very lonely part of the moors, not far from a road that lorries can come along to collect any goods carried out of here! There are some very deserted roads over these moors, running in the middle of miles of lonely moorland.'

'It's a clever organisation,' said Dick. 'Lorries stored at an innocent farm, full of goods for hiding in the tunnel-caves at a convenient time. The train comes out in the dark to collect the goods, and takes them back here, till the hue and cry after the goods has died down. Then out they go through this door on to the moorlands, down to the lorries which come to collect them and whisk them away to the black market!'

'I told you how I saw Peters late one night, locking up the barn, didn't I?' said Jock, excitedly. 'Well, he must have got the lorry full of stolen goods then – and the next night he loaded them on to the spook-train!'

'That's about it,' said Julian, who had been trying the door to see if he could open it. 'I say, this door's maddening. I can't make it budge an inch. There's no lock that I can see.'

They all shoved hard, but the door would not give at all.

It was very stout and strong, though rough and unfinished. Panting and hot, the four of them at last gave it up.

'Do you know what I think?' said Dick. 'I think the beastly thing has got something jammed hard against it on the outside.'

'Sure to have, when you come to think of it,' said Julian. 'It will be well hidden too – heather and bracken and stuff all over it. Nobody would ever find it. I suppose the lorry-drivers come across from the road to open the door when they want to collect the goods. And shut it and jam it after them.'

'No way of excape there, then,' said George in disappointment.

' 'Fraid not,' said Julian. George gave a sigh.

'Tired, old thing?' Julian asked kindly. 'Or hungry?'

'Both,' said George.

'Well, we've got some food somewhere, haven't we?' said Julian. 'I remember one of the men slinging my bag in after me. We've not had what we brought for tea yet. What about having a meal now? We can't seem to escape at the moment.'

'Let's have it here,' said George. 'I simply can't go a step further!'

They sat down against a big crate. Dick undid his kit-bag. There were sandwiches, cake and chocolate. The four of them ate thankfully, and wished they had something to wash down the food with. Julian kept wondering about Anne.

'I wonder what she did,' he said. 'She'd wait and wait, I suppose. Then she might go back to camp. But she doesn't know the way very well, and she might get lost. Oh dear – I don't know which would be worse for Anne, being lost on the moor or a prisoner down here with us!'

'Perhaps she's neither,' said Jock, giving Timmy his last bit of sandwich. 'I must say I'm jolly glad to have

486

Timmy. Honest, George, I couldn't believe it when I heard Tim whine, and then heard your voice, too. I thought I must be dreaming.'

They sat where they were for a little longer and then decided to go back to the tunnel where the train was. 'It's just possible we might find the switch that works the Open-Sesame bit,' said Julian. 'We ought to have looked before, really, but I didn't think of it.'

They went back to where the train stood silently on its pair of lines. It seemed such an ordinary old train now that the children couldn't imagine why they had ever thought it was queer and spooky.

They switched on the light again, then they looked about for any lever or handle that might perhaps open the hole in the wall. There didn't seem to be anything at all. They tried a few switches, but nothing happened.

Then George suddenly came across a big lever low down in the brick wall itself. She tried to move it and couldn't. She called Julian.

'Ju! Come here. I wonder if this has got anything to do with opening that hole.'

The three boys came over to George. Julian tried to swing the lever down. Nothing happened. He pulled it but it wouldn't move. Then he and Dick pushed it upwards with all their strength.

And hey presto, there came a bang from somewhere, as something heavy shifted, and then a clanking as if machinery was at work. Then came the sliding, grating noise and a great piece of the brick wall moved slowly back, and then swung round sideways and stopped. The way of escape was open!

'Open Sesame!' said Dick, grandly, as the hole appeared.

'Better switch off the light here,' said Julian. 'If there's anyone still in the tunnel they might see the reflection of it on the tunnel-wall beyond, and wonder what it was.'

487

He stepped back and switched it off, and the place was in darkness again. George put on her torch, and its feeble beam lighted up the way of escape.

'Come on,' said Dick, impatiently, and they all crowded out of the hole. 'We'll make for Olly's Yard.' They began to make their way down the dark tunnel.

'Listen,' said Julian, in a low voice. 'We'd better not talk at all, and we'd better go as quietly as we can. We don't know who may be in or out of this tunnel this evening. We don't want to walk bang into somebody.'

So they said nothing at all, but kept close to one another in single file, walking at the side of the track.

They had not gone more than a quarter of a mile before Julian stopped suddenly. The others bumped into one another, and Timmy gave a little whine as somebody trod on his paw. George's hand went down to his collar at once.

The four of them and Timmy listened, hardly daring to breathe. Somebody was coming up the tunnel towards them! They could see the pin-point of a torch, and hear the distant crunch of footsteps.

'Other way, quick!' whispered Julian, and they all turned. With Jock leading them now, they made their way as quickly and quietly as they could back to the place where the two tunnels met. They passed it and went on towards Kilty's Yard, hoping to get out that way.

But alas for their hopes, a lantern stood some way down the tunnel there, and they did not dare to go on. There might be nobody with the lantern – on the other hand there might. What were they to do?

'They'll see that hole in the wall is open!' suddenly said Dick. 'We left it open. They'll know we've escaped then. We're caught again! They'll come down to find us, and here we'll be!'

They stood still, pressed close together, Timmy growling a little in his throat. Then George remembered something!

'Julian! Dick! We could climb up that vent that I came down,' she whispered. 'The one poor old Timmy fell down. Have we time?'

'Where is the vent?' said Julian, urgently. 'Quick find it.'

George tried to remember. Yes, it was on the other side of the tunnel – near the place where the two tunnels met. She must look for the pile of soot. How she hoped the little light from her torch would not be seen. Whoever was coming up from Olly's Yard must be almost there by now!

She found the pile of soot that Timmy had fallen into. 'Here it is,' she whispered. 'But, oh Julian! How can we take Timmy?'

'We can't,' said Julian. 'We must hope he'll manage to hide and then slink out of the tunnel by himself. He's quite clever enough.'

He pushed George up the vent first and her feet found the first rungs. Then Jock went up, his nose almost on George's heels. Then Dick – and last of all, Julian. But before he managed to climb the first steps, something happened.

A bright glare filled the tunnel, as someone switched on the light that hung there. Timmy slunk into the shadows and growled in his throat. Then there came a shout.

'Who's opened the hole in the wall? It's open! Who's there?'

It was Mr Andrews's voice. Then came another voice, angry and loud: 'Who's here? Who's opened this place?'

'Those kids can't have moved the lever,' said Mr Andrews. 'We bound them up tightly.'

The men, three of them, went quickly through the hole in the wall. Julian climbed up the first few rungs thankfully. Poor Timmy was left in the shadows at the bottom.

Out came the men at a run. 'They've gone! Their ropes are cut! How could they have escaped? We put Kit down one end of the tunnel and we've been walking up this end. Those kids must be about here somewhere.'

'Or hiding in the caves,' said another voice. 'Peters, go and look, while we hunt here.'

The men hunted everywhere. They had no idea that the vent was nearby in the wall. They did not see the dog that slunk by them like a shadow, keeping out of their way, and lying down whenever the light from a torch came near him.

George climbed steadily, feeling with her feet for the iron nails whenever she came to broken rungs. Then she came to a stop. Something was pressing on her head. What was it? She put up her hand to feel. It was the collection of broken iron bars that Timmy had fallen on that morning. He had dislodged some of them, and they had then fallen in such a way that they had lodged across the vent, all twined into each other. George could climb no higher. She tried to move the bars, but they were heavy and strong – besides, she was afraid she might bring the whole lot on top of her and the others. They might be badly injured then.

'What's up, George? Why don't you go on?' asked Jock, who was next.

'There's some iron bars across the vent – ones that must have fallen when Timmy fell,' said George. 'I can't go any higher! I daren't pull too hard at the bars.'

Jock passed the message to Dick, and he passed it down to Julian. The four of them came to a full-stop!

'Blow!' said Julian. 'I wish I'd gone up first. What are we to do now?'

What indeed? The four of them hung there in the darkness, hating the smell of the sooty old vent, miserably uncomfortable on the broken rungs and nails.

'How do you like adventures now, Jock?' asked Dick. 'I bet you wish you were in your own bed at home!'

'I don't!' said Jock. 'I wouldn't miss this for worlds! I always wanted an adventure – and I'm not grumbling at this one!'

490

19

What an adventure!

And now, what had happened to Anne? She had stumbled on and on for a long time, shouting to Mr Luffy. And outside his tent Mr Luffy sat, reading peacefully. But, as the evening came, and then darkness, he became very worried indeed about the five children.

He wondered what to do. It was hopeless for one man to search the moors. Half a dozen or more were needed for that! He decided to get his car and go over to Olly's Farm to get the men from there. So off he went.

But when he got there he found no one at home except Mrs Andrews and the little maid. Mrs Andrews looked bewildered and worried.

'What is the matter?' said Mr Luffy gently, as she came running out to the car, looking troubled.

'Oh, it's you, Mr Luffy,' she said, when he told her who he was. 'I didn't know who you were. Mr Luffy, something queer is happening. All the men have gone – and all the lorries, too. My husband has taken the car – and nobody will tell me anything. I'm so worried.'

Mr Luffy decided not to add to her worries by telling her the children were missing. He just pretended he had come to collect some milk. 'Don't worry,' he said comfortingly to Mrs Andrews. 'You'll find things are all right in the morning, I expect. I'll come and see you then. Now I must be off on an urgent matter.'

He went bumping along the road in his car, puzzled. He had known there was something queer about Olly's Farm, and he had puzzled his brains a good deal over Olly's Yard and the spook-trains. He hoped the children hadn't got mixed up in anything dangerous.

'I'd better go down and report to the police that they're missing,' he thought. 'After all, I'm more or less responsible for them. It's very worrying indeed.'

He told what he knew at the police station, and the sergeant, an intelligent man, at once mustered six men and a police car.

'Have to find those kids,' he said. 'And we'll have to look into this Olly's Farm business, sir, and these here spook-trains, whatever they may be. We've known there was something funny going on, but we couldn't put our finger on it. But we'll find the children first.'

They went quickly up to the moors and the six men began to fan out to search, with Mr Luffy at the head. And the first thing they found was Anne!

She was still stumbling along, crying for Mr Luffy, but in a very small, weak voice now. When she heard his voice calling her in the darkness she wept for joy.

'Oh, Mr Luffy! You must save the boys,' she begged him. 'They're in that tunnel – and they've been caught by Mr Andrews and his men. I'm sure. They didn't come out and I waited and waited! Do come!'

'I've got some friends here who will certainly come and help,' said Mr Luffy gently. He called the men, and in a few words told them what Anne had said.

'In the tunnel?' said one of them. 'Where the spook-

492

trains run? Well, come on, men, we'll go down there.'

'You stay behind, Anne,' said Mr Luffy. But she wouldn't. So he carried her as he followed the men who were making their way through the heather, down to Olly's Yard. They did not bother with Wooden-Leg Sam. They went straight to the tunnel and walked up it quietly. Mr Luffy was a good way behind with Anne. She refused to stay with him in the yard.

'No,' she said, 'I'm not a coward. Really I'm not. I want to help to rescue the boys. I wish George was here. Where's George?'

Mr Luffy had no idea. Anne clung to his hand, scared but eager to prove that she was not a coward. Mr Luffy thought she was grand!

Meanwhile, Julian and the others had been in the vent for a good while, tired and uncomfortable. The men had searched in vain for them and were now looking closely into every niche at the sides of the tunnel.

And, of course, they found the vent! One of the men shone his light up it. It shone on to poor Julian's feet! The man gave a loud shout that almost made Julian fall off the rung he was standing on.

'Here they are! Up this vent. Who'd have thought it? Come on down or it'll be the worse for you!'

Julian didn't move. George pushed desperately at the iron bars above her head, but she could not move them. One of the men climbed up the vent and caught hold of Julian's foot.

He dragged so hard at it that the boy's foot was forced off the rung. Then the man dragged off the other foot, and Julian found himself hanging by his arms with the man tugging hard at his feet. He could hang on no longer. His tired arms gave way and he fell heavily down, landing half on the man and half on the pile of soot. Another man pounced on Julian at once, while the first climbed up the

493

vent to find the next boy. Soon Dick felt his feet being tugged at, too.

'All right, all right. I'll come down!' he yelled, and climbed down. Then Jock climbed down, too. The men looked at them angrily.

'Giving us a chase like this! Who undid your ropes?' said Mr Andrews, roughly. One of the men put a hand on his arm and nodded up towards the vent. 'Someone else is coming down,' he said. 'We only tied up three boys, didn't we? Who's this, then?'

It was George, of course. She wasn't going to desert the three boys. Down she came, as black as night with soot.

'Another boy!' said the men. 'Where did he come from?'

'Any more up there?' asked Mr Andrews.

'Look and see,' said Julian, and got a box on the ears for his answer.

'Treat 'em rough now,' ordered Peters. 'Teach 'em a lesson, the little pests. Take 'em away.'

The children's hearts sank. The men caught hold of them roughly. Blow! Now they would be made prisoners again.

Suddenly a cry came from down the tunnel: 'Police! Run for it!'

The men dropped the children's arms at once and stood undecided. A man came tearing up the tunnel. 'I tell you the police are coming!' he gasped. 'Are you stone deaf? There's a whole crowd of them. Run for it! Somebody's split on us.'

'Get along to Kilty's Yard!' shouted Peters. 'We can get cars there. Run for it!'

To the children's dismay, the men tore down the tunnel to Kilty's Yard. They would escape! They heard the sound of the men's feet as they ran along the line.

George found her voice. 'Timmy! Where are you? After them, Timmy! Stop them!'

494

A black shadow came streaking by out of the hole in the wall, where Timmy had been hiding and watching for a chance to come to George. He had heard her voice and obeyed. He raced after the men like a greyhound, his tongue hanging out, panting as he went.

These were the men who had ill-treated George and the others, were they? Aha, Timmy knew how to deal with people like that!

The policemen came running up, and Mr Luffy and Anne came up behind them.

'They've gone down there, with Timmy after them,' shouted George. The men looked at her and gasped. She was black all over. The others were filthy dirty too, with sooty-black faces in the light of the lamp that still shone down from the wall of the tunnel.

'George!' shrieked Anne in delight. 'Julian! Oh, are you all safe? I went back to tell Mr Luffy about you and I got lost. I'm so ashamed!'

'You've nothing to be ashamed of, Anne,' said Mr Luffy. 'You're a grand girl! Brave as a lion!'

From down the tunnel came shouts and yells and loud barks. Timmy was at work! He had caught up the men and launched himself on them one after another, bringing each one heavily to the ground. They were terrified to find a big animal growling and snapping all around them. Timmy held them at bay in the tunnel, not allowing them to go one step further, snapping at any man who dared to go near.

The police ran up. Timmy growled extra fiercely just to let the men know that it was quite impossible to get by him. In a trice each of the men was imprisoned by a pair of strong arms, they were being told to come quietly.

They didn't go quietly. For one thing Mr Andrews lost his nerve and howled dismally. Jock felt very ashamed of him.

'Shut up,' said a burly policeman. 'We know you're

only the miserable little cat's-paw – taking money from the big men to hold your tongue and obey orders.'

Timmy barked as if to say, 'Yes – don't you dare call him a *dog's* paw! That would be too good a name for him!'

'Well, I don't think I ever in my life saw dirtier children,' said Mr Luffy. 'I vote we all go back to my car and I drive the lot of you over to Olly's Farm for a meal and a bath!'

So back they all went, tired, dirty, and also feeling very thrilled.

What a night! They told Anne all that had happened, and she told them her story, too. She almost fell asleep in the car as she talked, she was so tired.

Mrs Andrews was sensible and kind, though upset to hear that her husband had been taken off by the police. She got hot water for baths, and laid a meal for the hungry children.

'I wouldn't worry overmuch, Mrs Andrews,' said kindly Mr Luffy. 'That husband of yours needs a lesson, you know. This will probably keep him going straight in future. The farm is yours, and you can now hire proper farm-workers who will do what you want them to do. And I think Jock will be happier without a stepfather for the present.'

'You're right, Mr Luffy,' said Mrs Andrews, wiping her eyes quickly. 'Quite right. I'll let Jock help me with the farm, and get it going beautifully. To think that Mr Andrews was in with all those black marketeers! It's that friend of his, you know, who makes him do all this. He's so weak. He knew Jock was snooping about in that tunnel, and that's why he wanted him to go away – and kept making him have a boy here or go out with him. I knew there was something queer going on.'

'No wonder he was worried when Jock took it into his head to go and camp with our little lot,' said Mr Luffy.

'To think of that old yard and tunnel being used again!' said Mrs Andrews. 'And all those tales about spook-trains – and the way they hid that train, and hid all the stuff, too. Why, it's like a fairy tale isn't it!'

She ran to see if the water was hot for the baths. It was, and she went to call the children, who were in the big bedroom next door. She opened it and looked in. Then she called Mr Luffy upstairs.

He looked in at the door, too. The five, and Timmy,

were lying on the floor in a heap, waiting for the bath-water. They hadn't liked to sit on chairs or beds, they were so dirty. And they had fallen asleep where they sat, their faces as black as a sweep's.

'Talk about black marketeers!' whispered Mrs Andrews. 'Anyone would think we'd got the whole lot of them here in the bedroom!'

They all woke up and went to have a bath one by one, and a good meal after that. Then back to camp with Mr Luffy, Jock with them, too.

It was glorious to snuggle down into the sleeping-bags. George called out to the three boys.

'Now don't you dare to go off without me tonight, see?'

'The adventure is over,' called back Dick. 'How did you like it, Jock?'

'Like it?' said Jock, with a happy sigh. 'It was simply – smashing!'

Enid Blyton's

FIVE GET INTO TROUBLE

ILLUSTRATED BY JOLYNE KNOX

CONTENTS

1
Five make a holiday plan

'Really, Quentin, you are *most* difficult to cope with!' said Aunt Fanny to her husband.

The four children sat at the table, eating breakfast, and looking very interested. What had Uncle Quentin done now? Julian winked at Dick, and Anne kicked George under the table. Would Uncle Quentin explode into a temper, as he sometimes did?

Uncle Quentin held a letter in his hand, which his wife had just given back to him after she had read it. It was the letter that was causing all the trouble, Uncle Quentin frowned – and then decided not to explode. Instead he spoke quite mildly.

'Well, Fanny dear – how can I possibly be expected to remember exactly when the children's holidays come, and if they are going to be here with us or with your sister? You know I have my scientific work to do – and very important it is too, at the moment. *I* can't remember when the children's schools break up or go back!'

'You could always ask *me*,' said Aunt Fanny, exasper-

ated. 'Really, Quentin – have you forgotten how we discussed having Julian, Dick and Anne here these Easter holidays because they all enjoy Kirrin and the sea so much at this time of the year? You said you would arrange to go off to your conferences *after* they had had their holidays – not in the very middle of them!'

'But they've broken up so late!' said Uncle Quentin. 'I didn't know they were going to do that.'

'Well, but you know Easter came late this year, so they broke up late,' said Aunt Fanny, with a sigh.

'Father wouldn't think of that,' said George. 'What's the matter, Mother? Does Father want to go away in the middle of our holidays, or what?'

'Yes,' said Aunt Fanny, and she stretched out her hand for the letter again. 'Let me see – he would have to go off in two days' time – and I must certainly go with him. I can't possibly leave you children alone here, with nobody in the house. If Joanna were not ill it would be all right – but she won't be back for a week or two.'

Joanna was the cook. The children were all very fond of her, and had been sorry to find her missing when they had arrived for the holidays.

'We can look after ourselves,' said Dick. 'Anne is quite a good little cook.'

'I can help too,' said George. Her real name was Georgina, but everyone called her George. Her mother smiled.

'Oh George – last time you boiled an egg you left it in the saucepan till it boiled dry! I don't think the others would like your cooking very much.'

'It was just that I forgot the egg was there,' said George. 'I went to fetch the clock to time it, and on the way I remembered Timmy hadn't had his dinner, and . . .'

'Yes, we know all about that,' said her mother with a laugh. 'Timmy had his dinner, but your father had to go without his tea!'

505

'Woof,' said Timmy from under the table, hearing his name mentioned. He licked George's foot just to remind her he was there.

'Well, let's get back to the subject,' said Uncle Quentin, impatiently. 'I've got to go to these conferences, that's certain. I've to read some important papers there. You needn't come with me, Fanny – you can stay and look after the children.'

'Mother doesn't need to,' said George. 'We can do something we badly wanted to do, but thought we'd have to put off till the summer hols.'

'Oh *yes*,' said Anne, at once. 'So we could! Do let's!'

'Yes – I'd like that too,' said Dick.

'Well – *what* is it?' asked Aunt Fanny. 'I'm quite in the dark. If it's anything dangerous, I shall say no. So make up your minds about that!'

'When do we *ever* do anything dangerous?' cried George.

'Plenty of times,' said her mother. 'Now, what's this plan of yours?'

'It's nothing much,' said Julian. 'It's only that all our bikes happen to be in first-class order, Aunt Fanny, and you know you gave us two small tents for Christmas – so we just thought it would be great fun sometime to go off on our bikes, taking our tents with us – and do a little exploring round the countryside.'

'It's grand weather now – we could have fine fun,' said Dick. 'After all, you must have meant us to use the tents, Aunt Fanny! Here's our chance!'

'I meant you to use them in the garden, or on the beach,' said Aunt Fanny. 'Last time you went camping you had Mr Luffy with you to look after you. I don't think I like the idea of you going off by yourselves with tents.'

'Oh, Fanny, if *Julian* can't look after the others he must be a pretty feeble specimen,' said her husband, sounding impatient. 'Let them go! I'd bank on Julian any time to

506

keep the others in order and see they were all safe and sound.'

'Thanks, Uncle,' said Julian, who was not used to compliments from his Uncle Quentin! He glanced round at the other children and grinned. 'Of course, it's easy to manage this little lot – though Anne sometimes is *very* difficult!'

Anne opened her mouth indignantly. She was the smallest and the only really manageable one. She caught Julian's grin – he was teasing her, of course. She grinned back. 'I promise to be easy to manage,' she said in an innocent voice to her Uncle Quentin.

He looked surprised. 'Well, I must say I should have thought that George was the only difficult one to . . .' he began, but stopped when he saw his wife's warning frown. George *was* difficult, but it didn't make her any less difficult if that fact was pointed out!

'Quentin, you never know when Julian is pulling your leg or not, do you?' said his wife. 'Well – if you *really* think Julian can be put in charge – and we can let them go off on a cycling tour – with their new tents . . .'

'Hurray! It's settled then!' yelled George, and began to thump Dick on the back in joy. 'We'll go off tomorrow. We'll . . .'

'GEORGE! There's no need to shout and thump like that,' said her mother. 'You know your father doesn't like it – and now you've excited Timmy too. Lie down, Timmy – there he's off round the room like a mad thing!'

Uncle Quentin got up to go. He didn't like it when meal-times turned into pandemonium. He almost fell over the excited Timmy, and disappeared thankfully out of the room. What a household it was when the four children and the dog were there!

'Oh Aunt Fanny – can we really go off tomorrow?' asked Anne, her eyes shining. 'It *is* such lovely April weather – honestly it's as hot as July. We hardly need to take any thick clothes with us.'

'Well, if you think that, you won't go,' said Aunt Fanny, firmly. 'It may be hot and sunny today – but you can never trust April to be the same two days together. It may be pouring tomorrow, and snowing on the next day! I shall have to give you money, Julian, so that you can go to an hotel any night the weather is bad.'

The four children immediately made up their minds that the weather would never be too bad!

'Won't it be fun?' said Dick. 'We can choose our own sleeping-place every night and put our tents there. We can bike half the night if it's moonlight, and we want to!'

'Ooooh – biking in moonlight – I've never done that,' said Anne. 'It sounds super.'

'Well – it's a good thing there is something you want to do while we are away,' said Aunt Fanny. 'Dear me – I've been married all these years to Quentin – and still he makes this kind of muddle without my knowing! Well, well – we'd better get busy today, and decide what you're to take.'

Everything suddenly seemed very exciting. The four children rushed to do their morning jobs of making the beds and tidying their rooms, talking at the tops of their voices.

'Who would have thought we'd be off on our own tomorrow!' said Dick, pulling his sheets and blankets up in a heap together.

'Dick! *I'll* make your bed,' cried Anne, shocked to see it made in such a hurried way. 'You can't possibly make it like that!'

'Oh, *can't* I!' cried Dick. 'You just wait and see! And what's more I'm making Julian's like that too, so you clear off and do your own, Anne – tuck in every corner, smooth the pillow, pat the eiderdown – do what you like with your own bed, but leave me to make mine my own way! Wait till we're off on our biking tour – you won't want to bother

508

about beds then – you'll roll up your sleeping-bag and that will be that!'

He finished his bed as he spoke, dragging on the cover all crooked, and stuffing his pyjamas under the pillow. Anne laughed and went to make her own. She was excited too. The days stretched before her, sunny, full of strange places, unknown woods, big and little hills, chattering streams, wayside picnics, biking in the moonlight – did Dick really mean that? How wizard!

They were all very busy that day, packing up into rucksacks the things they would need, folding up the tents into as small a compass as possible to tie on to their carriers, ferreting in the larder for food to take, looking out the maps they would want.

Timmy knew they were going off somewhere, and, of course, felt certain he was going too, so he was as excited as they were, barking and thumping his tail, and generally getting into everyone's way all day long. But nobody minded. Timmy was one of them, one of the 'Five', he could do almost everything but speak – it was quite unthinkable to go anywhere without dear old Timmy.

'I suppose Timothy can keep up with you all right, when you bike for miles?' Aunt Fanny asked Julian.

'Goodness yes,' said Julian. 'He never minds how far we go. I hope you won't worry about us, Aunt Fanny. You know what a good guard Timmy is.'

'Yes – I know,' said his aunt. 'I wouldn't be letting you go off like this with such an easy mind if I didn't know Timmy would be with you! He's as good as any grown-up at looking after you!'

'Woof, woof,' agreed Timmy. George laughed. 'He says he's as good as *two* grown-ups, Mother!' she said, and Timmy thumped his big tail on the floor.

'Woof, woof, *woof*,' he said. Which meant, 'Not two – but *three*!'

509

2

Away on their own

They were all ready the next day. Everything was neatly packed and strapped to the bicycles, except for the rucksacks, which each child was to carry on his or her back. The baskets held a variety of food for that day, but when it had been eaten Julian was to buy what they needed.

'I suppose all their brakes are in order?' said Uncle Quentin, thinking he ought to take some interest in the proceedings, and remembering that when *he* was a boy and had a bicycle, the brakes would never work.

'Oh Uncle Quentin – of course they're all right,' said Dick. 'We'd never dream of going out on our bikes if the brakes and things weren't in order. The Highway Code is very strict about things like that, you know – and so are we!'

Uncle Quentin looked as if he had never even heard of the Highway Code. It was quite likely he hadn't. He lived in a world of his own, a world of theories and figures and diagrams – and he was eager to get back to it! However,

510

he waited politely for the children to make last-minute adjustments, and then they were ready.

'Good-bye, Aunt Fanny! I'm afraid we shan't be able to write to you, as you won't be able to get in touch with us to let us know where you get fixed up. Never mind, enjoy yourselves,' said Julian.

'Good-bye, Mother! Don't worry about us – we'll be having a jolly good time!' called George.

'Good-bye, Aunt Fanny; good-bye, Uncle Quentin!'

'So long, Uncle! Aunt Fanny, we're off!'

And so they were, cycling down the lane that led away from Kirrin Cottage. Their aunt and uncle stood at the gate, waving till the little party had disappeared round the corner in the sunshine. Timmy was loping along beside George's bicycle, on his long, strong legs, overjoyed at the idea of a really good run.

'Well, we're off,' said Julian, as they rounded the corner. 'What a bit of luck, going off like this by ourselves. Good old Uncle Quentin! I'm glad he made that muddle.'

'Don't let's ride too many miles the first day – I always get so stiff if we do.'

'We're not going to,' said Dick. 'Whenever you feel tired just say so – it doesn't matter where we stop!'

The morning was very warm. Soon the children began to feel wet with perspiration. They had sweaters on and they took them off, stuffing them in their baskets. George looked more like a boy than ever, with her short curly hair blown up by the wind. All of them wore shorts and thin jerseys except Julian, who had on jeans. He rolled up the sleeves of his jersey, and the others did the same.

They covered mile after mile, enjoying the sun and the wind. Timmy galloped beside them, untiring, his long pink tongue hanging out. He ran on the grassy edge of the road when there was one. He really was a very sensible dog!

They stopped at a tiny village called Manlington-

Tovey. It had only one general store, but it sold practically everything – or seemed to! 'Hope it sells ginger-beer!' said Julian. 'My tongue's hanging out like Timmy's!'

The little shop sold lemonade, orangeade, lime juice, grape-fruit juice and ginger-beer. It was really difficult to choose which to have. It also sold ice-creams, and soon the children were sitting drinking ginger-beer and lime-juice mixed, and eating delicious ices.

'Timmy must have an ice,' said George. 'He does so love them. Don't you, Timmy?'

'Woof,' said Timmy, and gulped his ice down in two big, gurgly licks.

'It's really a waste of ice-creams to give them to Timmy,' said Anne. 'He hardly has time to taste them, he gobbles them so. No, Timmy, get down. I'm going to finish up every single bit of mine, and there won't be even a lick for you!'

Timmy went off to drink from a bowl of water that the shopwoman had put down for him. He drank and he drank, then he flopped down, panting.

The children took a bottle of ginger-beer each with them when they went off again. They meant to have it with their lunch. Already they were beginning to think with pleasure of eating the sandwiches put up into neat packets for them.

Anne saw some cows pulling at the grass in a meadow as they passed. 'It must be awful to be a cow and eat nothing but tasteless grass,' she called to George. 'Think what a cow misses – never tastes an egg and lettuce sandwich, never eats a chocolate eclair, never has a boiled egg – and can't even drink a glass of ginger-beer! Poor cows!'

George laughed. 'You do think of silly things, Anne,' she said. 'Now you've made me want my lunch all the more – talking about egg sandwiches and ginger-beer! I know Mother made us egg sandwiches – and sardine ones too.'

512

'It's no good,' chimed in Dick, leading the way into a little copse, his bicycle wobbling dangerously, 'it's no good – we can't go another inch if you girls are going to jabber about food all the time. Julian, what about lunch?'

It was a lovely picnic, that first one in the copse. There were clumps of primroses all round, and from somewhere nearby came the sweet scent of hidden violets. A thrush was singing madly on a hazel tree, with two chaffinches calling 'pink-pink' every time he stopped.

'Band and decorations laid on,' said Julian, waving his hand towards the singing birds and the primroses. 'Very nice too. We just want a waiter to come and present us with a menu!'

A rabbit lolloped near, its big ears standing straight up inquiringly. 'Ah – the waiter!' said Julian, at once. 'What have you to offer us today, Bunny? A nice rabbit-pie?'

The rabbit scampered off at top speed. It had caught the smell of Timmy nearby and was panic-stricken. The children laughed, because it seemed as if it was the mention of rabbit-pie that had sent it away. Timmy stared at the disappearing rabbit, but made no move to go after it.

'Well, *Timmy*! That's the first time you've ever let a rabbit go off on its own,' said Dick. 'You *must* be hot and tired. Got anything for him to eat, George?'

'Of course,' said George. 'I made his sandwiches myself.'

And so she had! She had bought sausage meat at the butchers and had actually made Timmy twelve sandwiches with it, all neatly cut and packed.

The others laughed. George never minded taking trouble over Timmy. He wolfed his sandwiches eagerly, and thumped his tail hard on the mossy ground. They all sat and munched happily, perfectly contented to be together out in the open air, eating a wonderful lunch.

Anne gave a scream. 'George! Look what you're doing! You're eating one of Timmy's sandwiches!'

'Urhh!' said George. 'I thought it tasted a bit strong. I must have given Timmy one of mine and taken his instead. Sorry, Tim!'

'Woof,' said Tim politely, and accepted another of his sandwiches.

514

'At the rate he eats them he wouldn't really notice if he had twenty or fifty,' remarked Julian. 'He's had all his now, hasn't he? Well, look out, everybody – he'll be after ours. Aha – the band has struck up again!'

Everyone listened to the thrush. 'Mind how you go,' sang the thrush. 'Mind how you go! Mind how you do-it, do-it, do-it!'

'Sounds like a Safety First poster,' said Dick, and settled down with his head on a cushion of moss. 'All right, old bird – we'll mind how we go – but we're going to have a bit of a snooze now, so don't play the band too loudly!'

'It *would* be a good idea to have a bit of a rest,' said Julian, yawning. 'We've done pretty well, so far. We don't want to tire ourselves out the very first day. Get off my legs, Timmy – you're frightfully heavy with all those sandwiches inside you.'

Timmy removed himself. He went to George and flumped himself down beside her, licking her face. She pushed him away.

'Don't be so licky,' she said, sleepily, 'just be on guard like a good dog, and see that nobody comes along and steals our bikes.'

Timmy knew what 'on guard' meant, of course. He sat up straight when he heard the words, and looked carefully all round, sniffing as he did so. Anyone about? No. Not a sight, sound or smell of any stranger. Timmy lay down again, one ear cocked, and one eye very slightly open. George always thought it was marvellous the way he could be asleep with one ear and eye and awake with the others. She was about to say this to Dick and Julian when she saw that they were sound asleep.

She fell asleep too. Nobody came to disturb them. A small robin hopped near inquisitively, and, with his head on one side, considered whether or not it would be a good thing to pull a few hairs out of Timmy's tail to line his new nest. The slit in Timmy's awake-eye widened a little

515

– woe betide the robin if he tried any funny tricks on Timmy!

The robin flew off. The thrush sang a little more, and the rabbit came out again. Timmy's eye opened wide. The rabbit fled. Timmy gave a tiny snore. Was he awake or was he asleep? The rabbit wasn't going to wait and find out!

It was half past three when they all awoke one by one. Julian looked at his watch. 'It's almost tea-time!' he said, and Anne gave a little squeal.

'Oh no – why we've only just had lunch, and I'm still as full as can be!'

Julian grinned. 'It's all right. We'll go by our tummies for our meals, not by our watches, Anne. Come on, get up! We'll go without you if you don't.'

They wheeled their bicycles out of the primrose copse and mounted again. The breeze was lovely to feel on their faces. Anne gave a little groan.

'Oh dear – I feel a bit stiff already. Do you mean to go very many miles more, Ju?'

'No, not many,' said Julian. 'I thought we'd have tea somewhere when we feel like it – and then do a bit of shopping for our supper and breakfast – and then hunt about for a really good place to put up our tents for the night. I found a little lake on the map, and I thought we could have a swim in it if we can find it.'

This all sounded very good indeed. George felt she could cycle for miles if a swim in a lake was at the end of it.

'That's a very nice plan of yours,' she said, approvingly. 'Very nice indeed. I think our whole tour ought to be planned round lakes – so that we can always have a swim, night and morning!'

'Woof,' said Timmy, running beside George's bicycle. 'Woof!'

'Timmy agrees too,' said George, with a laugh. 'But oh dear – I don't believe he brought his bathing-towel!'

516

3

A lovely day – and a
lovely night

The five of them had a lovely time that evening. They had
tea about half past five, and then bought what they
wanted for supper and breakfast. New rolls, anchovy
paste, a big round jam-tart in a cardboard box, oranges,
lime-juice, a fat lettuce and some ham sandwiches – it
seemed a very nice assortment indeed.

'Let's hope we don't eat it all for supper, and have no
breakfast left,' said George, packing the sandwiches into
her basket. 'Get down, Timmy. These sandwiches are not
for you. I've bought you a whacking big bone – *that* will
keep you busy for hours!'

'Well, don't let him have it when we settle down for the
night,' said Anne. 'He makes such a row, crunching and
munching. He'd keep me awake.'

'*Nothing* would keep *me* awake tonight,' said Dick. 'I
believe I could sleep through an earthquake. I'm already
thinking kindly of my sleeping-bag.'

'I don't think we need to put up our tents tonight,' said
Julian, looking up at the perfectly clear sky. 'I'll ask
someone what the weather forecast was on the radio at six.

Honestly I think we could just snuggle into our sleeping-bags and have the sky for a roof.'

'How smashing!' said Anne. 'I'd love to lie and look at the stars.'

The weather forecast was good. 'Fine and clear and mild'.

'Good,' said Julian. 'That will save us a lot of trouble – we don't even need to unpack our tents. Come on – have we got everything now? Does anyone feel as if we ought to buy any more food?'

The baskets were all full. Nobody thought it advisable to try and get anything more into them.

'We could get lots more in if Timmy would only carry his own bones,' said Anne. 'Half my basket is crammed with enormous bones for him. Why can't you rig up something so that Timmy could carry his own food, George? I'm sure he's clever enough.'

'Yes, he's clever enough,' said George. 'But he's much too greedy, Anne. You know that. He'd stop and eat all his food at once if he had to carry it. Dogs seem to be able to eat anything at any time.'

'They're lucky,' said Dick. 'Wish I could. But I just *have* to pause between my meals!'

'Now for the lake,' said Julian, folding up the map which he had just been examining. 'It's only about five miles away. It's called the Green Pool, but it looks a good bit bigger than a pool. I could do with a bathe. I'm so hot and sticky.'

They came to the lake at about half past seven. It was in a lovely place, and had beside it a small hut which was obviously used in summer-time for bathers to change into bathing-suits. Now it was locked, and curtains were drawn across the windows.

'I suppose we can go in for a dip if we like?' said Dick rather doubtfully. 'We shan't be trespassing or anything, shall we?'

518

'No. It doesn't say anything about being private,' said Julian. 'The water won't be very warm, you know, because it's only mid-April! But after all, we're used to cold baths every morning, and I daresay the sun has taken the chill off the lake. Come on – let's get into bathing-things.'

They changed behind the bushes and then ran down to the lake. The water was certainly very cold indeed. Anne skipped in and out, and wouldn't do any more than that.

George joined the boys in a swim, and they all came out glowing and laughing. 'Brrr, that was cold!' said Dick. 'Come on – let's have a sharp run. Look at Anne – dressed already. Timmy, where are you? *You* don't mind the cold water, do you?'

They all tore up and down the little paths by the Green Pool like mad things. Anne was getting the supper ready. The sun had disappeared now, and although the evening was still very mild the radiant warmth of the day had gone. Anne was glad of her sweater.

'Good old Anne,' said Dick, when at last he and the others joined her, dressed again, with their sweaters on for warmth. 'Look, she's got the food all ready. Proper little housewife, aren't you, Anne? I bet if we stayed here for more than one night Anne would have made some kind of larder, and have arranged a good place to wash everything – and be looking for somewhere to keep her dusters and broom!'

'You're so *silly*, Dick,' said Anne. 'You ought to be glad I like messing about with the food and getting it ready for you. Oh TIMMY! Shoo! Get away! Look at him, he's shaken millions and millions of drops of lakewater all over the food. You ought to have dried him, George. You know how he shakes himself after a swim.'

'Sorry,' said George. 'Tim, say you're sorry. Why must you be so *violent* about everything? If I shook myself like that my ears and fingers would fly off into the air!'

It was a lovely meal, sitting there in the evening light,

watching the first stars come out in the sky. The children and Timmy were all tired but happy. This was the beginning of their trip – and beginnings were always lovely – the days stretched out before you endlessly, and somehow you felt certain that the sun would shine every single day!

They were not long in snuggling into their sleeping-bags when they had finished the meal. They had set them all together in a row, so that they could talk if they wanted to. Timmy was thrilled. He walked solemnly across the whole lot, and was greeted with squeals and threats.

'Timmy! How dare you! When I've had such a big supper too!'

'TIMMY! You brute! You put all your great big feet down on me at once!'

'George, you *really* might stop Timmy from walking all over us like that! I only hope he's not going to do it all night long.'

Timmy looked surprised at the shouts. He settled down beside George, after a vain attempt to get into her sleeping-bag with her. George turned her face away from his licks.

'Oh Timmy, I do love you but I wish you wouldn't make my face so wet. Julian, look at that glorious star – like a little round lamp. What is it?'

'It's not a star really – it's Venus, one of the planets,' said Julian, sleepily. 'But it's called the Evening Star. Fancy you not knowing that, George. Don't they teach you anything at your school?'

George tried to kick Julian through her sleeping-bag, but she couldn't. She gave it up and yawned so loudly that she set all the others yawning too.

Anne fell asleep first. She was the smallest and was more easily tired with long walks and rides than the others, though she always kept up with them valiantly. George gazed unblinkingly at the bright evening star for a

520

minute and then fell asleep suddenly. Julian and Dick
talked quietly for a few minutes. Timmy was quite silent.
He was tired out with his miles and miles of running.

Nobody stirred at all that night, not even Timmy. He
took no notice of a horde of rabbits who played not far off.
He hardly pricked an ear when an owl hooted nearby. He
didn't even stir when a beetle ran over his head.

But if George had waked and spoken his name Timmy

521

would have been wide awake at once, standing over George and licking her, whining gently! George was the centre of his world, night and day.

The next day was fair and bright. It was lovely to wake up and feel the warm sun on their cheeks, and hear a thrush singing his heart out. 'It might be the very same thrush,' thought Dick, drowsily. 'He's saying, "Mind how you do-it, do-it, do-it!" just like the other one did.'

Anne sat up cautiously. She wondered if she should get up and have breakfast ready for the others – or would they want a bathe first?

Julian sat up next and yawned as he wriggled himself half out of his sleeping-bag. He grinned at Anne.

'Hallo,' he said. 'Had a good night? I feel fine this morning!'

'I feel rather stiff,' said Anne. 'But it will soon wear off. Hallo, George – you awake?'

George grunted and snuggled down farther in her sleeping-bag. Timmy pawed at her, whining. He wanted her to get up and go for a run with him.

'Shut up, Timmy,' said George from the depth of her bag. 'I'm asleep!'

'I'm going for a bathe,' said Julian. 'Anyone else coming?'

'I won't,' said Anne. 'It will be too cold for me this morning. George doesn't seem to want to, either. You two boys go by yourselves. I'll have breakfast ready for you when you come back. Sorry I shan't be able to have anything hot for you to drink – but we didn't bring a kettle or anything like that.'

Julian and Dick went off to the Green Pool, still looking sleepy. Anne got out of her sleeping-bag and dressed quickly. She decided to go down to the pool with her sponge and flannel and wake herself up properly with the cold water. George was still in her sleeping-bag.

The two boys were almost at the pool. Ah, now they

could see it between the trees, shining a bright emerald green. It looked very inviting indeed.

They suddenly saw a bicycle standing beside a tree. They looked at it in astonishment. It wasn't one of theirs. It must belong to someone else.

Then they heard splashings from the pool, and they hurried down to it. Was someone else bathing?

A boy was in the pool, his golden head shining wet and smooth in the morning sun. He was swimming powerfully across the pool, leaving long ripples behind him as he went. He suddenly saw Dick and Julian, and swam over to them.

'Hallo,' he said, wading out of the water. 'You come for a swim too? Nice pool of mine, isn't it?'

'What do you mean? It isn't really your pool, is it? said Julian.

'Well – it belongs to my father, Thurlow Kent,' said the boy.

Both Julian and Dick had heard of Thurlow Kent, one of the richest men in the country. Julian looked doubtfully at the boy.

'If it's a private pool we won't use it,' he said.

'Oh come on!' cried the boy, and splashed cold water all over them. 'Race you to the other side!'

And off all three of them went, cleaving the green waters with their strong brown arms – what a fine beginning to a sunny day!

4

Richard

Anne was astonished to find three boys in the Green Pool instead of two. She stood by the water with her sponge and flannel, staring. Who was the third boy?

The three came back to the side of the pool where Anne stood. She looked at the strange boy shyly. He was not much older than she was, and not as big as Julian or Dick, but he was sturdily made, and had laughing blue eyes she liked. He smoothed back his dripping hair.

'This your sister?' he said to Julian and Dick. 'Hallo there!'

'Hallo,' said Anne and smiled. 'What's your name?'

'Richard,' he said. 'Richard Kent. What's yours?'

'Anne,' said Anne. 'We're on a biking tour.'

The boys had had no time to introduce themselves. They were still panting from their swim.

'I'm Julian and he's Dick, my brother,' said Julian, out of breath. 'I say – I hope we're not trespassing on your land as well as on your water!'

Richard grinned. 'Well, you are as a matter of fact. But

I give you free permission! You can borrow my pool and my land as much as you like!'

'Oh thanks,' said Anne. 'I suppose it's your father's property? It didn't say "Private" or anything, so we didn't know. Would you like to come and have breakfast with us? If you'll dress with the others they'll bring you to where we camped last night.'

She sponged her face and washed her hands in the pool, hearing the boys chattering behind the bushes where they had left their clothes. Then she sped back to their sleeping-place, meaning to tidy up the bags they had slept in, and put out breakfast neatly. But George was still fast asleep in her bag, her head showing at the top with its mass of short curls that made her look like a boy.

'George! Do wake up. Somebody's coming to breakfast,' said Anne, shaking her.

George shrugged away crossly, not believing her. It was just a trick to make her get up and help with the breakfast! Anne left her. All right – let her be found in her sleeping-bag if she liked!

She began to unpack the food and set it out neatly. What a good thing they had brought two extra bottles of lime-juice. Now they could offer Richard one.

The three boys came up, their wet hair plastered down. Richard spotted George in the bag as Timmy came over to meet him. He fondled Timmy who, smelling that other dogs had been round Richard at home, sniffed him over with great interest.

'Who's that still asleep?' asked Richard.

'That's George,' said Anne. 'Too sleepy to wake up! Come on – I've got breakfast ready. Would you like to start off with rolls and anchovy and lettuce? And there's lime-juice if you want it.'

George heard Richard's voice, as he sat talking with the others and was astonished. Who was that? She sat up, blinking, her hair tousled and short. Richard honestly thought she was a boy. She looked like one and she was called George!

'Top of the morning to you, George,' he said. 'Hope I'm not eating your share of the breakfast.'

'Who are you?' demanded George. The boys told her.

'I live about three miles away,' said the boy. 'I biked over here this morning for a swim. I say – that reminds me – I'd better bring my bike up here and put it where I can see it. I've had two stolen already through not having them under my eye.'

He shot off to get his bike. George took the opportunity of getting out of her sleeping-bag and rushed off to dress. She was back before Richard was, eating her breakfast. He wheeled his bicycle as he came.

'Got it all right,' he said, and flung it down beside him. 'Don't want to have to tell my father this one's gone, like the others. He's pretty fierce.'

'My father's a bit fierce too,' said George.

'Does he whip you?' asked Richard, giving Timmy a nice little titbit of roll and anchovy paste.

'Of course not,' said George. 'He's just got a temper, that's all.'

'Mine's got tempers and rages and furies, and if anyone offends him or does him a wrong he's like an elephant – never forgets,' said Richard. 'He's made plenty of enemies in his lifetime. Sometimes he's had his life threatened, and he's had to take a bodyguard about with him.'

This all sounded extremely thrilling. Dick half-wished he had a father like that. I would be nice to talk to the other boys at school about his father's 'bodyguard'.

'What's his bodyguard like?' asked Anne, full of curiosity.

'Oh, they vary. But they're all big hefty fellows – they look like ruffians, and probably are,' said Richard, enjoying the interest the others were taking in him. 'One he had last year was awful – he had the thickest lips you ever saw, and such a big nose that when you saw him sideways you really thought he'd put a false one on just for fun.'

'Gracious!' said Anne. 'He sounds horrible. Has your father still got him?'

'No. He did something that annoyed Dad – I don't know what – and after a perfectly furious row my father chucked him out,' said Richard. 'That was the end of *him* . Jolly good thing too. I hated him. He used to kick the dogs around terribly.'

'*Oh!* What a beast!' said George, horrified. She put her arm round Timmy as if she was afraid somebody might suddenly kick him around too.

Julian and Dick wondered whether to believe all this. They came to the conclusion that the tales Richard told were very much exaggerated, and they listened with amusement, but not with such horror as the two girls, who hung on every word that Richard said.

'Where's your father now?' said Anne. 'Has he got a special bodyguard this very moment?'

'Rather! He's in America this week, but he's flying home soon – plus bodyguard,' said Richard, drinking the last of his lime-juice from the bottle. 'Ummm, that's good. I say, aren't you lucky to be allowed to go off alone like this on your bikes – and sleep where you like. My mother never will let *me* – she's always afraid something will happen to me.'

'Perhaps you'd better have a bodyguard too,' suggested Julian, slyly.

'I'd soon give him the slip,' said Richard. 'As a matter of fact I *have* got a kind of a bodyguard.'

'Who? Where?' asked Anne, looking all round as if she expected some enormous ruffian suddenly to appear.

'Well – he's supposed to be my holiday tutor,' said Richard, tickling Timmy round the ears. 'He's called Lomax and he's pretty awful. I'm supposed to tell him every time I go out – just as if I was a kid like Anne here.'

Anne was indignant. 'I don't have to tell anybody when I want to go off on my own,' she said.

'Actually I don't think we'd be allowed to rush off completely on our own unless we had old Timmy,' said Dick, honestly. 'He's better than any ruffianly bodyguard or holiday tutor. I wonder *you* don't have a dog.'

'Oh, I've got about five,' said Richard, airily.

'What are their names?' asked George, disbelievingly.

'Er – Bunter, Biscuit, Brownie, Bones – and er – Bonzo,' said Richard, with a grin.

'Silly names,' said George, scornfully. 'Fancy calling a dog *Biscuit*. You must be cracked.'

'You shut up,' said Richard, with a sudden scowl. 'I don't stand people telling me I'm cracked.'

'Well, you'll have to stand *me* telling you,' said George. 'I *do* think it's cracked to call a dog, a nice, decent dog, by a name like *Biscuit*!'

'I'll fight you then,' said Richard, surprisingly, and stood up. 'Come on – you stand up.'

George leapt to her feet. Julian shot out a hand and pulled her down again.

'None of that,' he said to Richard. 'You ought to be ashamed of yourself.'

'Why?' flared out Richard, whose face had gone very red. Evidently he and his father shared the same fierceness of temper!

'Well, you don't fight *girls*,' said Julian, scornfully. 'Or do you? Correct me if I'm wrong.'

Richard stared at him in amazement. 'What do you mean?' he said. 'Girls? Of course I don't fight girls. No decent boy hits a girl – but it's this boy here I want to fight – what do you call him? – George.'

To his great surprise Julian, Dick and Anne roared with laughter. Timmy barked madly too, pleased at the sudden

528

ending of the quarrel. Only George looked mutinous and
cross.

'What's up now?' asked Richard, aggressively. 'What's
all the fun and games about?'

'Richard, George isn't a boy – she's a *girl*,' explained
Dick at last. 'My goodness – she was just about to accept
your challenge and fight you, too – two fierce little fox-
terriers having a scrap!'

Richard's mouth fell open in an even greater astonishment. He blushed redder than ever. He looked sheepishly at George.

'Are you *really* a girl?' he said. 'You behave so like a boy – and you look like one too. Sorry, George. Is your name *really* George?'

'No – Georgina,' said George, thawing a little at Richard's awkward apology, and pleased that he had honestly thought her a boy. She did so badly want to be a boy and not a girl.

'Good thing I *didn't* fight you,' said Richard, fervently. 'I should have knocked you flat!'

'Well, I like *that*!' said George, flaring up all over again. Julian pushed her back with his hand.

'Now shut up, you two, and don't behave like idiots. Where's the map? It's time we had a squint at it and decided what we are going to do for today – how far we're going to ride, and where we're making for by the evening.'

Fortunately George and Richard both gave in with a good grace. Soon all six heads – Timmy's too – were bent over the map. Julian made his decision.

'We'll make for Middlecombe Woods – see, there they are on the map. That's decided then – it'll be a jolly nice ride.'

It might be a nice ride – but it was going to be something very much more than that!

5

Six instead of five

'Look here,' said Richard, when they had tidied up every-thing, buried their bits of litter, and looked to see that no one had got a puncture in a tyre. 'Look here – I've got an aunt who lives in the direction of those woods – if I can get my mother to say I can come with you, will you let me? I can go and see my aunt on the way, then.'

Julian looked at Richard doubtfully. He wasn't very sure if Richard really *would* go and ask permission.

'Well – if you aren't too long about it,' he said. 'Of course we don't mind you coming with us. We can drop you at your aunt's on the way.'

'I'll go straight off now and ask my mother,' said Richard, eagerly, and he ran for his bicycle. 'I'll meet you at Croker's Corner – you saw it on the map. That will save time, because then I shan't have to come back here – it's not much farther than my home.'

'Right,' said Julian. 'I've got to adjust my brakes, and that will take ten minutes or so. You'll have time to go home and ask permission, and join us later. We'll wait for you; at least we'll wait for ten minutes, at Croker's Corner. If you don't turn up we'll know you didn't get permission. Tell your mother we'll leave you safely at your aunt's.'

Richard shot off on his bicycle, looking excited. Anne began to clear up, and George helped her. Timmy got in everyone's way, sniffing about for dropped crumbs.

'Anyone would think he was half-starved!' said Anne. 'He had a lot more breakfast than I had. Timmy, if you walk through my legs again I'll tie you up!'

Julian adjusted his brakes with Dick's help. In about fifteen minutes they were ready to set off. They had planned where to stop to buy food for their lunch, and although the journey to Middlecombe Woods was a longer trip than they had made the day before, they felt able to cope with more miles on the second day. Timmy was eager to set off too. He was a big dog, and enjoyed all the exercise he was getting.

'It'll take a bit of your fat off,' said Dick to Timmy. 'We don't like fat dogs, you know. They waddle and they puff.'

'Dick! Timmy's *never* been fat!' said George, indignantly, and then stopped as she saw Dick's grin. He was pulling her leg as usual. She kicked herself. Why did she always rise like that, when Dick teased her through Timmy? She gave him a friendly punch.

They all mounted their bicycles. Timmy ran ahead, pleased. They came to a lane and rode down it, avoiding the ruts. They came out into a road. It was not a main road, for the children didn't like those; they were too full of traffic and dust. They liked the shady lanes or the country roads where they met only a few carts or a farmer's car.

'Now, don't let's miss Croker's Corner,' said Julian. 'It should be along this way somewhere, according to the map. George, if you get into ruts like that you'll be thrown off.'

'All right, I know that!' said George. 'I only got into one because Timmy swerved across my wheel. He's after a

532

rabbit or something. Timmy! Don't get left behind, you idiot.'

Timmy bounded reluctantly after the little party. Exercise was wonderful, but it did mean leaving a lot of marvellous wayside smells unsniffed at. It was a dreadful waste of smells, Timmy thought.

They came to Croker's Corner sooner than they thought. The signpost proclaimed the name – and there, leaning against the post, sitting on his bicycle was Richard, beaming at them.

'You've been jolly quick, getting back home and then on to here,' said Julian. 'What did your mother say?'

'She didn't mind a bit so long as I was with *you*,' said Richard. 'I can go to my aunt's for the night, she said.'

'Haven't you brought pyjamas or anything with you?' asked Dick.

'There are always spare ones at my aunt's,' explained Richard. 'Hurray – it will be marvellous to be out on my own all day with you – no Mr Lomax to bother me with this and that. Come on!'

They all cycled on together. Richard would keep trying to ride three abreast, and Julian had to warn him that cyclists were not allowed to do that. 'I don't care!' sang Richard, who seemed in very high spirits. 'Who is there to stop us, anyway?'

'*I* shall stop you,' said Julian, and Richard ceased grinning at once. Julian could sound very stern when he liked. Dick winked at George, and she winked back. They had both come to the conclusion that Richard was very spoilt and liked his own way. Well, he wouldn't get it if he came up against old Julian!

They stopped at eleven for ice-creams and drinks. Richard seemed to have a lot of money. He insisted on buying ice-creams for all of them, even Timmy.

Once again they bought food for their lunch – new bread, farm-house butter, cream cheese, crisp lettuce, fat

533

red radishes and a bunch of spring onions. Richard bought a magnificent chocolate cake he saw in a first-class cake-shop.

'Gracious! That must have cost you a fortune!' said Anne. 'How are we going to carry it?'

'Woof,' said Timmy longingly.

'No, I certainly shan't let *you* carry it,' said Anne. 'Oh dear – we'll have to cut it in half, I think, and two people can share the carrying. It's such an enormous cake.'

On they went again, getting into the real country now, with villages few and far between. A farm here and there showed up on the hillsides, with cows and sheep and fowls. It was a peaceful, quiet scene, with the sun spilling down over everything, and the blue April sky above, patched with great white cotton-wool clouds.

'This is grand,' said Richard. 'I say, doesn't Timmy *ever* get tired? He's panting like anything now.'

'Yes. I think we ought to find somewhere for our lunch,' said Julian, looking at his watch. 'We've done a very good run this morning. Of course a lot of the way has been downhill. This afternoon we'll probably be slower, because we'll be getting into hilly country.'

They found a spot to picnic in. They chose the sunny side of a hedge, looking downhill into a small valley. Sheep and lambs were in the field they sat in. The lambs were very inquisitive, and one came right up to Anne and bleated.

'Do you want a bit of my bread?' asked Anne, and held it out to the lamb. Timmy watched indignantly. Fancy handing out food to those silly little creatures! He growled a little, and George shushed him.

Soon all the lambs were crowding round, quite unafraid, and one even tried to put its little front legs up on to George's shoulders! That was too much for Timmy! He gave such a sudden, fierce growl that all the lambs shot off at once.

534

'Oh, don't be so jealous, Timmy,' said George. 'Take this sandwich and behave yourself. Now you've frightened away the lambs, and they won't come back.'

They all ate the food and then drank their lime-juice and ginger-beer. The sun was very hot. Soon they would all be burnt brown – and it was only April. How marvellous! Julian thought lazily that they were really lucky to have such weather – it would be awful to have to bike along all day in the pouring rain.

Once again the children snoozed in the afternoon sun, Richard too – and the little lambs skipped nearer and nearer. One actually leapt on to Julian as he slept, and he sat upright with a jerk. 'Timmy!' he began, 'if you leap on me again like that I'll . . .'

But it wasn't Timmy, it was a lamb! Julian laughed to himself. He sat for a few minutes and watched the little white creatures playing 'I'm king of the castle' with an old coop, then he lay down again.

'Are we anywhere near your aunt's house?' Julian asked Richard, when they once more mounted their bicycles.

'If we're anywhere near Great Giddings, we shall soon be there,' said Richard, riding without his handlebars and almost ending up in the ditch. 'I didn't notice it on the map.'

Julian tried to remember. 'Yes – we should be at Great Giddings round about tea-time – say five o'clock or thereabouts. We'll leave you at your aunt's house for tea if you like.'

'Oh no, thank you,' said Richard, quickly. 'I'd much rather have tea with *you*. I *do* wish I could come on this tour with you. I suppose I couldn't possibly? You could telephone my mother.'

'Don't be an ass,' said Julian. 'You can have tea with us if you like – but we drop you at your aunt's as arranged, see? No nonsense about that.'

They came to Great Giddings at about ten past five.

Although it was called Great it was really very small. There was a little tea-place that said 'Home-made cakes and jams', so they went there for tea.

The woman who kept it was a plump, cheerful soul, fond of children. She guessed she would make very little out of the tea she served to five healthy children – but that didn't matter! She set to work to cut three big plates of well-buttered slices of bread, put out apricot jam, raspberry, and strawberry, and a selection of home-made buns that made the children's mouths water.

She knew Richard quite well, because he had sometimes been to her cottage with his aunt.

'I suppose you'll be going to stay with her tonight?' she said to Richard, and he nodded, his mouth full of ginger cake. It was a lovely tea. Anne felt as if she wouldn't be able to eat any supper at all that night! Even Timmy seemed to have satisfied his enormous appetite.

'I think we ought to pay you double price for our gorgeous tea,' said Julian, but the woman wouldn't hear of it. No, no – it was lovely to see them all enjoying her cakes; she didn't want double price!

'Some people are so *awfully* nice and generous,' said Anne, as they mounted their bicycles to ride off again. 'You just can't help liking them. I do hope I can cook like that when I grow up.'

'If you do, Julian and I will always live with you and not dream of getting married!' said Dick, promptly, and they all laughed.

'Now for Richard's aunt,' said Julian. 'Do you know where the house is, Richard?'

'Yes – that's it over there,' said Richard, and rode up to a gate. 'Well, thanks awfully for your company. I hope I'll see you again soon! I have a feeling I shall! Good-bye!'

He rode up the drive and disappeared. 'What a sudden good-bye!' said George, puzzled. 'Isn't he *odd*?'

536

6

Odd happenings

They all thought it really was a little odd to disappear so suddenly like that, with just a casual good-bye. Julian wondered if he ought to have gone with him and delivered him safely on the door-step.

'Don't be an ass, Julian,' said Dick, scornfully. 'What *do* you think can happen to him from the front gate to the front door!'

'Nothing, of course. It's just that I don't trust that young fellow,' said Julian. 'You know I really wasn't sure he had asked his mother if he could come with us, to tell you the truth.'

'I thought that too,' said Anne. 'He did get to Croker's Corner so very quickly, didn't he? – and he had quite a long way to go really, and he had to find his mother, and talk to her, and all that.'

'Yes. I've half a mind to pop up to the aunt's house and see if she expected him,' said Julian. But on second thoughts he didn't go. He would feel so silly if the aunt was there with Richard, and all was well – they would think that he and the others ought to be asked in.

So, after debating the matter for a few minutes they all rode off again. They wanted to get to Middlecombe Woods fairly soon, because there were no villages between Great Giddings and Middlecombe, so they would have to find the woods and then go on to find a farm-house somewhere to buy food for supper and breakfast. They hadn't been able to buy any in the shops at Great Giddings because it was early closing day, and they hadn't liked to ask the tea-shop woman to sell them anything. They felt they had taken quite enough of her food already!

They came to Middlecombe Woods, and found a very fine place to camp in for the night. It was in a little dell, set with primroses and violets, a perfectly hidden place, secure from all prying eyes, and surely unknown even to tramps.

'This is glorious,' said Anne. 'We must be miles away from anywhere: I hope we can find some farm-house or something that will sell us food, though! I know we don't feel hungry now, but we shall!'

'I think I've got a puncture, blow it,' said Dick, looking at his back tyre. 'It's a slow one, fortunately. But I think I won't risk coming along to look for farmhouses till I've mended it.'

'Right,' said Julian. 'And Anne needn't come either. She looks a bit tired. George and I will go. We won't take our bikes. It's easier to walk through the woods. We may be an hour or so, but don't worry, Timmy will know the way back all right, so we shan't lose you!'

Julian and George set off on foot, with Timmy following. Timmy too was tired, but nothing would have made him stay behind with Anne and Dick. He must go with his beloved George!

Anne put her bicycle carefully into the middle of a bush. You never knew when a tramp might be about, watching to steal something! It didn't matter when Timmy was there, because he would growl if a tramp came within a

538

mile of them. Dick called out that he would mend his puncture now. He had found the hole already, where a small nail had gone in.

She sat near to Dick, watching him. She was glad to rest. She wondered if the others had found a farmhouse yet.

Dick worked steadily at mending the puncture. They had been there together about half an hour when they heard sounds.

Dick lifted his head and listened. 'Can you hear something?' he said to Anne. She nodded.

'Yes. Somebody's shouting. I wonder why!'

They both listened again. Then they distinctly heard yells. 'Help! Julian! Where are you? Help!'

They shot to their feet. Who was calling Julian for help? It wasn't George's voice. The yells grew louder, to panic-stricken shrieks.

'JULIAN! Dick!'

'Why – it must be Richard,' said Dick, amazed. 'What in the world does he want? What's happened?'

Anne was pale. She didn't like sudden happenings like this. 'Shall we – shall we go and find him?' she said.

There was a crashing not far off, as if somebody was making his way through the undergrowth. It was rather dark among the trees, and Anne and Dick could see nothing at first. Dick yelled loudly.

'Hey! Is that you, Richard! We're here!'

The crashing noise redoubled. 'I'm coming!' squealed Richard. 'Wait for me, wait for me!'

They waited. Soon they saw Richard coming, stumbling as fast as he could between the trees. 'Here we are,' called Dick. 'Whatever's the matter?'

Richard staggered towards them. He looked frightened out of his life. 'They're after me,' he panted. 'You must save me. I want Timmy. He'll bite them.'

'*Who*'s after you?' asked Dick, amazed.

'Where's Timmy? Where's Julian?' cried Richard, looking round in despair.

'They've gone to the farm-house to get some food,' said Dick. 'They'll be back soon, Richard. Whatever's the *matter*? Are you mad? You look awful.'

The boy took no notice of the questions. 'Where has

Julian gone? I want Timmy. Tell me the way they went. I can't stay here. They'll catch me!'

'They went along there,' said Dick, showing Richard the path. 'You can just see the tracks of their feet. Richard, whatever is . . .?'

But Richard was gone! He fled down the path at top speed, calling at the top of his voice, 'Julian! Timmy!'

Anne and Dick stared at one another in surprise. What had happened to Richard? Why wasn't he at his aunt's house? He must be mad!

'It's no good going after him,' said Dick. 'We shall only lose the way and not be able to find this place again – and the others will miss us and go hunting and get lost too! What *is* the matter with Richard?'

'He kept saying somebody was after him – *they* were after him!' said Anne. 'He's got some bee in his bonnet about something.'

'Bats in the belfry,' said Dick. 'Mad, dippy, daft! Well, he'll give Julian and George a shock when he runs into them – if he does! The odds are he will miss them altogether.'

'I'm going to climb this tree and see if I can see anything of Richard or the others,' said Anne. 'It's tall, and it's easy to climb. You finish mending your puncture. I should just love to know what happens to Richard.'

Dick went back to his bicycle, puzzled. Anne climbed the tree. She climbed well, and was soon at the top. She gazed out over the countryside. There was an expanse of fields on one side, and woods stretched away on the other. She looked over the darkening fields, trying to see if a farm-house was anywhere near. But she could see nothing.

Dick was just finishing his puncture when he heard another noise in the woods. Was it that idiot of a Richard coming back? He listened.

The noise came nearer. It wasn't a crashing noise, like

541

Richard had made. It was a stealthy noise as if people were gradually closing in. Dick didn't much like it. Who was coming? Or perhaps – *what* was coming? Was it some wild animal – perhaps a badger and its mate? The boy stood listening.

A silence came. No more movements. No more rustling. Had he imagined it all? He wished Anne and the others were near him. It was eerie, standing there in the darkening wood, waiting and watching.

He decided that he had imagined it all. He thought it would be a very good idea if he lighted his bicycle lamp, then the light would soon dispel his silly ideas! He fumbled about for it on the front of his handlebars. He switched it on and a very comforting little glow at once spread a circle of light in the little dell.

Dick was just about to call up to Anne to tell her his absurd fears when the noises came again! There was absolutely no mistake about them this time.

A brilliant light suddeningly pierced through the trees and fell on Dick. He blinked.

'Ah – so there you are, you little misery!' said a harsh voice, and someone came striding over to the dell. Somebody else followed behind.

'What do you mean?' asked Dick, amazed. He could not see who the men were because of the brilliant torch-light in his eyes.

'We've been chasing you for miles, haven't we? And you thought you'd get away. But we'd got you all the time!' said the voice.

'I don't understand this,' said Dick, putting on a bold voice. 'Who are you?'

'You know very well who we are,' said the voice. 'Didn't you run away screaming as soon as you saw Rooky? He went one way after you, and we went another – and we soon got you, didn't we? Now, you come along with us, my pretty!'

542

All this explained one thing clearly to Dick – that it was Richard they had been after, for some reason or other – and they thought *he* was Richard!

'I'm not the boy you're looking for,' he said. 'You'll get into trouble if you touch *me!*'

'What's your name, then?' asked the first man.

Dick told him.

'Oh – so you're Dick – and isn't Dick short for Richard? You can't fool us with that baby-talk,' said the first man. 'You're the Richard we want, all right. Richard Kent, see?'

'I'm *not* Richard Kent!' shouted Dick, as he felt the man's hand clutching his arm suddenly. 'You take your hands off me. You wait till the police hear of this!'

'They *won't* hear of it,' said the man. 'They won't hear anything at all! Come on – and don't struggle or shout or you'll be sorry. Once you're at Owl's Dene we'll deal properly with you!'

Anne was sitting absolutely petrified up in the tree. She couldn't move or speak. She tried to call out to poor Dick, but her tongue wouldn't say a word. She had to sit there and hear her brother being dragged away by two strange ruffians. She almost fell out of the tree in fright, and she heard him shouting and yelling when he was dragged away. She could hear the sound of crashing for a long time.

She began to cry. She didn't dare to climb down because she was trembling so much she was afraid she would lose her hold and fall.

She must wait for George and Julian to come back. Suppose they didn't? Suppose they had been caught too? She would be all by herself in the tree all night long. Anne sobbed up in the tree-top, holding on tightly.

The stars came out above her head, and she saw the very bright one again.

And then she heard the sound of footsteps and voices.

543

She stiffened up in the tree. Who was it this time? Oh let it be Julian and George and Timmy; let it be Julian, George and Timmy!

7

Richard tells a queer tale

Julian and George had managed to find a little farm-house tucked away in a hollow. A trio of dogs set up a terrific barking as they drew near. Timmy growled and the hair rose up on his neck. George put her hand on his collar.

'I won't go any nearer with Timmy,' she said. 'I don't want him to be set on by three dogs at once!'

So Julian went down to the farm-house by himself. The dogs made such a noise and looked so fierce that he paused in the farm-yard. He was not in the least afraid of dogs, but these looked most unpleasant, especially one big mongrel whose teeth were bared in a very threatening manner.

A voice called out to him. 'Clear off, you! We don't want no strangers here. When strangers come our eggs and hens go too!'

'Good evening,' called Julian, politely. 'We are four children camping out in the woods for the night. Could you let us have any food? I'll pay well for it.'

There was a pause. The man pulled his head in at the

window he was shouting from, and was evidently speaking to someone inside.

He stuck it out again. 'I told you, we don't hold with strangers here, never did. We've only got plain bread and butter, and we can give you some hardboiled eggs and milk and a bit of ham. That's all.'

'That'll do fine,' called Julian, cheerily. 'Just what we'd like. Shall I come and get it?'

'Not unless you want to be torn to pieces by them dogs,' came back the voice. 'You wait there. I'll be out when the eggs is done.'

'Blow,' said Julian, walking back to George. 'That means we'll have to kick our heels here for a while. What an unpleasant fellow! I don't think much of his place, do you!'

George agreed with him. It was ill-kept, the barn was falling to bits, rusty bits of machinery lay here and there in the thick grass. The three dogs kept up a continual barking and howling, but they did not come any nearer. George still kept her hand firmly on Timmy. He was bristling all over!

'What a lonely place to live in,' said Julian. 'No house within miles, I should think. No telephone. I wonder what they'd do if somebody was ill or had an accident and needed help.'

'I hope they'll hurry up with that food,' said George, getting impatient. 'It'll be dark soon. I'm getting hungry too.'

At last somebody came out of the tumble-down farmhouse. It was a bearded man, stooping and old, with long untidy hair and a pronounced limp. He had a grim and ugly face. Neither Julian nor George liked him.

'Here you are,' he said, waving his three dogs away behind him. 'Get back, you!' He aimed a kick at the nearest dog, and it yelped with pain.

'Oh don't!' said George. 'You hurt him.'

546

'He's my dog, ain't he?' said the man, angrily. 'You mind your own business!' He kicked out at another dog and scowled at George.

'What about the food?' said Julian, holding out his hand, anxious to be gone before trouble came between Timmy and the other dogs. 'George, take Timmy back a bit. He's upsetting the dogs.'

'Well, I like that!' said George. 'It's those other dogs that are upsetting *him*!'

She dragged Timmy back a few yards, and he stood there with all his hackles up on his neck, growling in a horrible way.

Julian took the food which was done up carelessly in old brown paper. 'Thanks,' he said. 'How much?'

'Five pounds,' said the old man, surprisingly.

'Don't be silly,' said Julian. He looked quickly at the food. 'I'll give you twenty-five pence for it, and that's more than it's worth. There's hardly any ham.'

'I said five pounds,' said the man, sullenly. Julian looked at him. 'He must be mad!' he thought. He held out the food to the ugly old fellow.

'Well, take it back,' he said. 'I haven't got five pounds to give you for food. Twenty-five pence is the most I can spare. Good night.'

The old man pushed the food back, and held out his other hand in silence. Julian fished in his pocket and brought out twenty-five pence. He placed them in the man's dirty hand, wondering why on earth the fellow had asked him for such a ridiculous sum before. The man put the money in his pocket.

'Clear off,' he said, suddenly, in a growling voice. 'We don't want strangers here, stealing our goods. I'll set my dogs on you if you come again!'

Julian turned to go, half-afraid that the extraordinary old man *would* set his dogs on him. The fellow stood there in the half-dark, yelling abuse at Julian and George as

547

they made their way out of the farm-yard.

'Well! We'll never go *there* again!' said George, furious at their treatment. 'He's mad as a hatter.'

'Yes. And I don't much fancy his food, either,' said Julian. 'Still, it's all we'll get tonight!'

They followed Timmy back to the woods. They were glad they had him, because otherwise they might have missed the way. But Timmy knew it. Once he had been along a certain route Timmy always knew it again. He ran on now, sniffing here and there, occasionally waiting for the others to catch him up.

548

Then he stiffened and growled softly. George put her hand on his collar. Somebody must be coming.

Somebody *was* coming! It was Richard on his way to find them. He was still shouting and yelling, and the noise he made had already come to Timmy's sharp ears. It soon came to Julian's, and George's too, as they stood there waiting.

'Julian! Where are you? Where's Timmy? I want Timmy! They're after me, I tell you; they're after me.'

'Listen – it sounds like *Richard*,' said Julian, startled. 'What in the world is he doing here? – and yelling like that too! Come on – we must find out. Something's happened. I hope Dick and Anne are all right.'

They ran up the path as fast as they could in the twilight. Soon they met Richard, who had now stopped shouting, and was stumbling along, half-sobbing.

'Richard! What's up?' cried Julian. Richard ran to him and flung himself against him. Timmy did not go to him, but stood there in surprise. George stared through the twilight, puzzled. What in the world had happened?

'Julian! Oh Julian! I'm scared stiff,' panted Richard, hanging on to Julian's arm.

'Pull yourself together,' said Julian, in the calm voice that had made a good effect on Richard. 'I bet you're just making a silly fuss. What's happened? Did you find your aunt was out or something? And come racing after us?'

'My aunt's away,' said Richard, speaking in a calmer voice. 'She . . .'

'*Away!*' said Julian, in surprise. 'But didn't your mother know that when she said you could . . .?'

'I didn't ask my mother's permission to come,' cried Richard. 'I didn't even go back home when you thought I did! I just biked straight to Croker's Corner and waited for you. I wanted to come with you, you see – and I knew my mother wouldn't let me.'

This was said with a great air of bravado. Julian was disgusted.

'I'm ashamed of you,' he said. 'Telling us lies like that!'

'I didn't know my aunt was away,' said Richard, all his sudden cockiness gone when he heard Julian's scornful voice. 'I thought she'd be there – and I was going to tell her to telephone my mother and say I'd gone for a trip with *you*. Then I thought I'd come biking after you and – and . . .'

'And tell us your aunt was away, and could you come with us?' finished Julian, still scornfully. 'A deceitful and ridiculous plan. I'd have sent you back at once; you might have known that.'

'Yes, I know. But I might have had a whole night camping out with you,' said Richard, in a small voice. 'I've never done things like that. I . . .'

'What I want to know is, what were you scared of when you came rushing along, yelling and crying,' said Julian, impatiently.

'Oh Julian – it was horrible,' said Richard, and he suddenly clutched Julian's arm again. 'You see – I biked down back to my aunt's gate – and out into the lane – and I was just going along the way to Middlecombe Woods when a car met me. And I saw who was in the car!'

'Well, *who*?' said Julian, feeling as if he could shake Richard.

'It was – it was Rooky!' said Richard, in a trembling voice.

'Who's he?' said Julian, and George gave an impatient click. Would Richard never tell his story properly?

'Don't you remember? – I told you about him. He was the fellow with thick lips and a huge nose that my father had for a bodyguard last year – and he chucked him out,' said Richard. 'He always swore he'd have his revenge on my father – and on me too because I told tales about him to Dad and it was because of that he was sacked. So when I

550

caught sight of him in the car I was terrified!'

'I *see*,' said Julian, seeing light. 'What happened then?'

'Rooky recognized me, and turned the car round and chased me on my bike,' said Richard, beginning to tremble again as he remembered that alarming ride. 'I pedalled for all I was worth – and when I got to Middle-combe Woods I rode into the path there, hoping the car couldn't follow. It couldn't, of course – but the men leapt out – there were three of them, two I didn't know – and they chased me on foot. I pedalled and pedalled, and then I ran into a tree or something and fell off. I chucked my bike into a bush, and ran into the thick undergrowth to hide.'

'Go on,' said Julian, as Richard paused. 'What next?'

'The men split up then – Rooky went one way to find me, and the other two went another way. I waited till I thought they were gone, then I crept out and tore down the path again, hoping to find you. I wanted Timmy, you see, I thought he'd go for the men.'

Timmy growled. He certainly would have gone for them!

'Two of the men must have been hiding, waiting to hear me start up again,' went on Richard. 'And as soon as I began to run, they chased after me. I put them off the trail, though – I dodged and hid and hid and dodged – and then I came to Dick! He was mending a puncture. But you weren't with him – and it was you and Timmy I wanted – I knew the men would soon be catching me up, you see, so I tore on and on – and at last I found you. I've never been so glad in my life.'

It was a most extraordinary story – but Julian hardly paused to think about it. An alarming thought had come into his head. What about Dick and Anne? What would have happened to them if the men had suddenly come across them?

'Quick!' he said to George. 'We must get back to the others! Hurry!'

8

What's the best thing to do?

Stumbling through the dark wood, Julian and George hurried as best they could. Timmy hurried too, knowing that something was worrying both his friends. Richard followed behind, half-crying again. He really had been very much afraid.

They came at last to the little dell where they had planned to spend the night. It was quite dark. Julian called loudly:

'Dick! Anne! Where are you?'

George had made her way to where she had hidden her bicycle. She fumbled for the lamp and switched it on. She took it off and flashed it round the dell. There was Dick's bicycle, with the puncture repair outfit on the ground beside it – but no Dick, and no Anne! What had happened?

'Anne!' yelled Julian, in alarm. 'Dick! Come here! We're back!'

And then a small trembling voice came down from the tree-top overhead.

'Oh Julian! Oh Julian! I'm here.'

'It's Anne!' yelled Julian, his heart leaping in relief. 'Anne – where are you?'

'Up in this tree,' called back Anne, in a stronger voice. 'Oh Ju – I've been so frightened, I didn't dare climb down in case I fell. Dick . . .'

'Where *is* Dick?' demanded Julian.

A sob came down to him. 'Two horrible men came – and they've taken him away. They thought he was Richard!'

Anne's voice became a wail. Julian felt that he must get her down the tree so that she could be with them and be comforted. He spoke to George.

'Shine that lamp up here. I'm going up to fetch Anne.'

George silently shone the light of the lamp on the tree. Julian went up like a cat. He came to Anne who was still clinging tightly to a branch.

'Anne, I'll help you down. Come on, now – you can't fall. I'm just below you. I'll guide your feet to the right branches.'

Anne was only too glad to be helped down. She was cold and miserable, and she longed to be with the others. Slowly she came down, with Julian's help, and he lifted her to the ground.

She clung to him, and he put his arm round his young sister. 'It's all right, Anne. I'm with you now. And here's George too – and old Timmy.'

'Who's *that*?' said Anne, suddenly seeing Richard in the shadows.

'Only Richard. He's behaved badly,' said Julian, grimly. 'It's all because of him and his idiotic behaviour that this has happened. Now – tell us slowly and carefully about Dick and the two men, Anne.'

Anne told him, not missing out anything at all. Timmy stood near her, licking her hand all the time. That was very comforting indeed! Timmy always knew when any-

553

one was in trouble. Anne felt very much better when she
had Julian's arm round her, and Timmy's tongue licking
her!

'It's quite clear what's happened,' said Julian, when
Anne had finished her alarming tale. 'This man Rooky
recognized Richard, and he and the other two came after

him, seeing a chance to kidnap him, and so get even with his father. Rooky was the only one who knew Richard, and he wasn't the man who caught Dick. The *others* got him – and they didn't know he wasn't Richard – and of course, hearing that his name was Dick they jumped to the conclusion that he was Richard – because Dick is short for Richard.'

'But Dick *told* them he wasn't Richard Kent,' said Anne, earnestly.

'Of course – but they thought he wasn't telling the truth,' said Julian. 'And they've taken him off. What did you say was the name of the place they were going to?'

'It sounded like Owl's Dene,' said Anne. 'Can we go there, Julian – if you told the men Dick was Dick and not Richard, they'd let him go, wouldn't they?'

'Oh yes,' said Julian. 'In any case, as soon as that fellow Rooky sets eyes on him he'll know there's a mistake been made. I think we can get old Dick away all right.'

A voice came out of the shadows nearby. 'What about *me*? Will you take me home first? *I* don't want to run into Rooky again.'

'I'm certainly not going to waste time taking *you* home,' said Julian, coldly. 'If it hadn't been for you and your tomfoolery we wouldn't have run into this trouble. You'll have to come with us. I'm going to find Dick first.'

'But I *can't* come with you – I'm afraid of Rooky!' wailed Richard.

'Well, stay here then,' said Julian, determined to teach Richard a lesson.

That was even worse. Richard howled loudly. 'Don't leave me here! Don't!'

'Now look here – if you come with us, you can always be dropped at a house somewhere, or at a police-station – and get yourself taken home somehow,' said Julian, exasperated. 'You're old enough to look after yourself. I'm fed up with you.'

555

Anne was sorry for Richard, although he had brought all this trouble on them. She knew how dreadful it was to feel really frightened. She put out a hand and touched him kindly.

'Richard! Don't be a baby. Julian will see that you're all right. He's just feeling cross with you now, but he'll soon get over it.'

'Don't you be too sure about that!' said Julian to Anne, pretending to be sterner than he really felt. 'What Richard wants is a jolly good hiding. He's untruthful and deceitful and an absolute baby!'

'Give me another chance,' almost wept poor Richard, who had never in his life been spoken to like this before. He tried to hate Julian for saying such things to him – but oddly enough he couldn't. He only respected and admired him all the more.

Julian said no more to Richard. He really thought the boy was too feeble for words. It was a nuisance that they had him with them. He would be no help at all – simply a tiresome nuisance.

'What are we going to do, Julian?' asked George, who had been very silent. She was fond of Dick, and was very worried about him. Where was Owl's Dene? How could they possibly find it in the night? And what about those awful men? How would they treat Julian if he demanded Dick back at once? Julian was fearless and straightforward – but the men wouldn't like him any the better for that.

'Well now – what *are* we going to do?' repeated Julian, and he fell silent.

'It's no good going back to that farm, and asking for help, is it?' said George, after a pause.

'Not a bit of good,' said Julian, at once. 'That old man wouldn't help anyone! And there's no telephone laid on, as we saw. No – that farm's no good. What a pity!'

'Where's the map?' said George, a sudden idea coming into her head. 'Would Owl's Dene be named on it, do you think?'

'Not if it's a house,' said Julian. 'Only places are named there. You'd want a frightfully big map to show every house.'

'Well, anyway – let's look at the map and see if it shows any more farms or villages,' said George, who felt as if she must *do* something, even if it was only looking at a map. Julian produced the map and unfolded it. He and the girls bent over it, by the light of the bicycle lamp, and Richard peered over their shoulders. Even Timmy tried to look, forcing his head under their arms.

'Get away, Tim,' said Julian. 'Look, here's where we are – Middlecombe Woods – see? My word, we *are* in a lonely spot! There's not a village for miles!'

Certainly no village was marked. The countryside was shown, hilly and wooded, with a stream here and there, and third-class roads now and again – but no village, no church, no bridge even was marked anywhere.

Anne gave a sudden exclamation and pointed to the contour of a hill on the map. 'Look – see what that hill's called?'

'Owl's Hill,' read out Julian. 'Yes – I see what you're getting at, Anne. If a house was built on that hill it might be called Owl's Dene, because of the name of the hill. What's more – a building *is* marked there! It hasn't a name, of course. It might be a farm-house, an old ruin – or a big house of some kind.'

'*I* think it's very likely that's where Owl's Dene is,' said George. 'I bet it's that very house. Let's take our bikes and go.'

A huge sigh from Richard attracted their attention. '*Now* what's the matter with you?' said Julian.

'Nothing. I'm hungry, that's all,' said Richard.

The others suddenly realized that they too were hungry. In fact, *terribly* hungry! It was a long, long time since tea.

Julian remembered the food he and George had brought from the farm. Should they have it now – or should they eat some on their way to Owl's Hill?

'Better eat as we go,' said Julian. 'Every minute we waste means a minute of worry for Dick.'

'I wonder what they'd do with him, if Rooky sees him and says he's not me, not the boy they want,' said Richard, suddenly.

'Set him free, I should think,' said George. 'Ruffians like that would probably turn him loose in a deserted countryside and not care tuppence if he found his way home or not. We've absolutely *got* to find out what's happened – whether he's at Owl's Dene, or been set free, or what.'

'I can't come with you,' suddenly wailed Richard.

'Why?' demanded Julian.

'Because I haven't got my bike,' said Richard, dolefully. 'I chucked it away, you remember – and goodness knows where it is. I'd never find it again.'

'He can have Dick's,' said Anne. 'There it is, over there – with the puncture mended too.'

'Oh yes,' said Richard, relieved. 'For one frightful moment I thought I'd have to be left behind.'

Julian secretly wished he *could* be left behind. Richard was more trouble than he was worth!

'Yes – you can take Dick's bike,' he said. 'But no idiotic behaviour with it, mind – no riding without handlebars, or any errand boy tricks like that. It's Dick's bike, not yours.'

Richard said nothing. Julian was always ticking him off. He supposed he deserved it – but it wasn't at all pleasant. He pulled at Dick's bike, and found the lamp was missing. Dick, of course, had taken it off. He hunted round for it and found it on the ground. Dick had let it fall,

558

and the switch had turned itself off when the lamp hit the ground. When Richard pressed the switch down the lamp lighted again. Good!

'Now, come on,' said Julian, fetching his bicycle too. 'I'll hand out food to eat as we go. We must try to find our way to Owl's Hill as quick as ever we can!'

9

Moonlight adventure

The four of them rode carefully down the rough, wood-land path. They were glad when they came out into a lane. Julian stopped for a moment to take his bearings.

'Now – according to the map, we ought to go to the right here – then take the left at the fork some way down, and then circle a hill by the road at the bottom – and then ride a mile or two in a little valley till we come to the foot of Owl's Hill.'

'If we meet anyone we could ask them about Owl's Dene,' said Anne, hopefully.

'We shan't meet anyone out at night in this district!' said Julian. 'For one thing it's far from any village, and there will be no farmer, no policeman, no traveller for miles! We can't hope to meet anyone.'

The moon was up, and the sky cleared as they rode down the lane. It was soon as bright as day!

'We could switch off our lamps and save the batteries,' said Julian. 'We can see quite well we're out of the woods and in the moonlight. Rather weird, isn't it?'

'I always think moonlight's queer, because although it shines so brightly on everything, you can never see much *colour* anywhere,' said Anne. She switched off her lamp too. She glanced down at Timmy.

'Switch off your head-lamps, Timmy!' she said, which made Richard give a sudden giggle. Julian smiled. It was nice to hear Anne being cheerful again.

'Timmy's eyes *are* rather like head-lamps, aren't they?' said Richard. 'I say – what about that food, Julian?'

'Right,' said Julian, and he fished in his basket. But it was very difficult to get it out with one hand, and try to hand it to the others.

'Better stop for a few minutes, after all,' he said at last. 'I've already dropped a hard-boiled egg, I think! Come on – let's stack our bikes by the side of the road for three minutes, and gulp down something just to satisfy us for now.'

Richard was only too pleased. The girls were so hungry that they too thought it a good idea. They leapt off their bicycles in the moonlit road and went to the little copse at the side. It was a pine-copse, and the ground below was littered with dry brown pine-needles.

'Let's squat here for a minute or two,' said Julian. 'I say – what's that over there?'

Everyone looked. 'It's a tumbledown hut or something,' said George, and she went nearer to see. 'Yes, that's all – some old cottage fallen to bits. There's only part of the walls left. Rather an eerie little place.'

They went to sit down under the pine-trees. Julian shared out the food. Timmy got his bit too, though not so much as he would have liked! They sat there in the pine shadows, munching hungrily as fast as they could.

'I say – can anyone hear what I hear?' said Julian, raising his head. 'It sounds like a car!'

They all listened. Julian was right. A car *was* purring silently through the countryside! What a bit of luck!

561

'If only it comes this way!' said Julian. 'We could stop it and ask it for help. It could take us to the nearest police-station at any rate!'

They left their food in the little copse and went to the roadside. They could see no head-lights shining anywhere, but they could still hear the noise of the car.

'Very quiet engine,' said Julian. 'Probably a powerful car. It hasn't got its head-lights on because of the bright moonlight.'

'It's coming nearer,' said George. 'It's coming down this lane. Yes – it is!'

So it was. The noise of the engine came nearer, and nearer. The children got ready to leap out into the road to stop the car.

And then the noise of the engine died away suddenly. The moon shone down on a big streamlined car that had stopped a little way down the lane. It had no lights at all, not even side-lights. Julian put out his hand to stop the others from rushing into the road and shouting.

'Wait,' he said. 'This is just a bit – queer!'

They waited, keeping in the shadows. The car had stopped not far from the tumbledown hut. A door opened on the off-side. A man got out and rushed across the road to the shadow of the hedge there. He seemed to be carrying a bundle of some kind.

A low whistle sounded. The call of an owl came back. 'An answering signal!' thought Julian, intensely curious about all this. 'I wonder what's happening?'

'Keep absolutely quiet,' he breathed to the others. 'George, look after Timmy – don't let him growl.'

But Timmy knew when he had to be quiet. He didn't even give a whine. He stood like a statue, ears pricked, eyes watching the lane.

Nothing happened for a while. Julian moved very cautiously to the shelter of another tree, from where he could see better.

562

He could see the tumbledown shack. He saw a shadow moving towards it from some trees beyond. He saw a man waiting – the man from the car probably. Who were they? What in the world could they be doing here at this time of night?

The man from the trees came at last to the man from the car. There was a rapid interchange of words, but Julian could not hear what they were. He was sure that the men had no idea at all that he and the other children were near. He cautiously crept to yet another tree, and peered from the shadows to try and see what was happening.

'Don't be long,' he heard one man say. 'Don't bring your things to the car. Stuff them down the well.'

Julian could not see properly what the man was doing, but he thought he must be changing his clothes. Yes – now he was putting on the others – probably from the bundle the first man had brought from the car. Julian was more and more curious. What a queer business! Who was the second man? A refugee? A spy?

The man who had changed his clothes now picked up his discarded ones and went to the back of the shack. He came back without them, and followed the first man across the lane to the waiting car.

Even before the door had closed, the engine was purring, and the car was away! It passed by the pine-copse where the children were watching, and they all shrank back as it raced by. Before it had gone very far it was travelling very fast indeed.

Julian joined the others. Well – what do you make of all that?' he said. 'Funny business, isn't it? I watched a man changing his clothes – goodness knows why. He's left them somewhere at the back of the shack – down a well, I think I heard them say. Shall we see?'

'Yes, let's,' said George, puzzled. 'I say, did you see the number on the car. I only managed to spot the letters – KMF.'

'I saw the numbers,' said Anne. '102. And it was a black Bentley.'

'Yes. Black Bentley, KMF 102,' said Richard. 'Up to some funny business, I'll be bound!'

They made their way to the ruined shack, and pushed through overgrown weeds and bushes into the backyard. There was a broken-down well there, most of its brick-work missing.

It was covered by an old wooden lid. Julian removed it. It was still heavy, though rotten with age. He peered down the well, but there was nothing at all to be seen. It was far too deep to see to the bottom by the light of a bicycle lamp.

'Not much to be seen *there*,' said Julian, replacing the lid. 'I expect it *was* his clothes he threw down. Wonder why he changed them?'

'Do you think he could be an escaped prisoner?' said Anne, suddenly. 'He'd have to change his prison clothes, wouldn't he? – that would be the most important thing for him to do. Is there a prison near here?'

Nobody knew. 'Don't remember noticing one on the map,' said Julian. 'No – somehow I don't think the man was an escaped prisoner – more likely a spy dropped down in this desolate countryside, and supplied with clothes – or perhaps a deserter from the army. That's even *more* likely!'

'Well, whatever it is I don't like it and I'm jolly glad the car's gone with the prisoner or deserter or spy, whatever he is,' said Anne. 'What a curious thing that we should just be nearby when this happened! The men would never, never guess there were four children and a dog watching just a few yards away.'

'Lucky for us they *didn't* know,' said Julian. 'They wouldn't have been at all pleased! Now come on – we've wasted enough time. Let's get back to our food. I hope Timmy hasn't eaten it all. We left it on the ground.'

Timmy hadn't eaten even a crumb. He was sitting

patiently by the food, occasionally sniffing at it. All that bread and ham and eggs waiting there and nobody to eat it!

'Good dog,' said George. 'You're very, very trustable, Timmy. You shall have a big bit of bread and ham for your reward.'

Timmy gulped it down in one mouthful, but there was no more for him to have. The others only just had enough for themselves, and ate every crumb. They rose to their feet in a very few minutes and went to get their bicycles.

'Now for Owl's Hill again,' Julian. 'And let's hope we don't come across any more queer happenings tonight. We've had quite enough.'

10

Owl's Dene on Owl's Hill

Off they went again, cycling fast in the brilliant moon-light. Even when the moon went behind a cloud it was still light enough to ride without lights. They rode for what seemed like miles, and then came to a steep hill.

'Is this Owl's Hill?' said Anne, as they dismounted to walk up it. It was too steep to ride.

'Yes,' said Julian. 'At least, I think so – unless we've come quite wrong. But I don't think we have. Now the thing is – shall we find Owl's Dene at the top or not? And how shall we know it *is* Owl's Dene!'

'We could ring the bell and ask,' said Anne.

Julian laughed. That was so like Anne. 'Maybe we'll have to do that!' he said. 'But we'll scout round a bit first.'

They pushed their bicycles up the steep road. Hedges bordered each side, and fields lay beyond. There were no animals in them that the children could see – no horses, sheep or cows.

'Look!' said Anne, suddenly. 'I can see a building – at least, I'm sure I can see chimneys!'

They looked where she pointed. Yes – certainly they were chimneys – tall, brick chimneys that looked old.

'Looks like an Elizabethan mansion, with chimneys like that,' said Julian. He paused and took a good look. 'It must be a big place. We ought to come to a drive or something soon.'

They pushed on with their bicycles. Gradually the house came into view. It was more like a mansion, and in the moonlight it looked old, rather grand and very beautiful.

'There are the gates,' said Julian, thankfully. He was

tired of pushing his bicycle up the hill. 'They're shut. Hope they're not locked!'

As they drew near to the great, wrought-iron gates, they slowly opened. The children paused in surprise. Why were they opening? Not for them, that was certain!

Then they heard the sound of a car in the distance. Of course, that was what the gates were opening for. The car, however, was not coming up the hill – it was coming down the drive on the other side of the gates.

'Get out of sight, quickly,' said Julian. 'We don't want to be seen yet.'

They crouched down in the ditch with their bicycles as a car came slowly out of the open gates. Julian gave an exclamation and nudged George.

'See that? It's the black Bentley again – KMF 102!'

'How mysterious!' said George, surprised. 'What's it doing rushing about the country at night and picking up stray men! Taking them to this place too. I wonder if it *is* Owl's Dene.'

The car went by and disappeared round a bend in the hill. The children came out of the ditch with Timmy and their bicycles.

'Let's walk cautiously up to the gates,' said Julian. 'They're still open. Funny how they opened when the car came. I never saw anyone by them!'

They walked boldly up to the open gates.

'Look!' said Julian, pointing up to the great brick posts from which the gates were hung. They all looked, and exclaimed at the name shining there.

'Well! So it *is* Owl's Dene, after all!'

'There's the name in brass letters – Owl's Dene! We've found it!'

'Come on,' said Julian, wheeling his bicycle through the gateway. 'We'll go in and snoop round. We might be lucky enough to find old Dick somewhere about.'

They all went through the gates – and then Anne clutched Julian in fright. She pointed silently behind them.

The gates were closing again! But nobody was there to shut them. They closed silently and smoothly all by themselves. There was something very weird about that.

'Who's shutting them?' whispered Anne, in a scared voice.

'I think it must be done by machinery,' whispered back Julian. 'Probably worked from the house. Let's go back and see if we can find any machinery that works them.'

They left their bicycles by the side of the drive and walked back to the gates. Julian looked for a handle or latch to open them. But there was none.

He pulled at the gates. They did not budge. It was quite impossible to open them. They had been shut and locked by some kind of machinery, and nothing and nobody could open them but that special machinery.

'Blow!' said Julian, and he sounded so angry that the others looked at him in surprise.

570

'Well, don't you see? – we're locked in! We're as much prisoners here as Dick is, if he's here too. We can't get out through the gates – and if you take a look you'll see a high wall running round the property from the gates – and I don't mind betting it goes the *whole* way round. We can't get out even if we want to.'

They went back thoughtfully to their bicycles. 'Better wheel them a little way into the trees and leave them,' said Julian. 'They hinder us too much now. We'll leave them and go snooping quietly round the house. Hope there are no dogs.'

They left their bicycles well hidden among the trees at the side of the wide drive. The drive was not at all well-kept. It was mossy and weeds grew all over it. It was bare only where the wheels of cars had passed.

'Shall we walk up the drive or keep to the side?' asked George.

'Keep to the side,' said Julian. 'We should easily be seen in the moonlight, walking up the drive.'

So they kept to the side, in the shadows of the trees. They followed the curves of the long drive until the house itself came into sight.

It really was very big indeed. It was built in the shape of the letter E with the middle stroke missing – E. There was a courtyard in front, overgrown with weeds. A low wall, about knee high, ran round the courtyard.

There was a light in a room on the top floor, and another one on the ground floor. Otherwise from that side the house was dark.

'Let's walk quietly round it,' said Julian, in a low voice. 'Goodness – what's that?'

It was a weird and terrible screech that made them all jump in alarm. Anne clutched Julian in fright.

They stood and listened.

Something came down silently and brushed George's hair. She almost screamed – but before she could, that terrible screech came again, and she put out her hand to quieten Timmy, who was amazed and scared.

'What is it, Ju!' whispered George. 'Something touched me then. Before I could see what it was it was gone.'

'Listen – it's all right,' whispered back Julian. 'It's only an owl – a screech owl!'

'Good gracious – so it was,' breathed back George, in great relief. 'What an ass I was not to think of it. It's a barn-owl – a screech owl out hunting. Anne, were you scared?'

'I should just think I was!' said Anne, letting go her hold on Julian's arm.

'So was I,' said Richard, whose teeth were still chattering with fear. 'I nearly ran for my life! I would have too, if I could have got my legs to work – but they were glued to the ground!'

The owl screeched again, a little farther away, and another one answered it. A third one screeched, and the night was really made hideous with the unearthly calls.

'I'd rather have a brown owl any day, calling To-whooo-oo-oo,' said George. 'That's a nice noise. But this screeching is frightful.'

'No wonder it's called Owl's Hill,' said Julian. 'Perhaps it's always been a haunt of the screech-owls.'

The four children and Timmy began to walk quietly round the house, keeping to the shadows as much as they could. Everywhere was dark at the back except two long windows. They were leaded windows, and curtains were pulled across them. Julian tried to see through the cracks.

He found a place where two curtains didn't quite meet. He put his eye to the crack and looked in.

'It's the kitchen,' he told the others. 'An enormous place – lighted with one big oil-lamp. All the rest of the room is in shadow. There's a great fire-place at the end, with a few logs burning in it.'

'Anyone there?' asked George, trying to see through the

crack too. Julian moved aside and let her take her turn.

'No one that I can see,' he said. George gave an exclamation as she looked, and Julian pushed her aside to look in again.

He saw a man walking into the room – a queer, dwarf-like fellow, with a hunched back that seemed to force his head on one side. He had a very evil face. Behind him came a woman – thin, drab and the picture of misery.

The man flung himself into a chair and began to fill a pipe. The woman took a kettle off the fire and went to fill hot-water bottles in a corner.

'She must be the cook,' thought Julian. 'What a misery she looks! I wonder what the man is – man-of-all-work, I suppose. What an evil face he's got!'

The woman spoke timidly to the man in the chair. Julian, of course, could not hear a word from outside the window. The man answered her roughly, banging on the arm of the chair as he spoke.

The woman seemed to be pleading with him about something. The man flew into a rage, picked up a poker and threatened the woman with it. Julian watched in horror. Poor woman! No wonder she looked miserable if that was the sort of thing that kept happening.

However, the man did nothing with the poker except brandish it in temper, and he soon replaced it, and settled down in his chair again. The woman said no more at all, but went on filling the bottles. Julian wondered who they were for.

He told the others what he had seen. They didn't like it at all. If the people in the kitchen behaved like that whatever would those in the other part of the house be like?

They left the kitchen windows and went on round the house. They came to a lower room, lighted inside. But here the curtains were tightly drawn, and there was no crack to look through.

They looked up to the one room high up that was lighted. Surely Dick must be there? Perhaps he was locked up in the attic, all by himself? How they wished they knew!

Dared they throw up a stone? They wondered if they should try. There didn't seem any way at all of getting into the house. The front door was well and truly shut. There was a side door also tightly shut and locked, because they had tried it. Not a single window seemed to be open.

'I think I *will* throw up a stone,' said Julian at last. 'I feel sure Dick's up there, if he has been taken here – and you're certain you heard the men say "Owl's Dene", aren't you, Anne?'

'Quite certain,' said Anne. 'Do throw a stone, Julian. I'm getting so worried about poor Dick.'

Julian felt about on the ground for a stone. He found one embedded in the moss that was everywhere. He balanced it in his hand. Then up went the stone, but fell just short of the window. Julian got another. Up it went – and hit the glass of the window with a sharp crack. Somebody came to the pane at once.

Was it Dick? Everyone strained their eyes to see – but the window was too far up. Julian threw up another stone, and that hit the window too.

'I think it *is* Dick,' said Anne. 'Oh dear – no it isn't after all. Can't *you* see, Julian?'

But the person at the window, whoever he was, had now disappeared. The children felt a bit uncomfortable. Suppose it hadn't been Dick? Suppose it had been someone else who had now disappeared from the room to go and look for them?

'Let's get away from this part of the house,' whispered Julian. 'Get round to the other side.'

They made their way round quietly – and Richard suddenly pulled at Julian's arm. 'Look!' he said. 'There's a window open! Can't we get in there?'

574

11

Trapped!

Julian looked at the casement window. The moonlight shone on it. It certainly was a little ajar. 'How did we miss that when we went round before?' he wondered. He hesitated a little. Should they try to get in or not? Wouldn't it be better to rap on the back door and get that miserable-looking woman to answer it and tell them what they wanted to know?

On the other hand there was that evil-looking hunchback there. Julian didn't like the look of him at all. No – on the whole it might be better to creep in at the window, see if it was Dick upstairs, set him free, and then all escape through the same open window. Nobody would know. The bird would have flown, and everything would be all right.

Julian went to the window. He put a leg up and there he was astride the window. He held out a hand to Anne. 'Come on – I'll give you a hand,' he said, and pulled her up beside him. He lifted her down on the floor inside.

Then George came, and then Richard. George was just

leaning out to encourage Timmy to jump in through the window too, when something happened!

A powerful torchlight went on, and its beam shone right across the room into the dazzled eyes of the four children! They stood there, blinking in alarm. What was this?

Then Anne heard the voice of one of the men who had captured Dick, 'Well, well, well – a crowd of young burglars!'

The voice changed suddenly to anger. 'How *dare* you break in here! I'll hand you over to the police.'

From outside Timmy growled fiercely. He jumped up at the window and almost succeeded in leaping through. The man grasped what was happening at once, and went to the open window. He shut it with a bang. Now Timmy couldn't get in!

576

'Let my dog in!' said George, angrily, and stupidly tried to open the window again. The man brought his torch down sharply on her hand and she cried out in pain.

'That's what happens to boys who go against my wishes,' said the man, whilst poor George nursed her bruised hand.

'Look here,' began Julian, fiercely, 'what do you think you're doing? We're not burglars – and what's more we'd be very, very glad if you'd hand us over to the police!'

'Oh, you would, would you?' said the man. He went to the door of the room and yelled out in a tremendous voice: 'Aggie! AGGIE! Bring a lamp here at once.'

There was an answering shout from the kitchen, and almost immediately the light of a lamp appeared shining down the passage outside. It grew brighter, and the miserable-looking woman came in with a big oil-lamp. She stared in amazement at the little group of children. She seemed about to say something when the man gave her a rough push.

'Get out. And keep your mouth shut. Do you hear me?'

The woman scuttled out like a frightened hen. The man looked round at the children in the light of the lamp. The room was very barely furnished and appeared to be a sitting-room of some kind.

'So you don't mind being given up to the police?' said the man. 'That's very interesting. You think they'd approve of you breaking into my house?'

'I tell you, we *didn't* break in,' said Julian, determined to get that clear, at any rate. 'We came here because we had reason to believe that you've got my brother locked up somewhere in this house – and it's all a mistake. You've got the wrong boy.'

Richard didn't like this at all. He was terribly afraid of being locked up in the place of Dick! He kept behind the others as much as possible.

The man looked hard at Julian. He seemed to be

577

thinking. 'We haven't a boy here at all,' he said at last. 'I really don't know what you mean. You don't suggest that I go about the countryside picking boys up and making them prisoners, do you?'

'I don't know what you do,' said Julian. 'All I know is this – you captured Dick, my brother, this evening in Middlecombe Woods – thinking he was Richard Kent – well, he's not, he's my brother Dick. And if you don't set him free at once, I'll tell the police what we know.'

'And dear me – *how* do you know all this?' asked the man. 'Were you there when he was captured, as you call it?'

'One of us was,' said Julian, bluntly. 'In the tree overhead. That's how we know.'

There was a silence. The man took out a cigarette and lighted it. 'Well, you're quite mistaken,' he said. 'We've no boy held prisoner here. The thing is ridiculous. Now it's very, very late – would you like to bed down here for the night and get off in the morning? I don't like to send a parcel of kids out into the middle of the night. There's no telephone here, or I'd ring your home.'

Julian hesitated. He felt certain Dick was in the house. If he said he would stay for the night he might be able to find out if Dick was really there or not. He could quite well see that the man didn't want them tearing off to the police. There was something at Owl's Dene that was secret and sinister.

'I'll stay,' he said at last. 'Our people are away – they won't worry.'

He had forgotten about Richard for the moment. His people certainly *would* worry! Still, there was nothing to do about it. The first thing was to find Dick. Surely the men would be mad to hold him a prisoner once they were certain he wasn't the boy. Perhaps Rooky, the ruffian who knew Richard, hadn't yet arrived – hadn't seen Dick? That must be the reason that this man wanted them to stay the night. Of course – he'd wait till Rooky came – and when Rooky said, 'No – he's not the boy we want!' they'd let Dick go. They'd have to!

The man called for Aggie again. She came at once.

'These kids are lost,' said the man to her. 'I've said I'll put them up for the night. Get one of the rooms ready – just put down mattresses and blankets – that's all. Give them some food if they want it.'

Aggie was evidently tremendously astonished. Julian guessed that she was not used to this man being kind to lost children. He shouted at her.

'Well, don't stand dithering there. Get on with the job. Take these kids with you.'

Aggie beckoned to the four children. George hung back. 'What about my dog?' she said. 'He's still outside, whining. I can't go to bed without him.'

'You'll have to,' said the man, roughly. 'I won't have him in the house at any price, and that's flat.'

'He'll attack anyone he meets,' said George.

'He won't meet anyone out there,' said the man. 'By the way – how did you get in through the gates?'

'A car came out just as we got there and we slipped in before the gates closed,' said Julian. 'How do the gates shut? By machinery?'

'Mind your own business,' said the man, and went down the passage in the opposite direction.

'Pleasant, kindly fellow,' said Julian to George.

'Oh, a sweet nature,' answered George. The woman stared at them both in surprise. She didn't seem to realize that they meant the opposite to what they said! She led the way upstairs.

She came to a big room with a carpet on the floor, a small bed in a corner, and one or two chairs. There was no other furniture.

'I'll get some mattresses and put them down for you,' she said.

579

'I'll help you,' offered Julian, thinking it would be a good idea to see round a bit.

'All right,' said the woman. 'You others stay here.'

She went off with Julian. They went to a cupboard and the woman tugged at two big mattresses. Julian helped her. She seemed rather touched by this help.

'Well, thank you,' she said. 'They're pretty heavy.'

'Don't expect you have many children here, to stay, do you?' asked Julian.

'Well, it's funny that you should come just after . . .' the woman began. Then she stopped and bit her lip, looking anxiously up and down the passage.

'Just after what?' asked Julian. 'Just after the other boy came, do you mean?'

'Sh!' said the woman, looking scared to death. 'Whatever do you know about *that*? You shouldn't have said that. Mr Perton will skin me alive if he knew you'd said that. He'd be sure I'd told you. Forget about it.'

'That's the boy who's locked up in one of the attics at the top of the house isn't it?' said Julian, helping her to carry one of the mattresses to the big bedroom. She dropped her end in the greatest alarm.

'Now! Do you want to get me into terrible trouble – and yourselves too? Do you want Mr. Perton to tell old Hunchy to whip you all? You don't know that man! He's wicked.'

'When's Rooky coming?' asked Julian, bent on astonishing the woman, hoping to scare her into one admission after another. This was too much for her altogether. She stood there shaking at the knees, staring at Julian as if she couldn't believe her ears.

'What do you know about Rooky?' she whispered. 'Is he coming here? Don't tell me he's coming here!'

'Why? Don't you like him?' asked Julian. He put a hand on her shoulder. 'Why are you so frightened and upset? What's the matter? Tell me. I might be able to help you.'

580

'Rooky's bad,' said the woman. 'I thought he was in prison. Don't tell me he's out again. Don't tell me he's coming here.'

She was so frightened that she wouldn't say a word more. She began to cry, and Julian hadn't the heart to press her with any more questions. In silence he helped her to drag the mattresses into the other room.

'I'll get you some food,' said the poor woman, sniffing miserably. 'You'll find blankets in that cupboard over there if you want to lie down.'

She disappeared. Julian told the others in whispers what he had been able to find out. 'We'll see if we can find

Dick as soon as things are quiet in the house,' he said. 'This is a bad house – a house of secrets, of queer comings and goings. I shall slip out of our room and see what I can find out later on. I think that man – Mr Perton is his name – is really waiting for Rooky to come and see if Dick is Richard or not. When he finds he isn't I've no doubt he'll set him free – and us too.'

'What about *me*?' said Richard. 'Once he sees me, I'm done for. I'm the boy he wants. He hates my father and he hates me too. He'll kidnap me, take me somewhere, and ask an enormous ransom for me – just to punish us!'

'Well, we must do something to prevent him seeing you,' said Julian. 'But I don't see why he *should* see you – it's only Dick he'll want to see. He won't be interested in what he thinks are Dick's brothers and sisters! Now for goodness' sake don't start to howl again, or honestly I'll give you up to Rooky myself! You really are a frightful little coward – haven't you any courage at all!'

'All this has come about because of your silly lies and deceit,' said George, quiet fiercely. 'It's all because of you that our trip is spoilt, that Dick's locked up – and poor Timmy's outside without me.'

Richard looked quite taken aback. He shrank into a corner and didn't say another word. He was very miserable. Nobody liked him – nobody believed him – nobody trusted him. Richard felt very, very small indeed.

12

Julian looks round

The woman brought them some food. It was only bread and butter and jam, with some hot coffee to drink. The four children were not really hungry, but they were very thirsty, and they drank the coffee eagerly.

George opened the window and called softly down to Timmy. 'Tim! Here's something for you!'

Timmy was down there all right, watching and waiting. He knew where George was. He had howled and whined for some time, but now he was quiet.

George was quite determined to get him indoors if she could. She gave him all her bread and jam, dropping it down bit by bit, and listening to him wolfing it up. Anyway, old Timmy would know she was thinking of him!

'Listen,' said Julian, coming in from the passage outside, where he had stood listening for a while. 'I think it would be a good idea if we put out this light, and settled down on the mattresses. But I shall make up a lump on mine to look like me, so that if anyone comes they'll think I'm there on the mattress. But I shan't be.'

583

'Where will you be, then?' asked Anne. 'Don't leave us!'

'I shall be hiding outside in that cupboard,' said Julian. 'I've a sort of feeling that our pleasant host, Mr Perton, will come along presently to lock us in – and I've no intention of being locked in! I think he'll flash a torch into the room, see that we're all four safely asleep on the mattresses, and then quietly lock the door. Well – *I* shall be able to unlock it when I come back from the cupboard outside – and we shan't be prisoners at all!'

'Oh – that really is a good idea,' said Anne, cuddling herself up in a blanket. 'You'd better go and get into the cupboard now, Julian, before we're locked up for the night!'

Julian blew out the lamp. He tiptoed to the door and opened it. He left it ajar. He went into the passage and fumbled his way to where he knew the cupboard should be. Ah – there it was. He pulled at the handle and the door opened silently. He slipped inside and left the door open just a crack, so that he would be able to see if anyone came along the wide passage.

He waited there about twenty minutes. The cupboard smelt musty, and it was very boring standing there doing absolutely nothing.

Then, through the crack in the door, he suddenly noticed that a light was coming. Ah – somebody was about!

He peered through the crack. He saw Mr Perton coming quietly along the corridor with a little oil-lamp held in his hand. He went to the door of the children's bedroom and pushed it a little. Julian watched him, hardly daring to breathe.

Would he notice that the figure on one of the mattresses was only a lump made of a blanket rolled up and covered by another blanket? Julian fervently hoped that he wouldn't. All his plans would be spoilt if so.

Mr Perton held the lamp high in his hand and looked

cautiously into the room. He saw four huddled-up shapes lying on the mattresses – four children – he thought.

They were obviously asleep. Softly, Mr Perton closed the door, and just as softly locked it. Julian watched anxiously to see if he pocketed the key or not. No – he hadn't! He had left it in the lock. Oh good!

The man went away again, treading softly. He did not go downstairs, but disappeared into a room some way down on the right. Julian heard the door shut with a click. Then he heard another click. The man evidently believed in locking himself in. Perhaps he didn't trust his other comrade, wherever he was – or Hunchy or the woman.

Julian waited a while and then crept out of the cupboard. He stole up to Mr Perton's room and looked through the keyhole to see if the room was in darkness or not. It was! Was Mr Perton snoring? Not that Julian could hear.

However Julian was not going to wait till he heard Mr Perton snore. He was going to find Dick – and he was pretty certain that the first place to look was in that attic upstairs!

'I bet Mr Perton was up there with Dick and heard me throwing stones at the window,' thought Julian. 'Then he slipped down and opened that window to trap us into getting in there – and we fell neatly into the trap! He must have been waiting inside the room for us. I don't like Mr Perton – too full of bright ideas!'

He was half-way up the flight of stairs that led to the attics now – going very carefully and slowly, afraid of making the stairs creak loudly. They did creak – and at every creak poor Julian stopped and listened to see if anyone had heard!

There was a long passage at the top turning at both ends into the side-wings. Julian stood still and debated – now which way ought he to go? – where exactly was that lighted window? It was somewhere along this long passage, he was certain. Well, he'd go along the doors and see if a light shone out through the keyhole, or under the door anywhere.

Door after door was ajar. Julian peeped round each, making out bare dark attics, or box-rooms with rubbish in. Then he came to a door that was closed. He peered through the keyhole. No light came from inside the room.

Julian knocked gently. A voice came at once – Dick's voice. 'Who's there?'

'Sh! It's me – Julian,' whispered Julian. 'Are you all right, Dick?'

There came the creak of a bed, then the pattering of feet across a bare floor. Dick's voice came through the door, muffled and cautious.

'Julian! How did you get here? This is marvellous! Can you unlock the door and let me out?'

Julian had already felt for a key – but there was none. Mr Perton had taken *that* key, at any rate!

'No. The key's gone,' he said. 'Dick, what did they do to you?'

'Nothing much. They dragged me off to the car and shoved me in,' said Dick, through the door. 'The man called Rooky wasn't there. The others waited for him for some time, then drove off. They thought he might have gone off to see someone they meant to visit. So I haven't seen him. He's coming tomorrow morning. What a shock for him when he finds I'm not Richard!'

'Richard's here too,' whispered Julian. 'I wish he wasn't – because if Rooky happens to see him he'll be kidnapped, I'm sure! The only hope is that Rooky will only see *you* – and as the other men think we're all one family, they may let us all go. Did you come straight here in the car, Dick?'

'Yes,' said Dick. 'The gates opened like magic when we got here, but I couldn't see anybody. I was shoved up here and locked in. One of the men came to tell me all the things

586

Rooky was going to do to me when he saw me – and then he suddenly went downstairs and hasn't come back again.'

'Oh – I bet that was when we chucked stones up at your window,' said Julian at once. 'Didn't you hear them?'

'Yes – so that was the crack I heard! The man with me went across to the window at once – and he must have seen you. Now, what about *you*, Ju? How on earth did you get here? are you all really here? I suppose that was Timmy I heard howling outside.'

Julian quickly told him all his tale from the time he and George had met the howling Richard to the moment he had slipped up the stairs to find Dick.

There was a silence when he had finished his tale. Then Dick's voice came through the crack.

'Not much good making any plans, Julian. If things go all right, we'll be out of here by the morning, when Rooky finds I'm not the boy he wants. If things go wrong at least we're all together, and we can make plans then. I wonder what his mother will think when Richard doesn't get home tonight.'

'Probably think he's gone off to the aunt's,' said Julian. 'I should think he's a very unreliable person. Blow him! It was all because of him we got into this fix.'

'I expect the men will have some cock-and-bull story tomorrow morning, about why they got hold of you, when they find you're not Richard,' went on Julian. 'They'll probably say you threw stones at their car or something, and they took you in hand – or found your hurt and brought you here to help you! Anyway, whatever they say, we won't make much fuss about it. We'll go quietly – and then we'll get things moving! I don't know what's going on here, but it's something queer. The police ought to look into it, I'm certain.'

'Listen – that's Timmy again,' said Dick. 'Howling like anything for George, I suppose. You'd better go,

Julian, in case he wakes up one of the men and they come out and find you here. Good-night. I'm awfully glad you're near! Thanks awfully for coming to find me.'

'Good-night,' said Julian, and went back along the corridor, walking over the patches of moonlight, looking fearfully into the dark shadows in case Mr Perton or somebody else was waiting for him!

But nobody was about. Timmy's howling died down. There was a deep silence in the house. Julian went down the stairs to the floor on which the bedroom was where the others lay asleep. He paused outside it. Should he do any further exploring? It really was such a chance!

He decided that he would. Mr Perton was fast asleep, he hoped. He thought probably Hunchy and the woman had gone to bed too. He wondered where the other man was, who had brought Dick to Owl's Dene. He hadn't seen him at all. Perhaps he had gone out in that black Bentley they had seen going out of the gate.

Julian went down to the ground floor. A brilliant thought had just occurred to him. Couldn't he undo the front door and get the others down, and send them out, free? He himself couldn't escape, because it would mean leaving Dick alone.

Then he gave up the idea. 'No,' he thought. 'For one thing George and Anne would refuse to go without me – and even if they agreed to get out of the front door, and go down the drive to the gates, how would they undo them? They're worked by some machinery from the house.'

So his brilliant idea came to nothing. He decided to look into all the rooms on the ground floor. He looked into the kitchen first. The fire was almost out. The moonlight came through the cracks of the curtains and lighted up the dark silent room. Hunchy and the woman had evidently retired somewhere.

There was nothing of interest in the kitchen. Julian went into the room opposite. It was a dining-room, with a

13
strange secret

long polished table, candlesticks on the walls and mantelpiece, and the remains of a wood fire. Nothing of interest
there either.

The boy went into another room. Was it a workroom, or
what? There was a radiogram there, and a big desk. There
was a stand with a curious instrument of some kind that
had a stout wheel-like handle. Julian suddenly wondered
if it would open the gates! Yes – that was what it was for.
He saw a label attached to it. Left Gate. Right Gate. Both
Gates.

'That's what it is – the machinery for opening either or
both of the gates. If only I could get Dick out of that room
I'd get us all out of this place in no time!' said Julian. He
twisted the handle – what would happen?

13

Strange secret

A curious groaning, whining noise began, as some kind of strong machinery was set working. Julian hurriedly turned the handle back. If it was going to make all that noise, he wasn't going to try his hand at opening the gates! It would bring Mr Perton out of his room in a rush!

'Most ingenious, whatever it is,' thought the boy, examining it as well as he could in the moonlight that streamed through the window. He looked round the room again. A noise came to his ears and he stood still.

'It's somebody snoring,' he thought. 'I'd better not mess about here any more! Where are they sleeping? Somewhere not far from here, that's certain.'

He tiptoed cautiously into the next room and looked inside it. It was a lounge, but there was nobody there at all. He couldn't hear the snoring there either.

He was puzzled. There didn't seem to be any other room nearby where people could sleep. He went back to the workroom or study. Yes – now he could hear that noise again – and it *was* somebody snoring! Somebody quite near – and yet not near enough to hear properly, or to see. Most peculiar.

Julian walked softly round the room, trying to find a place where the snoring sounded loudest of all. Yes – by this bookcase that reached to the ceiling. That was where the snoring sounded most of all. Was there a room behind this wall, next to the workroom? Julian went out to investigate. But there was no room behind the study at all – only the wall of the corridor, as far as he could see. It was more and more mysterious.

He went back to the study again, and over to the bookcase. Yes – there it was again. *Somebody* was asleep and snoring not far off – but WHERE?

Julian began to examine the bookcase. It was full of books jammed tightly together – novels, biographies, reference books – all higgledy-piggledy. He removed some from a shelf and examined the bookcase behind. It was of solid wood.

He put back the books and examined the big bookcase again. It was a very solid affair. Julian looked carefully at the books, shining in the moonlight. One shelf of books looked different from the others – less tidy – the books not so jammed together. Why should just one shelf be different?

Julian quietly took the books from that shelf. Behind them was the solid wood again. Julian put his hand at the back and felt about. A knob was hidden in a corner. A knob! Whatever was that there for?

Cautiously Julian turned the knob this way and that. Nothing happened. Then he pressed it. Still nothing happened. He pulled it – and it slid out a good six inches!

Then the whole of the back of that particular shelf slid quietly downwards, and left an opening big enough for somebody to squeeze through! Julian held his breath. A sliding panel! What was behind it?

A dim flickering light came from the space behind.

Julian waited till his eyes were used to it after the bright moonlight. He was trembling with excitement. The snoring now sounded so loud that Julian felt as if the snorer must be almost within hand's reach!

Then gradually he made out a tiny room, with a small narrow bed, a table and a shelf on which a few articles could dimly be made out. A candle was burning in a corner. On the bed was the snorer. Julian could not see what he was like, except that he looked big and burly as he lay there, snoring peacefully.

'What a find!' thought Julian. 'A secret hiding-place – a place to hide all kinds of people, I suppose, who have enough money to pay for such a safe hole. This fellow ought to have been warned not to snore! He gave himself away.'

The body did not dare to stay there any longer, looking into that curious secret room. It must be built in a space between the wall of the study and the wall of the corridor – probably a very old hiding-place made when the house was built.

Julian felt for the knob. He pushed it back into place, and the panel slid up again, as noiselessly as before. It was evidently kept in good working order!

The snoring was muffled again now. Julian replaced the books, hoping that they were more or less as he had found them.

He felt very thrilled. He had found one of the secrets of Owl's Dene, at any rate. The police would be *very* interested to hear about that secret hole – and perhaps they would be even more interested to hear about the person inside it!

It was absolutely essential now that he and the others should escape. Would it be all right if he went without Dick? No – if the men suspected any dirty work on his part – discovered that he knew of the secret hole, for instance – they might harm Dick. Regretfully Julian decided that there must be no escape for him unless everyone, including Dick, could come too.

He didn't explore any more. He suddenly felt very tired indeed and crept softly upstairs. He felt as if he simply must lie down and think. He was too tired to do anything else.

He went to the bedroom. The key was still in the lock outside. He went into the room and shut the door. Mr Perton would find the door unlocked the next morning, but probably he would think he hadn't turned the key properly. Julian lay down on the mattress beside Richard. All the others were fast asleep.

He meant to think out all his problems – but no sooner had he closed his eyes than he was fast asleep. He didn't hear Timmy howling outside once more. He didn't hear the screech owl that made the night hideous on the hill. He didn't see the moon slide down the sky.

It was not Mr Perton who awoke the children next morning, but the woman. She came into the room and called to them.

'If you want breakfast you'd better come down and have it!'

They all sat up in a hurry, wondering where in the world they were. 'Hallo!' said Julian, blinking sleepily. 'Breakfast, did you say? It sounds good. Is there anywhere we can wash?'

'You can wash down in the kitchen,' said the woman, sullenly, 'I'm not cleaning any bathroom up after you!'

'Leave the door unlocked for us to get out!' said Julian, innocently. 'Mr Perton locked it last night.'

'So he said,' answered the woman, 'but he *hadn't* locked it! It wasn't locked when I tried the door this morning. Aha! You didn't know that, did you? You'd have been wandering all over the house, I suppose, if you'd guessed that.'

'Probably we should,' agreed Julian, winking at the others. They knew that he had meant to go and find Dick in the night, and snoop round a bit – but they didn't know all he had discovered. He hadn't had the heart to wake them and tell them the night before.

'Don't you be too long,' said the woman, and went out of the door, leaving it open.

'I hope she's taken some breakfast up to poor old Dick,' said Julian, in a low voice. The others came close to him.

'Ju – did you find Dick last night?' whispered Anne. He nodded. Then, very quickly and quietly he told them all he had discovered – where Dick was – and then how he had heard the snoring – and discovered the secret panel – the hidden room – and the man who slept so soundly there, not knowing that Julian had seen him.

'Julian! How thrilling!' said George. 'Whoever would have thought of all that?'

'Oh yes – and I discovered the machinery that opens the gates too,' said Julian. It's in the same room. But come on – if we don't go down to the kitchen that woman will be after us again. I hope Hunchy won't be there – I don't like him.'

Hunchy, however, *was* there, finishing his breakfast at a small table. He scowled at the children, but they took absolutely no notice of him.

'You've been a long time,' grumbled the woman. 'There's the sink over there, if you want to wash, and I've put a towel out for you. You look pretty dirty, all of you.'

'We are,' said Julian, cheerfully. 'We could have done with a bath last night – but we didn't exactly get much of a welcome, you know.'

When they had washed they went to a big scrubbed table. There was no cloth on it. The woman had put out some bread and butter and some boiled eggs and a jug of steaming hot cocoa. They all sat down and began to help themselves. Julian talked cheerfully, winking at the others to make them do the same. He wasn't going to let the hunchback think they were scared or worried in any way.

'Shut up, you,' said Hunchy, suddenly. Julian took no notice. He went on talking, and George backed him up valiantly, though Anne and Richard were too scared, after hearing the hunchback's furious voice.

'Did you hear what I said?' suddenly yelled Hunchy, and got up from the little table where he had been sitting. 'Hold your tongues, all of you! Coming into my kitchen and making all that row! Hold your tongues!'

Julian rose too. 'I don't take orders from you whoever you are,' he said, and he sounded just like a grown-up. 'You hold your tongue – or else be civil.'

'Oh, don't talk to him like that, don't,' begged the woman, anxiously. 'He's got such a temper – he'll take a stick to you!'

'I'd take a stick to *him* – except that I don't hit fellows smaller than myself,' said Julian.

What would have happened if Mr Perton hadn't appeared in the kitchen at that moment nobody knew! He stalked in and glared round, sensing that there was a row going on.

'You losing your temper again, Hunchy?' he said. 'Keep it till it's needed. I'll ask you to produce it sometime today possibly – if these kids don't behave themselves!' He looked round at the children with a grim expression. Then he glanced at the woman.

'Rooky's coming soon,' he told her. 'And one or two others. Get a meal – a good one. Keep these children in here, Hunchy, and keep an eye on them. I may want them later.'

He went out. The woman was trembling. 'Rooky's coming,' she half-whispered to Hunchy.

'Get on with your work, woman,' said the dwarf. 'Go out and get the vegetables in yourself – I've got to keep an eye on these kids.'

The poor woman scuttled about. Anne was sorry for her. She went over to her. 'Shall I clear away and wash up for you?' she asked. 'You're going to be busy – and I've nothing to do.'

'We'll all help,' said Julian. The woman gave him an astonished and grateful glance. It was plain that she was not used to good manners or politeness of any sort.

'Yah!' said Hunchy, sneeringly. 'You won't get round *me* with your smarmy ways!'

Nobody took the slightest notice of him. All the children began to clear away the breakfast things, and Anne and George stacked them in the sink, and began to wash them.

'Yah!' said Hunchy again.

'And yah to you,' said Julian, pleasantly, which made the others laugh, and Hunchy scowl till his eyes disappeared under his brows!

14

Rooky is very angry

About an hour later there was a curious grinding, groaning noise that turned to a whining. Richard, Anne and George jumped violently. But Julian knew what it was.

'The gates are being opened,' he told them, and they remembered how he had described the machinery that opened the gates – the curious wheel-like handle, labelled 'Left Gate. Right Gate. Both Gates'.

'How do *you* know that?' asked Hunchy at once, surprised and suspicious.

'Oh, I'm a good guesser,' replied Julian airily. 'Correct me if I'm wrong – but I couldn't help thinking the gates were being opened – and I'm guessing it's Rooky that's coming through them!'

'You're so sharp you'll cut yourself one day,' grumbled Hunchy, going to the door.

'So my mother told me when I was two years old,' said Julian, and the others giggled. If there was any answering back to be done, Julian could always do it!

They all went to the window. George opened it. Timmy

was there, sitting just outside. George had begged the woman to let him in, but she wouldn't. She had thrown him some scraps, and told George there was a pond he could drink from, but beyond that she wouldn't go.

'Timmy,' called George, as she heard the sound of a car purring quietly up the drive, 'Timmy – stay there. Don't move!'

She was afraid that Timmy might perhaps run round to the front door, and go for anyone who jumped out of the car. Timmy looked up at her inquiringly. He was puzzled about this whole affair. Why wasn't he allowed inside the house with George? He knew there were some people who didn't welcome dogs into their houses – but George never went to those houses. It was a puzzle to him, too, to understand why she didn't come out to him.

Still, she was there, leaning out of the window; he could hear her voice; he could even lick her hand if he stood up on his hind legs against the wall.

'You shut that window and come inside,' said Hunchy, maliciously. He took quite a pleasure in seeing that George was upset at being separated from Timmy.

'Here comes the car,' said Julian. They all looked at it – and then glanced at each other. KMF 102 – of course!

The black Bentley swept by the kitchen windows and up to the front door. Three men got out. Richard crouched back, his face going pale.

Julian glanced round at him raising his eyebrows, mutely asking him if he recognized one of the men as Rooky. Richard nodded miserably. He was very frightened now.

The whining, groaning noise came again. The gates were being shut. Voices came from the hall, then the men went into one of the rooms, and there was the sound of a door being shut.

Julian wondered if he could slip out of the room unnoticed and go up to see if Dick was all right. He sidled to the door, thinking that Hunchy was engrossed in cleaning an array of dirty shoes. But his grating voice sounded at once.

'Where you going? If you don't obey orders I'll tell Mr Perton – and won't you be sorry!'

'There's quite a lot of people in his house going to be sorry for themselves soon,' said Julian, in an irritatingly cheerful voice. 'You be careful, Hunchy.'

Hunchy lost his temper suddenly and threw the shoe-brush he was using straight at Julian. Julian caught it deftly and threw it up on the high mantelpiece.

'Thanks,' he said. 'Like to throw another?'

'Oh don't,' said the woman, beseechingly. 'You don't know what he's like when he's in a real temper. Don't!'

The door of the room that the men had gone into opened, and somebody went upstairs. 'To fetch Dick,' thought Julian at once. He stood and listened.

Hunchy got another shoe-brush and went on polishing, muttering angrily under his breath. The woman went on preparing some food. The others listened with Julian. They too guessed that the man had gone to fetch Dick to show him to Rooky.

Footsteps came down the stairs again – two lots this time. Yes – Dick must be with the man, they could hear his voice.

'Let go my arm! I can come without being dragged!' they heard him say indignantly. Good old Dick! He wasn't going to be dragged about without making a strong protest.

He was taken into the room where the other three men were waiting. Then a loud voice was heard.

'He's not the boy! Fools – you've got the wrong boy!'

Hunchy and the woman heard the words too. They gaped at one another. Something had gone wrong. They went to the door and stood there silently. The children just

600

stood behind them. Julian edged Richard away very gradually.

'Rub some soot over your hair,' he whispered. 'Make it as black as you can, Richard. If the men come out here to see us, they're not likely to recognize you so easily if your hair's black. Go on, quick – while the others aren't paying attention.'

Julian was pointing to the inside of the grate, where black soot hung. Richard put his trembling hands into it and covered them with it. Then he rubbed the soot over his yellow hair.

'More,' whispered Julian. 'Much more! Go on. I'll stand in front of you so that the others can't see what you're doing.'

Richard rubbed soot even more wildly over his hair. Julian nodded. Yes – it looked black enough now. Richard looked quite different. Julian hoped Anne and George would be sensible enough not to exclaim when they saw him.

There was evidently some sharp argument going on in the room off the hall. Voices were raised, but not many words could be made out from where the children stood at the kitchen door. Dick's voice could be heard too. It suddenly sounded quite clearly.

'I TOLD you you'd made a mistake. Now you just let me go, see!'

Hunchy suddenly pushed everyone roughly away from the door – except poor Richard who was standing over in a dark corner, shaking with fright!

'They're coming,' he hissed. 'Get away from the door.'

Everyone obeyed. Hunchy took up a shoe-brush again, the woman went to peel potatoes, the children turned over the pages of some old magazines they had found.

Footsteps came to the kitchen door. It was flung open. Mr Perton was there – and behind him another man. No mistaking who *he* was!

Thick-lipped, with an enormous nose – yes, he was the ruffian Rooky, once bodyguard to Richard's father – the man who hated Richard because he had told tales of him and who had been sent off in disgrace by the boy's father.

Richard cowered back in his corner, hiding behind the others. Anne and George had given him astonished stares when they had noticed his hair, but neither of them had said a word. Hunchy and the woman didn't seem to have noticed any change in him.

Dick was with the two men. He waved to the others. Julian grinned. Good old Dick!

Rooky glanced at all four children. His eye rested for a moment on Richard, and then glanced away. He hadn't recognized him!

'Well, Mr Perton,' said Julian. 'I'm glad to see you've got my brother down from the room you locked him up in last night. I imagine that means he can come with us now. Why you brought him here as you did, and made him a prisoner last night I can't imagine.'

'Now look here,' said Mr Perton, in quite a different voice from the one he had used to them before, 'now look here – quite frankly we made a mistake. You don't need to know why or how – that's none of your business. This isn't the boy we wanted.'

'We *told* you he was our brother,' said Anne.

'Quite,' said Mr Perton, politely. 'I am sorry I dis-believed you. These things happen. Now – we want to make you all a handsome present for any inconvenience you have suffered – er – ten pounds for you to spend on ice-creams and so on. You can go whenever you like.'

'And don't try and tell any fairy stories to anyone,' said Rooky suddenly, in a threatening voice. 'See? We made a mistake – but we're not having it talked about. If you say anything silly, we shall say that we found this boy lost in the woods, took pity on him and brought him here for the night – and that you kids were – found trespassing in the grounds. You understand?'

'I understand perfectly,' said Julian, in a cool rather scornful voice. 'Well – I take it we can all go now, then?'

'Yes,' said Mr Perton. He put his hand into his pocket and took out some pound notes. He handed two to each of the children. They glanced at Julian to see if they were to take them or not. Not one of them felt willing to accept Mr Perton's money. But they knew they must take them if Julian did.

Julian accepted the two notes handed to him, and pocketed them without a word of thanks. The others did the same. Richard kept his head down well all the time, hoping that the two men would not notice how his knees were shaking. He was really terrified of Rooky.

'Now clear out,' said Rooky when the ten pounds had been divided. 'Forget all this – or you'll be very sorry.'

He opened the door that led into the garden. The children trooped out silently, Richard well in their midst. Timmy was waiting for them. He gave a loud bark of welcome and flung himself on George, fawning on her, licking every bit of her he could reach. He looked back at the kitchen door and gave a questioning growl as if to say, 'Do you want me to go for anyone in there?'

'No,' said George. 'You come with us, Timmy. We'll get out of here as quickly as we can.'

'Give me your pound notes, quick,' said Julian in a low voice, when they had rounded a corner and were out of sight of the windows. They all handed them to him wonderingly. What was he going to do with them?

The woman had come out to watch them go. Julian beckoned to her. She came hesitatingly down the garden. 'For you,' said Julian, putting the notes into her hand. 'We don't want them.'

The woman took them, amazed. Her eyes filled with

604

tears. 'Why – it's a fortune – no, no, you take them back. You're kind, though – so kind.'

Julian turned away, leaving the astonished and delighted woman standing staring after them. He hurried after the others.

'That was a very, very good idea of yours,' said Anne, warmly, and the others agreed. All of them had been sorry for the poor woman.

'Come on,' said Julian. 'We don't want to miss the opening of the gates! Listen – can you hear the groaning noise back at the house. Somebody has set the machinery working that opens the gates. Thank goodness we're free – and Richard too. That *was* a bit of luck!'

'Yes, I was so scared Rooky would recognize me, even though my hair was sooted black,' said Richard, who was now looking much more cheerful. 'Oh look – we can see the end of the drive now – and the gates are wide open. We're free!'

'We'll get our bikes,' said Julian. 'I know where we left them. You can ride on my crossbar Richard, because we're a bike short. Dick must have his bike back now – you remember you borrowed it? Look – here they are.'

They mounted their bicycles and began to cycle down the drive – and then Anne gave a scream.

'Julian! Look, look – the gates are closing again. Quick, quick – we'll be left inside!'

Everyone saw in horror that the gates were actually closing, very slowly. They pedalled as fast as they could – but it was no use. By the time they got there the two great gates were fast shut. No amount of shaking would open them. And just as they were so very nearly out!

15

Prisoners

They all flung themselves down on the grass verge and groaned.

'What have they done that for, just as we were going out?' said Dick. 'Was it a mistake, do you think? I mean – did they think we'd had time to go out, or what?'

'Well – if it was a mistake, it's easy to put right,' said Julian. 'I'll just cycle back to the house and tell them they shut the gates too soon.'

'Yes – you do that,' said George. 'We'll wait here.'

But before Julian could even mount his bicycle there came the sound of the car purring down the long drive. All the children jumped to their feet. Richard ran behind a bush in panic. He was terrified of having to face Rooky again.

The car drew up by the children and stopped. 'Yes, they're still here,' said Mr Perton's voice, as he got out of the car. Rooky got out too. They came over to the children.

Rooky ran his eyes over them. 'Where's that other boy?' he asked quickly.

606

'I can't imagine,' said Julian, coolly. 'Dear me – I wonder if he had time to cycle out of the gateway. Why did you shut the gates so soon, Mr Perton?'

Rooky had caught sight of Richard's shivering figure behind the bush. He strode over to him and yanked him out. He looked at him closely. Then he pulled him over to Mr Perton.

'Yes – I thought so – *this* is the boy we want! He's sooted his hair or something, and that's why I didn't recognize him. But when he'd gone I felt sure there was something familiar about him – that's why I wanted another look.' He shook poor Richard like a dog shaking a rat.

'Well – what do you want to do about it?' asked Mr Perton, rather gloomily.

'Hold him, of course,' said Rooky. 'I'll get back at his father now – he'll have to pay a very large sum of money for his horrible son! That'll be useful, won't it? And I can pay this kid out for some of the lies he told his father about me. Nasty little rat.'

He shook Richard again. Julian stepped forward, white and furious.

'Now you stop that,' he said. 'Let the boy go. Haven't you done enough already – keeping my brother locked up for nothing – holding us all for the night – and now you talk about kidnapping! Haven't you just come out of prison? Do you want to go back there?'

Rooky dropped Richard and lunged out at Julian. With a snarl Timmy flung himself between them and bit the man's hand. Rooky let out a howl of rage and nursed his injured hand. He yelled at Julian.

'Call that dog to heel. Do you hear?'

'I'll call him to heel all right – if you talk sense,' said Julian, still white with rage. 'You're going to let us all go, here and now. Go back and open these gates.'

Timmy growled terrifyingly, and both Rooky and Mr

607

Perton took some hurried steps backwards. Rooky picked up a very big stone.

'If you dare to throw that I'll set my dog on you again!' shouted George, in sudden fear. Mr Perton knocked the stone out of Rooky's hand.

'Don't be a fool,' he said. 'That dog could make mincemeat of us – great ugly brute. Look at his teeth. For goodness' sake let the kids go, Rooky.'

'Not till we've finished our plans,' said Rooky fiercely, still nursing his hand. 'Keep 'em all prisoners here! We shan't be long before our jobs are done. And what's more

I'm going to take that little rat there off with me when I go! Ha! I'll teach him a few things – and his father too.'

Timmy growled again. He was straining at George's hand. She had him firmly by the collar. Richard trembled when he heard Rooky's threats about him. Tears ran down his face.

'Yes – you can howl all you like,' said Rooky, scowling at him. 'You wait till I get you! Miserable little coward – you never did have any spunk – you just ran round telling tales and misbehaving yourself whenever you could.'

'Look, Rooky – you'd better come up to the house and have that hand seen to,' said Mr Perton. 'It's bleeding badly. You ought to wash it and put some stuff on it – you know a dog's bite is dangerous. Come on. You can deal with these kids afterwards.'

Rooky allowed himself to be led back to the car. He shook his unhurt fist at the children as they watched silently.

'Interfering brats! Little . . .'

But the rest of his pleasant words were lost in the purring of the car's engine. Mr Perton backed a little, turned the car, and it disappeared up the drive. The five children sat themselves down on the grass verge. Richard began to sob out loud.

'Do shut up, Richard,' said George. 'Rooky was right when he said you were a little coward, with no spunk. So you are. Anne's much pluckier than you are. I wish to goodness we had never met you.'

Richard rubbed his hands over his eyes. They were sooty, and made his face look most peculiar with streaks of black soot mixed with his tears. He tooked very woe-begone indeed.

'I'm sorry,' he sniffed. 'I know you don't believe me – but I really am. I've always been a bit of a coward – I can't help it.'

'Yes you can,' said Julian, scornfully. 'Anybody can

help being a coward. Cowardice is just thinking of your own miserable skin instead of somebody else's. Why, even little Anne is more worried about *us* than she is about herself – and that makes her brave. She couldn't be a coward if she tried.'

This was a completely new idea to Richard. He tried to wipe his face dry. 'I'll try to be like you,' he said, in a muffled voice. 'You're all so decent. I've never had friends like you before. Honestly, I won't let you down again.'

'Well, we'll see,' said Julian, doubtfully. 'It would certainly be a surprise if you turned into a hero all of a sudden – a very *nice* surprise, of course – but in the meantime it would be a help if you stopped howling for a bit and let us talk.'

Richard subsided. He really looked very peculiar with his soot-streaked face. Julian turned to the others.

'This is maddening!' he said. 'Just as we so nearly got out. I suppose they'll shut us up in some room and keep us there till they've finished whatever this "job" is. I imagine the "job" consists of getting that hidden fellow away in safety – the one I saw in the secret room.'

'Won't Richard's people report his disappearance to the police?' said George, fondling Timmy, who wouldn't stop licking her now he had got her again.

'Yes, they will. But what good will that do? The police won't have the faintest notion where he is,' said Julian. 'Nobody knows where we are, either, come to that – but Aunt Fanny won't worry yet, because she knows we're off on a cycling tour, and wouldn't be writing to her anyway.'

'Do you think those men will really take me off with them when they go?' asked Richard.

'Well, we'll hope we shall have managed to escape before that,' said Julian, not liking to say yes, certainly Richard would be whisked away!

'How *can* we escape?' asked Anne. 'We'd never get over those high walls. And I don't expect anyone ever comes by

610

here – right at the top of this deserted hill. No tradesman would ever call.'

'What about the postman?' asked Anne.

'They probably arrange to fetch their post each day,' said Julian. 'I don't expect they want anyone coming here at all. Or – there may be a letter-box outside the gate. I never thought of that!'

They went to see. But although they craned their necks to see each side, there didn't seem to be any letter-box at all for the postman to slip letters in. So the faint hope that had risen in their minds, that they might catch the postman and give him a message, vanished at once.

'Hallo – here's the woman – Aggie, or whatever he name is,' said George, suddenly, as Timmy growled. They all turned their heads. Yes, Aggie was coming down the drive in a hurry – could she be going out? Would the gates open for her?

Their hopes died as she came near. 'Oh, there you are! I've come with a message. You can do one of two things – you can stay out in the grounds all day, and not put foot into the house at all – or you can come into the house and be locked up in one of the rooms.'

She looked round cautiously and lowered her voice. 'I'm sorry you didn't get out; right down upset I am. It's bad enough for an old woman like me, being cooped up here with Hunchy – but it's not right to keep children in this place. You're nice children too.'

'Thanks,' said Julian. 'Now, seeing that you think we're so nice – tell us, is there any way we can get out besides going through these gates?'

'No. No way at all,' said the woman. 'It's like a prison, once those gates are shut. Nobody's allowed in, and you're only allowed out if it suits Mr Perton and the others. So don't try to escape – it's hopeless.'

Nobody said anything to that. Aggie glanced over her shoulder as if she feared somebody might be listening –

Hunchy perhaps – and went on in a low voice.

'Mr Perton said I wasn't to give you much food. And he said Hunchy's to put down food for the dog with poison in it – so don't you let him eat any but what I give you myself.'

'The brute,' cried George, and she held Timmy close against her. 'Did you hear that, Timmy? It's a pity you didn't bite Mr Perton too!'

'Sh!' said the woman, afraid. 'I didn't ought to tell you all this, you know that – but you're kind, and you gave me all that money. Right down nice you are. Now you listen to me – you'd better say you'd rather keep out here in the grounds – because if you're locked up I wouldn't dare to bring you much food in case Rooky came in and saw it. But if you stay out here it's easier. I can give you plenty.'

'Thank you very much,' said Julian, and the others nodded too. 'In any case we'd rather be out here. I suppose Mr Perton is afraid we'd stumble on some of his queer secrets in the house if we had the free run there! All right – tell him we'll be in the grounds. What about our food? How shall we manage about that? We don't want to get you into trouble – but we're very hungry for our meals, and we really could do with a good dinner today.'

'I'll manage it for you,' said Aggie, and she actually smiled. 'But mind what I say now – don't you let that dog eat anything Hunchy puts down for him! It'll be poisoned.'

A voice shouted from the house. Aggie jerked her head up and listened. 'That's Hunchy,' she said. 'I must go.'

She hurried back up the drive. 'Well, well, well,' said Julian, 'so they thought they'd poison old Timmy, did they? They'll have to think again, old fellow, won't they?'

'Woof,' said Timmy, gravely, and didn't even wag his tail!

16

Aggie – and Hunchy

'I feel as if I want some exercise,' said George, when Aggie had gone. 'Let's explore the grounds. You never know what we might find!'

They got up, glad of something to do to take their minds off their surprising problems. Really, who would have thought yesterday, when they were happily cycling along sunny country roads, that they would be held prisoner like this today? You just never knew what would happen. It made life exciting, of course – but it did spoil a cycling tour!

They found absolutely nothing of interest in the grounds except a couple of cows, a large number of hens, and a brood of young ducklings. Evidently even the milkman didn't need to call at Owl's Dene! It was quite self-contained.

'I expect that black Bentley goes down each day to some town or other, to collect letters, and to buy meat, or fish,' said George. 'Otherwise Owl's Dene could keep itself going for months on end if necessary without any contact with the outside world. I expect they've got stacks and stacks of tinned food.'

'It's weird to find a place like this, tucked away on a deserted hill, forgotten by everyone – guarding goodness knows what secrets,' said Dick. 'I'd love to know who that man was you saw in the secret room, Julian – the snorer!'

'Someone who doesn't want to be seen even by Hunchy or Aggie,' said Julian. 'Someone the police would dearly love to see, I expect!'

'I *wish* we could get out of here,' said George, longingly. 'I hate the place. It's got such a nasty "feel" about it. And I hate the thought of somebody trying to poison Timmy.'

'Don't worry – he won't be poisoned,' said Dick. 'We won't let him be. He can have half *our* food, can't you, Timmy, old fellow?'

Timmy agreed. He woofed and wagged his tail. He wouldn't leave George's side that morning, but stuck to her like a leech.

'Well, we've been all round the grounds and there's nothing much to see,' said Julian, when they had come back near the house. 'I suppose Hunchy sees to the milking and feeds the poultry and brings in the vegetables. Aggie has to manage the house. I say – look – there's Hunchy now. He's putting down food for Timmy!'

Hunchy was making signs to them. 'Here's the dog's dinner!' he yelled.

'Don't say a word, George,' said Julian in a low voice. 'We'll pretend to let Timmy eat it, but we'll really throw it away somewhere – and he'll be frightfully astonished when Timmy is still all-alive-o tomorrow morning!'

Hunchy disappeared in the direction of the cow-shed, carrying a pail. Anne gave a little giggle.

'I know what we'll pretend! We'll pretend that Timmy ate half and didn't like the rest – so we gave it to the hens and ducks!'

'And Hunchy will be frightfully upset because he'll

think they'll die and he'll get into a row,' said George. 'Serve him right! Come on – let's get the food now.'

She ran to pick up the big bowl of food. Timmy sniffed at it and turned away. It was obvious that he wouldn't have fancied it much even if George had allowed him to have it. Timmy was a very sensible dog.

'Quick, get that spade, Ju, and dig a hole before Hunchy comes back,' said George, and Julian set to work grinning. It didn't take him more than a minute to dig a large hole in the soft earth of a bed. George emptied all the food into the hole, wiped the bowl round with a handful of leaves and watched Julian filling in the earth. Now no animals could get at the poisoned food.

'Let's go to the hen-run now, and when we see Hunchy we'll wave to him,' said Julian. 'He'll ask us what we've been doing. Come on. He deserves to have a shock.'

615

They went to the hen-house, and stood looking through the wire surrounding the hen-run. As Hunchy came along they turned and waved to him. George pretended to scrape some scraps out of the dog's bowl into the run. Hunchy stared hard. Then he ran towards her, shouting.

'Don't do that, don't do that!'

'What's the matter?' asked George, innocently, pretending to push some scraps through the wire. 'Can't I give the hens some scraps?'

'Is that the bowl I put the dog's food down in?' asked Hunchy, sharply.

'Yes,' said George.

'And he didn't eat all the food – so you're giving it to my hens!' shouted Hunchy in a rage, and snatched the bowl out of George's hands. She pretended to be very angry.

'Don't! Why shouldn't your hens have scraps from the dog's bowl? The food you gave Timmy looked very nice – can't the hens have some?'

Hunchy looked into the hen-run with a groan. The hens were pecking about near the children for all the world as if they were eating something just thrown to them. Hunchy felt sure they would all be dead by the next day – and then, what trouble he would get into!

He glared at George. 'Idiot of a boy! Giving my hens that food! You deserve a good whipping.'

He thought George was a boy, of course. The others looked on with interest. It served Hunchy right to get into a panic over his hens, after trying to poison dear old Timmy.

Hunchy didn't seem to know what to do. Eventually he took a stiff brush from a nearby shed and went into the hen-run. He had evidently decided to sweep the whole place in case any poisoned bits of food were still left about. He swept laboriously and the children watched him, pleased that he should punish himself in this way.

'I've never seen anyone bother to sweep a hen-run

before,' said Dick, in a loud and interested voice.

'Nor have I,' said George at once. 'He must be very anxious to bring his hens up properly.'

'It's jolly hard work, I should think,' said Julian. 'Glad I haven't got to do it. Pity to sweep up all the bits of food, though. An awful waste.'

Everyone agreed heartily to this.

'Funny he should be so upset about my giving the hens any scraps of the food he put down for Timmy,' said George. 'I mean – it seems a bit *suspicious*.'

'It does rather,' agreed Dick. 'But then perhaps he's a suspicious character.'

Hunchy could hear all this quite plainly. The children meant him to, of course. He stopped his sweeping and scowled evilly at them.

'Clear off, you little pests,' he said, and raised his broom as if to rush at the children with it.

'He looks like an angry hen,' said Anne, joining in.

'He's just going to cluck,' put in Richard, and the others laughed. Hunchy ran to open the gate of the hen-run, red with anger.

'Of course – it's just struck me – he *might* have put poison into Timmy's bowl of food,' said Julian, loudly. 'That's why he's so upset about his hens. Dear, dear – how true the old proverb is – he that digs a pit shall fall into it himself!'

The mention of poison stopped Hunchy's rush at once. He flung the broom into the shed, and made off for the house without another word.

'Well – we gave him a bit more than he bargained for,' said Julian.

'And you needn't worry, hens,' said Anne, putting her face to the wire-netting of the run. 'You're not poisoned – and we wouldn't *dream* of harming you!'

'Aggie's calling us,' said Richard. 'Look – perhaps she's got some food for us.'

'I hope so,' said Dick. 'I'm getting very hungry. It's funny that grown-ups never seem to get as hungry as children. I do pity them.'

'Why? Do you *like* being hungry?' said Anne as they walked over to the house.

'Yes, if I know there's a good meal in the offing,' said Dick. 'Otherwise it wouldn't be at all funny. Oh goodness – is this all that Aggie has provided?'

On the window-sill was a loaf of stale-looking bread and a piece of very hard yellow cheese. Nothing else at all. Hunchy was there, grinning.

'Aggie says that's your dinner,' he said, and sat himself down at the table to spoon out enormous helpings of a very savoury stew.

'A little revenge for our behaviour by the hen-run,' murmured Julian softly. 'Well, well – I thought better than this of Aggie. I wonder where she is.'

She came out of the kitchen door at that moment, carrying a washing-basket that appeared to be full of clothes. 'I'll just hang these out, Hunchy, and I'll be back,' she called to him. She turned to the children and gave them a broad wink.

'There's your dinner on the window-sill,' she said. 'Get it and take it somewhere to eat. Hunchy and me don't want you round the kitchen.'

She suddenly smiled and nodded her head down towards the washing-basket. The children understood immediately. Their real dinner was in there!

They snatched the bread and cheese from the sill and followed her. She set down the basket under a tree, where it was well-hidden from the house. A clothes-line stretched there. 'I'll be out afterwards to hang my washing,' she said, and with another smile that changed her whole face, she went back to the house.

'Good old Aggie,' said Julian, lifting up the top cloth in the basket. 'My word – just look here!'

618

17

Julian has a bright idea

Aggie had managed to pack knives, forks, spoons, plates and mugs into the bottom of the basket. There were two big bottles of milk. There was a large meat-pie with delicious looking pastry on top, and a collection of buns, biscuits and oranges. There were also some home-made sweets. Aggie had certainly been very generous!

All the things were quickly whipped out of the basket. The children carried them behind the bushes, sat down and proceeded to eat a first-rate dinner. Timmy got his share of the meat-pie and biscuits. He also gobbled up a large part of the hard yellow cheese.

'Now we'd better rinse everything under that garden tap over there, and then pack them neatly into the bottom of the basket again,' said Julian. 'We don't want to get Aggie into any sort of trouble for her kindness.'

The dishes were soon rinsed and packed back into the basket. The clothes were drawn over them – nothing could be seen!

Aggie came outside to them in about half an hour. The children went to her and spoke in low voices.

'Thanks, Aggie, that was super!'

'You *are* a brick. We did enjoy it!'

'I bet Hunchy didn't enjoy his dinner as much as *we* did!'

'Sh!' said Aggie, half-pleased and half-scared. 'You never know when Hunchy's listening. He's got ears like a hare! Listen – I'll be coming out to get the eggs from the hen-run at tea-time. I'll have a basket with me for the eggs – and I shall have your tea in it. I'll leave your tea in the hen-house when I get the eggs. You can fetch it when I've gone.'

'You're a wonder, Aggie!' said Julian, admiringly. 'You really are.'

Aggie looked pleased. It was plain that nobody had said a kind or admiring word to her for years and years. She was a poor, miserable, scared old woman – but she was quite enjoying this little secret. She was pleased at getting the better of Hunchy too. Perhaps she felt it was some slight revenge for all the years he had ill-treated her.

She hung out some of the clothes in the basket, left one in to cover the dinner-things, and then went back into the house.

'Poor old thing,' said Dick. 'What a life!'

'Yes – *I* shouldn't like to be cooped up here for years and years with ruffians like Perton and Rooky,' said Julian.

'It looks as if we shall be if we don't hurry up and think of some plan of escape,' said Dick.

'Yes. We'd better think hard again,' said Julian. 'Come over to those trees there. We can sit on the grass under them and talk without being overheard anywhere.'

'Look – Hunchy is polishing the black Bentley,' said George. 'I'll just pass near him with Timmy, and let Timmy growl. He'll see Timmy's all alive and kicking then.'

So she took Timmy near the Bentley, and of course he

growled horribly when he came upon Hunchy. Hunchy promptly got into the car and shut the door. George grinned.

'Hallo!' she said. 'Going off for a ride? Can Timmy and I come with you?'

She made as if she was going to open the door, and Hunchy yelled loudly: 'Don't you let that dog in here! I've seen Rooky's hand – one finger's very bad indeed. I don't want that dog going for *me*.'

'Do take me for a ride with you, Hunchy,' persisted George. 'Timmy loves cars.'

'Go away,' said Hunchy, hanging on to the door-handle for dear life. 'I've got to get this car cleaned up for Mr Perton this evening. You let me get out and finish the job.'

George laughed and went off to join the others. 'Well, he can see Timmy's all-alive-o,' said Dick, with a grin. 'Good thing too. We'd find ourselves in a much bigger fix if we hadn't got old Timmy to protect us.'

They went over to the clump of trees and sat down. 'What was it that Hunchy said about the car?' asked Julian. George told him. Julian looked thoughtful. Anne knew that look – it meant that Julian was thinking of a plan! She prodded him.

'Ju! You've got a plan, haven't you? What is it?'

'Well – I'm only just wondering about something,' said Julian, slowly. 'That car – and the fact that Mr Perton is going out in it tonight – which means he will go out through those gates . . .'

'What of it?' said Dick. 'Thinking of going with him?'

'Well, yes, I was,' said Julian, surprisingly. 'You see – if he's not going till dark, I think I could probably get into the boot – and hide there till the car stops somewhere, and then I could open the boot, get out, and go off for help!'

Everyone looked at him in silence. Anne's eyes gleamed. 'Oh Julian! It's a wizard plan.'

'It sounds jolly good,' said Dick.

'The only thing is – I don't like being left here without Julian,' said Anne, suddenly feeling scared. 'Everything's all right if Julian's here.'

'*I* could go,' said Dick.

'Or I could,' said George, 'only there wouldn't be room for Timmy too.'

'The boot looks pretty big from outside,' said Julian. 'I wish I could take Anne with me. Then I'd know she was safe. You others would be all right so long as you had Timmy.'

They discussed the matter thoroughly. They dropped it towards tea-time when they saw Aggie coming out with a basket to collect the eggs. She made a sign to them not to come over to her. Possibly someone was watching. They stayed where they were, and watched her go into the hen-house. She remained there a short time, and then came out with a basketful of new-laid eggs. She walked to the house without looking at the children again.

'I'll go and see if she's left anything in the hen-house,' said Dick, and went over to it. He soon appeared again, grinning. His pockets bulged!

Aggie had left about two dozen potted-meat sandwiches, a big slab of cherry cake and a bottle of milk. The children went under the bushes and Dick unloaded his pockets. 'She even left a bone for old Tim,' he said.

'I suppose it's all right,' said George doubtfully. Julian smelt it.

'Perfectly fresh,' he said. 'No poison here at all! Anyway, Aggie wouldn't play a dirty trick like that. Come on – let's tuck in.'

They were very bored after tea, so Julian arranged some races and some jumping competitions. Timmy, of course, would have won them all if he had been counted as a proper competitor. But he wasn't. He went in for everything, though, and barked so excitedly that Mr Perton came to a window and yelled to him to stop.

'Sorry!' yelled back George. 'Timmy's so full of beans today, you see!'

'Mr Perton will be wondering why,' said Julian, with a grin. 'He'll be rowing Hunchy for not getting on with the poison job.'

When it began to grow dark the children went cautiously to the car. Hunchy had finished working on it. Quietly Julian opened the boot and looked inside. He gave an exclamation of disappointment.

'It's only a small one! I can't get in there, I'm afraid. Nor can you, Dick.'

'I'll go then,' said Anne, in a small voice.

'Certainly not,' said Julian.

'Well – *I'll* go,' said Richard, surprisingly. 'I could just about squash in there.'

'*You!*' said Dick. 'You'd be scared stiff.'

Richard was silent for a moment. 'Yes – I should,' he admitted. 'But I'm still ready to go. I'll do my very best if you'd like me to try. After all – it's me or nobody. You won't let Anne go – and there's not enough room for George and Timmy – and not enough for either you or Julian, Dick.'

Everyone was astonished. It didn't seem a bit like Richard to offer to do an unselfish or courageous action. Julian felt very doubtful.

'Well – this is a serious thing, you know, Richard,' he said. 'I mean – if you're going to do it, you've got to do it properly – go right through with it – not get frightened in the middle and begin howling, so that the men hear you and examine the boot.'

'I know,' said Richard. 'I think I can do it all right. I do wish you'd trust me a bit.'

'I can't understand your offering to do a difficult thing like that,' said Julian. 'It doesn't seem a bit like you – you've not shown yourself to be at all plucky *so* far!'

'Julian, I think *I* understand,' said Anne suddenly, and

she pulled at her brother's sleeve. 'He's thinking of *our* skins this time, not of his own – or at least he's trying to. Let's give him a chance to show he's got a bit of courage.'

'I only just want a chance,' said Richard in a small voice.

'All right,' said Julian. 'You shall have it. It'll be a very pleasant surprise if you take your chance and do something helpful!'

'Tell me exactly what I've got to do,' said Richard, trying to keep his voice from trembling.

'Well – once you're in the boot we'll have to shut you in. Goodness knows how long you'll have to wait there in the dark,' said Julian. 'I warn you it will be jolly stuffy and uncomfortable. When the car goes off it will be more uncomfortable still.'

'Poor Richard,' said Anne.

'As soon as the car stops anywhere and you hear the men get out, wait a minute to give them time to get out of sight and hearing – and then scramble out of the boot yourself and go straight to the nearest police-station,' said Julian. 'Tell your story *quickly*, give this address – Owl's Dene, Owl's Hill, some miles from Middlecombe Woods – and the police will do the rest. Got all that?'

'Yes,' said Richard.

'Do you still want to go, now you know what you're in for?' asked Dick.

'Yes,' said Richard again. He was surprised by a warm hug from Anne.

'Richard, you're nice – and I didn't think you were!' said Anne.

He then got a thump on the back from Julian, 'Well, Richard – pull this off and you'll wipe out all the silly things you've done! Now – what about getting into the boot immediately? We don't know when the men will be coming out.'

'Yes. I'll get in now,' said Richard, feeling remarkably

brave after Anne's hug and Julian's thump. Julian opened
the boot. He examined the inside of the boot-cover. 'I
don't believe Richard could open it from the inside,' he
said. 'No, he couldn't. We mustn't close it tight, then – I'll
have to wedge it a bit open with a stick or something. That
will give him a little air, and he'll be able to push the boot
open when he wants to. Where's a stick?'

Dick found one. Richard got into the boot and curled
himself up. There wasn't very much room even for him!

He looked extremely cramped. Julian shut the boot and wedged it with a stick so that there was a crack of half an inch all round.

Dick gave him a sharp nudge. 'Quick – someone's coming!'

18

Hunt for Richard!

Mr Perton could be seen standing at the front door, outlined in the light from the lamp in the hall. He was talking to Rooky, who, apparently, was not going out. It seemed as if only Mr Perton was leaving in the car.

'Good luck, Richard,' Julian whispered, as he and the others melted into the shadows on the other side of the drive. They stood there in the darkness, watching Mr Perton walk over to the car. He got in and slammed the door. Thank goodness he hadn't wanted to put anything in the boot!

The engine started up and the car purred away down the drive. At the same time there came the grating sound of the gate machinery being used.

'Gates are opening for him,' muttered Dick. They heard the car go right down the drive and out of the gateway without stopping. It hooted as it went, evidently a signal to the house. The gates had been opened just at the right moment. They were now being shut, judging by the grinding noise going on.

627

The front door closed. The children stood in silence for a minute or two, thinking of Richard shut up in the boot.

'I'd never have thought it of him,' said George.

'No – but you just simply never know what is in anybody,' said Julian thoughtfully. 'I suppose even the worst coward, the most despicable crook, the most dishonest rogue *can* find some good thing in himself if he wants to badly enough.'

'Yes – it's the "wanting-to" that must be so rare, though,' said Dick. 'Look – there's Aggie at the kitchen-door. She's calling us in.'

They went to her. 'You can come in now,' she said. 'I can't give you much supper, I'm afraid, because Hunchy will be here – but I'll put some cake up in your room, under the blankets.'

They went into the kitchen. It was pleasant with a log-fire and the mellow light from an oil-lamp. Hunchy was at the far end doing something with a rag and polish. He gave the children one of his familiar scowls. 'Take that dog out and leave him out,' he ordered.

'No,' said George.

'Then I'll tell Rooky,' said Hunchy. Neither he nor Aggie seemed to notice that there were only four children, not five.

'Well, if Rooky comes here I've no doubt Timmy will bite his other hand,' said George. 'Anyway – won't he be surprised to find Timmy still alive and kicking?'

Nothing more was said about Timmy. Aggie silently put the remains of a plum-pie on the table. 'There's your supper,' she said.

There was a very small piece each. As they were finishing, Hunchy went out. Aggie spoke in a whisper.

'I heard the wireless at six o'clock. There was a police message about one of you – called Richard. His mother reported him missing – and the police put it out on the wireless.'

628

'Did they really?' said Dick. 'I say – they'll soon be here then!'

'But do they know where you are?' asked Aggie, surprised. Dick shook his head.

'Not yet – but I expect we'll soon be traced here.'

Aggie looked doubtful. 'Nobody's ever been traced here yet – nor ever will be, it's my belief. The police did come once, looking for somebody, and Mr Perton let them in, all polite-like. They hunted everywhere for the person they said they wanted, but they couldn't find him.'

Julian nudged Dick. He thought *he* knew where the police might have found him – in the little secret room behind that sliding panel.

'Funny thing,' said Julian. 'I haven't seen a telephone here. Don't they have one?'

'No,' said Aggie. 'No phone, no gas, no electricity, no water laid on, no nothing. Only just secrets and signs and comings and goings and threats and . . .'

She broke off as Hunchy came back, and went to the big fire-place, where a kettle was slung over the burning logs. Hunchy looked round at the children.

'Rooky wants the one of you that's called Richard,' he said, with a horrible smile. 'Says he wants to learn him a few lessons.'

All the four felt extremely thankful that Richard was not there. They felt sure he wouldn't have liked the lessons that Rooky wanted to teach him.

They looked round at one another and then all round the room. 'Richard? Where *is* Richard?'

'What do you mean – where's Richard?' said Hunchy, in a snarling voice that made Timmy growl. 'One of you is Richard – that's all I know.'

'Why – there were five children – now there's only four!' said Aggie, in sudden astonishment. 'I've only just noticed. Is Richard the missing one?'

'Dear me – *where's* Richard gone?' said Julian, pretending to be surprised. He called him 'Richard! Hey, Richard, where are you?'

Hunchy looked angry. 'Now, none of your tricks. One of you's Richard. Which one?'

'Not one of us is,' answered Dick. 'Gracious, where *can* Richard be? Do you suppose we've left him in the grounds, Ju?'

'Must have,' said Julian. He went to the kitchen window and swung it wide open. 'RICHARD!' he roared. 'You're wanted, RICHARD!'

But no Richard answered or appeared, of course. He was miles away in the boot of the black Bentley!

There came the sound of angry footsteps in the hall and the kitchen door was flung open. Rooky stood there, scowling, his hand done up in a big bandage. With a delighted bark Timmy leapt forward. George caught him just in time.

'That dog! Didn't I say he was to be poisoned?' shouted Rooky, furiously. 'Why haven't you brought that boy to me, Hunchy?'

Hunchy looked afraid. 'He don't seem to be here,' he answered sullenly. 'Unless one of these here children is him, sir.'

Rooky glanced over them. 'No – he's not one of them. Where is Richard?' he demanded of Julian.

'I've just been yelling for him,' said Julian, with an air of amazement. 'Funny thing. He was out in the grounds all day with us – and now we're indoors, he just isn't here. Shall I go and hunt in the grounds?'

'I'll shout for him again,' said Dick, going to the window. 'RICHARD!'

'Shut up!' said Rooky. '*I'll* go and find him. Where's my torch? Get it, Aggie. And when I find him – he'll be sorry for himself, very, very sorry!'

'I'll come too,' said Hunchy. 'You go one way and I'll go another.'

630

'Get Ben and Fred too,' ordered Rooky. Hunchy departed to fetch Ben and Fred, whoever they were. The children supposed they must be the other men who had arrived with Rooky the night before.

Rooky went out of the kitchen door with his powerful torch. Anne shivered. She was very, very glad that Richard couldn't be found, however hard the men looked for him. Soon there came the sound of other voices in the grounds, as the four men separated into two parties, and began to search every yard.

'Where is he, the poor boy?' whispered Aggie.

'I don't know,' said Julian, truthfully. He wasn't going to give any secrets away to Aggie, even though she seemed really friendly to them.

She went out of the room and the children clustered together, speaking in low voices.

'I *say* – what a blessing it was Richard that went off in the Bentley and not one of *us*,' whispered George.

'My word, yes – I didn't like the look on Rooky's face when he came into the kitchen just now,' said Julian.

'Well, Richard's got a little reward for trying to be brave,' said Anne. 'He's missed some ill-treatment from Rooky!'

Julian glanced at a clock in the kitchen. 'Look – it's almost nine. There's a wireless on that shelf. Let's put it on and see if there's a message about Richard.'

He switched it on and twiddled the knob till he got the right station. After a minute or two of news, there came the message they wanted to hear.

'Missing from home since Wednesday, Richard Thurlow Kent, a boy of twelve, well-built, fair hair, blue eyes, wearing grey shorts and grey jersey. Probably on a bicycle.'

631

So the message went on, ending with a police telephone number that could be called. There was of course no message about Julian and the others. They were relieved. 'That means that Mother won't be worrying,' said George. 'But it also means that unless Richard can get help nobody can possibly find out we're here – if we're not missed we can't be searched for, and I don't really want to be here much longer.'

Nobody did, of course. All their hopes were now on Richard. He seemed rather a broken reed to rely on – but you never knew! He just might be successful in escaping unseen from the boot and getting to a police station.

After about an hour Rooky and the others came in, all in a furious temper. Rooky turned on Julian.

'What's happened to that boy? You must know.'

'Gr-r-r-r,' said Timmy at once. Rooky beckoned to Julian to come into the hall. He shut the kitchen door and shouted at Julian again.

'Well – you heard what I said – where's that boy?'

'Isn't he out in the grounds?' said Julian, putting on a very perturbed look. 'Good gracious – what *can* have happened to him? I assure you he was with us all day. Aggie will tell you that – and Hunchy too.'

'They've already told me,' said Rooky. 'He's not in the grounds. We've gone over every inch. Where is he?'

'Well, would he be somewhere in the house, then?' suggested Julian, innocently.

'How can he be?' raged Rooky. 'The front door's been closed and locked all day except when Perton went out. And Hunchy and Aggie swear he didn't come into the kitchen.'

'It's an absolute mystery,' said Julian. 'Shall I hunt all over the house? The others can help me. Maybe the dog will smell him out.'

'I'm not having that dog out of the kitchen,' said Rooky. 'Or any of *you*, either! I believe that boy's about somewhere, laughing up his sleeve at us all – and I believe you know where he is too!'

'I don't,' said Julian. 'And that's the truth.'

'When I *do* find him, I'll . . . I'll . . .' Rooky broke off, quite unable to think of anything bad enough to do to poor Richard.

He went to join the others, still muttering. Julian went thankfully back to the kitchen. He was very glad Richard was well out of the way. It was pure chance that he had gone – but what a very good thing! Where was Richard now? What was he doing? Was he still in the boot of the car? How Julian wished he knew!

19

Richard has his own adventure

Richard had been having a much too exciting time. He had gone with the car, of course, crouching in the boot at the back, with a box of tools digging into him, and a can of petrol smelling horribly nearby, making him feel sick.

Through the gates went the car, and down the hill. It went at a good pace, and once stopped very suddenly. It had gone round a corner and almost collided with a stationary lorry, so that Mr Perton had put the brake on in a hurry. Poor Richard was terrified. He bumped his head hard on the back of the boot and gave a groan.

He sat curled up, feeling sick and scared. He began to wish he had not tried to be a hero and get help. Being any kind of a hero was difficult – but this was a dreadful way of being heroic.

The car went on for some miles; Richard had no idea where it was going. At first he heard no other traffic at all – then he heard the sound of many wheels on the road, and knew he must be getting near a town. Once they must have gone by a railway station or railway line because Richard could distinctly hear the noise of a train, and then a loud hooting.

The car stopped at last. Richard listened intently. Was it stopping just for traffic lights – or was Mr Perton getting out? If so, that was his chance to escape!

He heard the car door slam.. Ah – Mr Perton was out of the car then. Richard pressed hard at the cover of the boot. Julian had wedged it rather tightly, but it gave at last, and the lid of the boot opened. It fell back with rather a noise.

Richard looked out cautiously. He was in a dark street. A few people were walking on the pavement opposite. A lamp-post was some way away. Could he get out now – or would Mr Perton be about and see him?

He stretched out a leg to slide from the boot and jump to the ground – but he had been huddled up in an awkward position for so long that he was too stiff to move. Cramp caught him and he felt miserably uncomfortable as he tried to straighten himself out.

Instead of jumping out and taking to his heels at once, poor Richard had to go very slowly indeed. His legs and arms would *not* move quickly. He sat for a half-minute on the open boot-lid, trying to make up his mind to jump down.

And then he heard Mr Perton's voice! He was running down the steps of the house outside which he had parked the car. Richard was horrified. It hadn't dawned on him that he would come back so quickly.

He tried to jump from the boot-cover, and fell sprawling to the ground. Mr Perton heard him, and, thinking someone was trying to steal something from his car he rushed up to the boot.

Richard scrambled up just in time to get away from his outstretched hand. He ran to the other side of the road as fast as he could, hoping that his stiff, cramped legs wouldn't let him down. Mr Perton tore after him.

'Hey, you, stop! What are you doing in my car?' shouted Mr Perton. Richard dodged a passer-by and tore on, panic-stricken. He mustn't be caught; he mustn't be caught!

Mr Perton caught up with him just under the lamp-post. He grabbed Richard's collar and swung him round roughly. 'You let me go!' yelled Richard, and kicked Mr Perton's ankles so hard that he almost fell over.

Mr Perton recognized him! 'Good gracious – it's you!' he cried. 'The boy Rooky wants! What are you doing here? How did you . . .?'

But with a last despairing struggle, Richard was off again, leaving his coat in Mr Perton's hands! His legs were feeling better now, and he could run faster.

He tore round the corner, colliding with another boy. He was off and away before the boy could even call out. Mr Perton also tore round the corner and collided with the same boy – who, however, was a bit quicker than before, and clutched Mr Perton by the coat, in a real rage at being so nearly knocked over again.

By the time Mr Perton had got himself free from the angry boy, Richard was out of sight. Mr Perton raced to the corner of the road, and looked up and down the poorly lighted road. He gave an exclamation of anger.

'Lost him! Little pest – how did he get here? Could he have been at the back of the car? Ah – surely that's him over there!'

It was. Richard had hidden in a garden, but was now being driven out by the barking of a dog. In despair he tore out of the gate and began running again. Mr Perton tore after him.

Round another corner, panting hard. Round yet another, hoping that no passer-by would clutch at him and stop him. Poor Richard! He didn't feel at all heroic, and didn't enjoy it a bit either.

636

He stumbled round the next corner and came into the main street of the town – and there, opposite, was a lamp that had a very welcome word shining on the glass.

POLICE

Thankfully Richard stumbled up the steps and pushed open the police station door. He almost fell inside. There was a kind of waiting-room there with a policeman sitting at a table. He looked up in astonishment as Richard came in in such a hurry.

'Now then – what's all this?' he asked the boy.

Richard looked fearfully back at the door, expecting Mr Perton to come in at any moment. But he didn't. The door remained shut. Mr Perton was not going to visit any police station if he could help it – especially with Richard pouring out a most peculiar story!

Richard was panting so much that he couldn't say a word at first. Then it all came out. The policeman listened in amazement, and very soon stopped Richard's tale, and called a big burly man in, who proved to be a most important police inspector.

He made Richard tell his tale slowly and as clearly as he could. The boy was now feeling much better – in fact he was feeling quite proud of himself! To think he'd done it – escaped in the boot of the car – got out – managed to get away from Mr Perton – and arrive safely at the police station. Marvellous!

'Where's this Owl's Dene?' demanded the Inspector, and the constable near by answered.

'Must be that old place on Owl's Hill, sir. You remember we once went there on some kind of police business, but it seemed to be all right. Run by a hunch-back and his sister for some man who is often away abroad – Perton, I think the name was.'

'That's right!' cried Richard. 'It was Mr Perton's car I came here in – a black Bentley.'

'Know the number?' said the Inspector, sharply.

637

'KMF 102,' said Richard at once.

'Good lad,' said the Inspector. He picked up a telephone and gave a few curt instructions for a police car to try to trace the Bentley immediately.

'So you're Richard Thurlow Kent,' he said. 'Your mother is very upset and anxious about you. I'll see that she is telephoned to straight away. You'd better be taken home now in a police car.'

'Oh but, sir – can't I go with you to Owl's Dene when

you drive up there?' said Richard, deeply disappointed. 'You'll be going there, won't you? – because of all the others – Anne, Dick, George and Julian.'

'We'll be going all right,' said the Inspector, grimly. 'But you won't be with us. You've had enough adventures. You can go home and go to bed. You've done well to escape and come here. Quite the hero!'

Richard couldn't help feeling pleased – but how he wished he could race off to Owl's Dene with the police. What a marvellous thing it would be to march in with them and show Julian how well he had managed his part of the affair! Perhaps Julian would think better of him then.

The Inspector, however, was not having any boys in the cars that were to go to Owl's Dene, and Richard was taken off by the young constable, and told to wait till a car came to take him home.

The telephone rang, and the Inspector answered it. 'No trace of the Bentley? Right. Thanks.'

He spoke to the young constable. 'Didn't think they'd get him. He's probably raced back to Owl's Dene to warn the others.'

'We'll get there soon after!' said the constable with a grin. 'Our Wolseley's pretty well as fast as a Bentley!'

Mr Perton had indeed raced off, as soon as he saw Richard stumbling up the police station steps. He had gone back to his car at top speed, jumped in, slammed the door and raced away as fast as he could, feeling certain that the police would be on the look-out for KMF 102 immediately.

He tore dangerously round the corners, and hooted madly, making everyone leap out of the way. He was soon out in the country, and there he put on terrific speed, his powerful headlights picking out the dark country lanes for half a mile ahead.

As he came to the hill on which Owl's Dene stood, he

hooted loudly. He wanted the gates opened quickly! Just as he got up to them they opened. Someone had heard his hooting signal – good! He raced up the drive and stopped at the front door. It opened as he jumped out. Rooky stood there, and two other men with him, all looking anxious.

'What's up, Perton? Why are you back so quickly?' called Rooky. 'Anything wrong?''

Mr Perton ran up the steps, shut the door and faced the three men in the hall.

'Do you know what's happened? That boy, Richard Kent, was in the car when I went out! See? Hidden in the back or in the boot, or somewhere! Didn't you miss him?'

'Yes,' said Rooky. 'Of course we missed him. Did you let him get away, Perton?'

'Well, seeing that I didn't know he was in hiding, and had to leave the car to go in and see Ted, it was easy for him to get away!' said Mr Perton. 'He ran like a hare. I nearly grabbed him once, but he wriggled out of his coat. And as he ended up finally in the police station I decided to give up the chase and come back to warn you.'

'The police will be out here then, before you can say Jack Robinson,' shouted Rooky. 'You're a fool, Perton – you ought to have got that boy. There's our ransom gone west – and I was so glad to be able to get my hands on the little brute.'

'It's no good crying over spilt milk,' said Perton. 'What about Weston? Suppose the police find *him*. They're looking for him all right – the papers have been full of only two things the last couple of days – Disappearance of Richard Thurlow Kent – and Escape from Prison of Solomon Weston! And we're mixed up with both these. Do you want to be shoved back into prison again, Rooky? You've only just come out, you know. What are we going to do?'

'We must think,' said Rooky, in a panic-stricken voice. 'Come in this room here. We must *think*.'

640

20

The secret room

The four children had heard the car come racing up the drive, and had heard Mr Perton's arrival. Julian went to the kitchen door, eager to find out what he could. If Mr Perton was back, then either Richard had played his part well, and had escaped – or he had been discovered, and had been brought back.

He heard every word of the excited talk out in the hall. Good, good good! – Richard had got away – and was even now telling his tale to the police. It surely wouldn't be very long before the police arrived at Owl's Dene then – and what surprising things they would find there!

He tiptoed out into the hall, when he heard the men go into the room near by. What were their plans? He hoped they would not vent their rage on him or the others. It was true they had Timmy – but in a real emergency Rooky would probably think nothing of shooting the dog straightaway.

Julian didn't at all like what he heard from the room where the men talked over their plans.

'I'm going to bang all those kids' heads together as hard as I can, to start with,' growled Rooky. 'That big boy – what's his name? – Julian or something – must have planned Richard Kent's escape – I'll give him a real good thrashing, the interfering little beast.'

'What about the sparklers, Rooky?' said another man's voice. 'We'd better put them in a safe hidingplace before the police arrive. We'll have to hurry.'

'Oh, it'll be some time before they find they can't open that gate,' said Rooky. 'And it'll take a little more time before they climb that wall. We'll have time to put the sparklers into the room with Weston. If *he's* safe there, they'll be safe too.'

'Sparklers!' thought Julian, excited. 'Those are diamonds – so they've got a haul of diamonds hidden somewhere. Whatever next?'

'Get them,' ordered Mr Perton. 'Take them to the Secret Room – and be quick about it, Rooky. The police may be here at any minute now.'

'We'll spin some tale about that kid Richard and his friends,' said the voice of a fourth man. 'We'll say they were caught trespassing, the lot of them, and kept here as a little punishment. Actually, if there's time, I think it would be best to let the rest of them go. After all – they don't *know* anything. They can't give away any secrets.'

Rooky didn't want to let them go. He had grim plans for them, but the others argued him over. 'All right,' he said sullenly. 'Let them go, then – if there's time! You take them down to the gate, Perton, and shove them out before the police arrive. They'll probably set off thankfully and get lost in the dark. So much the better.'

'You get the sparklers then, and see to them,' said Mr Perton, and Julian heard him getting up from his chair. The boy darted back to the kitchen.

It looked as if there would be nothing for it but to let themselves be led down to the gates and shoved out and

Julian decided that if that happened they would wait at the gateway till the police arrived. They wouldn't get lost in the dark, as Rooky hoped!

Mr Perton came into the kitchen. His eyes swept over the four children. Timmy growled.

'So you made a little plan, did you, and hid Richard in the car?' he said. 'Well, for that we're going to turn you all out into the night – and you'll probably lose yourselves for days in the deserted countryside round here – and I hope you do!'

Nobody said anything. Mr Perton aimed a blow at Julian, who ducked. Timmy sprang at the man, but George had hold of his collar, and he just missed snapping Mr Perton's arm in two!

'If that dog had stayed here a day longer I'd have shot him,' said Mr Perton, fiercely. 'Come on, all of you, get a move on.'

'Good-bye, Aggie,' said Anne. Aggie and Hunchy watched them go out of the kitchen door into the dark garden. Aggie looked very scared indeed. Hunchy spat after them and said something rude.

But, when they were half-way down the drive, there came the sound of cars roaring at top speed up the hill to the gates of Owl's Dene! Two cars, fast and powerful, with brilliant headlights. Police cars, without a doubt! Mr Perton stopped. Then he shoved the children roughly back towards the house. It was too late to set them free and hope they would lose themselves.

'You look out for Rooky,' he said to them. 'He goes mad when he's frightened – and he's going to be frightened now, with the police hammering at the gates!'

Julian and the others cautiously edged into the kitchen. They weren't going to risk meeting Rooky if they could help it. Nobody was there at all, not even Hunchy or Aggie. Mr Perton went through to the hall.

'Have you put those sparklers away?' he called, and a

643

voice answered him: 'Yes. Weston's got them with him. They're O.K. Did you get the kids out in time?'

'No – and the police are at the gates already,' growled Mr Perton.

A howl came from someone – probably Rooky. 'The police – already! If I had that kid Richard here I'd skin him alive. Wait till I've burnt a few letters I don't want found – then I'll go and get hold of the other kids. I'm going to put somebody through it for this, and I don't care who.'

'Don't be foolish, Rooky,' said Mr Perton's voice. 'Do you want to get yourself into trouble again through your violent temper? Leave the kids alone.'

Julian listened to all this and felt very uneasy indeed. He ought to hide the others. Even Timmy would be no protection if Rooky had a gun. But where could he hide them?

'Rooky will search the whole house from top to bottom if he loses his temper much more, and really makes up his mind to revenge himself on us,' thought Julian. 'What a pity there isn't another secret room – we could hide there and be safe!'

But even if there was one he didn't know of it. He heard Rooky go upstairs with the others. Now, if he and the other children were going to hide somewhere in safety, this was their chance. But WHERE could they hide?

An idea came to Julian – was it a brilliant one, or wasn't it? He couldn't make up his mind at first. Then he decided that brilliant or not they had got to try it.

He spoke to the others. 'We've got to hide. Rooky isn't safe when he's in a temper.'

'Where shall we hide?' said Anne, fearfully.

'In the secret room!' said Julian. They all gaped at him in amazement.

'But – but somebody else is already hidden there – you told us you saw him last night,' said George at last.

644

'I know. That can't be helped. He's the last person to give us away, if we share his hiding-place – he wouldn't want to be found himself!' said Julian. 'It will be a frightful squash, because the secret room is very, very small – but it's the safest place I can think of.'

'Timmy will have to come too,' said George firmly. Julian nodded.

'Of course. We may need him to protect us against the hidden man!' he said. 'He may be pretty wild at us all invading his hiding-place. We don't want to have him calling Rooky. We'll be all right once we're in the room, because Timmy will keep him quiet. And once we're in he won't call out because we'll tell him the police are here!'

'Fine,' said Dick. 'Let's go. Is the coast clear?'

'Yes. They're all upstairs for some reason or other,' said Julian. 'Probably destroying things they don't want found. Come on.'

Hunchy and Aggie were still not to be seen. They had probably heard what the scare was about and were hidden away themselves! Julian led the way quietly to the little study.

They stared at the big, solid wooden bookcase that stretched from floor to ceiling. Julian went quickly to one shelf and emptied out the books. He felt for the knob.

There it was! He pulled it out, and the back panel of the shelf slid noiselessly downwards, leaving the large hole there, like a window into the secret room.

The children gasped. How queer! How very extraordinary! They blinked through the hole and saw the small room behind, lit by a little candle. They saw the hidden man too – and he saw them! He looked at them in the very greatest astonishment.

'Who are you?' he said, in a threatening voice. 'Who told you to open that panel? Where's Rooky and Perton?'

'We're coming through to join you,' said Julian quietly. 'Don't make a noise.'

He shoved George up first. She slid through the narrow opening sideways and landed feet-first on the floor. Timmy followed immediately, pushed through by Julian.

The man was up on his feet now, angry and surprised. He was a big burly fellow, with very small close-set eyes and a cruel mouth.

'Now look here,' he began in a loud voice. 'I won't have this. Where's Perton? Hey, Per . . .'

'If you say another word I'll set my dog on you,' said George, at a sign from Julian. Timmy growled so ferociously that the man shrank back at once.

'I – I . . .' he began. Timmy growled again and bared all his magnificent teeth in a snarl. The man climbed up on the narrow bed and subsided, looking astonished and furious. Dick went through the opening next, then Anne. By that time the small room was uncomfortably crowded.

'I say,' said Julian, suddenly remembering something, 'I shall have to stay outside the room – because the books have got to be put back, otherwise Rooky will notice the shelf is empty and guess we're hiding in the secret room. Then we'll be at his mercy.'

'Oh Ju – you must come in with us,' said Anne, frightened.

'I can't, Anne. I must shut the panel and put the books back,' said Julian. 'I can't risk your being discovered till the police have safely caught that madman Rooky! I shall be all right, don't you worry.'

'The police?' whispered the man in the secret room, his eyes almost falling out of his head. 'Are the police here?'

'At the gates,' answered Julian. 'So keep quiet if you don't want them on top of you at once!'

He pushed the knob. The panel slid back into place without a sound. Julian replaced the books on the shelf as fast as he could. Then he darted out of the study, so that the men would not even guess what he had been up to. He was very thankful that Rooky had kept away long enough for him to carry out his plan.

Where should he hide himself? How long would it take the police to get over the wall, or break down the great gates? Surely they would soon be here?

There came the sound of footsteps running down the stairs. It was Rooky. He caught sight of Julian at once. 'Ah – there you are! Where are the others? I'll show you what happens to children who upset my plans. I'll show you what . . .'

Rooky carried a whip in his hand and looked quite crazy. Julian was afraid. He darted back into the study and locked the door. Rooky began to hammer at it. Then such a crash came on the door that Julian guessed he was smashing it down with one of the hall chairs. The door would be down in a moment!

21
A very exciting finish!

Julian was a courageous boy, but just at that minute he felt very scared indeed. And what must the children hidden in the secret room beyond be thinking? Poor Anne must be feeling terrified at Rooky's shouts and the crashing on the door.

And then a really marvellous idea came to Julian. Why, oh why hadn't he thought of it before? He could open the gates himself for the police to come in! He knew how to do it – and there was the wheel nearby in the corner, that set the gate machinery working! Once he had the gates open it would not be more than a few minutes, surely, before the police were hammering at the front door.

Julian ran to the wheel-like handle. He turned it strongly. A grinding, whining noise came at once, as the machinery went into action.

Rooky was still crashing at the door with the heavy chair. Already he had broken in one panel of it. But when he suddenly heard the groaning of the machinery that opened the gates, he stopped in panic. The gates were being opened! The police would soon be there – he would be caught!

He forgot the beautiful stories he had arranged to tell, forgot the plans that he and the others had made, forgot everything except that he must hide. He flung down the chair and fled.

Julian sat down in the nearest chair, his heart beating as if he had just been running a race. The gates were open – Rooky had fled – the police would soon be there! And, even as he sat thinking this, there came the sound of powerful cars roaring up the wide drive. Then the engines stopped, and car doors were thrown open.

Someone began to hammer at the front door. 'Open in the name of the law!' cried a loud voice, and then came another hammering.

Nobody opened the door. Julian unlocked the half-broken door of the study he was in, and peered cautiously into the hall. No one seemed to be about.

He raced to the front door, pulled back the bolts, and undid the heavy chain, afraid each moment that some of the men would come to punch him away. But they didn't.

The door was pushed open by the police, who swarmed in immediately. There were eight of them, and they looked surprised to see a boy there.

'Which boy's this?' said the Inspector.

'Julian, sir,' said Julian. 'I'm glad you've come. Things were getting pretty hot.'

'Where are the men?' asked the Inspector, walking right in.

'I don't know,' said Julian.

'Find them,' ordered the Inspector, and his men fanned out up the hall. But before they could go into any room, a cool voice called to them from the end of the corridor.

'May I ask what all this is?'

It was Mr Perton, looking as calm as could be, smoking a cigarette. He stood at the door of his sitting-room, seeming quite unperturbed. 'Since when has a man's house been broken into for no reason at all?'

'Where are the rest of you?' demanded the Inspector.

'In here, Inspector,' drawled Mr Perton. 'We were having a little conference, and heard the hammering at the door. Apparently you got in somehow. I'm afraid you'll get into trouble for this.'

The Inspector advanced to the room where Mr Perton stood. He glanced into it.

'Aha – our friend Rooky, I see,' he said, genially. 'Only a day or two out of prison, Rooky, and you're mixed up in trouble again. Where's Weston?'

'I don't know what you mean,' said Rooky, sullenly. 'How should I know where he is? He was in prison last time I knew anything about him.'

'Yes. But he escaped,' said the Inspector. 'Somebody helped him, Rooky. Somebody planned his escape for him – friends of yours – and somebody knows where the diamonds are that he stole and hid. I've a guess that you're going to share them with him in return for getting your friends to help him. Where is Weston, Rooky?'

'I tell you I don't *know*,' repeated Rooky. 'Not here, if that's what you're getting at. You can search the whole house from top to bottom, if you like. Perton won't mind. Will you, Perton? Look for the sparklers, too, if you want to. I don't know anything about them.'

'Perton, we've suspected you for a long time,' said the Inspector, turning to Mr Perton, who was still calmly smoking his cigarette. 'We think you're at the bottom of all these prison escapes – that's why you bought this lonely old house, isn't it? – so that you could work from it undisturbed? You arrange the escapes, you arrange for a change of clothes, you arrange for a safe hiding-place till the man can get out of the country.'

'Utter nonsense,' said Mr Perton.

'And you only help criminals who have been known to do a clever robbery and hide the stuff before they're caught,' went on the Inspector, in a grim voice. 'So you know you'll make plenty of profit on your deals Perton. Weston is here all right – and so are the diamonds. Where are they?'

'They're not here,' said Perton. 'You're at liberty to

651

look and see. You won't get anything out of *me*, Inspector. I'm innocent.'

Julian had listened to all this in amazement. Why, they had fallen into the very middle of a nest of thieves and rogues! Well – *he* knew where Weston was – and the diamonds too! He stepped forward.

'Tell your story later, son,' said the Inspector. 'We've things to do now.'

'Well, sir – I can save you a lot of time,' said Julian. 'I know where the hidden prisoner is – and the diamonds too!'

Rooky leapt to his feet with a howl. Mr Perton looked at Julian hard. The other men glanced uneasily at one another.

'You don't know anything!' shouted Rooky. 'You only came here yesterday.'

The Inspector regarded Julian gravely. He liked this boy with the quiet manners and honest eyes.

'Do you mean what you say?' he asked.

'Oh yes,' said Julian. 'Come with me, sir.'

He turned and went out of the room. Everyone crowded after him – police, Rooky and the others; but three of the policemen quietly placed themselves at the back.

Julian led them to the study. Rooky's face went purple, but Perton gave him a sharp nudge and he said nothing. Julian went to the bookcase and swept a whole shelf of books out at once.

Rooky gave a terrific yell and leapt at Julian. 'Stop that! What are you doing?'

Two policemen were on the infuriated Rooky at once. They dragged him back. Julian pulled out the knob and the panel slid noiselessly downwards, leaving a wide space in the wall behind.

From the secret room four faces gazed out – the faces of three children – and a man. Timmy was there too, but he was on the floor. For a few moments nobody said a single word. The ones in the hidden room were so surprised to see such a crowd of policemen looking in at them – and the ones in the study were filled with amazement to see so many children in the tiny room!

'WELL!' said the Inspector. 'Well, I'm blessed! And if that isn't Weston himself, large as life and twice as natural!'

Rooky began to struggle with the policemen. He seemed absolutely infuriated with Julian.

'That boy!' he muttered. 'Let me get at him. That boy!'

'Got the diamonds there, Weston?' asked the Inspector, cheerfully. 'May as well hand them over.'

Weston was very pale indeed. He made no move at all. Dick reached under the narrow bed and pulled out a bag. 'Here they are,' he said, with a grin. 'Jolly good lot they feel – heavy as anything! Can we come out now, Ju?'

All three were helped out by policemen. Weston was handcuffed before he was brought out. Rooky found that he also had handcuffs on all of a sudden, and to Mr Perton's angry surprise he heard a click at his own wrists too!

'A very, very nice little haul,' said the Inspector, in his most genial voice, as he looked inside the bag. 'What happened to your prison clothes, Weston? That's a nice suit you've got on – but you weren't wearing that when you left prison.'

'I can tell you where they are,' said Julian, remembering. Everyone stared in amazement, except George and Anne, who also knew, of course.

'They're stuffed down a well belonging to an old tumble-down shack on a lane between here and Middlecombe Woods,' said Julian. 'I could easily find it for you any time.'

Mr Perton stared at Julian as if he couldn't believe his ears. 'How do you know that?' he asked roughly. 'You can't know a thing like that!'

'I do know it,' said Julian. 'And what's more you took him a new suit of clothes, and arrived at the shack in your black Bentley, didn't you – KMF 102? I saw it.'

'That's got you, Perton,' said the Inspector, with a pleased smile. 'That's put you on the spot, hasn't it? Good boy, this – notices a whole lot of interesting things. I shouldn't be surprised if he joins the police force some day. We could do with people like him!'

Perton spat out his cigarette and stamped on it viciously, as if he wished he was stamping on Julian. Those children! If that idiot Rooky hadn't spotted Richard Kent and gone after him, none of this would have happened. Weston would have been safely hidden, the diamonds sold, Weston could have been sent abroad, and he, Perton, would have made a fortune. Now a pack of children had spoilt everything.

'Any other people in the house?' the Inspector asked Julian. 'You appear to be the one who knows more than anybody else, my boy – so perhaps you can tell me that.'

'Yes – Aggie and Hunchy,' said Julian, promptly. 'But don't be hard on Aggie, sir – she was awfully good to us, and she's terrified of Hunchy.'

'We'll remember what you say,' promised the Inspector. 'Search the house, men. Bring along Aggie and Hunchy too. We'll want them for witnesses, anyway. Leave two men on guard here. The rest of us will go.'

It needed the black Bentley as well as the two police cars to take everyone down the drive and on to the next town! The children's bicycles had to be left behind, as they could not be got on the cars anywhere. As it was, it was a terrific squash.

'You going home tonight?' the Inspector asked Julian. 'We'll run you back. What about your people? Won't they be worried by all this?'

'They're away,' explained Julian. 'And we were on a

cycling tour. So they don't know. There's really nowhere we can go for the night.'

But there was! There was a message awaiting the Inspector to say that Mrs Thurlow Kent would be very pleased indeed if Julian and the others would spend the night with Richard. She wanted to hear about their extraordinary adventures.

'Right,' said Julian. 'That settles that. We'll go there – and anyway, I want to bang old Richard on the back. He turned out quite a hero after all!'

'You'll have to keep around for a few days,' said the Inspector. 'We'll want you, I expect – you've a very fine tale to tell, and you've been a great help.'

'We'll keep around then,' said Julian. 'And if you could manage to have our bikes collected, sir, I'd be very grateful.'

Richard was at the front door to meet them all, although by now it was very late indeed. He was dressed in clean clothes and looked very spruce beside the dirty, bedraggled company of children that he went to greet.

'I wish I'd been in at the last!' he cried. 'I was sent off home, and I was wild. Mother – and Dad – here are the children I went off with.'

Mr Thurlow Kent had just come back from America. He shook hands with all of them. 'Come along in,' he said. 'We've got a fine spread for you – you must be ravenous!'

'Tell me what happened, tell me at once,' demanded Richard.

'We simply *must* have a bath first,' protested Julian. 'We're filthy.'

'Well, you can tell me while you're having a bath,' said Richard. 'I can't wait to hear!'

It was lovely to have hot baths and to be given clean clothes. George was solemnly handed out shorts like the boys, and the others grinned to see that both Mr and Mrs

Kent thought she was a boy. George, of course, grinned too, and didn't say a word.

'I was very angry with Richard when I heard what he had done,' said Mr Kent, when they were all sitting at table, eating hungrily. 'I'm ashamed of him.'

Richard looked downcast at once. He gazed beseechingly at Julian.

'Yes – Richard made a fool of himself,' said Julian. 'And landed us all into trouble. He wants taking in hand, sir.'

Richard looked even more downcast. He went very red, and looked at the table-cloth.

'But,' said Julian, 'he more than made up for his silliness, sir – he offered to squash himself into the boot of the car, and escape that way, and go and warn the police. That took some doing, believe me! I think quite a bit of Richard now!'

He leaned over and gave the boy a pat on the back. Dick and the others followed it up with thumps, and Timmy woofed in his deepest voice.

Richard was now red with pleasure. 'Thanks,' he said, awkwardly. 'I'll remember this.'

'See you do, my boy!' said his father. 'It might all have ended very differently!'

'But it didn't,' said Anne happily. 'It ended like this. We can all breathe again!'

'Till the next time,' said Dick, with a grin. 'What do *you* say, Timmy, old boy?'

'Woof,' said Timmy, of course, and thumped his tail on the floor. 'WOOF!'